SHADOWS OF A DREAM

SL HARBY

*Don't Dream
In The Shadows
SL H*

COVER ART BY
GILBERT ARTHUR

ILLUSTRATIONS BY
GILBERT ARTHUR & ISABEL ADORNO

CONTENTS

To my wife, muse and biggest fan, Jessica, without which Shadows of a Dream would never have become reality. At every step, your quiet confidence in my words gave me the courage to continue.

CAST OF CHARACTERS

<u>Earth</u>
Stephen's Current Gaming Group

Stephen Moses – the hero of our story
Alan Lightner –Steven's friend, Jeffery's son
Michael Ryan –Steven's friend, Beatrice's stepson
Robert Maris –Steven's friend, Roger's brother

Stephen's Original Gaming Group

Jeffery Lightner – Deceased, Stephen's mentor
George Lightner – Deceased, Jeffery's brother
Beatrice Ryan – Deceased, Michael and Nell's mother
Roger Maris – He is still with us, Robert's brother

Other Important Characters of Note

Veronica/Ronni Moses –Stephen's wife
Nell Ryan –Michael's sister
Alice Rohm –Jeffery's widow (before she married Fredrick) and
Fredrick's wife, Alan's mother
Fredrick Rohm –Alice's husband, Alan's stepfather
Samantha Marcheur –Alice and Jeffery's friend
Jared Horne – Stephen's employer

Taerh

Band of Six

Alexei Silvermoon – Jeffery's Reflection / Forester
Mika – Beatrice's Reflection / Mantrian Warrior
Ret – Roger's Reflection / Rangor Warrior
Marcus the Green – George's Reflection / Mage
Hollis the Slender – Stephen's Reflection / Thief
Haedren – Priest of Olm

Band of Four

Hollis the Slender – Stephen's Reflection / Thief
Renthroas – Alan's Reflection / Half Blood Elf
Rhyzzo – Michael's Reflection / Priest of Olm
Ulrych – Robert's Reflection / Rangor Warrior

Gods and Goddesses

Olm – God of Justice, Creation. Twin Brother of Umma. Known as the Father of Justice, Lord of the Dawn
Umma – Goddess of Nature, Knowledge. Twin Sister of Olm. Known as the Mother of the Forrest, Lady of Light
Sharroth – God of Shadow, Deception. Younger Brother of Olm and Umma. Known as the Master of Beasts, Father of Lies, Bringer of Shadows'

PART ONE

A DEATH IN THE FAMILY

"The two most important days in your life are the day you were born and the day you find out why."

-Mark Twain

CHAPTER ONE
AN INAUSPICIOUS PRECEDENT

The sound of the trap sliding into place was faint, but still the crouching figure's ears detected the slightest click coming from inside the door. Using the torque to hold the lock's cylinder in place with his left hand, Hollis gestured to his companions to back up with a quick motion of the fingers of his free hand before turning his attention back to the lock in front of him. The thick stone door contained a patinated panel that dominated a quarter of its central surface. In the center of the plate was an ancient lock. Its wide keyhole made it seem easy to pick but there was more than enough room to hide a nasty, poison-tipped needle. The key that had been designed for it was wide at the base, the goal of which was likely to prevent any unfortunate incidents when it was opened. The young man didn't have the key that fit this lock, so he would have to depend on his sensitive touch and quick reflexes. It was an exhilarating feeling.

Holding his left hand still in order to maintain pressure on the mechanism, he placed the thin hook-pick that he held in his right, next to his knee. Hollis felt in his pouch for another hook-pick, thicker than the one beside him. His left hand was now quivering slightly. The hook on this pick ended at a steeper angle, allowing for a better leverage on the larger pins within the lock. He bent his head down closer to the opening of the keyhole. In the dim light of Rhyzzo's torch, Hollis spotted the dark, viscous substance that was clinging to the tiny needle. In his heart, he knew it was poison and he doubted that time had dulled its potency.

Shifting his gaze sideways, he brought the thicker hook-pick into his line of sight, mentally measuring the angle. His left hand was beginning to shake a little more insistently, and a dull burning was building in his forearm. He peered down at the mechanism that was holding the needle in place. He needed at least another few degrees of an angle to not trip the stop that was preventing it from being loosed into his face as he pushed the needle back into a safe position. As he felt around in the pouch at his side for the correct pick, the burning in his forearm worked its way into the back of his left hand.

Ever so slowly, he brought his right hand upwards, placing the pick into the lock. His hand now blocked the needle's path to his face but if it was coated with poison, a puncture to his hand would be no less deadly. And, to add to his misfortune, his view of the mechanism was now blocked completely. He would need to maneuver around the catch and move the needle by touch alone.

The burning settled in his left hand, working its tendrils deep into his palm.

He felt the mechanism's resistance against his pick; but was it the catch or the needle itself? He pushed up and to the left, feeling as the mechanism ...

"Stephen!"

.. as the mechanism began to ...

"Stephen!"

Stephen looked up from his character sheet, his dice clenched in his hand as Hollis's picks were clenched in his. "What?" He'd gathered around the worn table with his friends every Sunday for almost three years now, yet his wife had interrupted their role-playing games each and every time.

"Do you have a second? I need to talk to you!"

Stephen peered around the table at his friends. Although each of them was on the verge of graduating high school and he was more than a decade removed from it, they were more his friends than anyone else in his life. "I'm sorry, guys. This should only take a second." As he got up from the table, he tossed his dice down more harshly than he'd intended. He took a swig from the water bottle in front of him before realizing that it was Alan's. His friend tried to catch the bottle before it reached his lips but failed.

Robert rolled his eyes and sighed heavily, "Whatever, dude." Of the three teens, Robert was the one that least appeared to be a 'typical role-player'. Tall and broad, the boy had the broad shoulders and strong stance of a football player. He had played in his freshman and sophomore years, but soon lost interest as he did in most things. His chiseled chin and deep brown eyes made him popular with each of his girlfriends of the moment, until he inevitably lost interest in them as well. Even his interest in the game had begun to wane in the last few months. As he became less and less invested, Stephen began to see his cynicism.

Alan, who was playing the part of the Game Master that evening, smiled, kicking Robert under the table, of all of them, he was most put off by the changes in his friend. "It's okay, Stephen. Do what you need to do." The boy had such a gentle bearing about him, from his always slightly tousled light brown hair and soft hazel eyes to his steady demeanor.

Stephen grimaced as the flavor of the water hit him. Alan was always infusing his water with one vegetable or another; last week it had been cucumber and this week it seemed to be e skunk weed or something equally as foul. Mike barely stifled a childlike giggle as he watched Stephen's face crinkle up with disgust. Hair and eyes the color of mud after a spring rainstorm, Mike seemed to embrace the art of being overlooked in both appearance and demeanor. When he allowed the cloud of insecurity around him drop and laughed; Mike's entire face lit up. It suited him.

Unable to meet the eyes of his friends, Stephen turned and rushed up the stairs from his basement 'Man Cave'. He found his wife, Veronica standing at the top, her hands planted on her hips.

He didn't need his character's keen senses see the severe set of her jaw. She was clearly unhappy. With her voice in a tense whisper, she said, "You've been playing for four hours and you told me you'd take the garbage out before your friends got here."

She had been the most beautiful girl Stephen had ever seen when they met. Her hair was the color of black velvet, making her topaz blue eyes more striking. Her expressions of disappointment, silent and verbal eroded that beauty as sure as a river devours its banks. Stephen could not put his finger on exactly when her plump lips had begun to migrate to the perpetual downturn in which they dwelt now.

He nodded, whispering as well, "I'm sorry, I forgot, and Alan got here early ..." His wife shook her head sadly, her mouth a tight line, "I'm only hearing excuses, Stephen. I don't understand what you even see in these guys. You're almost thirty and still playing *games*." The last word dripped with disdain and disgust.

"It's only once a week, Ronni." he explained, "I work hard all week ..."

"For less money than you're worth, but do you say anything to your boss? Do you stand up for yourself? You need to do something about your life, Stephen." Stephen saw the irony of her accusations given that she counted on him not standing up to her; but knew better than to interrupt. "I thought you would give up these *games*," the disdain didn't lessen with repetition, "when we got married, and when you became an adult. I don't know why I even ..." She didn't finish her thought; she didn't need to. He had heard it before and would hear it again soon, no doubt. "Do what you want, I'm going out."

His stomach contracted, a mixture of his dread and anger clenching it into a tightly twisted ball. "Ronni," he called out tentatively, before turning and descending the stairs. His friends were already packing away their books and dice. Mike and Robert shook their heads disappointedly as he appeared.

Robert spoke first, "We calling it for the night, boys?" He

didn't wait for Stephen's slow nod before throwing his backpack over his shoulder. He'd seen this same scenario playing out far too many times.

Stephen's voice was quiet, "I'm sorry, guys."

Alan's understanding smile soothed the bite of the others' scowls, "No worries, Stephen. It's a good stopping point anyway." The lie was almost believable. He placed a hand on Stephen's shoulder, "See you next week?" Stephen could only nod, not trusting the embarrassment that burned in his chest to allow him to speak. Alan's eyes said the words that he would never voice, *You deserve better than this.*

Used to these sudden ends to their weekly games, the three men left quickly.

When Stephen emerged from the basement, Veronica was sitting on the couch, waiting for him. Unbidden, the words fell from his mouth, "I'm sorry, Ronni ... "

She just shook her head, "I just don't understand. My brother invited us over for dinner; I honestly don't know what to tell him anymore."

"I know, just tell him I had friends over."

"I don't even understand what it is you do... neither does he."

His stomach clenched again. "I invited you to play with us ... "

The frown was back, almost as if it were a part of her permanent expression. "I don't have time to *play*." The disdain sounded even worse when it colored that word. He settled in for an argument. "I have things to do ... grown up things. Those kids are more than ten years younger than you are ... don't you see that it's time to grow up?"

He opened his mouth to speak but simply settled for a nod. He remembered a time when she smiled. Her smile was so beautiful, especially when it was directed at him. He had missed it like a long-lost friend. "Do you still want to go to your brother's?"

She sighed, before closing her eyes for a moment. When she

opened them, they bored into him. "Only if you want to." The words contradicted her expression.

He forced a smile to his lips, "Of course, Ronni ..."

~

By the time they returned home, her good spirits had returned. It was almost as if she fed upon his joy like a leech, leaving him sad and weary. Veronica's brother, Vince, was what she called '*a man's man,*' or when she was feeling particularly mean spirited just '*a man,*' drawing the obvious contrast to her opinion of Stephen. He was not sure why his wife held up her brother as the example of manhood; he did not compare favorably whatever the reason. Evenings at Vince's home were filled with finished home-improvement projects (*Why can't you do things around the house?*), car '*talk*' (*Why aren't you handy like that?*) and awkward attempts to explain gaming, (*I just don't understand*).

Stephen dropped his wallet and keys into the wooden bowl by the door as he headed for the bedroom. As he began to get undressed, he caught sight of himself in the full-length mirror that hung on the back of the door. Over the years his hairline had regressed so that it only maintained a horseshoe shaped garrison around the top of his head. As his hair receded, his waistline had expanded. He wasn't fat by conventional standards, but he carried the evidence of a decade spent behind a desk around his middle. Even after the evening's frustration, his dark brown eyes possessed the warmth of a spirit not completely crushed. After placing his jeans and t shirt into the hamper beside his dresser, Stephen turned off the light and climbed into bed. As she often did, Roni would fall asleep on the couch, lulled into slumber by the droning television.

As little as he was looking forward to work the next day, he was looking forward less to the inevitable post-Vince discussion with Ronni. She really had refined kicking a man when he was down to an art form. When she turned on the light, he looked up at her sleepily. Her brows furrowed slightly as she murmured, 'Good night,'', and shut the light off and left him to his thoughts. Maybe the night wouldn't end so badly after all.

Stephen lay awake and alone in his bed, the soft voices on the television in the living room just brushing his consciousness. He was briefly tempted to join his wife on the couch; but each time he had extended an olive branch to Roni in the last decade, she took the opportunity to turn it into an argument about how his life had not lived up to her expectations. No matter how often the man tried to find the common ground that he was sure they had once shared, his wife seemed to find a way to turn it into a punishment.

The clenching in his stomach had evolved into a pit of fear and dread as he remembered that another weekend had passed and in seven short hours he would need to get up for work. It wasn't that he didn't like his job, he loved the interaction with people and when you worked tech support, people were always happy to see you. His company, on the other hand, was a level of hell that, even in his gaming, his characters had never ventured into. His bosses believed in the advantages of negative reinforcement. If you kept a person down, they would do good work out of fear or you would find someone else who could.

In the dismal economy, any job one could get, one should keep. Somehow, despite the dread of work on his mind, Stephen was able to drift off to sleep.

Hollis stood on a gently sloping hill, staring down into the valley. He knew this place well, for he had visited it each time his travels took him through the kingdom of Slazè. In the valley, stood a farmhouse among a small copse of trees, a thin line of smoke drifting from the small chimney. The first time he looked upon the valley it was much different than

what lie before him. The gently sloping hills were covered in trees, surrounding a claptrap barn and small one room house, which was more of a hut. Over the years, the owner had expanded the homestead; first plowing meager fields but eventually the surrounding land was cleared and had become the rolling pastures that now stretched as far as the eye could see.

A soft wind blew against his back, blowing through the grass and causing it to tickle the back of his calves. Several groups of cattle grazed placidly before him. Although, the intense contrast between the valley now and when he first laid eyes upon it was stark, the decades did not dull the memories of that night. The small house, far as it was from the village of Ghath, had become the unfortunate victim of a passing band of orcs. From what Hollis's mentor, Silvermoon, could tell, it had been bad luck that sometime during the night, the orcs had badly beaten the couple that dwelled in the house. The man died of his injuries Hollis and his companions could save him.

By the time they had made their way overland to the source of the smoke, there had been nothing the three of them could do. But they had hunted the beasts to a cave that served them as a temporary lair, sheltering them from the light of the sun they so hated.

It had served them just as well as a tomb, as none of them lived to see the fall of the following night. Flush with the spoils of raiding, they were made careless by their temporary success. One moment of carelessness was all it took for the man and his companions to creep into their dark hole and deliver them unto justice.

Despite the victory that day, Hollis always carried with him a measure of guilt that Silvermoon, Mika and he had not arrived quickly enough to save the woman's husband. He took a deep breath of the cool early morning air; many years separated the man from that unfortunate night.

He closed his eyes and savored the feeling of the breeze against his face. The wind was crisp and clean; just breathing it sapped the last vestiges of stress from his body. He had not realized the tension he had held until it was gone. His left hand brushed against the hilt of his short, single bladed sword. Without looking down, he could picture it in his mind.

It was an Uteli blade called Talis Fahr in their clipped language. It translated as 'Tall Knife' and that was, as most things in Uteli, a precise and direct description of the weapon. Made as one would a knife, it was simply longer and a bit thinner in relation to its length. Although it had only a single sharpened edge, there was a smaller edge on the opposite side of the blade that allowed limited cutting near the tip. The hilt was made of two rectangular strips of ivory flanking the full steel tang of the blade. Contrary to Uteli custom, Hollis had wrapped it in sharkskin and silver wire, hiding both ivory and steel. It was a gift of his mentor, Silvermoon, long gone and was closer to him than her. But who was she? Hollis had neither wife nor betrothed; nor did he have a lover for the time span of longer than a few days. The closest thing he had to either was the woman who lived in the farmhouse before him.

As it always did when he thought of her, a smile lifted the edges of his mouth. Although years had passed, Hollis's fondness for the widow had never waned. When he reached the house, she was standing in the doorway watching him approach. Her raven locks framed her sweet smile like a work of art. The linen dress accentuated her curves rather than hid them. Only a year or so older than the thief, she now had the full, mature body of a woman rather than the boyish frame of a girl.

"Hollis, I did not expect to see you again so soon." He found that he enjoyed the sight of his name on her lips as much as the sound of it. "I did not think you ventured forth from the shelter of your teeming city home after the leaves began to color." Her smile tightened into a wry smirk. Her soft features mirrored her amusement as she seemed to smile with her entire being.

"Hello, Maggie," he said, a matching smirk coming to his lips, "I have business south." His hand reached out unbidden to take hers. "Standing here, with you...I wonder why I stayed away so long." The words fell from him almost without thought.

Maggie brought her free hand up to her chest as she bit back a gasp, as if the breath had been taken from her by his words. Her ruse fell apart almost immediately as she dissolved into laughter. "Truly, Hollis, do the ladies of Oizan fall for such things? I suppose cosmopolitan does not always equate to wise."

The man raised an eyebrow and smiled softly. "You would be surprised. Not every woman is as keen of eye and cold of heart as you are."

"Cold of heart? I do not remember you complaining of any such thing when last we saw each other."

Hollis shrugged, still holding her hand, "Circumstances were different."

"Mmm hmm, I do seem to recall they were." She pulled herself into his arms, wrapping her own around his waist, saying simply, "I have missed you," before burying her face in his chest. He put his finger beneath her chin and lifted her lips to his own. Her mouth was warm and willing; her passion was a physical thing calling forth his own. As they kissed, their bodies crushed together to make two one. It was many long moments before they separated the emotion exhausting in its intensity. "You should come in before the hired hands begin to talk." Maggie took Hollis by the hand again, leading him into the house, "Are you hungry? I did not expect company, but I am sure I can find something for you."

Hollis lay on his back, with his arms behind his bare head. Years before, when his hairline began its steady march away from his face, he had decided to take his destiny into his own hands and shaved his head to the skin. At the same time, he cultivated the goatee below which his often-mischievous smile was nestled.

Beside him, Maggie's soft breaths, deep and regular in sleep, brought him comfort. In the close dimness of the woman's bedroom, he felt a peace that had eluded him for most of his life. For as long as he could remember, the thief had spent his life balanced on a razor's edge. His youth was spent first under the thumb of a bitter, unpredictable *father and then living hand-to-mouth in the streets of the slums of Oizan, better known as the Ash. Even after his 'discovery' by the guild, his existence did not grow any more secure. He simply traded the physical dangers of the streets for the political ones of the guild house.*

His quick wits and apparent talent for the arts practiced in the shadows earned him respect and no small amount of financial security, although neither made his life any less frenetic. If anything, as the stakes increased, so did the pressure to prove himself to be faster and more cunning than those around him.

Were it not for the timely intervention of the forester, Alexei Silvermoon, he might very well have been devoured by the life lain out before him. Silvermoon had become more of a father to him than the man from whose loins he came ever was. The man had been dead for more than a decade, yet Hollis could feel the judgement of his patient eyes upon him whenever the world around him grew still.

His eyes shifted to Maggie's form beside him as her regular breathing changed. The only good thing his actual father had left him was an above average night-vision; honed by necessity throughout the thief's life, and it had developed into quite a remarkable asset. More times than he cared to remember, the difference between detection and escape had been the fact that Hollis saw someone a split second before they saw him. On more than one occasion, it had saved him from having his warm, brown eyes closed forever.

The woman muttered sleepily, "What is wrong, Hollis?"

He gently rubbed her shoulder, "Nothing, Maggie, go back to sleep."

True to her nature, she ignored his command, and sat up. "I can count on one hand the number of times that you have lain awake in the years that we have known one another."

"I was visiting with ghosts of my past." His hand slid down her arm to tuck her into his side as he rested his cheek against the top of her head. "Not all of them are the joyful type."

"I understand; that is a burden we all carry at one time or another."

13

As Hollis lay there, with the woman curled up against him, he wondered, not for the first time, why he had even left. Impulsively he began, "Maggie, answer me a question?" She tilted her head to regard him from beneath his cheek, her agreement assumed. "Why have we never made more of ... this?"

Maggie let out a soft exhalation of amusement before beginning, "Which reason would you like, my dear? I recall you having as many excuses as I over the years."

He chuckled slightly, "You are not incorrect. Is there a possibility that we have erred?"

Hollis felt her shrug against his ribs, "Perhaps. Both of us have lived full lives ... containing joy and pain in equal measure, but full, nonetheless. Do you feel an absence of something?"

It was his turn to shrug, "I am not certain." It was not his way to mourn decisions made, nor had he ever regretted the sacrifice of home and hearth for his freedom. These feelings were a stranger to him.

"Was it not you who explained to me in this very bed two years ago that were you to give up your life in the city or I to give up my pastoral existence, it would lead to resentment on one or both of our parts?"

The thief grumbled, "Certainly sounds like me."

"If you also recall, I could not disagree with you."

He raised an eyebrow, "That certainly does not sound like you."

Maggie poked him sharply in the ribs, "You tempt fate, old man ... sans armor and weapon as you are." She kissed him gently where his throat met with his shoulder, "I am not innocent in this, my own excuses equal your own. I have made a life for myself here. I could not bring myself to abandon everything I have built for a life on the road or even as a society matron among the gardens of Oizan. This land is as much in my blood as the alleys of your home are in yours."

"Why have you not..."

"... found another husband? I will echo your own words: I would only consider adding another to my life if it were you ... but our lives are so disparate as to be discordant. Living one of our lives together would undoubtedly lessen the other."

14

Despite the pragmatic wisdom, Hollis still felt that something was missing from his life. "I can be wise when I choose to be."

"... *when you choose to be*," she repeated in a low, slightly mocking rumble. With her head tucked under his chin, she could not see his glare; but he was certain she could feel it. "Have you ever reconsidered finding someone more suited to the haphazard epic that is your own life?" She pulled away from him a little to study his face in the early morning shadows.

"I refer you to my previous ... and quite honestly stunningly wise statement." Hollis looked down into her face, his memories filling in the features hidden by those same shadows. "So here we are."

"Here we are," she agreed.

Despite the inevitable solitary nature of each of their lives, the thief did not find himself disheartened. He truly enjoyed his way of life. Living by his wits, coming and going as he pleased, when he pleased suited him. His life was rarely quiet; Hollis hated the quiet. In Maggie, he had a companion soul, if not truly a kindred one.

These moments recharged them both, giving him a still port in the storm of his existence and her the knowledge that she was not the cold, calculating cattle baroness the townspeople saw in her.

Unbidden a sense of guilt rolled through his gut like a frigid stream, leaving his heart chilled in its wake. For a moment, he could not shake the thought that lying beside here, beside one of his oldest friends, he in turn betrayed another.

As quickly as it came, the feeling faded.

Hollis's instincts had served him well from childhood, however; he was never one to ignore their warnings, no matter how trivial. He turned inward, seeking the source of the strange emotion. Neither the thief nor the woman beside him had made any promises of exclusivity, nor had either expected any. The question then remained, from what or who originated the sense of betrayal?

At the back of his mind, a memory flickered just beyond his perception. When Hollis attempted to chase it, the memory flitted away like a

15

butterfly in the summer sun. A frustrated frown found its way to his lips.

Maggie misunderstood the gesture. "Have you had a change of heart?" She gently rubbed his arm, watching him with a concerned expression. He wondered what she was thinking and felt guilty for worrying her.

The thief shook his head absently, "It's not that ... it just ..." Through force of will, he brought the elusive memory to heel. The issue was that he had no idea what he had caught. He could see in his mind's eye a woman, and a severe frown stamped upon her face like a minted coin. Hollis did not recognize the woman; but her very image brought with it feelings of shame and frustration.

The conversation fled his mind as further memories crushed on him from every direction. He saw the stern woman dressed in white, the dark wood of a church surrounding her. He felt the weight of words he did not comprehend falling on him, bringing with them humiliation and anger. Although he could not identify the woman, she seemed familiar to him. Then it dawned on him like a rush of cold water.

Stephen realized that he was dreaming. A loud, chirping cut the air like a scream ... the fear came rushing back ... and the dread began to crush him again.

His eyes opened slowly, hesitantly as he tried to hold on to the sensation and the emotion. For a long second, he could still feel the breeze on his face. He could smell the earthy scent of Maggie's skin. More importantly, he could feel the passion deep in his being and the hollow longing for its touch again.

He lay in bed alone; Ronni must not have come to bed. He was secretly glad for that fact, almost as if her presence would tarnish Maggie's memory. His hand found the switch to silence his alarm clock before pushing himself into a sitting position. He took a deep breath to steady himself for the day to come and found that the air tasted somehow thin, almost artificial compared to the world of the dream.

Stephen dressed quickly, pulling on dress pants and a polo shirt before making his way quietly to the bathroom. He ran his fingers along his jaw; he could go another day without shaving; but his boss would no doubt use that as another reason for not giving him a raise, or a promotion, or any sort of positive feedback. He stripped off his shirt and pulled his razor from the medicine cabinet.

$\sim$

The day passed quickly; his boss favoring him with disinterested apathy rather than the honest venom he was quite capable of. As he passed through the toll booth on to the New Jersey Turnpike, Stephen slipped his blue tooth into his ear and thumbed open the contacts on his phone. Beneath Ronni on his favorites, he touched Alan's number. The electronic chirping ring sounded a half dozen times before he heard a click: "You've reached Alan's phone. No doubt I'm doing something more interesting. Leave your name, number and a brief message and I'll get back to you as soon as I can *beep*."

"Hey, Alan … It's Stephen … I just wanted to apologize again for last night. I'm looking forward to this weekend. Give me a call when you get a chance. See you later, brother."

He ended the call and tossed his Bluetooth on the passenger seat, sitting back and settling in for his two-hour drive home. His mind returned to the dream. It had felt so real, more real than any dream he could think of in recent memory. A smile came unbidden to his lips when he thought about how vibrant it was, how much brighter and intense the colors seemed, how much fuller the air tasted, how much sweeter time spent with Maggie was. He shook his head, now he was cheating on his very real wife with a dream. *How sad was that?*

His fingers turned the radio on and quickly cycled through the stations, ending on an oldies station playing Asia. He chuckled, "*Heat of the Moment*" was his favorite song in the 80's; it was the soundtrack to his summers spent at that small day camp. What was its name, Pine Something? He did remember clearly the lazy days of swimming and capture the flag.

He could smell the scent of damp pine trees and fresh cut grass.

And The Game. That camp was where he first learned about The Game from some older campers.

He could sense the excitement in the pit of his stomach as he took his first steps into the world of his imagination.

He remembered how he made his parents go out and buy it that weekend. How his father promised to play it with him but changed his mind when he found that there was no board, no playing pieces.

He could remember how different he felt in that moment; but it did not dull the unbridled joy that The Game brought him.

His parents supported his playing the game; but neither really understood it.

He could imagine how hard it must have been; most boys his age were playing pickup football games or little league baseball. Their son spent those hours alone in his room reading and taking furious notes in an old marble notebook.

When camp ended that summer, so too did The Game. No one at school knew about it, much less played it. When he tried to explain it, they just laughed at him. He became more of an outcast – the weird kid in class.

He could feel the way their laughter and words of derision bit into him like a physical thing.

But that did not dull his love of The Game. No one understood how it made him feel, how for the first time in his life, he belonged. He felt that he could truly influence things and not be just another ineffectual nobody.

He could recall the wonder and satisfaction of The Game driving from his heart the shadows cast by the other children.

That was when summers became magical for Stephen. From June to August, he felt like he belonged. He was with people that understood him, people that were as passionate about The Game as he was.

He could hear the voices of his friends, calling to him, the ache of the school year would fall from his shoulders like a summer rain the moment he stepped from his father's car onto the grounds of camp.

CHAPTER TWO
AN UNBEARABLE TRAGEDY

Stephen pulled into his driveway as the sun was starting to set. Ronni wasn't home yet. Perhaps she had stopped somewhere on the way home, or perhaps she was at her brother's house. He put his Bluetooth into his jacket pocket and took out his laptop bag from the back seat. The house was cool and quiet as he stepped inside; it almost seemed ominous, like a tomb. Stephen liked the quiet; he liked the dim light, but this was different. Moving around the house in the pre-dawn hours, before Ronni awoke, it felt calming; but this felt like the eye of a storm. He had the sense that everything would break loose at any moment. The feeling made him uneasy.

His jacket chirped a split second before his cell phone rang, making him jump. It rang twice more, before he fished it from his pocket and put it to his ear, "Hello?"

"Stephen, dude, something happened last night." It was Robert's voice. He sounded uncharacteristically somber

"I know, bro. I already said I was sorry."

"No, not that ... Mike was driving Alan home from your house."

The uneasy feeling in his stomach built up, and it filled him with fear. A flash of heat passed through Stephen's body, leaving his skin tingling with dread, "And, what happened?" He had asked the question, although he knew he didn't want to hear the answer.

"There was an accident. The car flipped over. Mike's in the hospital."

"What about Alan?" There was silence on the line. "Rob, what about Alan?"

"He's gone." Stephen heard the hitch in his friend's voice. "The police said it was quick; but he's ..." Robert took a deep breath but couldn't continue.

Stephen felt as if a hole had opened in his chest, stealing the breath from his lungs as he stood in his darkened living room, with his phone pressed to his ear. Silence hung in the air for a minute before he finally was able to speak, "I can't believe it." The revelation of his friend's death felt like a physical thing, crushing him beneath its weight. At a loss for anything else to say, he repeated, "I can't believe it."

"His folks are having something on Wednesday at Beckett's."

Stephen's grandparents both had their funerals at that parlor. "I know where it is. I'll be there." Although he had no idea how he was going to get off from work with such short notice. *Screw it, I'll call in sick,* he thought, *it's not like they ever showed me any loyalty.* "What about Mike? Which hospital is he in?"

"Saint Margret's."

"Okay let me get changed and I'll head over. Do you need me to pick you up on the way?"

"No. I have to wait until my mom gets home with the car; but I will be there as soon as I can."

"Okay, see you there." Stephen hung up. He didn't know how long he stood there with his phone in his hand before heading to his bedroom to get changed. He heard the front door open as he was pulling on his jeans. Tugging a tee shirt over his head, he walked out into the living room.

"Why's it so dark in here? Is it so much to ask that you turn on the lights when you get home, so I don't trip over something and kill myself?" Ronni asked, as she put her tote down on a chair. He hadn't heard her come in.

"Alan's dead." Stephen blurted out more harshly than he had intended.

"I'm sorry, he was so young." She put her hand on his chest, the anger draining from her face. "What happened?"

"Mike crashed his car last night on the way home."

"From here?" she asked. Stephen nodded, feeling deflated once again. Ronni's face tightened into a scowl. "Had he been home with his family rather than playing that damned game that would never have happened." She shook her head sadly, "His mother must be beside herself."

Stephen reeled in shock, "You can't possibly be blaming the game for this." She always managed to make him feel worse than he already did. He hadn't thought it possible, but here he was.

She shook her head; but her face told another story, "I'm just saying that if he had been home like a ..."

"Normal kid," Stephen finished for her. He pushed past her, a little more roughly than he'd planned. "Mike's in the hospital. I may be late."

"Stephen, I didn't mean ... "

"Yes, you did." He did not turn to face her; he didn't know if he could handle it. "You did mean to ... even now, you can't let it drop. I'll be late. Don't wait up." With that he walked through the door, closing it behind him. He thought he heard her speak to him through the door, but he wasn't sure that he could stand it if her words only contained more venom.

∿

As the automatic doors opened, the air-conditioned air hit Stephen like a bucket of cold water, burning his sinuses for a moment. Even now, with his best friend lying dead in some

23

funeral parlor and another lying in a hospital bed, his mind returned to the dream. The tomb-like air here was cold and sharp, but it had no soul, no anima, nothing to give it anything of substance. Not like the wind on that hill side, the wind outside Maggie's cottage. He shook his head, *that was just a dumb dream; and this is real life. For all you know, Mike could be dying too, and you stand here thinking about a stupid fantasy,* he scolded himself.

He stepped up to the desk, "I'm here to see Michael Ryan." He forced a smile that he did not feel to his face, "Can you tell me what room he's in?"

The woman looked up at him and then tapped a few keys on her computer, "He's in room 672; but that's intensive care. Only family are permitted. I'm sorry, sir." To her credit, she did seem to feel for him.

He nodded slowly, and he was now at a loss as to what to do next. Across the lobby, the elevator doors opened, and Mike's stepsister Nellie emerged. He could see her eyes were red from crying. She had been a sophomore when he graduated high school. Stephen had known her mother. The two shared their dark auburn locks and soulful, chestnut brown eyes. "Thank you, Miss," he said absently to the receptionist before hurrying across the floor to where Nellie stood. She smiled sadly when she recognized him. "I'm so sorry, Nell. How is he?"

She wrapped her arms around his neck, "Oh, Stephen, he's just lying there; tubes sticking out of him. They say he may never," her voice caught for a moment, "never wake up."

He rubbed her back lightly, "It'll be okay, Nell ... It'll be okay." Stephen had known Nellie for more than a decade; he had spent a lot of time at her house, as her mother and he had played the Game together. She had never been the emotional type; even when her mother died suddenly in her junior year, Stephen couldn't remember her crying. She had looked sad, sure; but she was a rock for her father. Protective and kind to a fault, Nellie always wore a strong face for those around her. Mike's accident was hitting her hard.

"Let me buy you a coffee?"

She thought about it for a quick second and then nodded.

∾

"He just lies there, Stephen ... he hit his head during the crash, but they can't find signs of a serious concussion. They did a CT scan and an MRI; both came back inconclusive." Nellie sat with her hands wrapped tightly around her cup, clutching it like it was her lifeline.

Stephen reached across the table and touched her arm, "Then he should wake up soon, right?" He wanted to be comforting, although there wasn't much that he knew he could do.

She nodded quickly and smiled a little, as if trying to reassure him that she was okay. "He should've woken already but he just ... he just doesn't. He can breathe on his own but that's it. He doesn't react to pain or light or anything." She gritted her teeth so fiercely that he thought he heard a crack as she repeated, "He just lies there."

"I tried to get up to see him; but they're only allowing family."

She shook her head, "Follow me. Maybe it will be good for him to hear your voice. I've been talking to him all afternoon." She rose from the table in a single movement, her posture defeated, "I don't know if it does any good, but I don't know what else to do."

Stephen followed her to the elevator, "I'll give it the old college try." He smiled sadly at her, but she was focused on a spot beyond his face, lost in her own thoughts. They emerged from the elevator on the sixth floor. He followed her to the right, down a hall marked by slate grey room numbers and black clipboards. She stopped in front of the one marked 672; Mike's name was written in marker above it. She nodded towards the room, her eyes welling up again, before turning her face from him. Stephen stepped into the room; the smell of excrement barely covered by antiseptic assaulting his senses. He settled into a chair that had been pulled beside the bed, no doubt by Nellie.

"Hey buddy, I imagine you've had better days, huh?" Suddenly he felt a little foolish, his voice echoing a bit inside the tomb like room. "Nell says that there's no reason you should be asleep ... so maybe you go ahead and wake up?" The words felt awkward as they rolled from his lips, but he continued to babble, at a loss about how to proceed. As much as he hoped that his voice brought his friend comfort, part of him hoped that he couldn't hear him rambling. He paused, truly looking at Mike for the first time. A bandage was wrapped loosely around his head and a large gauze pad was taped to his left forearm; but, as Nell had said, other than that, he looked like he was in good shape. His breathing was slow and steady, as if he was merely sleeping rather than deep in a coma.

Stephen's eyes went from his friend's face to the bank of machines to which he was connected. His heart rate seemed normal, if not a little slow. His blood pressure as of a few minutes ago looked normal; certainly, more normal than his own the last time he had gone to the doctors. Mike's chart hung on the foot of his bed; almost inviting him to look. Ignoring the fact that Stephen would not know a medical chart from a pie graph, it was also the best way to get himself thrown out of the room. Hospitals take HIIPPA pretty seriously.

Just as he was going to pick it up anyway, he heard a pair of voices in the hall. He sat back in his chair. He watched Mike again, suddenly at a loss for words.

"Did the lab have any more luck with the second set of blood panels?" It was a woman's voice, her tone soft and inquisitive.

A Nurse or Doctor? Stephen thought.

"No, Doctor Freeman." A man's voice responded then. "They think it may be some sort of narcotic that put his Thyroid levels into a tailspin; but they have no idea what it is. How'd you know to even ask for them to test that?"

There was a pause, as if the woman was contemplating something, "A couple of detectives came in just as my shift was starting and asked about it. Something they found with his friend, the DOA." The voices faded as the pair walked further down the hallway. The last thing Stephen heard clearly was Doctor Freeman saying, "Shame about kids these days."

~

As Stephen walked Nellie to the elevator, he stopped her, "Nell, I have to ask you something … it's about Mike."

She turned to face him, his tone snapping her out of her funk for a moment, "What's that, Stephen?"

"Do you know if he was taking, you know … anything?"

She frowned, understanding what he was asking but not wanting to. "Like medicine or …"

"Or."

Rage filled her expression. She pointed a finger at him, a little too close to his face for his liking. He'd never seen her like this, and it worried him. "Stephen, I'm going to chalk this up to you being upset about Mike and Alan and looking for a way to make sense of all this; but don't you ever accuse my brother of being an addict. He was … is a good kid." She punched the down button and turned away from him.

"I didn't mean to …" He laid his hand on her arm; but she shrugged him off. It was a very quiet seven floors down in the elevator. Stephen was almost glad when the doors opened. Robert was waiting in the lobby; Stephen assumed that Nell was going to take him up next. He caught Robert's arm for a moment, "Call me later," before releasing it.

Stephen walked through the automatic doors into the humid night; it was like walking into a wet towel. He stood on the curb, his mind spinning as he tried to make sense of it all. If the police were correct, Alan had the same chemical in his system that was causing Mike's coma; but he knew for sure that Alan was not taking drugs. Stephen had never met a more anti-drug proponent than Alan. His father, Jeff, had died from an overdose the same day Nell's mother was hospitalized for her brain embolism. His uncle drank himself to death later that same year. Stephen felt for the entire family, who had suffered such tragedy through the years. Now, Alan had been added into the equation, and for what?

It just didn't make sense. There was something missing, but he couldn't put his finger on it. He found himself in the parking lot, his feet leading him to his car on their own. Unlocking the door, he slid into the driver's seat and started the car; still not knowing where he would go. He didn't want to go home quite yet; Ronni was there and with time to stew, he could be in for a pretty huge fight if he was home before she was asleep.

He put the car in reverse and backed out of the parking spot, clicking the shifter twice, putting it in drive.

He parked in front of Alan's house without realizing his destination and sat in the quiet car for a moment. Asking Nell about Mike's possible drug use had gone sideways like their damaged car, and there was little chance that asking Alan's parents the same thing would go any better. Perhaps he would do it clearly and tell them about the conversation he'd overheard between the doctor and nurses. He stepped out of the car and walked to the door. It took a few minutes for Alan's stepfather to answer the door.

"Stephen, we were wondering when you'd be by." Alan's family's acceptance of their son's friendship with a man almost ten years his senior had always made Stephen happy. Coming from a small family, the connection that he had made with Alan's father,

Jeff, had made his high school experience more bearable. Stephen had been small and unpopular; he never could understand what made Jeff, his freshman history teacher, extend his friendship and hospitality to the boy. After Stephen's own parents' deaths Alice and Jeff had become almost surrogate parents to him. When Jeff passed, Stephen tried to give the same support to Alan that his father had extended to him.

"Fredrick, I'm so sorry. Do you and Alice need anything?"

Alan's step-father shook his head solemnly "Having you here is enough. Please come in." He stepped back to allow Stephen to step inside. "Alice is lying down; the doctor gave her something to help her sleep." He walked back towards the kitchen, "Can I get you anything? Soda, beer?"

Stephen shook his head, "No, sir, thank you, I'm fine." He leaned against the counter, watching the man only a handful of years older than himself open the refrigerator, looking for something he would never find. The dark-skinned man's normally warm, calm face was filled with grief and worry. Conspicuous by its absence was the ever-present smile that seemed to always be nested among the grey depths of his thick beard. His normally clean-shaven head was beginning to sprout a salt and pepper stubble that the fastidious man would never have allowed, under normal circumstances. "Do they know what caused the accident?"

Fredrick shrugged, pulling an infusion pitcher out and pouring Stephen a glass before continuing. Stephen watched him, grateful even though he'd refused any kind of beverage. "They say that Alan was on something ... you know my Alan ... our Alan would never take that junk. His father, his uncle's death, they almost broke him ... almost broke both him and Alice."

Although it had no scent, the glass contained the same foul infusion as his friend's bottle had the night before. He shook his head and took another swig. This one went down easier than the first. Alan had always stayed lean, a direct contrast to Stephen's ever-expanding waistline. Perhaps his friend could do him one final service and force him to take his health more seriously. Unfortunately, drinking this concoction may very well drive a man to wish to see his friend sooner than expected.

Stephen nodded, "I remember. Jeff's death was a shock to all of us." Alan's father had been his freshman History teacher and the first adult that had understood The Game and his obsession with it. Before his death, Jeff had also been the Game Master for a group that included Stephen, Nell's mother, Beatrice and Robert's older brother, Roger. Occasionally, Jeff's brother, George would join them; but usually the game consisted of the four of them.

After the closing of his childhood camp, it was the first time Stephen had felt that same sense of belonging. No matter what misery high school brought him all week, Sundays always washed it away. Those hours of playing The Game shored up his defenses for the week to come. He knew it was just pretend; but the sense of pride he felt at defeating a black thaumaturge or slaying a dragon based on nothing, but his wits and the known qualities written on his character sheet was very real.

When he began, he had asked to play a thaumaturge. The idea of playing an intellectual being, weak of body but powerful in ways the jocks and popular kids in school could never understand appealed to him. Alan's father had insisted he play Hollis, however; he had even generated the character before his first session. Being the child of a very moral upbringing, the idea of playing a thief didn't resonate with him; but Jeff had been very adamant. Stephen grew to like Hollis over the next several sessions; playing him became like slipping on a comfortable sweater. Now he would feel uncomfortable playing anything else; it would seem somehow wrong.

When Jeff passed away suddenly, Stephen was heartbroken. Robert's brother, Roger had said that the group was unlucky; first Jeff overdosed, and Beatrice died of a ruptured brain embolism a day later. Roger never played The Game again. Roger now sold industrial heating and air conditioning systems. He'd been adamantly opposed to his brother joining the group; but Robert had always been independent and played anyway.

Lucky for us, Stephen had thought, *The Game always feels best with four. Three and a Game Master, the magic number.*

"Stephen? Stephen, are you alright?" Fredrick asked.

He had zoned out, lost himself in the past, "Yes ... yes, I'm alright, Fredrick. I'm sorry, it's just all so sudden."

The man nodded, "It's hard on all of us. Alan was such a good boy ... young man. I wasn't his father but that never stopped me from loving him .... from being proud of him." Fredrick wiped away a tear, turning to hide the motion.

"Did the police say what they found in his system?"

Fredrick frowned a bit but answered slowly, "No. They just asked if he'd been having issues with drugs ... acting strangely. Things like that."

Stephen sighed, "I hate to ask this, knowing Alan like I did; but did you notice anything unusual? I was just in the hospital, visiting Mike, and I overheard..."

The look of disappointment in Fredrick's eyes hit him harder than Nell's anger. To his credit, he answered, "Nothing like that. He'd been going through his father's things in the attic recently. I figured it was just that he didn't want to forget him ... wanted to feel close to him as he went off to college."

Stephen put his hand on Fredrick's shoulder, squeezing it lightly, "I'm sure they're wrong. Alan wasn't that kind of kid." He couldn't help but think there was some kind of connection. At the back of his mind there was an itch, the beginning of an idea. It was almost as if there was something, he should have known but could not recall. The idea was like something seen out of the corner of your eye; but when you turn it is gone. It could only be known in the periphery of his memory.

The clock above the stove read 11:30 and that same fear gripped his stomach; he had to be up for work in less than six hours. "Listen, Fredrick, you have my number. Call me anytime if you or Alice need anything. I'll come by tomorrow night." to check on you." He caught the man's eye. "Both of you."

Fredrick nodded again and followed him to the door. A quick handshake was all Alan's stepfather could manage; Stephen could see the tears he barely held back.

CHAPTER THREE
AN UNCOMFORTABLE REALIZATION

H ollis was standing on the crowded street, taking advantage of the shade granted by a vendor's awning; the bazaar before him spread out like a quilt of brightly colored stalls. The smell of baking bread and cooking meat filled his senses; beneath it hid the heavy scent of massed humanity. While not pleasant, the sour and earthy smells of sweat at least felt real, complete. Not like ... like what? Hollis closed his eyes for a moment, chasing the wisps of an idea as it faded into nothingness.

He shook his head and opened his eyes; it must have been nothing.

Even under the shade granted by the stall, the day was scorching. By the position of the sun, it could not be later than two hours before noon and already a thin sheen of sweat had built on his crossed forearms. For a moment a touch of fear caressed him, raising the hairs on the back of his neck with that familiar tingle. At first, he could not remember where he was or how he came to be here; but then the realization came to him.

The independent city of Oenigh stood to the southeast of the kingdom of Slazè, just outside the desert wastes known as the Expanse. It was the last vestige of civilization before entering the fifty-league desert between here and the Dwarven city of Drunmarch, nestled among the Grey Spire Mountains. Dwarven steel and its value in markets throughout the known realms made the journey worth it, despite the toll it could take on a caravan. It was from these caravans that Oenigh derived its wealth.

Hollis had come here in search of Renthroas Halfborn, a sometimes-comrade and full-time friend. Hollis had found Ren half-starved and bloody in one of the twisted alleys of the Slum District of Oizan almost five years previous. The half elven – or half human depending on your point of view – boy had run afoul of one of the many gangs who had divided the District up amongst themselves for as long as Hollis could remember. Beneath the grime and blood, Ren showed signs of wealth; his nails were smooth and clean, his hair and face groomed. The boy did not volunteer any information at the time and his rescuer did not ask. It was not until much later that Hollis found out that his friend was the bastard son of a traveling elvish diplomat and the daughter of a minor noble family. The hushed comments and shameful glances of his mother's family drove him from his home and onto the streets.

Their loss was Hollis's gain; never had he had as loyal a companion as Renthroas Halfborn. Hollis reached into his pouch and pulled forth a wrinkled letter that had seen better days. It had found him just over a month ago, left for him at a dead drop the pair often used in Oizan. Unfolding it before shifting his eyes from the bazaar, Hollis scanned the words. He knew them by heart.

My friend,

News of my father has reached my ears by way of the Fair Folk. Although I know you would accompany me at a moment's notice, time is not a patient mistress and the trail grows cold. Rhyzzo has agreed to travel with me to Drunmarch, where he was last seen. We will leave word of our intended destination should we not find him in the dwarven city. Join us when you can. I believe that his disappearance holds significance for us all; else I would not travel with so much haste and such little caution.

Your Friend

Something nagged at the edge of Hollis's consciousness. It was something he should know, something that would shed light on the letter; but it fled from his thoughts as he tried to make sense of the feeling, the same way a shadow flees from the light.

Hollis vaguely remembered the week's journey to Oenigh from Maggie's farm in the north of Slazè. The details blurred in the fog of his memory; the heat must have been having more of an effect on him than he first believed. Perhaps it was the shock of the day's events, as well. He froze, a cold sense of realization countering the harsh glare of the sun for a moment. He could see Rhyzzo lying motionless in a bed, strange machines attached to him by brightly colored cables; an insistent noise demanding attention, its rhythm strong and regular. Beep. Beep. Beep.

As suddenly as it came upon him, the vision dissipated; leaving him frightened and confused. Fear turned to violence as a hand touched his arm. Without a thought, Hollis had drawn his needle thin stiletto and turned to face the man to whom that hand belonged. The plump caravan master paled two shades beneath his keffiyeh, as he pulled his hand back as if it had burned him.

"I had not meant to startle you, Sayyid. I realize we were to meet here as the sun crested the mountains; I apologize for the delay."

Hollis allowed the point of his blade to drop, flushing a bit in embarrassment, "Of course, Aamir. Forgive me, I have much on my mind and time escaped me this morning as well." Silently he cursed himself; had it been an enemy rather than the fat caravan master, he would have no longer needed to worry about Rhyzzo or Ren. He would have never needed to worry about anything again. Ever.

The man bowed slightly, "It is nothing, Sayyid. There is not much that gets a man's blood pumping before a long trip better than threatened death. That is what my mother always said." Hollis nodded absently. "We have finished procuring supplies and should be ready to leave soon. Do you think you will be prepared by then?" And then a little quieter, more tentative, "Do you think you will have the payment?"

Hollis sheathed his weapon and pulled a fat pouch from the folds of his vest. "As agreed, Aamir," he nodded, tossing it to the other man. His left hand rested on the hilt of his short sword. "I trust there will not be any, shall we say, unexpected surprises? Also, as agreed?"

Aamir nodded quickly, "No one will see you leave, and my cousin will spread word of seeing you in various cantinas over the next few weeks." He smiled broadly; although the gesture reminded Hollis more of a shark than anything designed to bring him comfort.

"Very good. Then I am ready to leave when you are." He shouldered his pack and followed the man from the bazaar.

Aamir led Hollis through the winding alleys of Oenigh as if he were navigating his own home. He turned seemingly randomly through the patchwork of laundry lines and grit-lined streets, never slowing his constant chatter. He took note of his guide's eyes as he rambled on, watching to ensure that the faces behind them did not look too familiar.

When they finally reached his home, he pulled the curtain hanging in the threshold back, allowing Hollis to enter the squat daub building before him. The thief's hand again rested upon the sharkskin wrapped hilt of his sword out of habit; but nothing more threatening than Aamir's four children awaited him. They squealed and surrounded him. The oldest, a boy of the advanced age of ten, touched the leather that was wrapped around his sword like a second skin with hesitant fingers.

Hollis reached down to swat the boy's hand from the sheath with his left hand and his right caught Aamir's daughter's wrist, her own fingers already halfway into the folds of his vest. "There is nothing there for you, boy ... you either, little Princess." He winked in her direction, eliciting a deep blush from her cheeks, "Although, I do commend the effort." Aamir came in behind him, opening his mouth to protest, only to be cut off by a shake of the thief's head and an easy smile, "Do not do either of us the dishonor. Like understands like... and I have, on occasion, been accused of having wandering fingers. No harm done." He released the girl's wrist and gestured, "After you, Sayyid," stressing the last word. He saw her rubbing the offended body part briskly out of the corner of his eye as the two men made their way through the kitchen and back out into the city.

"Nice children," Hollis commented.

Aamir shrugged as he walked, setting a slower pace, "They are my beloved wife's." Hollis raised an eyebrow but remained silent, waiting for the man to continue. "She is my dearest desert flower and the sun upon my life. If she says that they come from our bed, I do not argue." He continued to watch Aamir through hooded lids. "But the camel whose hoof had a not so intimate interaction with a very intimate portion of my body as a child may indicate otherwise." The man's smile

39

never dimmed as he shrugged again, and added, "As I said, she is my sun."

Hollis felt pity for the man initially; but that pity turned to a touch of envy. To love someone so much must be a freeing state of being... not like...what?

Again, on the edge of his mind, a thought danced. He still had not caught it when the two reached the small caravan, tucked behind a bleached, empty building. Hollis could picture the tight confines of the cantina within its walls, always filled despite the lack of a sign or a name. With practiced, light steps, the thief climbed into the back of a wagon covered in bright silks. The inside was close and hot; but soon the shade would be a boon companion.

He settled back, closing his eyes. His relief at being out of the sun washed over him; it was then that the thought that had been plaguing him for most of the morning came into startling clarity. This was not his life, not his real life.

Stephen realized that this was just another dream and soon he would awaken to find his wife beside him, that sour look upon her face, even in sleep. He would need to face another day in a job he hated and another night with the woman who hated him. That same sense of dread rose in his stomach as he prepared for the dream to fade and life to once again impose its will upon him.

Except that it did not do so.

He still felt the hard, wooden floor of the wagon beneath him rather than the soft surface of his bed and the oppressive heat of a city on the verge of the Expanse rather than the slight chill of his air-conditioned bedroom. Besides the panic he still felt in his belly, his mind could not tell the dream from reality. His thumb ran along his palm, rubbing the rough calluses found there ... calluses that Stephen did not possess. He could smell the close-ness of the wagon and beneath it the sickly-sweet smell of horse dung and fresh bread. Once more, his mind turned to how rich the air smelled as opposed to the thin, sanitized scent of his house, his office ... his world.

A smile came to his lips, thinking that if he was not going to suddenly awaken, he might as well enjoy the dream for as long as it lasted.

That was when he heard the voices. At first, they were hushed, although their tone belied their volume. Over them, he could hear Aamir's voice calling out in protest, louder than necessary. "There is nothing in the wagon, but goat's milk and cheese bound for Sharroth's Point Oasis."

Stephen frowned slightly; but deep inside his mind a voice screamed to him, the pangs of panic from his waking world being replaced by fear from this one. It is just a dream, he assured himself.

He climbed from the back of the wagon and heard Aamir shout, "No, Sayyid!" a split second before he was thrown to the ground.

The dirt rushed to meet Stephen as a pair of rough hands gave him a short shove. Reactions he did not command caused him to tuck his shoulder and roll as he fell, coming to his feet in one effortless movement, facing his attacker. With a smooth, practiced motion, his sword was free of its sheath and its tip leveled with the man's breastbone. It was a toss-up who was more shocked, his attacker or Stephen himself. The three men wore the pale-yellow uniform of Oenigh's city guard and the two behind Stephen's attacker each drew scimitars from sheaths at their waists. The third remained very still, his hands open and extended slightly towards him.

One of his companions turned to Aamir, "This is goat's milk and bread bound for Sharroth's Point Oasis?"

Aamir's eyes darted to meet Stephen's, hard and dark; but his tone remained light, "You never gave me a chance to finish. This is my cousin... my wife's cousin, really, from the north. He is not all that bright and cannot speak a word." He stressed the last five words before continuing, "He is good for lifting heavy things and little else."

The guard, obviously the leader of his band of three nodded gravely, "He may not speak; but he has made his intentions known in Oenigh before." His gaze never leaving Stephen, "Do you honestly believe I could forget the man whose actions forced me to the streets, Slender One?"

Stephen froze, as unbidden, memories and instinct that were not his own flooded his mind. He felt another consciousness surge forward, relegating him to the position of observer once more.

Over the years, Hollis's youthful frame had broadened. His love of fine food and drink left him with an expanding waistline, earning him the sarcastic moniker Hollis the Slender. From the depths of these memories, came a recollection of the desert city-state. He had stolen a necklace from around the throat of the favored daughter of the Emir and then left the city with the daughter in her entirety. He chuckled softly at the thought.

The leader snapped, "Do you find something funny?"

He bit his lip slightly and shook his head, "No, sir. I am just afraid you have me confused for someone else ..." Aamir frowned deeply as Hollis realized his mistake.

"Not a word hmm?"

Stephen thought he remembered his name was Omar, or was it from Hollis's memory? He couldn't be sure, his memories and those of the thief he inhabited mixed together in a confusing rush of images and thoughts.

"The Emir had a few questions for you, I believe. They begin with the location of his favored daughter and end with how long you will scream on the tip of a spear."

Stephen felt the cold hand of fear creep into his stomach but as the rain washed away the dust of a summer's day, a cool feeling of confidence asserted itself atop the dread. He could still feel the fear but Hollis's faith in his skills with sword and dirk dulled it.

"Your companions are more than two yards from me but, alas, my steel is a whore's conscience from your heart. Should they stir even that

much, you will be telling this tale to Olm himself before they can raise their blades." With a slow, sure motion, he drew his emerald pommeled stiletto from its sheath with his left hand.

Omar swallowed slowly one time, as if his throat was suddenly drier than the desert that surrounded them and then again with more effort.

"Now, I have places to be ... places that include neither Oenigh nor yourselves. We find ourselves at a fork in the road, in a philosophical sense. Both lead to the same place, although the paths taken differ quite substantially." He pointed east with the tip of his dagger, "The first path leads me into the Expanse immediately with no further issues or discussion with any of the three of you. Everyone is content, if not exactly happy, and more importantly able to go our separate ways in the same state we are now."

"You are a fool if you believe we will let that happen." Omar had found his voice again.

The thief shook his head slowly, his eyes remaining focused on the three men.

The tip of Hollis's short sword traced a small circle on Omar's chest. "In that case you will be wanting to hear about the second path. This one, too, leads me into the Expanse but, unfortunately, it takes me through the three of you. Omar's concern for his Emir dictated punishment ceases to be a concern immediately. Both of his fellow guards will rush me; but in a street so clogged with men, wagons and beasts, my short, light weapons will serve me far better than your large heavy ones, especially when you need to mind each other as well as make an, no doubt earnest, attempt on my life. It is my honest opinion that both of you will end your day in a pool of your own life's blood, right here on this street." A small smirk came to his lips like the touch of an angel's feather. "I honestly have no strong feelings either way; so, it is up to you three... take your time."

The sound of sand beneath a sandal behind him was the only warning he had before something heavy and mightily swung collided with his temple.

43

Stephen's only thought before the darkness rose up with the street to consume him was that he had a sudden need to finish the job the camel started on Aamir.

~

The heat of the dream was more obvious by its absence, as Stephen came to himself in the darkness of his own bed, the drone of the window air-conditioner filling his ears that, only a moment ago, were ringing from Aamir's cudgel blow. His hand went to his right temple but didn't find any tenderness at all.

What his elbow found was Roni's ribs. "What the fuck, Stephen?!?" she exclaimed, as she rolled over, "I swear, you can't even sleep like a normal person."

"I'm sorry, Roni." Stephen rubbed her shoulder gently as she drifted back to sleep. He normally would feel a mixture of shame and anger in response to her words but the mixture of fear and excitement from his dream stayed with him. Despite knowing it was a dream, he still couldn't shake the feeling of trepidation over Hollis's fate. He sat up, hanging his legs over the edge of the bed. His eyes went to his bedside clock; it almost shouted 4:09 at him in an angry red hue. He rubbed his face with both hands as the reality of the previous day crashed into him again.

He rose from the bed, stopping to pull a shirt and pair of pants from his dresser before closing the bedroom door behind him. He stood beneath the scalding spray of the shower for what seemed like forever; thinking about the fact that he would never see his best friend again, never hear his carefree laugh, never share their joy and their pains. It all seemed unreal to him; but the weight of truth sat upon his heart like a mountain. His mind kept going back to that night. Alan hadn't left the table for the hours that they were playing; nor had he been acting strangely. The only thing he had been drinking was his water.

Despite the heat of the shower, Stephen's skin chilled.

44

It had been the same water that he himself had drank by mistake, and the same water he had drunk again in his friend's kitchen while consoling Fredrick. He tried to remember if Mike had drunk from Alan's bottle as well.

Could whatever he was infusing into his water be the narcotic that caused the accident?

Stephen turned the shower off with fumbling hands and dried his body quickly. The thoughts of what could have been in Alan's water continued to haunt him as he padded down the stairs into the house's small kitchen. As he did every day, Stephen filled the coffee maker with grounds and started it on its daily task. He did not drink the bitter beverage, but Roni could not start her day without her morning dose. It was a small thing, but the ritual of preparing his wife's morning coffee was one of the few holdovers from happier times.

He crept up the stairs and quietly opened the door to the couple's bedroom. In the dim predawn light, Roni slept peacefully. In slumber, her features became placid, like the surface of a still pond. Stephen remembered the day of their wedding; they were so much in love back then. Roni was beautiful in her off white gown; the subtle pink tones of the fabric complemented the soft red of her lips. In those days, her lips always looked beautiful, drawn into a smile as they often were. A smile came to Stephen's face as he thought of their first dance as husband and wife before family and friends.

They swayed slowly to Bruno Mars' *Just the Way You Are,* her arms wrapped loosely around his neck. It was as if nothing existed for them except the music and each other. As they circled leisurely, they spoke of a future in hushed tones. Stephen was unsure where the fault lie for the present they now experienced. In the soft light of their shared space, he was sure that neither was more to blame than the other. He made a promise to himself to put the effort into their relationship that the young man in his memories would want him to.

By the time the coffee had filled the glass carafe, Stephen had returned to the kitchen to pull a protein bar from the cabinet above the machine. After verifying that the machine was set to keep the coffee warm, he rushed upstairs to face his day

∽

These questions plagued him throughout the day as he tried to get through his nine hours of work. On his lunch break, he used Google to research narcotics and hypothyroidism. His research showed that few to no narcotics cause hypothyroidism, although quite a few chemotherapy drugs, along with dopamine as well as glucocorticoids, which were used for high blood pressure and asthma treatment respectively. None of them, however, could explain the sudden onset in Mike nor cause him to be incapable of driving. He did read that hypothyroidism caused fatigue in some patients and if Mike had lost consciousness before the crash not as a result of it, it would explain his lack of injuries. Many intoxicated drivers emerge from otherwise fatal crashes with minimal injuries. Some studies that Stephen read attributed this to them being relaxed or unconscious at the time of impact.

If Mike's condition was a result of whatever caused Alan's low thyroid levels rather than the impact, it could go a long way toward explaining things.

Approaching it from the side of the symptoms themselves, drugs such as Eszopiclone aided in sleeping and could, given large doses be used recreationally. They could cause hallucinations and fainting but didn't have the side effect of lowering thyroid levels. A few steroid antibiotics, again taken in larger than recommended doses could cause the same side effects along with euphoria; but had reports of hypothyroidism in less than a tenth of a percent of users but none within a few months much less a few hours.

Unless he was mistaken, Mike had not been exposed more than the once.

46

The question of what was in that bottle remained. Stephen resolved to keep his promise to visit Alice and Fredrick after work.

The water was the only commonality. Delirium was one of the symptoms of Hypothyroidism; it could explain the dreams he'd been having since that night. His research kept coming across the fact that sudden onset Hypothyroidism was so rare as to enter the realm of the impossible in three people almost simultaneously. He was so focused on his theory that he didn't realize his boss had come up behind him; he had no idea how long he had been there.

Jared Horne was quite possibly the worst human being that Stephen had ever had the dishonor of knowing. Their company's contract with the financial brokerage firm was signed years ago and as best Stephen could tell, both sides have spent those intervening years trying to cheat each other out of anything and everything they can. Horne & Hew Consulting seemed to be ahead by a quite a large margin. Weighted estimates and outright theft had made Jared a very rich man.

There is a saying that the rich stay that way by making sure that once they have money in their grasp, it never leaves. Jared Horne was a prime example of that. He hired unqualified employees for substantially less than their job would be worth, trained them just enough to not jeopardize his business and took every opportunity to remind them that they couldn't be hired anywhere else.

In times gone by, he would be labeled a tyrant. Actually, even now, the label seemed appropriate. Within The Game, Hollis would have dealt with Horne much before now; but, Stephen could only endure the man's abuse.

"Stephen? Don't you have better things to do than surf the web?"

His eyes darted to the task bar, verifying that he indeed did still have twelve minutes left until his hour lunch was over. "Oh, hello, Jared, I was just looking something up while I'm still on lunch," he said, as he turned to face his boss.

The man was just over six feet tall, skinny but not fit. He looked like he should have been no more than five foot eight but had been stretched to make the last four or five inches. His hair was salt and pepper grey, but it made him look old rather than distinguished, an illusion furthered by the smug, leering smile that he always wore. He sighed and said, "People who want to keep their jobs don't take lunch, Stephen. You want to continue with us, right?" Stephen nodded slowly, not trusting himself to speak for fear of the truth slipping out.

"Your support ticket closure times are in such a state that surely you'd use an extra hour to catch up, rather than take breaks, don't you think?"

Jared always did that, phrasing statements as questions, as if he were speaking to a child. Stephen nodded again. Horne's smile widened, only causing him to appear more patronizing, "Good. There are plenty of people nowadays that would like the chance to make their way up the corporate ladder."." Stephen lowered his gaze to hide his disgust. There was no one in Horne & Hew management that wasn't in some way related to Jared, or who wasn't a friend of Jared's. He turned his chair and closed his web browser; the rest of the day was going to be one of those afternoons.

CHAPTER FOUR
AN ESSENTIAL CROSSROAD

True to his prediction, Jared made his life miserable for the next five hours; Stephen stopped counting at seventeen separate emails asking for statuses on issues that he knew hadn't been dealt with, each with a snarky statement of how a certain level of performance was expected in their employees. He felt like he had been in an actual fight when the elevator opened into the parking garage.

He walked quickly through the oppressive, urine-scented heat to his car, closing the door quickly to shut out both the smell and the contents of his day.

As the door closed, a sense of relief washed over him. Between Alan's wake and funeral, he didn't anticipate having to deal with Jared or work until Thursday afternoon.

It took him twenty minutes to navigate out of Jersey City and onto the New Jersey Turnpike. His hand instinctively reached for his Bluetooth to call Alan; but hovered above it as the realization hit him again. He clenched his fist and punched the roof above his head with all his might.

With people like Jared in the world, how could good, honest people like Alan be gone so soon?

He hit it again before the effects of the first strike reached his brain. Strangely he relished the pain; it was something he could seize onto, something real, a mirror to the agony that filled his heart. He rode in silence for the better part of an hour, rubbing his aching knuckles and allowing the theory he had been developing, to rotate inside his brain.

If whatever Alan had been infusing in his water was the cause of both the accident and Stephen's own startlingly realistic dreams, *what was it? Where did he get it?* Most importantly, even if whatever he was infusing could cause hallucinations and fainting, *how did it affect both himself and Mike so quickly and completely?* There were so many unanswered questions and he had neither medical nor psychology training. *Could this be nothing more than a tragedy and his wild theory be his way of dealing with the senselessness of it all?* That would be the simplest explanation; the one that his mind knew must be the truth.

He should comfort his friend's family, be there for Nellie and focus on keeping a roof over his head and food on his family's table; but his heart told him something very different. There was something beyond a random accident at work here and he owed it to both Alan and Mike as well as the friendship Alan's father had shown him years ago to follow it to its conclusion, no matter where it led him.

Stephen pulled up in front of Alan's house again, no surer of how to proceed than he was when he left work two hours ago. He took a steadying breath and opened his door. The humid summer air hit him like a physical thing; but he climbed out into it anyway. If The Game taught him nothing else, it taught him to think on his feet; he would figure out what to say when he was in the moment. His heart had gotten him into this; it would have to get him out of it as well.

As he walked up the stone steps leading to the front door, he noticed that the curtains had been pulled shut and the house stood dark. Alice had always loved the natural light, insisting that it buoyed the spirit and sharpened the mind.

Having gone through Jeff's death with her and Alan, he didn't relish the thought of seeing her deal with losing her son as well. *Here goes nothing*, he thought to himself as he raised his hand to knock. His knuckles moaned in protest; the pain from his ill-advised show of temper having cooled suddenly flared back to life. He could hear muted voices inside, but it took a few moments for the door to open.

Fredrick again greeted him, "Stephen, it's good to see you. Thank you for coming by; I think it will do Alice well to have someone else in the house." He gestured into the shadowed depths of the living room, where he could just make out her silhouette in a large armchair. Taking a deep breath, he tried to fight down his own grief as he entered the room.

"Hey Ali. How are you holding up?" He smiled softly and offered her his hand. "Whatever you need, I'm here." Alice's short blonde hair was streaked in places with grey, made more apparent by its uncombed appearance. Her blue eyes sparkled with moisture in the dim light of the room. For a moment, he thought the woman would hold it together but then she dissolved into tears as she collapsed into his arms.

"Oh, Stephen ... he was my light ... First Jeff and now Alan ... I don't know if I can make it through this ... I just don't know."

He rubbed her back gently, "It'll be okay. Not now, but someday ... You are a strong woman, Ali ... strongest I have ever known. You will get through it and go on with your life ... because you are strong and that is what he would want. He loved you more than anything else, it would break his heart to know that he brought you any sort of pain at all." Her tears burned against his skin as he cradled her head, "It's alright, let it out. I'm not going anywhere. Fredrick's not going anywhere. In times like this, family has to stick together."

She looked up at him, "You are, you know? Jeff always thought of you as a son, even though we were also blessed with ... Alan." She could barely let the name pass her lips before falling into tears again.

"I know, Ali ... Jeff was always more than my teacher and you made me feel welcome the moment we met. I thought of the two of you as a second family after my parents passed. They couldn't see me get married; but with the two of you there, it was almost as if they had." This didn't calm her crying in the least, and he feared it had only made things worse.

Fredrick entered the room, setting a glass of water down on the coffee table before squeezing his shoulder lightly. Stephen mouthed his thanks, before continuing to speak softly to Alice. "I took the day off tomorrow," which was not quite the truth, as he intended on calling in sick, "I will be there with you both the entire time, for as long as you need me." He turned to Fredrick, "Why don't you take a break? I can sit with her for a while." A look of relief crossed the other man's face and he nodded.

"Alice, I'll be just upstairs, okay?"

"Thank you, Stephen."

They sat in that darkened room for hours talking about Alan; and a few times, a smile even came to her lips. As the sun was beginning to touch the horizon, she asked for her pills and reached for the glass of water that sat forgotten on the table. Stephen quickly snatched it up, making the excuse that it had gone warm and would get her a cold glass to wash her pills down. He poured it down the drain with relief and pulled a fresh glass from the cabinet above the sink, filling it from a Poland Spring jug in the refrigerator. He smelled it twice and dipped in a finger before bringing it back into the living room.

It didn't take even fifteen minutes for Alice to begin softly snoring in her chair. He pulled the quilt from the back off the couch and covered her up gently before taking the glass into the kitchen. It took him a few minutes to wash it and the other dishes that sat in the sink before drying his hands on a dish towel. He checked once more on her before moving towards the door. His hand hovered above the knob as an idea occurred to him. He could hear Fredrick's bear-like snores from above and Alice's puppy-like ones from the living room. There would be no better time.

With as much stealth as he could muster, Stephen crept up the stairs and past the room where Fredrick slept. Slowly, he opened the door to Alan's room and slipped inside; sliding his hand along the wall to locate the light switch. After assimilating to the dim interior of the house, the glaring light momentarily blinded him. He closed his eyes against it and inhaled instinctively; a scent that brought images of Alan to his mind assaulted him. A mixture of his cologne and incense that was such a part of him that it might have been baked into his skin hung in the room. He opened his eyes slowly, his grief rising to the surface once again. The room was just as he'd left it. His textbooks were piled on the oak desk in the corner and the bookshelves were filled with the fathers of modern fantasy: Tolkien and Lieber ... Howard and Lovecraft. In the center of the room, however, was something new ...something different.

Stephen recognized the steamer trunk that sat like a petulant toad on the floor as belonging to Jeff. It was where he kept his most treasured things: his books. In his ten-year friendship with the man, he had only seen the inside of it a hand full of times.

Stephen's curiosity picked at him; but he resisted. Somewhere in this room lay the solution to the questions that had been plaguing him since that terrible night.

Two hours passed like two minutes; but he had no more answers than when he entered the room. The only thing he hadn't searched was the trunk. *Could that hold the answer?*

Fredrick had said that Alan had suddenly become very interested in his father's things recently. Perhaps Jeff's trunk held the key to understanding what had happened to his son. He approached it with a trepidation that he couldn't explain. Again, his mind told him that it was only an old trunk and couldn't contain anything frightening; but his heart was beating fast. His hand trembled as he pushed back the lid, its hinges having gone far too long without oil and it let out a shrill screech. It echoed in the room and then faded into silence.

Stephen paused, listening for the sure tones of Fredrick's snores. He could hear his pulse in his ears but then the bass drone came to them and he breathed a sigh of relief.

He turned his attention back to the trunk; the answer he sought blatantly obvious. Sitting atop the neatly stacked books was a fat velvet pouch, the corner of a plastic bag poking out from its top. A wave of disappointment flowed through Stephen as he reached for it.

Oh, Alan, he thought. Pulling open the drawstrings, he tugged free the zip lock bag and let it sit in his palm. The bag contained some sort of leaves, no bigger than his thumbnail. They were dark green with a darker purple vein running through them, although at first look, both appeared black. He recognized them from the infusion bottle in the refrigerator. A soft squeeze verified that whatever they were, they were fresh. In the bottom of the pouch was a smaller, yellowed plastic sandwich bag. He shook this free into his hand as well and opened it. The same leaves were in this bag as well; but they crumbled at his touch, quite obviously dried with age.

He placed the older bag back into the pouch and turned his attention back to the fresh leaves, bouncing the sealed bag in his palm. The mystery was solved. Whatever else these leaves were, they were what Alan was infusing into his water. It could be a harmless herb but deep in his heart he knew the truth. With his left hand, he drew his cell phone from his pocket and unlocked it. He took a quick picture of the leaves and set them down.

A quick image search returned a match: hieracium venosum or rattlesnake weed. It supposedly had the effect of increasing circulation and combating the venom of snakes; but nowhere was it mentioned that it caused hallucinations or fainting, although it could be classed as a narcotic. The leaves he had, however, were a third the size of those typical to the plant and much darker. Perhaps this was an off shoot of some sort?

He placed the bag back within the velvet pouch and set it aside, ruminating on whether to mention it at all. Perhaps it would be better for him to let it all drop. Alice deserved to bury the son she remembered, and Nellie deserved to tend to the brother she believed Mike was. The doctors would end up declaring their tests inconclusive; most didn't care enough to chase something they were having issues catching. Alan had been a good friend to him; good enough to carry this to the grave with him. As he thought, he began to examine the books on which the pouch had lain. The top layer of books were leather-bound but sans any markings or titles.

Stephen picked up the first and flipped through it casually, still struggling with his dilemma. The pages were all handwritten. He instantly realized that the writing belonged to Jeff and seemed to be written in the first person.

It seemed to him at first that it was notes for The Game; but they seemed too detailed, to specific. *Perhaps he was writing a novel?*

May 8, 2010

We are still on his trail, although despite traveling deep into the night and forgoing sleep for the advantage, we remain three days behind him. Marcus believes he is using the ring properly; but the Walker was so rushed in her explanation, we can't be sure. Mika continues to harp on the fact that while we chase the words of the Herald, our quarry may be getting further away. Besides splitting up, I can think of no other options, however. Should Haeren command a fraction of the power that Theamon was capable of, I am not sure that any one of us could best him. Although I would never tell the others, I am unsure that even the three of us will be able to slay him and take the relic. If we had Ret's axe, I would feel more confident.

Stephen recognized the names; they belonged to the original campaign that Jeff had run. Beatrice had played Mika, Rodger had played Ret and on the odd occasion that Jeff's brother George had played, he used a thaumaturge by the name of Marcus the Green. He felt a small pang of resentment; Hollis wasn't included. He turned the page and nearly dropped the book.

I only wish that I could have made Roger believe our wild tale or had been able to convince the others to allow me to tell Stephen. He is young; but what Stephen lacks in worldliness is offset ten times by Hollis's guile. I was tempted to approach Hollis himself on this side; but I could not in good conscience pull him into a potentially deadly situation without knowing what effect it may have on Stephen on the other. I am sure that if he knew what was at stake, he would agree without a second thought and jump in with both feet. Perhaps that is why it is wise to exclude him; he has too much life left to live. If this all falls apart and goes wrong, at least I can live with the thought that he will have the bright future that I know he is capable and deserving of.

It seemed more like a journal than a novel to Stephen and seeing his name in this context raised chills on his skin and filled his belly with apprehension.

The adder root began to fade that night, although I yearned to see Alice and Alan again; I dreaded what we would come back to after half a day. I could only hope that we are still in pursuit of Haeren and that my fear that we do not have the ability to defeat him does not come to fruition while I pass the day on this side. I worry what would become of us if while on this side, our personas on that were to die.

The more Stephen read, the more it seemed to be Jeff's recollections and less an actual story. He closed the book with a sharp snap. This was ridiculous; Stephen couldn't believe that he was even contemplating the possibility that any of this was true.

The Game was fantasy, an escape from the pressures of life for a few hours. It was a hobby, a passionate one but a hobby, nonetheless. He picked up the velvet pouch again and weighed it in his hands. *But what if the plants within were indeed the adder root that Jeff wrote about? What if his dreams of the last few nights were not dreams at all...?*

This was foolishness. Ronni was right – he should have given up the Game a long time ago. It was time to give up childish things before he lost his mind completely.

He was almost thirty years old and should know better than to believe something like this. He closed the trunk quickly and left Alan's room. After writing a quick note for Alice and Fredrick, he locked the door behind him and drove home.

CHAPTER FIVE

AN EXTENDED BRANCH

Ronni was on the couch when Stephen walked through the door. "Hello," she said, never taking her eyes from the television screen. He thought to walk by her and down the stairs into the kitchen. With her attention focused squarely on the television, she did not notice that he had sat beside her until his spoke.

"How was your day?" It felt awkward but the question was as good of a place to start as any. He had started this same conversation many times over the years with results ranging from luke-warm to down-right hostile.

She turned to regard him as she extended the remote towards the screen and paused her show. "Fine?" What should have been a statement came out as a question.

"Did anything interesting happen?"

"No." The statement was quick and clipped but she turned to face him rather than unpausing her show. That was a good sign.

"Would you mind if I watched TV with you for a little while?"

She shrugged and turned back to the screen, "Suit yourself." They sat in silence, passive observers of a half dozen couples' struggle to find love on some tropical island or other. As the credits rolled, Stephen spoke again.

"This is nice. How long has it been since we just sat and hung out?" Ronni shrugged and brought up the channel guide. As she browsed through the options, Stephen said, "It's been a while."

"You don't like my shows and I don't want to watch yours"

"Maybe we can find something we both like." He pointed to the screen, "Look. Top Chef. Do you remember when we took that cooking class at the community college?"

A small smile turned up the corner of her mouth, "We burned that lasagna within an inch of its life."

Stephen chuckled, "I don't know. It wasn't that bad."

She squinted at him, her smile dimming already, "We must not have eaten the same thing."

Stephen shrugged, "I like to think of it as crunchy style."

Ronni exhaled with a sharp breath, "No one else's was 'crunchy style'." Her mouth snapped down into a scowl. "If you remember, I told you that it was 325 not 425. Why don't you ever just listen to me?"

He frowned, a wave of despondency descended over him like a damp blanket, "I think it was actually supposed to be 375. That is what I used when I made it for dinner Saturday."

"It was over-done then too." Ronni turned back to the television, continuing to scroll through the listings.

"Ronni, can't we just try to get along for one evening?"

Her only response was a shrug. She chose the home improvement channel from the list and set the remote on the side table away from Stephen.

"Ronni?" he pressed quietly.

"Why can't you do something like that?" She nodded towards the screen. "I would love to have laminate flooring in the bedroom rather than that dull brown carpet."

"You loved that carpet when we picked it out. You said it brought out the red in the trim."

"That was three years ago, people are not carpeting anymore."

She pointed to the screen, "They're putting in hard wood. We can't afford that, but I would settle for laminate."

"Settle for?"

She scrunched her face as if she smelled something foul, "I've gotten good at that." Stephen had seen this before. Here is where their 'evening' went downhill. The only thing missing was a mention of his wife's paragon of masculinity, her brother. "I am sure that Vince would be glad to help you put it in, he did it in his extra bedroom last summer. You won't ask him, though, you never do." There is was.

Stephen stood slowly, "Okay, Ronni. I'm going to go downstairs to grab a snack."

"I didn't have dinner, get me some of that lasagna. It's better than nothing."

As it had countless times before, the couple's evening ended in each going to their neural corners. Stephen remembered when these skirmishes were more frequent but as the years passed, both of them settled into a rhythm more like tolerance than anything else.

CHAPTER SIX
AN INESCAPABLE CALL

S tephen crawled into bed after Ronni was already asleep, having spent the remainder of the evening in his 'man cave'; but sleep wouldn't find him for a long time that night. On the edge of his consciousness, the thrill of the possibility teased him. He focused on Ronni's breathing and cursed himself for an idiot. Eventually sleep did claim him, although his dreams weren't remarkable, and he woke the next morning almost disappointed.

He rose just as the sun did and slipped from the bed, padding downstairs and into the kitchen. After starting Roni's coffee, two pieces of bread found their way into the toaster and he poured himself a glass of orange juice. He simply stared at the toaster, allowing his thoughts to wander. Today was Alan's wake but all he could think about was the journals and the velvet bag. Still feeling ridiculous for contemplating the possibility that they held what Jeff had written, it was all that he could think about.

With a pop, the toast sprang up, breaking him from his reverie. Mechanically, he slathered butter on each and chewed them without really tasting either. He caught the time displayed on the microwave, realizing that he still had to call out of work. He returned to the bedroom where his wife slept. Sometimes, in the right light, she retained some of the sweet girl he fell in love with. This was one of those times; but as it always did, the moment was too short. Her sweet smile turned to scowl, even in the throes of sleep. He unplugged his phone from his bedside charger and closed the door behind him.

He stood on the porch, enjoying the dawn air as he left a message for his boss. He was simply glad that Jared didn't care enough to answer his call; it made it easier to lie convincingly. As he ended the call, he looked out over the porch railing at his postage stamp sized property; the porch's neglected state mirrored his hand to mouth existence. Jeff had written about his bright future; but that prediction never quite came to pass.

He worked a job he hated for a man he did not respect to support a wife that didn't respect him. His only real accomplishment was not being a complete failure; but deep in his heart, he believed he was capable of so much more.

His lips formed themselves into a determined line as he slowly shook his head.

Today was going to be hard; there was no need to make it more difficult by feeling sorry for himself. Alice would need him to be strong today; no matter how many times Ronni told him what a disappointment he was, he wouldn't disappoint Alice.

He rose swiftly and went back into the house.

The day was already warm when he parked in front of Alan's house, dressed smartly in his suit and tie. He left his jacket hanging in the car and walked up the steps. He noticed there were already a few other cars parked in the driveway. Stephen was glad that Alice had a support system; she deserved all the well wishes she could get. A woman he didn't recognize answered the door, "Good Morning."

Stephen nodded, "Good Morning, Ma'am … my name is…"

He heard Fredrick's voice from inside, "Stephen! Theresa, let him in. He is family." The woman stepped back to allow him to enter. He flashed her a small smile before Fredrick wrapped him in a hug, "I'm sorry about last night."

Stephen shook his head, "Don't worry about it. Both of you needed some time free of worry about the other. It's the least I could do."

"Thanks," was all he could manage before his voice caught in his throat.

Stephen patted him on the back and allowed him to retreat to compose himself. He entered the living room and waved lightly to Alice, who was surrounded by three women dressed in black. She began to rise, and he waved her off, "Sit. There is plenty of time." As the woman settled back into the overstuffed chair, Stephen forced a smile to his lips, "Ronni sends her best. She was unable to get the day off from work."

Alice nodded, her patient eyes holding a sadness that had nothing to do with the death of her son.

"I think she will come to the evening visitation." He looked up the stairs, contemplating what to do next. "Would you mind if I go upstairs to see his room?" She shook her head as she turned her attention back to the women at her side. He was grateful to be out from underneath her compassionate gaze.

What am I doing? Stephen asked himself as he climbed the stairs. The trunk and the journals it contained pulled at him the very moment he stepped in the house. He needed to see them again, re-read them. Part of him believed it was to prove it was just a mental exercise of Jeff's. He wanted to believe that in one of them, he would find something to make him feel less foolish; but a larger portion of him wanted them to be just as they seemed.

The room was just as he had left it the previous night, the trunk's lid shut, waiting for him. He closed the door behind him and sank to the floor. His hands found the latch and lifted the lid.

The velvet bag sat atop the leather journals, as if it was watching him.

Stephen set it aside and pulled the journals from the trunk. There were five in all; they were all bound in similar brown faux leather but were of disparate size and thickness, so it took him a few moments to find the first one.

April 9, 2008

I have been having such strange dreams of late. At first, I believed it was an overactive imagination and a side effect of the plants that Alice's friend, Samantha, had given me for my heart.

The dreams are so vibrant that I wake each morning believing that our world is the dream and that Taerh is the real world. I feel that it may behoove me to write down my impressions each morning, as many give credence to the theory that dreams serve as a way for our subconscious to communicate to our waking selves. These dreams are likely to be a case of an active fantasy life, as I have been spending a great deal of time as of late with the new game George and I discovered a week or so ago. George seems less taken with it than I; but I am truly fascinated by the lack of boundaries it offers. For a boy that was raised on Tolkien and Howard, the thought of writing my own tale of heroic legend does indeed hold a great deal of attraction.

Last night's dream was the third in a row, and all of them were set in the same location. In the dreams, I play the part of some sort of forester or ranger in the vein of Tolkien's Strider. I seem to dwell in a village typical of Europe circa the 13th or 14th century; but everything seems so much more l real. It's like I've been sucked into one of my favorite fantasy books, but for the first time, I'm really living in that world and breathing the same air as those characters and experiencing the same turmoil. When I wake, I am always struck by the fact that all the colors are deeper, the scents are fuller. Compared to my recollections of the dreams, my daytime activities seem like they are painted in watercolors. Another unusual characteristic of these dreams is that I seem to recall them with perfect clarity; where before a week or so ago, most of my dreams faded like smoke from my mind within the time it took for me to get up from the bed to the bathroom in the morning.

The forester's name is Alexei Silvermoon and his village is called Two Bridges. It seems like an idyllic community based around an inn and some sort of stables. I have gotten the sense that Two Bridges horses are of good quality and sought after throughout at least the local area. Alexei is a widower; his wife having died at the hands of some sort of raiding monsters (Orcs or the like) from what I have gathered. His neighbors seem to shy away from the subject in my presence. He seems to be an exceptional shot with a bow and based upon the well-worn hand and half sword that hangs above his mantle; his skills are not limited to hunting. As of yet, I have not ventured beyond the locality of the village; but I overheard in the Bough's Shadows Inn, during last night's dream, mention of a larger city called Oizan.

As far as I can tell, Silvermoon does not seem to have an occupation but his home contains a wooden trunk in which I found several bags containing various coins of what I assume to be silver and gold. Each bag held coins that appeared to be currencies from different countries. My cursory examination found at least five distinct shades of coins.

Last night, the innkeeper, a rather pleasant man by the name of Van Garrey, passed on a letter brought to him by a caravan guard that day. I questioned the guard at length; he claimed a woman by the name of Mika had asked him to deliver it to Two Bridges on his way through enroute to Oizan. I asked him for a description of the woman; but obviously he has been away from the fairer sex for too long, as he seemed to recall a great deal about her physical assets and little else.

The letter itself was marked in a simple script with my his name and sealed with a dull red wax. But there was no mark or seal impressed into it.

I took my leave of the Inn and returned to Alexei's home to read the letter, somewhere I would befree of his nosey neighbors. What struck me immediately was the lack of contractions in the language known simply as Trade Tongue, both in its written and spoken forms. Although my thoughts translated seamlessly from English into the language, any contraction translated directly into a more formal phrasing.

I do not recall the specific words contained in the letter, but I will attempt to paraphrase as best I can remember:

Silvermoon,

I hope this letter finds you well. Ret and I have arrived in Oenigh from the Expanse. If only Hollis could see us now, he would be unable to contain his mirth. Two of the famed Band of Six reduced to guarding a caravan of Dwarven steel across the desert. We did have some thrilling moments, for which I will exact a price equal to the cost of dinner and a beer when I arrive in your sleepy little village. Ret has some business in Slazè that he would like my help with; so, I am sending this in advance of my arrival. Dain is a good man; honest enough that I trust that it will find you before I would.

Stay well until we meet again,

Mika

I can only extrapolate that Alexei is some sort of mercenary or adventurer, which would certainly track with an overactive imagination. Who would dream they were a farm hand or stable boy?

As I was contemplating that less than great mystery, I saw a map through another's eyes, held by hands very much like my own. The wasteland known as the Expanse, that Mika had written of lay to the east of a small continent, a great mountain range between it and the sea. The mountains continue north into the isthmus Shire of Utel. To the east lays the Kingdom of Slazè and to the south the Confederation of Kiel. North of Slazè, across a broad bay was the Stewardship of Granatyr, where the town of Two Bridges was located. A narrow strait separated the stewardship and the rest of the continent from the Lathe of Mantry and the Rangor northlands beyond.

This wash of knowledge took me by surprise, both by its speed and *completeness. Beyond the vision of the carefully drawn map, I felt as if I had seen these places firsthand. I could almost feel the unyielding humidity of the jungles of Kiel and the biting cold of the northlands. I could almost taste the rich taste of Slazèan noodles and see the vaulted cathedrals that dominate Mantrian cities.*

A mixture of amazement and fear filled my heart; I could still feel the pounding of it in my chest as I awoke.

April 10, 2008

Last night's dream seemed to have skipped ahead almost a month and began during a conversation with a woman I immediately recognized as Beatrice. Her skin was deep bronze, and she had a lithe grace to her shape that was startling; but it was her.

I let her speak as I gathered my wits and attempted to find my place in the conversation. Thank the lord their relationship seemed to be platonic; I am not sure if I could have dealt with the guilt of cheating on Alice, even in a dream.

Lucky for me, she was describing an ambush that she and the Ret she had written of, which they had thwarted during their time in the Expanse. From context, I assumed it to be the desert she had mentioned in her letter. The casual way she discussed the killing of the men who attacked their caravan was jarring, especially given Beatrice's personality. I have seen the woman take ten minutes to capture a spider and usher it outside to avoid having to squash it. This same woman regaled me in detail, running her sword through another human being, and all the time, her eyes shone with a mixture of pride and amusement.

Towards the end of her story, she picked up on the fact that something was amiss. Eying me skeptically, she continued, but even as she spoke, she studied me. It was in those eyes, that I truly saw Beatrice's keen mind working.

To distract her, I asked if she had heard from any of the others, assuming that a group known as the Band of Six indeed may have more than three members. That particular gambit seemed to bear fruit, as she explained to me that this was indeed the reason behind her visit. Again, I will paraphrase to the best of my ability, as I feel I may have missed some subtleties in the conversation, and it may allow me to ferret them out.

"Hollis has supposedly located the Hand in Mantry; but with last year's fishing dispute between them and Granatyr, he felt uncomfortable traveling there alone." I nodded, encouraging her to continue. "I believe that he fears actually finding Theamon all by himself.".".

"Who would not?"

She squinted at me for a moment and I thought I had erred, but then her face broke into a bashful smile. "I am glad you said it, Moon, as I did not want to be the first. Perhaps the simple life agrees with you; the Silvermoon of a year or so ago would never have made such an admission." She sat back, visibly relaxing, "Haeren and Marcus assure me that they can meet us in Oizan within the week. With Ret a few days behind me, we could leave the city in four days' time." Again, I nodded. "Hollis has hired a captain that should be able to get us across the strait into Mantry; but neither myself nor Haeren are likely any more welcome there than when we left. The Mantrians do not count forgiveness among their damnable Four Virtues. What they lack in forgiveness, they make up for in memory, so we cannot depend on their good intentions." Her eyes shifted nervously as she looked expectedly at me. "Do you still remember the game trail you used the last time?"

A knot of fear formed in my gut before an image sprung to mind unbidden. I could picture a rocky beach surrounded by evergreens; and a narrow trail that led from the rocks into the woods. I sat up a little straighter, filled with excitement. The image wavered a bit but then solidified along with a sense of confidence, whose source is a mystery to me. I felt a smile come to my lips, "I am sure I can manage." This seemed to visibly calm her agitation. I relaxed slightly. "Where are Marcus and Haeren coming from?"

Immediately, I realized I had made a mistake.

She frowned at me, "He is your brother, Moon, why are you asking me?"

I shrugged, thinking quickly, "You obviously have spoken to him more recently than I", trying to sound as casual as I could.

She sneered, "I never know where he or that zealot, Haeren, get off to. If I could trade a tenth of his fanaticism for gold, I certainly would not have needed to sweat my ass off for a month in the Expanse."

"You could settle down," I offered, settling into banter that I was only half aware of. Words flowed from my lips that I was not entirely sure were my own. "There is a piece of land on the other side of the Bartram farm that I am sure I could convince him to part with."

She laughed loudly, drawing stares from some of the other patrons, "Moon, this life is yours. I am too fond of the comforts that a steady stream of coin brings, not to mention a little too long on vices and short on attention span for a town like this." She caught the eye of one the men who had not yet averted his gaze. "Not enough here to hold my interest." With a wink, she turned back to me. "Not all of us can stay on the farm once we have seen the wonders the wide world offers."

I felt myself nod, "True, I suppose. But you say they should be able to join us within a few days' time? They must not be coming from that far."

She shrugged absently, turning back to the bowl in front of her. "Truth be told, as much as his holier than thou attitude gets under my skin, if Theamon is bringing the Master of Beasts with him, I will feel more at ease having one of Olm's faithful beside us." I watched all eyes in the common room turn to us as the room grew silent. Beatrice's double turned, meeting the eyes of a few of the closest men before speaking again; every one of them averted their gaze. "It is simply a name; I assure you it only contains the power you give it." Turning back to me, her lips were curled into a sneer, "Sheep, Silvermoon. You live among sheep. Just as dumb and twice as easily spooked." She did not lower her voice, and none present so much as looked towards our table.

Much like the previous night, the rush of thoughts not of my own experience caused my heart to pound in my ears and I awoke in my own bed, gasping for air.

April 11th, 2008

When I dreamt this evening, some time had passed again. I estimate at least a few weeks had passed since my dream the night before last, based on overheard conversations of my dream comrades. I came to my senses in front of a low burning fire. I was wrapped in a blanket, my head pillowed on a rolled-up cloak of some kind. I could make out three other shapes near me in the darkness. Across the fire from me was Beatrice's double, Mika, and a young man I did not recognize. From where I lay, I estimated his age as late teens to early twenties; but his eyes held not the folly of youth. I remained as still as I could and simply listened.

"...last I heard, he was traveling with a group of ten to fifteen men," it was the boy's voice, "Light and fast, horses and no wagons." I heard the rustle of paper and a finger tapping against the ground, "He will avoid the major cities. The Mantrians are crazy but even they will not have dealings with Sharroth's chosen."

"Thank Olm for small favors," Beatrice's Mika's voice, "He is here for something; I doubt a brisk ride through the Mantry countryside is its own reward."

The boy chuckled and said, "As you say. There are three towns along this route, assuming he does not travel cross-country." I heard him tap three times, "Two farming villages and a glorified inn. Past them, there is nothing of note before the border with the Northlands. You do not think ...?"

Mika finished his thought, "The Rangor barbarian tribes. If I were looking for an army of blood thirsty men, there are few more suited for the task." I heard her snort and say, "He cannot reach them, Hollis."

"He will not." Hollis did not sound convinced, although he continued. "Silvermoon can guide us through the wilds. Even with fifteen men, cross-country in these forests would be slower than going the long way via the roads. The six of us can make time, through the woods here, where the road bends. If we do not get ahead of him, we should be closer at least."

"I certainly hope we are lucky enough to get ahead of them; our six against their fifteen plus Theamon, we will need every advantage we can manage."

"The road narrows here, we could easily..." I heard a soft pop from beyond the fire and Mika hissed for Hollis to be silent. I could see both figures turned away from the fire and squinting into the woods. With a slow, methodical motion, Hollis reached beside him, pulling a crossbow into his lap. He tapped Mika's arm with his free hand and nodded back towards where I slept, before setting a bolt in the crossbow and slowly drawing it back.

Mika lightly toed me in the ribs, bringing her finger to her lips and then motioning towards the sound. She moved on, repeating her actions with each of the other three sleeping figures. My heart was in my throat as the reality of what could be happening dawned on me. Again, however, there was a wave of calm the descended over my heart, almost as if my emotions were not my own. As I rolled over to rise, a thick wooden bow bumped my knee. I gripped it tightly in my left hand as I felt my heartbeat thudding in my ears.

The others were on their feet with a speed that belied their obvious fatigue, beginning their own preparations almost as if by rote. A husky man buckled a sword to his hip before hefting a large single edged axe. He rolled his shoulders and rocked his head back and forth, loosening his muscles made tight by sleep. Mika assisted another man with a breast plate, her fingers speeding over the buckles as he held it to his chest with one hand and flexed the fingers of the other. As she finished, he picked up a huge two-handed mace and swung it slowly from side to side.

The third figure finished strapping a thin short sword to his waist

73

and then crouched next to me. Even beyond the thin, well-kept beard he wore, I could not fail to recognize my own brother. George leaned in and placed his face so close to mine that our beards meshed. His words were the barest of whispers, "The trees are too close for fire; anything else I have at my disposal will require me to be very close." I nodded dumbly, overwhelmed by the entire experience.

That is when it broke through the trees. The creature was something out of a nightmare; almost seven feet tall and covered by scaly skin, broken by patches of unkempt fur. It had a small snout filled with razor sharp teeth and eyes that reflected the dim light that was shed by the fire. A fear washed through me in a white-hot wave, stealing my breath for a second as it opened its mouth, letting out what was like half hiss and half growl. Its mouth opened wider than I would have thought possible, and the light from the fire glinted off the wet, viciously serrated teeth.

Hollis brought the crossbow to his cheek and fired a bolt into the thing's open maw before backing towards the others. Bracing the stock against his hip, his hand fit another bolt into the crossbow and cocked it again with one continuous movement. Even in retreat, the boy's movements were like water over stone; at no point did he stumble or misstep and at no point did the crossbow waver as he fired a second shot. This one struck the thing in the chest, its tip only penetrating a few inches. The arrow hung there for a moment before falling to the ground.

Hollis dropped the crossbow and drew a thick bladed short sword and needle-like dagger. A large figure rushed past me in the darkness, his axe raised above his head. They collided on the other side of the fire, man and beast all at once. He drove it back through the sheer ferocity of his charge; but struggled to bring the axe up before the creature wrapped its arms around his chest, locking their bodies together and knocking him to the ground. Mika turned and drew her sword, before stalking towards the creature. She was mirrored by the man hefting the huge mace. I heard George's double mumbling something beneath his breath as he rose. I could not make out the words,

74

but the sound resonated in my chest, beating a counter-rhythm to my heart. Like twin shadows, George's double and Hollis followed in Mika and the other's footsteps. Although I could no longer hear the syllables he muttered, I could still feel the force of the words in my chest.

The creature's mouth opened even further before snapping shut on its victim's shoulder, far too close to his throat for my liking.

"Ret!" Mika yelled, before closing the distance between them with a sudden charge

I heard her partner curse beneath his breath and launch himself at the intertwined pair, sliding his right hand halfway up the shaft of his mace. A few feet before he reached the creature, he sank to one knee and slid the remaining distance. Using the head of the mace as a battering ram, he struck the beast squarely in the right knee. It released its bite on Ret to let out a roaring scream, turning its attention to this new attacker. It threw Ret's body to the ground, where it bounced once, and he lay still.

It surprised me that Mika did not stop her charge to see to her friend; she simply leapt over his motionless form and pointed with her free hand.

Hollis dropped into a baseball slide beside the man, thrusting his sword and dagger into the dirt before grabbing him roughly and beginning to drag him free.

Mika placed her both of hands on the hilt of her sword and drove it into the creature's back with all her momentum. Again, the thing roared; but it did not turn to face her. Its jaw opened further, impossibly wide until its head rested against its back, regarding her from upside down. It forced its arms backwards, so that sickening pops filled the air as both shoulder and elbow hyperextended.

I saw her face twist in horror as its claws sank into her flesh.

George's double dropped to his knees beside the mace wielding man, his muttering reaching a crescendo. "Haedren, mind your step ..." He slammed both of his palms into the dirt. Haedren immediately stepped back, the ground already clinging to his feet.

The beast sank six inches into the ground that was, only a moment ago, as firm as stone. Hollis propped Ret against a tree and then ran back to where his weapons impaled the earth. His arm pistoned and his dagger embedded itself in the creature's throat, as if by magic. Haedren took another step back and fished an amulet from beneath his armor with his left hand, continuing to keep the head of his mace between him and the beast.

I heard George's voice, "Any time, Alexei!" The creature's head had returned to its original position and one of its hyper extended arms was folding back, accompanied by the same sickening sound as it reached for my brother's double. I felt him muttering again, but it abruptly stopped when he was forced to dive to the ground, the creature's claws missing his face by mere inches.

I saw that the beast had sunk to its knees in the ground, which was now bog-like. Loud squelching sounds reached my ears as it attempted to pull its leg free in order to pursue George.

Hollis reached Mika's side, his sword piercing the thing's arm just above the wrist. The sound reminded me of the leg that was pulled from a Thanksgiving turkey. It withdrew the injured arm, still reaching for George.

Mika slumped but refused to fall, shrugging off Hollis's supporting arm. She drove her blade into the thing's back again with all her might.

Haedren held the amulet aloft and hissed, "Turn away, beast! Return to the darkness of your master's cage. You are not meant to walk in the light of Olm's ever burning sight."

The amulet began to glow, only slightly at first. At first, I thought my mind was playing tricks on me. The light drove back the shadows of the forest, taking the ghastly image of the beast's substance with it. I swore I could see the trees through its body as it took on a ghostly pallor.

In a panic, the thing flailed at Haedren, connecting with the amulet itself. I heard a sizzle, like the sound of bacon on a hot griddle, but it was enough to knock the offending object away from the man's hand. Instantly, the light was extinguished, and the beast's form regained solidity.

Haedren dropped to his knees, searching for it. The creature loomed over him, raising the claw on his unmarred arm to strike down. As quick as a thought, three feathered shafts appeared in the thing's neck, buried to the fletching. I looked down and saw the long bow in my hand, the other reflexively pulling another shaft from where they stood impaling the dirt at my feet. By instinct, I let the next arrow fly, and I didn't stop until there were no more to pull.

Haedren stood with the amulet again in his hands. Rather than shying away from the creature, he stepped forward and. sank to his knees in the mire that George's double had created. Without hesitation, he pressed the now- blinding object against the beast's chest. The scent of burning offal filled my nostrils and overwhelmed my eyes, which started to water. But, I still could not look away.

"Mistake! Abomination! If you stand before the righteous light of Olm's judgement! You will burn!" Haedren pulled the amulet away from the creature momentarily and then drove it hard into its body with ease, as if the beast were no more than smoke. "Burn!" The creature's flesh ignited from within, a raging inferno that blazed for a space of a thought and then was gone, leaving only the stench of burning filth in its wake.

As suddenly as it began, the combat was over. The putrid scent filled the air, as well as the sweat of those who had battled here. As suddenly as it began, the combat was over. The putrid scent filled the air, as well as the sweat of those who had battled here.

Marcus had anchored himself on a tree and was helping Haedren extricate himself from the mud that sought to drag him into the depths of the earth. Once he was free, Haedren quickly made his way to his fallen comrade and knelt beside him, wiping the mud-saturated ash from the surface of his amulet with the hem of his tabard.

Holding it before his face, close enough to his mumbling lips to kiss its surface, he covered the vicious tear in Ret's neck. "Olm, eldest of the get of Galen and bringer of light to dark places, grant your servant the grace to soothe the depredations visited upon this man by the Master of Beasts and Father of Lies. His light, a gift of your ever-present mercy, still drives back the shadows from places lost to Sharroth's darkness."

Ret began to stir, moaning softly.

Mika placed her hand on his other shoulder speaking to him too softly for me to hear.

So transfixed was I by what was I observed, I did not notice that George's double had come up beside me. When he spoke, I must have jumped a foot in the air because he smirked and said, "I know that the shot takes you not the other way around, but perhaps you could nudge it along a little next time. That thing almost clawed my face off."

I turned my attention to him, barely restraining an unmanly shriek. "Do not sneak up on me like that." I covered my heart and went on, still reeling from the shock of it. "You nearly scared me out of my skin."

George's double laughed in a way I had not heard since before our mother passed. He always took so much on to his shoulders, being the older of us. "No more than you scared me when I had a face full of ugly and no-ranged doom to be seen."

Hollis approached, with a fist full of arrows in one hand. He handed them to me absently as he spoke to my brother's double, "Are you alright, Marcus? That thing certainly did not appreciate the made-to-order swamp you conjured for him." He smiled brightly, as if the last few minutes had never happened. "All the flavors of arcane and you pull out something I could do with a dozen or so water skins?"

George Marcus snorted, "I'd like to see you try. Those who cannot, criticize."

I stepped away from them and moved closer to Haedren and Ret. The big man was now on his feet, his fingers tenderly probing where his neck met with his shoulder.

"Do not fuss with it," Haedren counseled him, watching the

Rangor closely. "The pain will fade in a few moments, once your body realizes that it is no longer injured."

Ret wore his hair and beard wild and unkempt, which made recognizing Roger beneath it all difficult; but once I made the connection, I am not sure how I could have missed it earlier. Ret was massive in comparison to my college roommate but his mannerisms and that self-satisfied smirk could not be hidden.

"I never said anything about pain, Olmite. I hurt myself worse than that pulling my prick out for a piss in the morning."

Haedren raised an eyebrow, "If that thing holds your manhood daily, I should give you much more credit than I do ..."

"I did not mean..."

Mika stepped in, turning the big man from Haedren, "No you did not, Ret... you also did not think. What possessed you to charge that thing, not knowing if it was man or beast?"

Ret snorted, "Neither man nor beast drives fear into a Rangor."

She laughed, that same silver bell-like laugh that brought to mind barbeques and Christmas parties. I had to remind myself that this was not Beatrice, at least not the one I knew. "Fear? No. His teeth? His claws? Yes, on both counts."

"I still live." He spoke these words as if they were the answer to everything.

"...because of Haedren."

Ret blew air out past tight lips, "His god helped, sure; but a Rangor warrior cannot be stopped by a little nip such as that." She simply patted him on the bicep and walked away, with a smile painted on her lips.

Haedren began to speak, "Little nip? You self-important, bloated..."

Mika grasped his elbow and turned him to walk with her, "Let it go, Priest ... Young Rangor prove their worth by smashing their heads against trees to gather firewood. If half-frozen branches cannot crack their thick skulls, your words have no hope." She winced slightly; but it did not dim her smile.

"Let me have a look at your side, Soldier. It is my hope that you will be a more cooperative patient."

She laughed, "More cooperative? I want that spoken at my funeral, Priest, 'She is more cooperative than an unconscious Rangor.' I think it sums up my life very concisely."

I watched Haedren work his talents on the furrows in Mika's side and it was nothing short of miraculous. He placed his hand over the wound and after his prayer was done, the skin beneath his palm seemed like it had been healing for a few weeks rather than a few moments. The area was pink and raw; however, blood ceased to flow, and a solid scab had formed.

As he worked, Mika turned to me, "Very nice shots, Moon... Perhaps we should discuss timing, however. Age and the good life seem to have dulled your reflexes a bit."

Thinking quickly, I responded, "The shot takes you, not the other way around, Mika."

She shook her head, laughing lightly, "So you have said."

My eyes were glued to the apparent miracle that Haedren had performed. Once again, revelations I recognized as Silvermoon's memories took over my own. Servants of the three gods of Taerh could not truly heal wounds as depicted in legends of our own world. But what they could do was speed the body's own healing process exponentially. A wound that would have taken a month to heal, would only take a week once they had channeled the power of their deity upon it.

Silvermoon had recovered from a sword-stroke through his lung in a matter of weeks thanks to Haedren's blessed touch. In a world devoid of hospitals or any real medicine as our world would consider it, the collapsed lung and massive internal bleeding should have brought the forester to his end.

Instead, he spent less than a score of days laid up in an Uteli public house; it had been an uncomfortable experience, for sure, but much preferable to the alternative.

Again, I woke with heart palpitations and a shortness of breath.

Alice fears my heart condition has returned. I'm afraid that she is correct.

April 15, 2008

Alice's concern led me to visit the cardiologist, leading in turn to a few days spent as a lab rat in St Margret's. The strange thing is for the first time in more than a week, I had no dreams of the other world. Perhaps it was, as I thought just an active fantasy life, now pushed aside by more immediate concerns.

Alice's friend, Samantha, has suggested I expand the amount of Adder root tea I use to twice the dosage she originally gave me. The doctors do not seem to know what is causing the palpitations, so it certainly cannot hurt.

One of the nurses even went so far as to suggest that the root is the cause of my episodes. They have prescribed some pills to jump start my thyroid; but have no medicine to offer to fix the actual problem.

So, Adder root remains my hope.

Stephen had been so engrossed in the journal that he'd lost track of time. The opening door caused him to jump out of his skin. His gaze turned to the figure in the doorway like a child caught with his hand in the cookie jar. The face in the doorway was carefully painted and powdered to hide the years that it had seen. At first glance, its owner seemed to be only a few decades Stephen's senior; but on closer examination, he presumed she was well into her sixties. Even her hair was styled to hide the wiry wisps of grey among its stark red tones. But her eyes were what caught his attention. The piercing green orbs stabbed into him like emerald knives.

He recovered quickly but the woman frowned for a moment before speaking. "We are getting ready to leave for the funeral parlor." Her eyes moved from Stephen's expression to the journal clenched in his hand. "Are you coming?"

Stephen nodded, before managing the words, "Of course... I'll be down in a moment."

He swore the woman smiled before stepping back and closing the door. He managed to locate a gym bag and stuffed the journals and the velvet bag inside before closing the trunk.

Guilt crept through him, into his chest. His best friend laid in a wooden box a few miles away, yet all he could think about was those journals.

CHAPTER SEVEN
A HEREDITARY CONDITION

T he wake was worse than he had imagined. As they entered the building, Stephen could see Alice's spirit break as if it were a physical thing. Only Fredrick's grasp stopped her from collapsing to the floor. Stephen stepped up to lend his own strength to her husband's. To tell the truth, he felt the bitterly cold tendrils of grief wrap themselves around his heart as well. He was able to take a deep, fortifying breath to steady himself; he repeated to himself one mantra. *You must be strong for her. You must be strong for her.* The afternoon-viewing was light but still the faces blurred before him.

His eyes kept straying to the open casket; his thoughts returning to the day a decade before when friends and family had gathered to bury his father. To have to bury two friends in the span of five years, much less a husband and son, was more than you could expect anyone to bear. Alice held up as well as could be expected, but the watching it from such a close place was heartbreaking.

Nellie and Robert came together, most likely from the hospital; Stephen could still smell the antiseptic that was clinging to their clothes. "How is Mike?" he asked Nellie gently, hoping to not push her too hard.

Nellie's brows tightened; obviously she hadn't forgotten his questions from his last visit to the hospital.

Robert spoke up as if he sensed the tension between them. "He's still the same. The doctors cannot seem to figure out why he won't wake up." Nellie offered him the kindness of nodding. "The police were there again today asking questions."

Nellie seized Stephen's eyes for a moment but remained silent.

"I am sorry, Nell, that must be really hard." He broke eye contact first and took a deep breath. "Listen, I'm sorry ..."

"Stop. Now is neither the time nor the place." She was never one for emotional outbursts or known for expressing her feelings. Stephen could tell he'd hurt her, but he wasn't sure if she'd decided to let the matter drop. He hoped it was the later; but still carried guilt over making a terrible situation more difficult for a woman he considered a friend.

He simply nodded, turning back to Robert, "I found some things in Alan's room. Come find me after you have seen Alice, if you don't mind."

Robert nodded and made his way towards Alan's mother.

Stephen reached out and squeezed Nellie's arm. Her lips curled into a tight smile, the only response she gave.

Robert found him on the covered porch in front of the funeral parlor, "Rough," was all he had to say.

Stephen nodded slowly, "Rough."

"Do I want to know what you found? Is it something that the cops are going to ask me about?" Stephen shrugged, thinking of the journal and wondering what they would make of what he'd found. "Jesus, that bad?"

"I'm not sure yet." Stephen remained non-committal, still debating how much to share with his friend. He blew his lips out, before making a quick decision, "Come with me, I have it in my car."

Robert nodded and followed him. When they reached Stephen's Honda, Robert spoke, "Is this something we should just dump in the trash and never talk about?"

"Most likely, but I don't think it's a decision I should make myself, too much of a burden." Stephen attempted a half-hearted smile and added, "Congratulations, you've been appointed my coconspirator. Is there anyone you would like to thank in your acceptance speech?"

He shook his head, as if he'd lost his patience. "Just show it to me." Stephen reached into the gym bag and pulled out the velvet pouch. A quick tug of the draw strings and the plastic bag fell into his palm. "Is that pot?"

"I don't think so. At least no pot I have ever seen." He watched Robert's face, studying him in anticipation of his reaction. "Have you ever heard of Adder root?"

The other man shook his head, still studying the leaves inside the clear plastic.

"Are you sure? Maybe something your brother may have mentioned?" Stephen saw him tense, once again he over played his hand.

"What are you trying to say, Steve?"

"Nothing, just asking a question."

"My brother wouldn't have anything to do with this, especially after what happened to Jeff and George." He looked back towards the building. "You're batting a thousand, aren't you?"

"Seems like it. Something just doesn't add up, Robert. Neither Alan nor Mike fooled around with drugs; but the police seemed to think they played a part in the accident. I found this in Jeff's old trunk, right in Alan's room." He took a deep breath, before continuing, "Tell me how that could be a coincidence."

Robert pressed the bag into Stephen's chest, perhaps harder than he had intended, "I'll tell you... I'll tell you to drop this in the nearest dumpster and walk away. Forget that you found it...forget we had this conversation. I know that I sure as hell will." He turned to walk away, speaking over his shoulder, "You wanted my advice. That's it."

Stephen watched his friend walk down the sidewalk towards the building, realizing that he had gotten so focused on the adder root and forgotten to mention the journals. He watched him walk inside, still holding the adder root against his chest. At the back of the parking lot, he saw a looming green dumpster. Less than two dozen steps separated him from taking Robert's advice. He could be rid of the evidence and bring this secret to his grave. Alice could bury her son in peace. It was the right thing to do, what he should do.

Then why did he tuck the Root back into the velvet pouch and tighten the draw strings?

Why did he put it back atop the journals and zip everything up inside the gym bag?

The rest of the night passed in a fog. Stephen said the right things, did what was expected of him; but always in the forefront of his thoughts was the contents of that pouch. At some point, Roni arrived. She appeared out of the crowd, laying her hand on the crook of his elbow. To her credit, she greeted him with a sympathetic smile rather than the sour face she normally showed him. She wore a simply grey and black flowered dress that swirled about her knees when she moved. He could almost see the girl he once loved in the woman before him. Ronni stayed by Stephen's side throughout the night, caressing his arm gently when emotion threatened to overtake her husband. The irony lay in the fact that her actions, supportive or otherwise, faded into the wash of the evening.

He felt a pang of guilt when he thought that he spent more

time inside his own thoughts than keeping his word to lend his strength to Alice, but she seemed more at peace as the funeral director closed the casket and reminded them that the funeral was to be held at 8am the following morning.

Stephen nodded absently as people began to filter out, offering platitudes to both Alice and himself. A firm hand on his shoulder brought him out of his own mind. A woman stood in front of him, her eyes locked deeply with his. She was the woman that had interrupted him as he read the journals in Alan's room earlier that day. "I am so sorry for your loss, Stephen." It was her use of his name that shook him free and his confusion was evident. "Jeff mentioned you on numerous occasions, as did Alan. I feel as if I know you. My name is Samantha Marcheur. Alice and I have been friends for almost twenty years."

"Thank you," Stephen muttered back, his brow furrowing slightly. Had Jeff written of Samantha in his *books? Journals?* For some reason he couldn't quite quantify, this woman made him uncomfortable. Perhaps it was the way she insisted on maintaining eye contact, almost as if she were peering into his soul. Perhaps it was the strange lilt to her words; they were just a beat too slow but had a certain rhythm to them that was both intriguing and alarming.

"We met at Jeff's funeral; but I suppose you do not recall." She also seemed to avoid contractions when speaking, keeping her language almost formal. She smiled warmly; but he thought it took a split second to reach her eyes, "Have no fear, I take no offense. It was, after all, a very difficult time for all involved." She continued to stare into his eyes, as if looking for something. Stephen felt suddenly uncomfortable, like he was standing revealed in her gaze.

He broke her gaze, looking to his shoes briefly to shake the discomfort. "I'm terribly sorry. Of course, I remember you, Ma'am." Her grip on his shoulder tightened momentarily as she chuckled briefly.

"Of course, you do not. It does you a disservice to mislead an old woman, Stephen; but do not think I do not appreciate the intent." His eyes darted back to hers as she continued, almost softly now, "I have known men far more accomplished at deception than you; but practice will hone your talent, I suppose."

"Ma'am..."

She held up her free hand, palm towards him, "It is nothing; I am sorry I mentioned it." Still her deep blue eyes bore into the depths of his own, "Perhaps once you have processed recent events, we can talk again in a more...comfortable environment." He nodded absently, more ill at ease than he had been a moment ago. She pressed a business card into his palm and then disappeared into the group of people funneling out of the building.

Perhaps once you have processed recent events; those words seemed off to him. The words themselves made sense; but he couldn't help the feeling that there was a meaning buried within them. He looked at the card, cradled in the palm of his hand. *Samantha Marcheur, Florist and Holistic Medicine, it read.* The address indicated that her business was only a mile or so from his home; but he couldn't recall seeing it.

Another hand found its way to his arm, causing him to flinch. Ronni looked at him with an expression of pity, "It's been a long day, Stephen. Why don't you say your goodbyes and we can head home?" He nodded once and disengaged from his wife's grip.

It didn't take him too long to find Alice and Fredrick. The man held his wife's arm as she spoke softly to the last of those in attendance. He had observed her over the last few days and hated seeing her look so exhausted, but at the same time he saw the strength that he knew dwelled within. This would bring her pain; it may come close to breaking her; but he knew in his heart that it wouldn't. Not fully.

Stephen's father passed the day after Christmas of his senior year of high school, followed six months later by his mother. Both had been heavy smokers and the habit had caught up with them.

Although he had been eighteen when his mother passed, Stephen was not prepared for a life lived alone. Jeff and Alice had taken him in as if he were their own blood. Stephen had idolized Jeff since he first met the man on his first day of high school; but it was not until his greatest loss that he saw the strength of his mentor's wife. For years, Stephen had wondered what had brought Alice and Jeff together. He was outgoing and gregarious, while she was quiet to the point of appearing shy.

Alice's strength lay in whispered words of encouragement and a confidence that everything would work one that was infectious. Her kindness and support healed the pain of Stephen's loss by inches rather by miles. That is how she did everything, she was a quiet cove in the tempest of life, allowing those around her to heal from its wounds in peace. Stephen was sure that it was through this strength that Jeff was able to blossom as he had, and it was the same with Alan. Losing his father at such an impressionable age could have scarred the young man. Through Alice's quiet but unbreakable support, Alan came to grips with the loss and become a better person for it. In the same vein, she had affected Fredrick's life. Her current husband had been in the military for most of his life, through his wife's still support, he was able to adjust to civilian life.

Stephen had managed to keep his emotions in check since receiving Robert's call on Monday. Watching Alice, a rock amid swirling storms for those around her once again beset by the vicious waves of tragedy, he felt the burning of tears in the backs of his eyes. He snorted once, before gaining control of himself quickly. He wouldn't give her one more reason to despair on this already tragic day.

Stephen laid his hand on her shoulder and squeezed gently. Alice turned and gave him a sad smile before resting her head on his chest. Simply, she said, "Thank you," but he knew there was a deeper meaning beyond the words, which lifted his spirits, just as she always did.

He kissed her lightly atop her head, "I will see you tomorrow, Alice." She looked up at him with a smile, "I know you will. Go home and sleep, I've been very worried about you." He smiled at the paradox of her comforting him as she continued, "I thought we were going to lose you a few times tonight; you just seemed to be in your own world."

He felt as if talons were clawing at his heart again, a feeling of love and relief that he'd always felt when he was around her. "Thank you for your concern, Alice... I'll be fine." He raised her hand to his lips and kissed it gently, before turning to Fredrick, "Take care of her."

Fredrick nodded, "You know I will," before leading her towards the sidewalk.

Ronni took his arm and walked with him to his car. As he fished his keys from his pocket, she said simply, "I'm sorry." In that moment, all the pain and resentment fell from him. Suddenly, he was in her arms, her face pressed against his heart. She became a solid center in the maelstrom of the last few days, and he clung to her. She let him, rubbing his back gently as the tears finally came. He didn't know how long he stood in the summer's dimness sobbing like a child. At some point the two bodies separated, the moment passing. When he looked upon his wife, her mask of dispassion was again firmly in place. Ronni's lips were drawn into a hard line of impatience as her eyes searched beyond him to where her own car was parked. "We should go. I will see you at home," and she was gone.

She was so easy to love when she let herself be loved; but few and far between were those moments.

CHAPTER EIGHT
AN INEVITABLE RETURN

Stephen waited for Ronni's breathing to become slow and regular before slipping from their bed, lifting the gym bag in a single movement as he padded to the bedroom door. The stairs creaked lightly as he made his way to the kitchen table and set it down. He pulled a bottle of water from the refrigerator and took a seat, with his eyes on the bag. The journals within, taunted him from the canvas depths. His hand rose and fell a few times before he could bring himself to unzip the bag and pull forth a journal.

April 16, 2008

It cannot be a coincidence that I resumed the Adder root and the dreams returned. I never thought I would admit it; but after last night, part of me wishes they had not. I came to my senses, while crouched in a loam-scented forest overlooking a road formed from packed dirt. To my left, with his back to the trunk of a large tree, sat my brother's other-self, Marcus. I could see by the last rays of day that his lips were moving, repeating a series of words that fled my mind as soon as I understood them. His eyes were tightly closed, and his brow bore wrinkles of intense concentration.

Unbidden, memories came to mind – memories of conversations with my brother's double. The sensation of sharing recollections that were not of my own life caused my head to spin. As sure as I remembered sharing a beer with George on the Fourth of July last year, I could picture Marcus lecturing Silvermoon on the subtleties of magic. The way he explained it, magic seemed to be more of a science than the art in which it's normally assumed.

As an apprentice, a thaumaturge learned specific words and gestures that could draw upon the potential energy around the caster to be formed into the desired effect, whether it be causing an object to glow or throwing a stream of fire. In my understanding of the process, these words and gestures serve purely as mnemonic devices for words of power hidden within them. These devices seem to resist memorization, almost as if they had sought to remain hidden. A thaumaturge had to work very hard at forcing the magical trappings to imprint on their brain.

A caster could memorize multiple series of words and gestures, but each additional set was exponentially more difficult to hold in the back of one's mind. Only the most accomplished thaumaturge could hold more than a handful at one time. Marcus described the sensation of having, for the lack of a better term, a spell memorized as an intense itching in one's mind. It constantly rubbed against his thoughts, as sand would rub against skin. The spell seemed to have a will of its own, and it wished nothing but freedom.

As a thaumaturge grew in power and knowledge, they were able to separate the words of power, known as Baenu in Trade Tongue, contained within those learned rotes from the chaff that aided in memorization. This distillation revealed a powerful pseudo language with the potential of rewriting reality itself. I can remember ... or should I say that I saw in Silvermoon's memories when Marcus learned the first Baenu, the word for fire. I can remember the same look of pride in George's face when he finished his first half marathon. Both tasks were great accomplishments in their own right.

While the words of this language did not come with the downfalls of their source spells (difficulty of memorization, limitation of options, etc.), their utterance drew power from the thaumaturge themselves as opposed to the energy of the surrounding area. An unwary thaumaturge could literally cast themselves to death. This side effect led most casters to utilize a mixture of rote and hard-won words of power in their craft.

A few wielders of magic could perfect Baenu to such a degree that they could draw upon the effects created by another and twist it to their own uses. Most thaumaturges, Marcus included, had never moved beyond the rudimentary use of these words of power. Silvermoon has heard tales of men and women who had. These are known in Taerh simply as Mages, the most powerful among them are called the Heralds.

I could feel my heart like thunder in my chest, the pounding of it deafening in my ears. Closing my eyes, I willed my heart to slow. I focused on the smell of the rich loam beneath me, the sound of crickets in the distance and the sensation of the gentle breeze across my exposed skin. At first, I thought I would wake breathless like I had each time I had accessed Silvermoon's memories. Slowly, the pounding softened and then faded, leaving me firmly in the other world.

Impaling the dirt beside my knee stood at least two dozen arrows. The same sword that had hung above Silvermoon's mantle lay beside the simple rosewood bow. Across the road, among the old growth trees, I could just make out the figures of Mika, Haedren and Ret, with their weapons at the ready. There was a sense of determination in the air, but also a lingering fear. In my prior dreams, fear was always subsumed by a sense of confidence and excitement; but in this instance, the fear seemed to be the stronger emotion.

Marcus's eyelids began to flicker, his lips slowing and coming to a stop as they opened. He smiled softly; but the trepidation was clear beneath the thin veil of bravado.

At the sound of hoof beats, I realized they were already there, simply growing louder as they approached. Marcus stood slowly, pulling from a bag hanging from his shoulder what appeared to be peat moss. He stopped beside me for a moment and said, "Perhaps you take some shots as 'the' shot is deciding to take itself, hmm?" before moving closer to the road and taking cover behind the thick trunk of a tree. He bent to speak to Hollis, craftily camouflaged among the leaves and brush. The boy nodded once, unwinding and rewinding a rope around his wrist. The rope snaked out into the road, where its length was buried in the packed surface. I could see the other end looped around a tree on the opposite side.

It was apparent even to my out of sort mind that this was indeed an ambush. I had to assume it was planned for whoever rode towards our position. The sharp talons of fear clawed at my heart as I barely made out the dust rising from around the bend to my right. I reached down beside me, gripping the bow in my left hand, while pulling an arrow from the dirt with my right. Their solidity combined with that familiar sense of confidence helped calm my nerves as the first horse came into view. The arrow was knocked through pure muscle memory and its fletching caressed my cheek like the familiar touch of a long-lost lover. My left eye squinted slightly, focusing my sight on the lead horse like a razor's edge.

I saw Hollis's hand gripping the rope more tightly through the dim perception of my squinted eye, but he made no move to interfere with the rider and I chose to follow his lead and hold my shot. I had always assumed that the proper archery technique was to close one eye to focus your attention. Here, I found that keeping both eyes open gave a clearer field of vision, while not dulling my target. I was also amazed how easily it was to hold the arrow to my cheek; my arm did not as much as tremble. Silvermoon seemed to be a true master of his art, if one killing could be called an art form.

Two more horses stormed by, with nary a twitch from the boy lying prone at the roadside. As a group of six horses approached, I made out the subtle movements of Hollis's arm as he prepared to act.

My right thumb flicked softly at the green feather fletching of the shaft as I chose its target. There was a large figure dressed in a combination of leather and what I assumed to be chainmail. He wore a steel helmet that covered his head and most of his face, but there was a small gap between helmet and armor. I took aim on that, but something beneath the surface of my consciousness told me it was unwise. I redrew a bead on the man's center mass, noting how high he held his arms as his hands held the reins. Once he drew up perpendicular to me, his arm pits and the entirety of his torso would present itself. After estimating his height and speed, I shifted my aim to a spot in front of him, focusing on where he would be rather than where he was.

That was what Silvermoon must have meant about the shot taking you, not the other way around.

As the first of the six reached Hollis's position, he lurched backwards and settled his feet against the tree hiding him from the men's sight. The rope snaked its way out of a shallow trench that had hidden it in an explosion of dust and dirt. I saw him wrap the free end of the rope around a low-cut stump and brace himself. The two leading horsemen didn't act react quickly enough to avoid the rope. The horses went down with a terrible cacophony of screams both human and equine. I watched Marcus step out from behind the tree, his words already heavy in my chest. My target drew even with my position, just as sparks rose up behind him and a line of flames leapt to life. I released the shaft and in a quick succession, another joined it in flight. Both struck the man under the arm, the first sunk six inches into his body; but the second only a half an inch above it was driven to its fletching. He fell from his panicked horse before he could register the first arrow.

My three comrades emerged from the woods across the road at a run, with their weapons in motion. Haedren swung his huge mace in a low arc as he passed the first of the downed horsemen. The sound was both wet and sharp at the same time; his screams ceased instantly.

Ret charged past the second, hurdling the prone body of my own target and stood before the sheet of flame that had risen from the line of sparks thrown by my 'brother', his feet planted shoulder-width apart. He did not need to wait long.

As Mika speared the second fallen horseman with her wicked sword, two additional men came charging through the fire. Their long hair, and the manes of their horses were already set alight.

Ret's axe swung right and left, and the first swing caught a horse's leg just below its barrel chest, causing it to tumble headfirst to the ground. The second swing struck the other man in the stomach, opening his body from ribs to hip. His horse carried him free of the axe's deadly reach. Ret spun and planted his axe between the neck and shoulder of the tumbling horse's rider before turning back to the already fading curtain of fire.

I drew a quick bead on the retreating back of Ret's fleeing opponent; two shafts appeared between his shoulder blades. I am unsure if it was my arrows or Ret's cleaving stroke catching up to him, but he slumped from the saddle as his horse continued its panic driven rush. Marcus stepped into the road; his hands already raised in the direction of the horse's flight.

Again, I felt the words in my chest as the fog brought on by nightfall thickened. I could not help but be entranced by the mist's almost sentient movements as the sound of more hoof-beats came to my ears, this time from both my right and left. The scouts must have pieced together what was happening. As my brother stepped into the woods on the far side of the road, I drew a bead on the thick rolling bank of fog.

Out of my peripheral vision, I found Mika and Ret making short work of the last horseman in this group. Mika grasped the man's belt, pulling him from his horse and in a fluid motion, took his place. Her left hand quickly brought the animal under control as she circled around to face the last flickers of flames. I heard shouts from my right; but could not spare a glance as the fog was split by the nose of the first returning horse. Taking aim at where I could just make out a silhouette of a man, I let loose a shaft and adjusted my aim as the rider broke through as well. Two more arrows sped through the air, before finding their place in his chest. His breast plate absorbed their impact more deftly than his companions' chainmail; but each sunk down a few inches into the metal surface. Two more shapes began to emerge from the fog.

I felt the cold fingers of indecision touching my stomach, my attention vacillating between finishing the armored target and moving onto the new threats. My decision was made as a flash of movement erupted from my left.

Hollis emerged from the tree line, his left arm pistoning forward. The knife appeared in the shoulder of the lead horse. The wound was slight but still brought the animal to a halt. Hollis continued his momentum, his short sword piercing the rider at the hip below the breastplate. Ducking low, he moved down beneath the horse, avoiding a sweeping sword stroke in the process. I heard his sword driven home a second time, but the horse's body hid the details from my eyes. I turned my attention back to the two figures fully emerged from the mist.

One went down quickly under a trio of arrows, but the second charged forward to aid his comrade, hard pressed by Hollis. A pair of what appeared to be fireflies darted from the darkening depths of the woods across from me. They veered in midair and seemed to intercept the second horseman's path. I heard a sickening hiss as they collided with the man's body, followed by a cry of agony. He pulled hard on the reins, causing the horse to rear to a halt, turning slightly. Where there were two fireflies, now there were two dozen boring into the man's abdomen. What I thought to be hissing was instead the chittering of the glowing insects, doubling in number as I watched with horror-filled fascination. His chainmail appeared unbroken; but the padding and flesh underneath seemed to erode under their malicious attentions. Beneath the bone-chilling screams of terror and pain, I could almost hear my brother's voice. I could just make out his shape amid the trees, his hands outstretched towards the man and his infestation.

I turned my attention back to my other companion. Hollis's opponent swung at him a bit too vigorously and lost his seat. I took in the realization and resignation in the man's expression. As he crashed to the ground, the boy was upon him, his sword driving itself into the fallen soldier's body twice before he bounced the first time. He was dead as he rolled to a stop.

More than the sudden violence before me, the look in Hollis's eyes caused me to pause. I had seen that look before in my students during gym-class or even my own son when he played on his PlayStation. He was having fun; it was as if this maelstrom of death and pain were nothing more than a game. He winked at me as he disappeared into the dimness of the woods across the road, fading as if he had never been.

I turned my attention back to where Ret and Haedren was standing. Mika's horse was stamping impatiently behind them. A smaller dust cloud could be seen around the bend, resolving itself into a trio of men on horseback. From somewhere deep within me, a sense of dread began to take hold. The first horseman was without a doubt the largest man I have ever seen, so large that I was amazed that his horse could bear him at all much less at the run it maintained. Dressed in thick furs, most likely wolf or bear, he looked more beast than man. This appearance was only enhanced by the scar that ran from the corner of his mouth, through a milky dead eye and into his thick hairline. The scar caused the corner of his mouth to pull back in a perpetual sneer, revealing a vicious canine. It seemed that time slowed to a crawl as he rounded the bend, followed by a second figure.

He seemed at first glance to be nothing of import – he was on the thin side of average, his brown traveling cloak pulled tightly against his side despite the warm summer night. A shock of brown hair hid his face as he held his head down against the rocking motion of his mount. As he came into view, his right hand drew up and pulled the hair out of his eyes, holding it atop his head for a moment. Those dull brown eyes held everything and nothing all at once. Even from thirty yards, those eyes burned into me before shifting to each of my companions. I could not see them; but I could indeed feel their effect.

What I could see, however, was the small, tight smile that came to his lips as he pulled lightly on the reins. His horse reacted with incredible alacrity, pulling to a stop. His burly companion spurred his mount to a more breakneck speed, causing Ret and Haedren to leap out of its path.

Mika kicked at the flanks of her stolen horse and met the horseman's charge, her sword held low like a short lance. The horseman reached out and batted the sword aside with his bare hand, slamming the same elbow into Mika's temple as he pulled his horse to a stop between my position and hers.

I shook off my shock and put two arrows in the air like it was breathing. Both shafts struck true; one sank into his shoulder, the other three inches closer to his spine. He never looked back, simply reaching back to pull the arrow from his shoulder as you or I would pluck a splinter from our finger. Through sheer will alone, Mika retained her seat although she shook her head slowly, trying to regain her senses. Marcus stepped into the road, his words already resonating in my chest. They echoed in the air as the light evening clouds began to gather into bruised masses in the night sky. I released another two arrows, both sinking to the fletching in his back above the kidney. I might as well have been throwing pencils at him for the amount that he flinched.

The plain-faced man sat astride his motionless horse watching the scene unfold, as a third horseman charged by him, with his own mace raised high in his right hand.

Ret and Haedren rushed towards him. Ret's axe drove deeply into his horse's front leg. As the horse fell and rolled to a stop, Haedren used his momentum to add to the force of his mace's blow. The fallen horseman raised his own weapon at the last second, catching the cleric's shaft on his own.

The downed man spoke in a soft almost lisp, "Father of Lies, grant your servant the strength that served you so well in weathering the persecution of your siblings." I think it could have been my imagination; but it was as if a shadow fell over the pair for the briefest of seconds. Haedren's weapon was pushed aside as his opponent slowly rose to his feet.

Ret charged to Mika's aid as she gathered her wits. The beast-man dropped heavily to the ground, slapping his horse on the flank as he did so. Ret collided with the mountain of a man, making the Rangor warrior appear small in comparison. "Gorack, I thought it was your foul stench I sensed on the wind."

Gorack pushed Ret backwards a step, drawing a wickedly serrated sword from where it had been sheathed on his hip. "Little cousin, have you lost weight? I thought by the sway of your hips and your girlish figure, I may have had a night of enjoyment ahead of me." His laugh sounded more akin to a cough than an expression of amusement.

The thunder that mirrored my brother's words began to build in both volume and frequency as his timbre became clipped. I saw the concern on his face before he shifted his attention to the still mounted observer at the bend.

Ret growled, "You will find much enjoyment in Sharroth's Cage this evening, but I do not believe it will be yours." He lunged ahead, his axe leading the way.

Gorack grunted and was forced to surrender ground before his opponent's rage filled rush. "I am sure you will see the 'Cage before I do, runt," Gorack swung his sword in short chopping arcs.

On the defensive as he was, there was little power behind any of the strikes and Ret took them against his shoulders and chest as his armor turned the blade easily. He brought the end of his axe up into Gorack's chest, driving him back another half of a step.

"You call me cousin, traitor, but you are no kin to me. My kin would not wither before love taps such as these. A true Rangor accepts these as the southerners accept the clasping of hands." He brought the blade of his axe up to follow the haft, aiming for Gorack's hip. Again, he gave ground, thrusting with his sword to achieve some distance from his attacker.

"We are simply beginning the dance, 'cousin'," Gorack taunted as he took another step back towards the woods. The Rangor followed him to press his advantage, to his harm. As Ret lunged forward to reclaim the distance his retreat had taken, Gorack also lunged forward. The lunge carried the beast past Ret's guard and planted that wicked sword into his side. "Come now, do all of your kin wither so easily after only one thrust?"

Ret roared and gathered himself to swing his axe, not bothering to remove the serrated blade from his body. "We will see who is withered when the sun falls upon their corpse!"

I spotted movement behind Ret's opponent, and it brought me out of my thoughts. Hollis stepped out from behind a tree and sank his short sword to the hilt in the Gorack's back.

Ret bellowed, "He is! mine!" In his rage, he failed to notice the lack of effect that three feet of steel had on his opponent.

Gorack pulled his sword from Ret's side, twisting his wrist, "Perhaps the return stroke will bring you too your premature end, runt."

A low growling scream was wrenched from Ret's throat. The sound echoed into the woods like the clarion call of a hunting horn.

Ignoring his friend's words, Hollis withdrew his sword and plunged it again into the beast's body. I saw the tip emerge from his chest, but it elicited no more than a grunt from him. Gorack stared back at the thief and with a sudden, violent motion elbowed him in the face. I heard bones break as Hollis fell into the road. With a slow, sure motion, Gorack's hand found the hilt of Hollis's sword, drew it from his body and tossed it aside.

I launched another two arrows, drawing Gorack's attention as they slammed home into his chest. Still, the mountain of a man showed no pain or distress. It gave Ret a chance to recover, so that when Gorack shifted his focus back to him, he was prepared. He launched an overhead chop fueled with pain and rage, and the beast staggered. A second chop drove Gorack to his knees.

I fired another two shots, the last of my arrows. Both struck home in Gorack's hip, putting an end to his rage-filled rise. I took the moment to examine the struggle between Haedren and his foe.

Haedren took a step back slowly to free his mace from the grasp of his opponent, his own free hand finding the chalice symbol of Olm lying against his chest. He spoke quickly, as if to himself, "Father of Justice and Lord of the Dawn, grant me a measure of the burning light of your truth." As he spoke, the chalice around his neck glowed softly between his fingers, further eroding the shadows surrounding Sharroth's priest's body. Pressing his advantage, Haedren swung his mace in a probing arc, causing the other priest to retreat, and in turn, his shadows fell back with him.

I was transfixed by the strengthening of the brilliant aura surrounding the man, growing brighter by the second. As he shifted his left hand from the symbol to the haft of his weapon, I saw the shadows as they were ripped from his opponent's body, pooling behind him as if Haedren were the sun itself.

"Mercy," the Haedren's foe croaked weakly as he collapsed before the almost- blinding brilliance that radiated from the chalice around Haedren's neck.

He raised his mace above his head and screamed "Death is the only mercy I can offer Children of the Beast!" His opponent cringed, covering his face. I never saw the still mounted figure move his horse closer to the melee; but the soft thump of boots against dirt drew my attention. His hair had fallen to partially hide his features again; but the small smile that colored his lips was quite clear. It was not a pleasant expression.

I heard my brother's voice cut across the battlefield, "Incoming!" Ret stepped back quickly, burying his face in his elbow. I saw Mika draw her cloak over her head and across her mount's eyes. Even Hollis rolled over with a groan and covered his head. Before I could process these sights, my vision exploded with blinding light as the bolt of lightning struck Gorack and then a second pulse of light erupted again before the first rumble of thunder could be heard.

I fell backwards, clawing at my eyes as the scent of ozone and burning flesh filled my nostrils.

I could hear Haedren's opponent's voice again, "Mercy! I understand now..."

"I will grant you mercy..." Haedren's voice was strong and sure; but held the conviction of a child, compared to the voice that followed.

The tone was soft; but held power like I had never heard before. One word cut across the battlefield like a knife. "No."

My vision began to clear. The figure standing in the center of the road held his left hand out before him, half of it lost in a shadow with no source. The only detail I could make out clearly was the dark metal brooch that he grasped between the fingers of his right hand. Upon its surface was a skeletal cameo cast in glittering metal. Amid the growing darkness, the cameo alone retained its brilliance. He slowly and methodically closed his left hand into a fist. As he clenched his hand, the shadows around his right hand faded like they had never been, but deeper shadows appeared around Haedren's body, blotting out the light emerging from his holy symbol. Once his right fist was free of shadow, he lowered his left down to his side.

Haedren's form was driven into the hard-packed dirt of the road. Through the shifting darkness, I saw Haedren struggling against the force that held him. He may well have been a willow fighting against an avalanche. His mace fell from his fingers as he grasped the symbol around his neck with both hands. "Bastion of Justice and Father of Light, grant your servant strength in this his time of need." But his voice lacked the confidence that had been there only a moment ago, and now it seemed more desperate plea than command. The shadows only grew darker around his form, which was now forced into a crumpled kneeling posture in the center of the road.

The non-descript man simply clicked his tongue as a parent would to his child, "Poor man, it never brings me joy to see the light of faith fade from a man's eyes when he realizes what the sacrifices he has made in the name of that faith actually earn him." He stepped closer to Haedren, as his fist reached his side, driving the prostrate man into the dirt.

Mika wheeled her horse around and kicked it into a charge, "Release him, monster!"

He turned his head casually and watched her approach. "I assure you, milady, I have no hold upon him. Not compared to the dispassion of his sworn deity, at any rate." He deliberately raised his hand again, opening his fingers as he did so. At first, I thought it was my still flash blind eyes, but Mika's mount began to stumble as it bore down on the man. It released a heart wrenching cough as it fell to the ground mere feet from its target, pinning Mika beneath its bulk, its grey chest marred by a perfect jet palm print. Just as slowly, he turned his back on her and her horse, seizing the quickly recovering priest of Sharroth in his gaze.

"Theamon, allow me to strike down the foolish priest of Olm... in the name of our master." As he picked up his horseman's mace from the road, Theamon chuckled softly; a gesture that even from fifty feet away, even I could see his companion misinterpreted. His own laughter joined that of the slim man.

"Oh, my dear Coitae, Theamon owes fealty only to Theamon. No man. No god. No one." He slowly drew the long, thin blade he wore at his side. "You see, I have no more use for you than I have for the Olmite." His companion's laughter faded with his smile.

"But Theamon...my lord... "

Theamon shook his head and said, "I am not your lord, Coitae... not in any real way. You will always serve the Father of Lies, even above his Hand on Taerh."

I spotted Ret trying to heave the horse off Mika's unconscious body and knew I should do something; but I was so transfixed by the scene before me. Theamon spoke again, his voice barely above a whisper, although clearly heard from where I stood. "Tell me, priest, whose power is greater? The deity bound in a cage of his siblings' making deep in the earth or he who acts in his name in the world? When one cannot handle his own affairs and is forced to give a share of his power to a vessel, is it still truly his own power? What if that vessel decided to keep that power? Well, there would be little that so-called deity could truly do about it."

Fear filled Coitae's eyes now. "Lord Theamon, this is madness. You are the Hand of Lies, Sharroth's most potent and favored vessel."

Theamon pressed the tip of his sword against Coitae's chest. He tried to raise his mace to brush it aside, but it was as if he were pushing through water. "There you go again, attributing my actions to a will not my own." He caught the man's eyes. "You should endeavor to not repeat that mistake." The tip of his blade dimpled the leather that covered Coitae's heart. "Although, I am not sure I would not worry much about it." With a soft pop, the sword broke the surface of the armor and split the flesh beneath. "You will not live long enough to learn that particular lesson. Do give my regards to your master, though." With a slow and deliberate motion, Theamon sank the blade into his companion's heart, his eyes never leaving Coitae's until the man's life had faded from them.

The sound of the man's body falling to the dirt broke whatever remained of my awe. I saw Ret pull Mika from beneath the horse and lay her beside it. He swept his axe from the ground and charged at the unprotected back of the slim man. I felt in my chest that my brother had begun casting again as I pulled my own sword from its sheath of earth and ran towards Theamon as well.

I felt another vibration in my chest, beating a counter point to the words spoken by George's other self. This rhythm seemed off somehow; like just experiencing it made me feel dirty somehow. I saw Theamon's brow furrow in concentration as he turned to face Ret's furious charge. His slim sword was driven into Ret's chest by his own momentum; the slim man's smile disappeared as that same momentum threw him to the ground and tore the blade from his hand.

Ret roared as he pulled the offending object from his body and tossed it aside, "Enough of your words, monster! A Rangor speaks with steel... he convinces with blood and fire!" To his credit, Theamon's lips turned upward into a deeper smile; the counter vibration I

105

could feel in my chest never wavered. "Have you nothing to say? Do even your words pale in the face of my steel?"

Out of the corner of my eye, I saw Marcus turn pale as his lips ceased to move but the warring vibrations in my chest continued unabated. I came to the realization that Theamon was more than the Hand of Lies, he was also a Mage. "Ret, get away from him! He has taken control of my spell! Run!"

The huge man turned to regard Marcus with a crooked smile as the clouds began to part, his white teeth shining in the moonlight. "Worry not, spell-slinger, his words hold no fear for me. His tricks are at an end."

Again, Theamon's soft voice cut through the night, "Not quite."

As the beams of moonlight broke through the clouds, they seemed to take on almost an unbearable luminesce. Anywhere that a beam fell on Ret, his armor sparked into flames, followed quickly by the scent of burning flesh. His words morphed into screams as he was engulfed in flames. I closed the distance, bringing my sword down on the slim man's form. At first, I felt resistance and then a split second later my blade bit deep into his shoulder. He turned; an expression of shock painted on his face. Marcus's stolen illusion faded with Theamon's concentration. The flames that had surrounded Ret disappeared as if they had never been, but his unburned form still lay motionless.

"Kill him, Alex!" It was Marcus's voice, weakened by the strain of running towards Ret's prone form. "Kill him before he gathers his wits!"

I raised my sword again but now felt what Coitae must have experienced. Everything around me seemed to move at a lightning pace, while I moved at that of a snail. "Fascinating. What, pray tell, are you? You are the forester and yet... not." He began to climb to his feet; to my senses, he moved with staggering alacrity. I strained to swing my blade but felt as if I fought a hurricane force wind. "Let your mind be at peace, good forester, of all your friends, you shall survive. I believe you to be a quite remarkable being."

I laid my eyes on each of my companions, the other selves of my closest and dearest friends. Ret lay motionless, despite Marcus shaking him and yelling his name at the top of his voice. Mika was crumpled next to her dead horse, so I was unsure whether she still breathed. Even the boy, Hollis lay broken in the road. Haedren seemed to be the only member of our band besides George's other self that clung to consciousness; but he was curled in the fetal position, his eyes wide and unseeing.

I looked back to Theamon and saw that his smile had returned. I took a deep fortifying breath and felt my teeth grind together, before I said, "You smug son of a bitch."

"Smug and certain are two distinct things..." Even with his hood pulled back, Theamon's features did not become more distinct to my eyes. I expected the Hand of Lies to appear more sinister somehow. He looked like any number of men I have passed on the street without even noticing. His arrogant smirk was the only thing that made him stand out in my mind.

I felt my anger as a physical thing that burned in my chest. I did not belong here; it was a terrible dream that I just wanted to wake from. Or did I? Dream or not, this man was a being of evil, of that I was sure. Could I escape into the waking world and leave these people to die? Even if it were my imagination, could I live with myself knowing that, even in my own mind, I could not be the man my friends and family needed me to be?

"Give me a moment to deal with some small things," he looked to Marcus and said, "...and we will be on our way."

Something happened that I can still not completely quantify; as I accepted that this world was as real as the waking one, even if just in this moment, the world slowed around me. A cloak of calm descended upon me, as I had experienced during the fight with the demon a few weeks ago. With that calm, whatever spell had fallen over me faded.

Theamon had turned his back on me and was walking over to my brother. Every inch of my skin burned with rage – I was completely in this moment, this place. I drove my sword into the slim man's back with all my might. His blood sprayed across Marcus's face as the tip exploded from his chest. "Not today, monster... Never again," I muttered, more to myself than to Theamon or anyone else around me. I will never forget the look of disbelief in his eyes as the life fled from them.

Stephen closed the journal with a soft snap, his hand already reaching for another. He immediately noticed the difference. Where the first journal was heavy and obviously old, this one was more compact and its surface less worn. The book fell to the floor with an echoing slap as it slipped from nerveless fingers.

A loose sheet of paper inside the cover read:

Stephen,

If you are reading this, things have no doubt gone horribly wrong. I think I found my father and I am going after him.

CHAPTER NINE
AN AGONIZING FAREWELL

Stephen had to read the line several times before the shock wore off. Despite the gathering warmth of the summer evening, chills rose on his skin as his tear-filled eyes shifted between the words on the page and the zip-lock bag sitting atop the other journals. Gnawing fingers of pain burrowed into his gut as his all too fresh grief surged in him.

Could these dreams, these stories from Jeff's journals really be true? A wave of fear swept through him; but it was replaced by a surge of hope. On one hand, this is what he had dreamed of since first playing 'The Game' so many years ago; never believing that it could be possible. On the other, those closest to him: Jeff, Alan, Beatrice, Mike had suffered terrible fates, their only commonality being the world of Taerh.

Stephen,

If you are reading this, things have no doubt gone horribly wrong. I think I found my father and I am going after him. My father's death always seemed so senseless and without reasonable explanation. The coincidence of Uncle George and Beatrice dying within weeks of my father's passing was too much. As I was preparing to leave for college, I felt so far from him. Samantha suggested that I go through his things as a way to take a piece of him with me... to convince myself that he would be proud of me. I found so much more. Read his journals, as I did. The world that he created for us was not based on his imagination; but instead a real place, a place he'd seen. Once I tried the Adder root, the old leaves I found in the trunk, I could not hold on to the delusion that it wasn't true.

I know it is hard to believe; but if anyone will believe me, it will be you. The old leaves have lost most of their potency; I convinced Samantha to give me more in order to see for myself. I was surprised at how readily she agreed. It is everything my father wrote about and more. My nightly visits to that world seem a million times more real than anything while awake. I have come to believe that our world is the pale reflection and that one the true waking world. Each of the three of you has a reflection there, all unaware of your existences.

Following in my father's footsteps, I began to guide the three of you through events I, myself, experienced while dreaming. As my father prepared Uncle George, Beatrice and Roger to reflect, I did the same for you, Mike and Robert. I know I should have told the group everything, most especially you; but I was afraid you would think I was crazy. I had thought to show you once you were ready; but things have changed. Walker has told me that my father is alive, that the key to bringing him back lies with the Well of Worlds.

Robert wouldn't believe me without a great deal of convincing, even if I showed him. Mike is the most open minded and loyal of us, which is fortunate because I don't think I have time to fully warn him before we reflect. God forgive me for what I am about to do to him. You, as the oldest and quite frankly smartest of us, are most suited to pour over the journals for anything that I may have missed. Also, you knew the others as a group better than the three of us.

Please, convince Robert of the truth and follow us when you can. I know this is a tremendous thing to ask; but I do not feel that Mike and I can do it alone. The recommended dosage is two small leaves in a cup of tea or six in a pitcher of water, but after speaking with Samantha, I believe twice that dosage will guarantee a longer reflec-

tion. I hope that this letter is not necessary, and I can explain this to you in person; but if something goes wrong, you may be our only hope.

Regardless of what you decide, know that you have always been my closest friend, just as you were to my father.

Alan

Stephen closed his eyes and took a few deep breaths before reading the letter in its entirety one more time. He almost jumped out of his skin as the alarm on his phone split the silence that ruled the kitchen. He flailed at it, silencing it on the second try, his eyes going to the stairs. He could hear Ronni stir but then fall into silence again. Another deep breath settled his nerves. The rush of his recent realization warred with the dread of the day to come. Despite the hopeful tone of his letter, they were burying Alan today. He would have to sit beside Alice, her hand clutched in his own, carrying this secret. He didn't know who Walker was, but if they spoke the truth, he was the only chance Alan and his father had of returning to this world.

Questions pricked at the back of his mind: *How does one return when your dead body is buried, in Jeff's case for a decade? What happens to the body of a person in this world when he is killed in the other?* It was then that a realization struck him. When last he dreamt of the other side, Hollis was in dire straits. *Would he even still be alive? If his consciousness possessed Hollis's body while under the influence of Adder root, what would happen if Hollis were no more?* Fear seized him. The Game was the one place Stephen took chances. There, he had Hollis's strength and character. He wished he could see himself in the way he valued the thief. It was ironic how Hollis was his reaction, yet Stephen felt nothing like him at all. In his real life, he only ever made the safe choice, the one with the least risk. At each juncture in his life, he always chose the route of least danger. His job... his marriage... even his choice of a car.

This situation left so many questions unanswered, and there were so many chances for things to go awry. The fear inside him intensified. It would be so easy to do as Robert bid him, to put the journals and adder root in the trash and carry on with his safe – if not mildly uncomfortable – life. He could convince himself that Jeff and Alan had been the victim of drug-addled hallucinations and these journals were nothing but flights of fancy. It struck him in those moments that at some point it had become necessary to convince him that this insanity was not the truth and not his reasonable concept of reality.

In the storm of these emotions, an eye formed slowly. The sound of his heart beating in his ears began to quiet and the cold burning feeling of fear began to dull. Just as in the dreams, a calm descended upon him. If he concentrated, he was aware of the feelings; but it was as if a warm blanket were wrapped around his heart, keeping the cold at bay. Mike and Alan were his friends. Jeff, Beatrice and George were his friends.

Despite the risks, he could not look at himself in the mirror from this morning to the end of his life knowing that he abandoned them because he was afraid. His eyes seized upon the Adder root and a slow smile came to his lips.

Stephen pulled at his tie for what seemed like the hundredth time in the already stifling heat. He wasn't sure if he could attribute all his discomfort to the silk noose around his neck or the heat. Making a choice does not come close to making the repercussions of that choice any easier. He had come close to unburdening his soul to Alice on more than one occasion, most recently when the tears began to stream from her already reddened and swollen eyes. Each time, he stopped himself with the rationalization that if he were wrong... if he gave her false hope, he could never forgive himself.

The graveside service was truly heartbreaking. The finality of it all struck those present like a hammer. Alice clenched Fredrick's hand with both of hers. Stephen laid his arm across her shoulders, his thumb rubbing her arm soothingly. Stephen looked around and saw that even Robert's stoic façade had shifted slightly.

The only face on which the pain of grief was not etched was that of Samantha Marcheur; where every eye in the group was seized on the deep brown wooden surface of the casket being lowered into the ground, her eyes were fixed firmly upon Stephen's. Despite her previously kind demeanor, there was something disquieting in that stare. He was forced, just as in the funeral home the night before, to break contact first.

A stifled gasp from Alice brought his attention back to the matter at hand. He squeezed her shoulder gently, opening his mouth to offer some platitude; but found himself bereft of one. He settled for kissing her softly on the cheek. She turned her head and mouthed, "Thank you," before turning back to the cavernous grave containing the body of her son.

Alice's pastor spoke quietly, "Any who wish to approach and say their final good-byes to Alan may do so." People began to shuffle forward, each clutching a white rose. "Alice and Fredrick would like to thank each of you for coming and invite you to join them at their home for a repast at one o'clock."

Stephen watched Robert drop his rose into the grave, his other hand firmly clasping Nell's free one. As she dropped her rose into the grave, Nell rested her head on his broad shoulder. Stephen couldn't help but smile; she was eight years his senior, but they looked good together. He was glad that something positive could come out of this tragedy.

He was briefly seized with doubt. There was no denying that the other world had taken more than its fair share of blood. It occurred to him, for the first time strangely enough, that everyone he knew who *reflected*, as Alan had termed it, except for himself, had eventually not returned. *Even if he could convince Robert of the truth of the journals, could he bring himself to threaten to take Robert from Nell, just as it seemed they had found each other? Did it make him selfish that he feared facing the unknown alone?* He told himself that it was Alan's last request, that two had a better chance of accomplishing what needed to be done, but in his heart, he knew it was his fear again forcing his hand. In the end, Stephen made the choice to leave Robert to his happiness.

Stephen did not see the two approach; he was so lost in thought... lost in doubt. "Something on your mind, Steve?" Robert looked down at him, his eyes seeming to plead to his friend to say no. A wave of loneliness swept through him as he realized even if he told his friend about the journals, he was not sure Robert would want to know.

"No, Rob, just processing is all."

"Did you take my advice?" He reached up with his free hand to cradle Nell's chin with a tenderness Stephen wasn't aware he was capable of. He watched some of the tension flow from her body at his touch. Guilt overcame fear in that moment, no matter what happened, this would end with him.

Stephen nodded slowly, "Yes, thank you." He even managed a smile. "It was best for everyone."

Robert smiled, his relief evident, "Good. I'll see you at Alice and Fredrick's?"

He nodded and they were gone into the swirl of mourners. The crowd soon began to thin, and Stephen rose, squeezing Alice's shoulder one more time. "Alice, I'm going to take a moment. Do you mind?"

She shook her head slowly, managing, "You are coming back to the house? We have so much food... "

He smiled; Alice could always be counted on to be Alice. Especially in times like this, she drew a certain strength from taking care of others. "Of course, I heard some sausage and peppers calling my name from across town." She smiled, at least a small measure of weight seeming to lift from her shoulders.

When he turned around, Samantha was standing a small distance away, her eyes still fixed upon him, "Good Afternoon, Stephen. How are you holding up?"

He continued to study her as he responded almost by rote, "As well as can be expected. It's a tragedy and my heart goes out to Alice and Fredrick, of course."

She nodded her head politely, solemnly. "A tragedy indeed. Alice is a strong woman, as much as her heart is breaking, she will carry on as she always has. I know Fredrick will take good care of her."

Stephen met her eyes again and was taken aback by the intensity of them. "Of course."

She smiled with something that seemed to approach satisfaction, "Is this truly what you wanted to speak about, Stephen? I can sustain small talk as long as you like; but in the end, I am not sure you have the time, do you?"

He took a step back, his brow furrowing. Cynicism crept through him, and he was slightly offended at her rudeness. "Excuse me?"

"When I went into Alan's room to take back the Root he had not used, it was gone along with several of the journals. It was a simply bit of deduction as to who had both." Stephen tried to speak but found himself without words, and she continued. "I was surprised when Alan came to me, to be sure. I had debated for years on how to help dear Jeffery. It is a rather difficult pill to swallow, precluding me from enlisting aid from anyone else and, alas, I am too frail to reflect any longer." She shrugged slightly, "It demands a cost that I simply can no longer pay."

"You knew?"

"More than that, I searched for Jeffery for more than a year after his disappearance .... "

"Death," he corrected.

She let out a short, sharp laugh, although her eyes remained hard, "Concepts such as that are mutable, Stephen, especially in

Taerh." She clearly saw his confusion, because she smiled with amusement and continued, "The other side, son."

"You mean the other side that claimed that woman's husband and son? That other side?" His voice remained quiet but was filled with accusation, "She's your friend. How could you let her suffer like that?" As the words left his mouth, he was already aware of the hypocrisy of them. *Wasn't that exactly what he was doing now?*

Samantha frowned briefly. "The same way you hid that fact from her this afternoon. It would do her no justice to give her hope when I have no way to remedy the situation. And, that is assuming that I could get her to believe me in the first place."

He nodded slowly and said, "I see your point, I guess; but it's been five years, Miss Marcheur."

"Please, Stephen, call me Samantha."

"Samantha, it's been five years. In all that time, you couldn't find a moment ...a way to ease her mind?"

"Do you not think I wanted to? Do you not think I tried to find a way to bring her husband back to her? To bring Alan's father back to him? Especially in this case, things are far more difficult done than said." She laid a hand on his forearm and stared harder into his eyes, if it was possible. "Until now, at least."

Stephen's eyes darted to her hand and then back up to her eyes. "How did you ... I mean, what do you mean?"

"I have said before, son, I have had more practiced liars than you attempt to deceive me; do not waste either of our time trying." Her fingers dug into his flesh, holding his arm in place when he tried to pull away. "You have decided to go after your friends. Well, with my aid, you may very well be successful. Alan disregarded my advice of patience and..." She released his arm to gesture to the grave as he rubbed it vigorously. "... You can see the consequences of that."

"I have so many questions."

"Come to the florist tomorrow morning and I will do my best to answer them all." She laid her hand on his arm again, this time with a gentleness that surprised him. "We can do this, Stephen. I honestly believe that; just be patient, please."

He laid his hand over hers. "I have to work tomorrow ... "

"... and that will be the first sacrifice you will make. I wish I could say that it will be the last." She pulled her hand from his grasp, turning to leave, "This is an important moment, Stephen. This is the moment you decide to either wither in mediocrity or risk everything you have to do what you know you must." She began to walk towards the parking lot, "I will see you tomorrow... or I will continue to look for another solution."

Stephen watched her back for a moment and then turned, approaching the gravesite. He stood looking down at the casket, its surface speckled with the white flowers, for a moment. He brought his own to his nose and inhaled deeply to cover a small catch in his throat. As he dropped the rose into the grave he whispered, "Hold on, Brother. I'm coming."

CHAPTER TEN
A CONTEMPTUOUS CAPTOR

Hollis woke on the stone floor, with his back pressed against the corner of his tiny, night-black cell. The dull ache in his left hand throbbed, as the small spasm that had woken him raced through his forearm. A moment of panic seized him as he tried to make sense of his surroundings but faded as the memory of Aamir's betrayal dawned upon him. He was unsure how many days he had been a guest of the Emir; they ran together in a drone of darkness and pain.

He slowly flexed his hand and was rewarded with a shock of pain that bolted right up into his elbow. Beneath the pain, was a sense of satisfaction when he felt his fingers move, even with the damage to the hand itself. If he found a way out of this cell and someone to set it, there was a fair chance that it could regain part of the dexterity that it once was capable of. His hands were his livelihood, so no matter how slim the chance, he had to seize it. The alternative was not something he preferred to dwell on.

They no longer shackled him, whether due to laziness or faith that a one-handed thief posed no threat of escape he was unsure. He would make them regret either. Reaching under the filthy pile of straw that served as the only furniture in his ever-so-modest home, Hollis pulled out the torque and hook-pick he had been shaping – agonizingly slowly

119

— from two ragged splinters. He had acquired them from the rough wooden bowl his captors filled with weevil-infested slop when it suited them. They believed keeping him in darkness was simply another way to break his spirit, but the man was decidedly more comfortable without light. It served him well in covering his activities from the eyes of his captors.

He held a small piece of mortar, pried from between the stones of his cell, as tightly as he could stand in his left hand, and ran the torque along its surface. Every few strokes, he brought it up against his lips, testing the angle. It was by no means perfect, but it would have to do. He had complained when his mentor, Seran, insisted he learn to pick a lock with only one hand and then the other; but the skill was now as natural to him as breathing and he reveled in it.

When the pain became too great in his left hand, he returned the picks and mortar to their place under the straw and stood slowly, stretching first his arms and then his back. Prisoners often fall into depression while in captivity, leading to a decline in strength and health that has nothing to do with torture or poor nutrition. When one's spirit gives up, one's body tends to follow suit; but the opposite can also be true. In Hollis's line of work, incarceration is an ever-present risk. If your captors do not execute you on the spot, the chance of release is always there, whether voluntary or not. Any city with a respectable thieves-guild would throw a thief in a dark hole long enough to 'teach them a lesson'; but as long as the target of your crime was not too highly placed and you were a member in good standing, eventually your release would be negotiated. In that case, you simply had to wait and hope it did not take too long. When in a city that took their morals a little more seriously or your target was someone of import, the chances of release become less certain.

In either case, it is in one's best interest to keep sharp, both mentally and physically. Shackles make this more difficult but not impossible. Being free of such restraints, Hollis started by pacing out his cell, focusing on keeping his steps uniform and steady. His cell was three strides by three strides, which from exploration was a little longer than he was tall. He used the same stride whenever he was taken from his cell to his 'meetings' with the Emir's inquisitor.

From this he knew that the corridor leading from his cell was fifteen strides, ending in a T with a guard post at the dead end. From there, he was taken another thirty strides to a room on the right side of the corridor. Cells lined both corridors; of which only three were occupied. As he paced his cell, he reviewed this information until it was second nature. Once he could picture the layout of his route, he moved to the center of the room and sat with his legs out before him.

Beginning at the waist, he bent forward, stretching each muscle group one at a time until his chest pressed against his thighs. Ignoring the slight burning in his back, he slowly relaxed each group in reverse, returning to an upright position. He repeated this process ten times before laying back against the stone floor and drawing his legs to his chest with the same deliberate pace, stressing the muscles in the core of his body. Once the burning in his stomach became noticeable, he rolled over, wincing as his left hand took too much of his weight. As best he could, he pushed against the stone floor, taking most of his weight on his good hand. When he could stand the pain in his bad hand no longer, he sank to the floor once more.

He lay against the cold stone, focusing on keeping his breathing slow and steady; despite his desire to gulp air as a starving man wolfs down food. Soon his heart slowed, and the desire left him. Only then did he roll to his back and rise, taking a half step to the right, bringing him back to his straw bed. A smile crossed his lips as he sank down cross-legged on the straw. He picked up three pieces of straw and began braiding them with only his right hand.

He was on his third braid when his captors came for him.

≈

After the darkness of his cell and the hood they forced him to wear in transit, the light of the inquisitor's 'workshop' was jarring, even through closed eyes. Hollis forced himself to remain calm, his eyes closed until they adjusted behind his eyelids, but it was difficult when the first backhanded slap tore across his face.

Slowly, his eyes flickered open, boring into those of the inquisitor. Just as he had in each other meeting, it was not Hollis who first broke eye contact. It earned him another vicious slap, but the victory was undeniable. He noticed the small hesitation before the inquisitor locked an iron cuff around his right wrist. "I told you he was to be brought to me restrained," he growled at the guard standing next to the door.

Hollis chuckled softly.

The inquisitor, made a little bolder now that the man was chained, turned to him and snarled, "Something funny, pig?"

Hollis shook his head. "Not a thing... more sad than funny." This earned him another jaw-jarring slap. "It seems ..." He shook his head to try to stop the ringing before continuing, "... it seems that I make you uncomfortable, Sayyid, so uncomfortable that you can barely contain the tremors in your hand when you fasten a chain about my wrist."

"So, I fear you, do I?"

Hollis shook his head. "I said nothing about fear... only you can testify to that. I said discomfort." The man seized his left hand and slammed it against the heavy wooden table beside him. Hollis gritted his teeth, not wanting to give the man the satisfaction of crying out. No doubt, that satisfaction would come later. "For that I apologize; that is quite rude of me. Your hospitality to this point has been beyond reproach, I should endeavor to be a better guest."

"You seem to be very impressed with yourself, Slender One."

Hollis's grimace turned into a pained smile. "Just a little bit." He watched the man's face turn crimson as the guard tried to contain his smile. Hollis considered this little humiliation payment in advance of what was about to happen.

"If you have the breath to make quips, you have the breath to scream." The inquisitor picked up a blunt-edged chisel from the table. It was useless for its intended purpose, but it was perfect for what the man had in mind. With a swift downward motion, he drove the implement into the thief's hand, just beneath his first knuckle. The sudden,

excruciating pain drew a short scream from Hollis, who clenched his teeth to silence it. It turned into a soft whimper instead. "Do you think you can mock me?" He drove the chisel into Hollis's hand again. "Do you?" The inquisitor snatched up a small hammer, putting it to chisel with a sickening sound of metal on metal followed by a liquid crunching. "You have nothing to say? No clever words for me?"

Hollis's eyes, a moment ago clenched against the pain, opened suddenly. His smile was gone. "You and I will meet on more even terms... no chains... no guards. There, in the dark, we will balance our books. Count on it." Again, hammer met chisel; Hollis screamed, "Count... on... it!"

～

They did not even replace his hood before they dragged his half-conscious body back to his cell. When the stone floor came up to meet him, Hollis did not have the strength to raise an arm to cushion his fall. He simply lay in a heap mumbling to himself through swollen and blood-flecked lips. The guard laughed loudly, "You are not so funny now, are you?" before closing the door with a loud click.

Hollis painfully curled into a ball, his least swollen eye on the door and continued to mumble. "Torch every ten steps... Two guards... spears...on rack...two steps of light, then darkness." Those same lips pulled back into a smile. He tried to rise but could not muster the strength. As he sank back down, he began again: "Thirteen strides of darkness... two strides of light...Two guards with knives...three spears on a rack behind...behind them...Right turn...thirty strides to the workshop...ten strides between torches...half a stride of darkness between torchlight..."

～

Before he had opened his eyes, Hollis knew something was different. This time they chained both of his wrists as well as his legs before removing the hood. Without waiting for his eyes to adjust, he flickered them open to see two figures sitting well out of arms reach, even were he not shackled. Hollis felt his heart drop a little as he saw Omar, a self-satisfied smirk painted on his lips, standing behind a seated man dressed from head to toe in silken finery. This, no doubt, was the Emir.

The inquisitor grabbed the chained man by his beard, pulling his eyes up to meet his own, "We have had enough of your petulance, pig. You will tell me where the Emir's daughter is, now!"

Hollis regarded him through hooded lids, "What makes you think today is any different from yesterday? Or was it the day before? I can never be sure."

A fist slammed into Hollis's gut, doubling him over in his chair. "I am losing my patience!" The inquisitor's fist struck him across the back of the head, making his head ring. "You will not...!"

A quiet voice cut through the room. "Enough." Hollis raised his head, his vision beginning to clear. The Emir had raised his hand slightly, "Altair, I have given you enough time with this man..." His voice was conversational and calm. Hollis took this for a bad sign, if people were yelling there was an opportunity to capitalize on their passion. When a man is calm, it indicated he had made a decision, normally not to one's benefit.

Hollis met his eyes and saw within them why the Emir ruled the city unconditionally. They did not float or falter with indecision. This was a man who was comfortable in his own skin as well as the strength of his own counsel. Facing such eyes, it was Hollis who faltered.

"Hollis of Oizan, called Hollis the Slender, you have stolen from me. You have taken something of value that I would have returned." The tone was so reasonable, so sure that the cold fingers of fear began to run down the bound man's spine.

"The necklace is gone by now, sold by your daughter long ago."

"I do not refer to that paltry trinket."

Hollis took a deep breath, steadying his nerves, "Kalilah left me as she left you, not long after we fled the city. I would not even hazard a guess as to where she is now."

The Emir stood, waving Omar's protests to silence, "Although I will have my daughter found, cutpurse, she is also not what I refer to." He stood in front of Hollis's chained form before sinking to one knee, putting his eyes on level with the seated man. "I want my reputation back... I want the tales of the man who stole from me to come to an end." He seized his chin in his surprisingly strong hand, "I would have them replaced... replaced with tales of what happens to those who cross me. I want the city to ring out with a message to anyone who dares act counter to my wishes, whether they are noble or gutter rat." He released Hollis's chin and turned his back on him, "Would you care to guess what that message should be?"

"My guess would be: Not to?"

The Emir turned, no sign of annoyance clouding his features. This was without a doubt a dangerous man. "After a fashion, yes. I would like to not be forced to send this message again, if I can help it. That is where you come in."

"Of course, how better to repay your hospitality?"

He turned to face Hollis, "Excellent, then we are in agreement. You shall deliver this message for me, hopefully at the top of your lungs...as you hang eviscerated from the walls of the palace." Again, his voice did not rise in pitch or volume, as if he were discussing the affairs of the day. "I have a man at my disposal that can make sure you take your time in dying; depending on how convincing your voice is you could be dead by sunrise or live long enough to be choked by the scent of your own rotting entrails." He gestured with a casual flick of his fingers to Omar, "Take the day to decide for yourself. We will speak again at nightfall; I have chosen a place that offers a rather stunning view of the moon rising over the Expanse." As frightening of an opponent as the Emir was, he had made one mistake; but it was a crippling one.

Hollis had until nightfall to escape.

~

Almost as soon as the door slammed, Hollis was on his feet. He forced his breathing to slow as he paced out his cell, going over his plan one final time. The guards would not be back until sunset, giving him ample time to prepare and execute his escape. He repeated his mental map of the prison three times as he circumnavigated the cell before easing himself to the floor and loosening his muscles. Most people would be tempted to execute their plan as quickly as possible; Hollis certainly felt the temptation as well. He did not relish the thought of ending his life hanging from a wall, intestines flowing from his gut like honey from a broken beehive. He pushed the temptation, along with that image, down with some effort. Proper preparation would provide more success than speed.

Once he felt that his muscles were loose and warm, he pulled his makeshift picks from beneath the straw and rolled them across his knuckles a few times to limber out his fingers. While he did this, he worked his jaw slowly, miming a chewing motion. After a few moments, Hollis placed the torque into his ear carefully, rotating it to coat the end with ear wax. He repeated the process with the wooden hook-pick before running the wax along the length of each, making them tacky to the touch. There was a plethora of ways his plan could go awry but if he dropped either the torque or the pick, it would be over before it began. The wax would give him the best possible grip given the circumstances, even considering he would only be working with one hand.

He took three slow, fortifying breaths and then stepped up to the door, snaking his arm through the small viewing window at eye level. Despite the weight and age of the mechanism, he opened it in only a moment. He forced himself to relax and listen for a full minute before pulling his arm back through the window and easing the door open. After placing the torque into his unkempt beard, he held the pick in his right hand, its length along his extended thumb as a makeshift thumb knife. The hallway was in darkness; but to his left, the corridor opened into the T. At the end of it sat two guards in a pool of light shed by the low burning torch.

True to his preparation, the darkness extended thirteen strides from his cell to where the light began. Hollis sat and watched the guards for a moment, choosing his opportunity. It came when the larger of the two guards announced that he was hungry and entered the hallway. Hollis was on him before he took his second step, the pick lodged in his throat. The man's blood was hot on his arm as he pulled the pick free and wrapped his hand around the back of his neck. Hollis's human shield took a spear thrust meant for him as he reached down to pull the man's dagger from his belt. In the heat of the combat, he instinctively grabbed it with his left hand. Clenching his teeth to cut off the cry of pain, he pushed the dead weight of his shield towards his companion and scooped the dagger from the ground with his good hand. By the time the second guard had freed himself from the tangle of dead friend and spear, Hollis was on him, slitting his throat with deadly accuracy.

Again, he crouched in the alcove, listening for any sign that the struggle had been overheard. He forced his breathing to return to normal and waited for silence to reign over the sound of his heartbeat. Once he was satisfied, he pulled the other man's dagger free of his belt and appraised both men for a second before stripping the larger of his pants, shirt and boots.

Now more appropriately attired, Hollis tucked one dagger into his belt, the other into the padding of his new boot and pulled a spear from the rack. It would be useless to him in melee while his hand was still broken, but it could be used as a missile and supported his disguise, at least until closer inspection.

His brief trip down the hallway sans hood had shown him that the corridor past Altair's workshop turned to the right and was much more brightly lit. Getting out of the dungeon would not be the most difficult phase of his escape, but he focused on what was in front of him for now. Dodging from shadow to shadow, he made his way down the corridor. When he was halfway to the workshop, he heard voices. He thought that Altair may have a visitor in his workshop; visitors meant the possibility of a weapon more effective than the poorly crafted daggers he took from the guards.

Hollis stopped in the last shadow between him and the door and readied himself. Normally Altair posted one guard just inside the door to the right and another behind his workspace. He gingerly eased the dagger from his belt with his left hand, only exerting enough pressure to keep it clutched there, despite the agony even that caused. He sprinted the last few feet and drove the door open with his shoulder. Altair looked up from his work, which in this instance was carving deep furrows into the chest of a bound Kieli woman. Hollis threw the spear with all his might before switching the knife from his left hand to his right.

Altair fell like a pole-axed steer when the spear impaled his thigh, his scream shrill and loud. It echoed through the room and no doubt into the hallway. Hollis could not afford to worry about that now, as the guard to the right of the door had already drawn his scimitar and began it swinging in a low arc. He stepped inside the blade's swing, the hilt striking him hard in his already-bruised ribs. Hollis's first strike was an upward stab into the guard's hip, causing him to list to the right. He did not have to adjust his aim; the man's descent put his chest in line as he reached out to break his fall. As he lifted his arm, the thief's blade drove into his armpit. He had to withdraw the dagger quickly to prevent it from being torn from his grasp. He reversed his grip, stabbing the guard a third time, this time in the opposite side of his neck. Whether dead or unconscious, the man did not rise again.

Altair still lay on the floor screaming for help at the top of his lungs, but Hollis could not take the time to silence him now. The second guard charged at him, scimitar buzzing in an overhead chop. With no time to get inside the deadly arc, he was forced to dive to the left. He tucked his shoulder and rolled to his feet, again using his left hand, this time to soften his fall. His vision was tinted red as he rose, his hand screaming in protest. The guard laughed, swinging his sword before him in slow, sweeping patterns as he positioned himself between Hollis and the door. His posture demonstrated confidence that his superior reach would hold the thief at bay until help arrived. He wore that confident smile unto death as Hollis's thrown dagger bisected his sinuses and continued into his brain.

He kicked the door closed and looked around for something to wedge under it to buy a little more time. Altair's cries for aid continued unabated. Not finding anything of use, Hollis turned on the inquisitor. "Remember that later conversation we spoke of?" Altair tried to scramble backwards but the motion caused the spear's weight to shift in his leg; he doubled over in pain. "So curious. Someone so comfortable causing pain would be so uncomfortable on the other side of it." Hollis stepped on the shaft, shifting the tip again in the man's leg. He was rewarded by another scream.

"Please.... I am sorry, I had no choice! It was the Emir's will."

Hollis nodded, "Of course it was." He stepped on the shaft a little closer to the point, bringing out another scream from Altair.

"I can help you... I can get you out."

He shook his head and said, "No, Altair ... no you cannot." A third step brought him close enough to grip the inquisitor's hair. "Your child-like screams have attracted attention, so our conversation, fortunately for you, will be short." With a sudden motion, Hollis drove his dagger behind Altair's left ear. He did not scream again.

A quick search of the inquisitor's belt found a ring of keys and after only one incorrect guess, Hollis was able to free his fellow prisoner. The woman looked like she had been in Altair's care for a while. Her hair, arranged in what were no doubt tight braids at one time, hung in her face like a greasy curtain. Several wounds of varying ages crisscrossed her dark-skinned chest and a few of them had already begun to scar. Each one seemed to dissect a tattoo of Kieli origin.

"Can you stand?" Hollis asked.

The woman nodded and tried to do so; the thief caught her as she wavered. Her deep brown eyes shone with a mixture of gratitude and defiance.

He released her arm and continued, "We will be having some company very soon... I am leaving tonight, help me deal with what comes through that door and I will take you with me." The woman nodded again.

As if on cue, the referred to company burst through the door. Three yellow-cloaked soldiers, with their scimitars already drawn pressed through the door. Before Hollis could say another word, his fellow prisoner snatched the spear from the inquisitor's still warm body and met their charge. The leading soldier swung his blade in a left to right slash at waist height. The woman swung the spear in the same direction; allowing its momentum to carry her around as well as she compressed her body and sank to the floor. The spear's tip slashed across the soldier's knees, laying them open to the bone. She continued her circular momentum, rising again as she drove the point of the spear under the man's ribs, lifting him off the ground and into his companions. Hollis watched in awe as the silent woman went from victim to predator.

Before they could react, she thrust the spear outward, allowing it to slide through her hands until she gripped it on the last third of the shaft. The thrust did not have enough power to do any real harm but caused the second soldier to duck out of its path...and into the path of the follow-up thrust, which took him under the chin. The third man began to back away, his sword thrust out before him. Hollis's fellow prisoner drew the spear from her second victim, rotating as she did. Her bare foot rose as she spun, catching the retreating soldier in the side of the face, driving him to the ground. She snagged the man's leg with the tip of the spear, flipping him face up and then drove the tip into the man's heart.

So sudden was this display of brutality that Hollis did not have time to react, much less lend aid. He still wore a look of shock on his face when the woman casually walked back to him offering him the spear; all the thief could manage was, "Keep it, friend."

"Aristoi."

"I beg your pardon?"

"Aristoi. My name is Aristoi."

Hollis stared at the woman in awe and then regained some of his composure. "I shall call you anything you want as long as you keep that up until we are clear of the palace. You may call me Hollis."

The woman's face split into a smile, "Then it is an accord, Hollis."

Hollis began stripping the soldiers of their cloaks, wrapping one around his shoulders and tossing the other to Aristoi.

"Although we need to make a stop before we leave," she continued slowly, and gazed around, as if in thought, or as if looking for something.

The thief looked up as he tucked another dagger into his belt, "Indeed?"

"They have something that belongs to me."

"Me as well... my freedom. Anything else can be re-acquired."

She shook her head. "Not this, it was my mother's and her mother's before her."

Hollis sighed, "Do you even know where to begin looking for it?"

Aristoi nodded, "In the armory, no doubt with the rest of my weapons."

The thief's eyes shifted between the shoddy daggers tucked in his belt and the large, unwieldy scimitars scattered about the floor, "Lead the way... "

CHAPTER ELEVEN
AN UNLIKELY COMRADE

B y the time the two had fought their way to the armory, Hollis could hear the peals of the alarm echoing through the stone corridors of the palace. This was not the stealthy escape he had planned in his eight by eight stone cell over the last week. "Would you hurry up," he snapped more harshly than he had intended, "I am a big man, but I cannot hold this door indefinitely." His ivory hilted short sword once again rode his left hip, which certainly was something at least. He had found it rather quickly. The spear, on the other hand...

"Patience, Hollis, it must be here somewhere. I just need a few... "The last of her words were drowned out by a thunderous crash against the door, and the impact of it drove the man back a few steps. A heavily muscled arm snaked through the gap, gripping the door jamb for leverage, leverage that he would not maintain long with Hollis's dagger in his wrist. Hollis sliced along the hand, and its owner let out a pained shout and withdrew his arm, allowing the thief to slam the door closed again.

"Do not take too long, I think they may be using one of those statues we passed of the Emir's dearly departed third wife as a battering ram. He will be so put out about that." He felt another powerful impact that shook him to his bones. "I heard she was his favorite."

"I have it!" Aristoi exclaimed, holding up an object that could only marginally be called a spear. It looked to Hollis to be more of a short sword on a stick. The blade itself must have exceeded two feet, wickedly sharp on one edge of its broad surface. From tip to butt, it measured six feet, only an inch or so shorter than the woman herself. She spun the weapon a few times, reacquainting herself with its weight and balance before joining Hollis at the door.

Hollis raised an eyebrow. "We came all this way for that? No offense to your mother and 'her mother before her...'" The door shook again, driving him back. Aristoi slipped the spear into the gap and she was rewarded by the wet sound of steel in flesh. She worked the spear in a motion that seemed to the thief more like stirring than fighting, but when the door slowly swung open, four men lay on the floor in various states of laceration. "... and totally worth it." The woman simply smiled through her unkempt hair and stepped over the pile of bloody flesh.

Hollis inexplicably felt queasy looking at it. He had slain his fair share of men and spilled more blood than this in his three decades of life, but for some reason the sight shocked him. Shaking his head to clear the feeling, he stepped over the mass of bodies and followed his companion. The corridor was thankfully clear of guards for the moment, allowing the two to reach the stairs at the far end of the hallway.

The sense of wrongness continued to plague the thief as they quickly dispatched another two guards that had been rushing to aid those at the armory door. Truth be told, Aristoi did most of the work, and Hollis simply administered the coup de grace to one as he ran past. He remembered his weeks in the dungeon, under the not so tender care of Altair; but he also could clearly remember a grave... a dark wooden coffin peppered with white roses... the soft sobs of a widow? A mother? The harder he tried to capture the image, the more elusive it became.

They reached a shuttered window and threw them open to reveal Oenigh at dusk, the sun setting over the scrub grass plains that bordered the city on the west. A quick look down showed a ten-foot drop to the roof of an outbuilding and a few hundred yards to the palace wall *itself. Hollis could hear shouts and the building thunder of booted feet in the distance; when he turned back, Aristoi was already in the air, landing with a clumsy roll on the opposite roof, her spear wedged between two slate shingles, anchoring her. She looked up and smiled as she waved the thief on.*

After taking a few steps back, Hollis surged forward; but a light-headedness swept over him, causing him to slide to a stop at the window. The drop seemed to possess a cavernous depth. The distance to the nearest rooftop seemed to stretch forever. He shook his head again; he had made leaps further than this as a child and was almost as comfortable scaling a building as he was in the shadows. His trepidation made no sense, especially given the approaching footfalls. He climbed into the open window frame and tried to calm his mind. Perhaps he was simply over thinking this; he closed his eyes for a second to center himself.

An image came unbidden to his mind's eye.

A young woman's face painted with concern and lit with rapidly shifting colors. The sweet scent of fried sugar and greasy meat almost overwhelmed him. He could feel her hand in his, squeezing it in reassurance; but the fear blotted everything else out. Out of the corner of his eye, he could see the tents far below him, stretching out into the night. The carefree sound of an organ played counter point to the quickened thunder of his heart in his ears.

At Aristoi's voice, his eyes snapped open. "Jump for Umma's sake! Even I can hear them coming!"

In one sudden lunge, Hollis was out of the window and free-falling to the roof below. Once again, the vertigo overtook him as he could not seem to get his bearings in midair. He hit the tiled roof hard, saved from sliding down into the darkness only by his companion's quick reflexes. His knee where it had struck the terracotta shingles sang an aria of agony; Hollis thanked the gods for its brevity. Anchored by her spear, Aristoi pulled him to a standing position, favoring him with a raised eyebrow before ascending the roof with sure steps. Hollis looked over his shoulder to see the guards gathered at the window before following in her footsteps.

The next jump was easier, from one rooftop to another, but he did not look down, instead he focused his attention on the spot where he wanted to land. He felt his confidence return as his feet touched the roof and his momentum carried him to the peak with steps as light as a mouse's. The next was as easy as breathing; a familiar sense of exhilaration forced out the fear. The wall was in sight; two steps and one last leap carried him to where he could pull himself to its top. Hollis almost lost his grip when the streaks of agony shot up his arm from his ruined left hand. His right still held enough strength to pull his weight up onto the wall before turning to help Aristoi the rest of the way.

"Rough start, Hollis; but I cannot complain about the smooth finish," Aristoi muttered as she caught her breath.

He smiled down at his companion, before quipping, "I had to give you a head start, did I not?" His easy tone hid the uneasiness in his gut as Hollis looked over the wall into the city proper.

This thirty-foot height was barely half that of the Ferris wheel years ago, but it invoked the same cold rush of fear Stephen had experienced that summer's night.

Hollis paused as he and his reflection truly met for the first time.

Sometime later, Stephen would try to explain the sensation of having two distinct personalities in his head. It was more uncomfortable than painful or frightening, the mental equivalent of switching from briefs to boxers. Nothing really felt any different, there was just more of everything that made a person what they are. Both he and Hollis thought it would be more a rush of voices, each screaming to be heard, but they did not so much have discussions as know what the other was feeling, instantly and completely.

The memories of these alternating personalities did not war with each other for dominance; instead they coexisted as separate but equal recollections. The most remarkable thing about the situation was that rather than feeling frightened, both felt a sense of peace. Stephen had been searching for something his entire life, to some measure only *finding it when playing 'The Game'.; Hollis, on the other hand, had tried to achieve this sense of completeness through the acquisition of objects, both physical and emotional. He never understood why he could never steal enough to fill that space inside of him or why no friendship or love from a woman could make him feel whole. Both had felt hollow until this moment. Just as a face is incomplete without its reflection, so too Stephen was lessened without Hollis.*

All of this happened within the space between breaths; Aristoi had rolled over and pushed herself to her feet as Hollis came to his senses, with Stephen in the back of his mind. The sense of vertigo faded, lost in the wash of contentment, truly the first in either of their lives. "What are you smiling about?" His companion looked over her shoulder quickly and then back to the three-story drop, "They are not going to give up so easily. We still have a way to go before we are truly safe."

"It is alright, my friend." He squeezed her arm and smiled more deeply; his eyes filled with his joy. "Things are just starting to go our way." His companion looked at him doubtfully but did not voice her disbelief. Patting her on the shoulder, Hollis dropped down and pulled his boots off. "Drop your spear and put your hands and feet where I do. We will be down before you know it." He tossed his boots to the ground and draped his legs over the wall. "You may want to ditch your boots as well. Toes find smaller cracks than does leather." Aristoi could not figure out if the man's change in attitude was more encouraging or frightening. She decided that it was both in equal measure.

True to his word, Hollis's toes found small cracks in the mortar of the wall and even using one hand scrambled down the thirty feet almost as fast as he could have fallen. His companion's descent was a controlled plunge, landing in a heap as Hollis rolled out of the way. He pulled on his boots as Aristoi verified that nothing had been broken in the fall and searched for her own.

As Hollis moved to press his back against a nearby building, Stephen could not help but smile at the sheer ease at which he moved from shadow to shadow with footsteps so light they barely stirred the dust from the road. Once again, he was entranced by how much more intense everything was on this side. Even the throbbing pain in his left hand felt more real, although he could have done without that sensation.

When Aristoi joined him in the shadows, Hollis leaned over to whisper against her ear, "If you continue in that direction," pressing his finger into the woman's stomach, indicating the quickest route to the west gate, "You will find a daub building taller than the rest a few hundred yards to the south of the gate itself. From there, you should be able to pull yourself onto the wall. This early in the evening, the guards are not all that focused; you should be able to drop down and be on your way with them none the wiser."

He felt Aristoi shake her head slowly, "I go where you do." There was a certain finality in her voice.

"I am bound for the Expanse, my friend. That is not a journey to be taken lightly if at all."

"Were it not for you, I would never make that journey or any other ever again." She pushed Hollis's hand from her belly. "I owe you both my freedom," she said, hefting her spear before continuing, "and my honor. I will travel with you until I feel I have paid for both."

Hollis wanted to argue but he could deny neither the woman's skill nor the wisdom of a traveling companion in the Expanse. He nodded, "Fair enough; but now I have one stop to make."

Aamir's children slept on the roof of his simple home to combat the heat; but so softly did Hollis land upon the surface that none of them stirred. He was forced to take to the rooftops as the streets became host to the search for both himself and Aristoi. It made no difference to the thief, as their pitched surface was as much of a home to him as the hard-packed surface below. Stephen's consciousness had settled into the background as Hollis practiced his trade. He lowered himself one-handed to the alley outside the small kitchen that he remembered from the day of his capture.

The curtains that usually kept the daytime's dust at bay were pulled back to admit as much of the night air as possible. Hollis slid into the oppressive silence of the house, his eyes adjusting quickly. The building was simple, containing only three rooms, of which Hollis had seen two. Finding where Aamir slept was a simple matter. Stephen cringed as Hollis slowly drew one of his stolen daggers and pressed it to the fat caravan master's throat. With the barest whispers he warned, "This is between us, Sayyid, I have no interest in involving your sun and flower; but I will if pressed." He felt the man nodding carefully. "You will rise without waking her and lead me to your strong box. Nod again if you understand me." Aamir nodded again. Hollis stepped back slightly, allowing the man to rise; but the blade never wavered from its position.

The two walked into the common room where Aamir folded back a carpet, revealing a hole dug in the dirt floor; inside sat an iron bound chest. "I have children, Hollis, have mercy," he whispered, his tone pleading.

Hollis smiled, a malicious glint coming to his eye, "They are not yours, as we have already discussed."

The man paled, swallowing slowly, "I had no choice."

"We both know that is a lie. Your cudgel was the deciding factor in that conflict. You saw the chance to keep my money and collect what I can only assume was a significant reward. You took that gamble, betting that once I entered the Emir's dungeons, I would never emerge. That was an unwise wager." He pressed the blade deeper into Aamir's throat, creasing the skin, "Open the chest."

"Of course, Sayyid." His hands trembled as he pulled the key from a hidden pocket and turned it slowly.

Hollis heard the soft click of the lock opening and Aamir tried to take a step back. Hollis clicked softly and shook his head. "If you would be so kind as to open it for me, I would be most appreciative. I have my hands full." He shifted the knife slightly. He could see the man's shoulders slump as he reached in, lifted the lid a small way and pulled a catch to the side, disarming the poison-needle trap. He looked up at

139

Hollis with something that could have passed for an apology. The thief shrugged and nodded appreciatively but did not comment.

"You cannot carry all this, Hollis," Aamir whispered in clipped tones.

"I do not have to. Give me what I paid you and what is left of the reward you collected."

The man did as he was asked with as much speed as he could muster with a knife at his throat, "It was nothing personal, simply a sound business decision."

"It felt kind of personal to me, Aamir."

"Please accept my sincerest apologies, Sayyid. Here is all I have left and the pouch you gave me with not an iron drab missing. Does this make us even?"

Hollis growled low and deadly, "Not even close, Aamir." He pressed the blade further into the caravan master's throat, drawing a thin crimson line in the flesh, "Remember this blade," as he removed it from his neck, he held it before the man's eyes. "I will keep it with me until we meet again. When that happens, I will kill you with it, so it will be as if no time has passed." Hollis tapped him on the chest with the tip of the dagger. "Were I you, I would make it my business to ensure that I never see you again." He casually sheathed the weapon and turned on his heel, moving towards the kitchen. Over his shoulder he whispered, "Now that is a sound business decision."

CHAPTER TWELVE
AN INEXORABLE CONFLICT

Stephen's eyes fluttered open slowly as he brought his hand to his face. His neck was stiff and his back ached a bit, but he seemed none the worse for spending the night on the old couch that dominated his basement 'man cave'. In the pre-dawn light, he made out the empty cup that had contained the adder root tea six hours ago. It made him a little dizzy trying to reconcile his clear memories of a week in the Emir's dungeon with those of finishing the bitter concoction and lying down early in the evening. Time between this world and the other seemed to be fluid and not at all consistent; he made a mental note to search through Jeff's journals for his theory on that phenomenon, a sort of Theory of Otherworldly Relativity.

He pushed himself to a seated position, expecting the burning pain in his left hand that did not come. In the back of his mind, Stephen felt Hollis's presence everywhere and nowhere at once. Still firmly in his reflection's mindset, he felt a tinge of worry that, although he had set his hand, it would never be the same. Too much time had passed and besides some basic tricks Hollis had picked up here and there and Stephen's basic knowledge of first aid, neither of them claimed to be a doctor... or stitch as they were known in Taerh.

Stephen pushed the worry away as he lifted his empty cup from the table and carried it into the kitchen. As he absently rinsed it, he debated calling in sick again. He'd already made up his mind.

Jared's voicemail picked up on the fourth ring and Stephen left a short, vague message promising to be in later that morning and hung up before he thought too deeply about it. No doubt when he eventually arrived in the office, he would be in for a lecture at best and outright threat to his job at worst. He surprised himself with how little he cared, he had always fretted so about taking the safe path through life. The last week spent in Taerh convinced him that the journals were not flights of fancy. Samantha's words gave him hope that he was finally doing something of worth, much more so than resetting a lost password or replacing a burned-out mouse. Alan, Mike and Jeff depended on him.

A quick check of the clock above the stove revealed that it was a little after six a.m. Samantha's florist didn't open until nine, which gave him three hours to pour over the journals again before meeting her. He sat down at the kitchen table and reached into the duffel bag, pulling a journal out at random.

April 25, 2008

When I came to my senses in Taerh, I found myself on horseback traveling the Lord's Road in Granatyr. I am always amazed by the ease with which I assimilate upon reflection now. I find it almost like second nature to access Silvermoon's memories of the time I am away, and slide into our symbiosis.

Lately however, I must work very hard to separate where he ends and I begin, since we seem to be different sides of the same coin.

Haedren's condition has worsened, although every healer we have found has assured us that, physically, he is in perfect health. His connection to Olm has not returned and I believe this is what has hit him hardest. I had hoped that after a month, the lingering effects of our battle with Theamon would at least begin to fade. Hollis was back on his feet the quickest, the worst of his injuries a concussion and a broken nose. Mika's sprained ankle and dislocated shoulder took a little longer to mend. Ret's wounds were superficial at worst, but the psychological damage done by Marcus' hijacked illusion lingered for weeks, with the northerner complaining of phantom pains until only a few days ago.

Haedren, however, remained in a semi-catatonic state. He would answer direct questions if pressed, but for the most part he simply stared into space with a blank expression. Several gold plates bought the services of a diviner of some experience to verify my brother's findings that the priest was under no spell or curse. So, we rode towards Oizan to consult with the head of Haedren's order.

The Grand Cathedral of Dawning Light is the center of Olm's power on Taerh and if anyone could help us cure what was plaguing our friend, they would be found there. I felt Silvermoon's reticence, being what I would term a lapsed Olmite, but Haedren was a friend and we would do everything in our power to restore his sanity. I was greatly anticipating seeing the great city state of Oizan for myself, rather than in Silvermoon's memories.

The city came into sight a few hours after dawn on the next day, a huge, walled fortress backed by a monstrous river. I have stood beside the Mississippi River in Memphis, but from where we first viewed the river called the Granatyr Serpent, I felt no less in awe. At more than a quarter mile distant, I felt the rumble of its passing waters in my chest.

I could also feel Silvermoon's discomfort rising as he vastly preferred the wilderness to the confines of the city. Hollis, on the other hand, looked much like Alan as Christmas approaches. From my recollections, the boy was raised in the streets of Oizan and it was the closest thing he had to a true home. The closer we drew to the gates, the further his horse began to out distance the rest of us.

So great was his lead, that when we finally arrived at the gates, he was chatting casually with a guard beside the southern check point. Clapping the man on the shoulder, Hollis climbed aboard his horse and waved us through. When I raised a querying eyebrow, his only explanation was a sad smile and the words, "Trace and I shared a lot of the same alleys as a child. It is truly unfortunate that he ended up on the wrong side of the law." I could not help but chuckle.

I had pressed to travel directly to the Cathedral, perhaps due to Silvermoon's unease; but the rest of my companions assured me that our business would not be quick and felt it best to find rooms first. Travel on the main thoroughfares was quite comfortable, but once Hollis led us into the maze of alleys that crisscrossed the city, I felt positively claustrophobic and soon lost any sense of direction.

It was to my great surprise, not to mention relief when we emerged from one of these passages into the clear, mostly clean air of the Dock District.

Shirtless men raced this way and that among the various slips loading and unloading cargo from the tall ships moored there. The river must be deep indeed to not cause even these ships to run aground this close to the city. The current in this natural harbor was remarkably calm, given that only a few thousand yards to the north, the river churned like a boiling pot. Hollis led us past the bustle of activity to a large, solid looking building of stone, painted in such a dark green that it appeared black except in the most direct rays of the sun. Hanging above the massive twin oak doors was a painting of a mermaid sprawled on a rock in a quite compromising posture.

"Welcome," Hollis purred through a wide smile, "To the Virgin Mermaid." Without waiting for any of us to react, he pushed his way into the dark, smoke-filled building. It took my eyes a moment to adjust to the dim interior; but my other senses were stimulated in the meantime. The inn was close and warm, almost like being wrapped in a wet washcloth, and the scent of cooking meat battled with pipe and wood smoke for dominance. The bar as well as the tables I could see through the shadows and miasma of vapors were made of dark oak stained with age and use. As early as it was, there were still an impressive amount of people filling the tables, with the hint of more out of sight in the corners, out of reach of the fire's light.

Hollis approached the bar, waving lightly to the chubby man on the far side of it. The closer he came, the more cherub-like he appeared. He wore an easy smile and rosy cheeks, both of which put me at ease. When he spoke the illusion was broken, his voice rough and gritty, like gravel poured from a glass jar. From only a few feet away, I could not miss the thick scar that marred his throat just under his second chin. "Is it too much to hope that you have more than vague promises and impassioned pleas with which to rent a room this time, Hollis?"

The thief placed his hand upon his heart, a sly smirk coming to his lips, "Gabby, my dear and valued friend, you wound me...truly you do. When have I ever..."

The man interrupted, "Neither of us has the time for me to list them all. As to your grievous wounds, what makes me think that the miraculous cure for these will be an ale or three...? On the house, of course?"

"Because you are a wise and generous man, Gabby."

"I am neither."

Hollis reached into the pouch at his belt and pulled free a trio of silver nobles and laid them on the surface of the bar. "Then, allow me to purchase some of both."

The man's hand tapped each of the coins against the bar before dropping them into a pocket. "Am I to assume that along with your wisdom, you would like dinner and a room?"

Hollis nodded, "Three rooms, although only one needs to be nice." This earned him a stiff elbow from Mika. "I mean three of your best rooms for the night." She nodded quickly before turning to survey the room. Gabby chuckled but didn't say a word.

"I am hungry. Get us some food as well." Ret requested.

Hollis smiled at Gabby as he pulled another trio of silver nobles from his pouch, "...and breakfast?" The man nodded. He turned back to the Northerner, "Happy?"

145

Ret grumbled, "Not yet... still hungry" He collapsed into a chair that audibly groaned as it accepted his weight.

After feeding Ret and stowing our things, all but Ret traveled to the University District. He remained behind with our baggage and a flagon of mead. Once there, Mika and Marcus split off for the Great Library as Hollis and I – with Haedren trailing dutifully behind – approached the Cathedral. The structure was larger than even Silvermoon recalled and its façade seemed to be carved out of a single piece of marble. With the way the noonday sun reflected off its pristine surface, it seemed to glow from within.

I let Hollis speak to the Templars of Olm who were standing before the imposing double doors. After some convincing and the lure of two gold plates, we were admitted to the foyer. This room was crowded with a cross section of Oizan society; Nobles and farmers alike were represented. The sturdy cherry wood benches that lined each wall were packed to the brim with waiting petitioners and at least twice that number stood restlessly in the center.

Hollis waded through the press of humanity and soon returned with a large red wooden disk. "As best I can tell, they are taking green now. I saw a fair amount of blue in the crowd; so, I can only assume that red is after that." I watched the cogs of his young mind working. "If I had to hazard a guess, we may be seen tomorrow or the day after." His face lit up suddenly, and he said, "Unless ... "

I shook my head, ready to scald him as if he were only a young child. "No, Hollis. These people have been patient as well; we can wait our turn."

Hollis's stubbornness shone through. "They are here about sick cows and love-struck daughters. Haedren is broken; that has to push him to the front of the line." I shook my head again. "Suit yourself; but I am certainly not waiting here all day. You would not ask the fox to wait in the henhouse, would you?"

I looked around the room and even with the crowd, could see the white and gold tabards of the Templars scattered among those waiting. "Wiser words I have not heard spoken in a while. Why do you not go back and keep Ret company?"

"Eventually. I have some old friends to visit while we have some spare time." His smile broadened at my withering glare.

"Stay out of trouble."

His look of injury appeared almost genuine as he faded into the gathered mass of people.

True to Hollis's prediction, it took almost two days for our petition to come before the Hand of Dawn, Olm's chosen servant on Taerh. I heard Hollis's name and our number called by a young acolyte dressed in white and gold robes. Hollis and I, with Haedren in tow navigated the crowd and stood before the acolyte. She favored Hollis with a smile before gesturing through the gilded inner door; another acolyte led us through the labyrinth of corridors. I lost my way after the third switchback, but Hollis seemed abnormally alert, taking note of every twist and turn.

Before we knew it, we were ushered into a cavernous hall, its vaulted ceilings lined with the palest platinum and the darkest yellow sapphire. A dozen Templars in gleaming breast plates flanked a carpet of golden thread set against the white marble floor.

Sitting in an imposing, cherry wood chair was a frail man, whose form was almost lost within his pure white robe. Despite his advanced age, his keen eyes and confident posture made his authority undeniable; I could not help but share the reverence of the gathered soldiers as I approached. His sense of power fell upon me as the sun falls upon the morning dew laden grass. Any doubt of his identity evaporated from my mind as the cool remembrances of the evening fade before the dawn's light.

The Hand of Dawn watched us approach, his voice belying his sunken cheeks and paper-thin skin, "Olm's light be upon your path, Brothers."

Hollis responded with the expected, "So too, may the Lord illuminate your way." The Hand of Dawn nodded, waiting for Hollis to continue. "We come before you to ask for intercessions for our comrade, Haedren. He has walked the Lord's path as a member of his clergy; but was set upon by a foul acolyte of the Father of Lies." He gestured to Haedren's bowed head. "He seems to be under some sort of spell; he will only respond when prompted but won't give anything else away."

The Hand of Dawn nodded slowly; but it was obvious that his thoughts were far from the audience chamber., "What is it that you expect us to do for your friend?" His voice dripped with impatience.

Hollis ignored his patronizing tone, "Haedren has devoted his life to the service of the light; the cheap shadow tricks of the Caged God can no doubt not hold when exposed to the purifying light of Olm."

The Hand nodded again, "If you wish to leave your friend here, we can see to his needs as befits a member of the clergy."

Hollis opened his mouth to argue further; but to his surprise, Haedren stepped forward, raising his head to seize the man's eyes. "When, brother, did his light leave you?" Haedren's voice was his own but contained a raspy quality that raised the hair on the back of my neck.

"You overstep yourself, Brother Haedren. We will not be spoken to in that manner."

A sharp laugh erupted from Haedren's throat, "We? Why do you speak as if your absentee god stands with you? He has left your side, just as he abandoned me in the time of my greatest need."

"Watch your tone; you speak to the Hand of Dawn!" The frail man extended his long, boney finger in the direction of our companion.

Again, Haedren laughed, "I speak to the Hand of Nothing. You have not the strength to restore your own faith; much less anyone else's." I saw the same shadow from our final confrontation with Theamon on that lonely road fall upon my companion, "It was not until this moment that the true extent of their malicious neglect became clear to me."

I watched the old man begin to sweat, his angry countenance trying to hide the clearly uncomfortable, nervous swallow. "Your *friend is taxing our patience, boy." The Hand's eyes bore into Hollis's before shifting back to Haedren's. I am not sure if anyone else in that room saw what was exchanged wordlessly between the two. I saw the anger in the man's eyes turn to trepidation and then to unreasoning terror. "We tire of his presence. Take him from our sight." I could hear the tremble in the Hand's previously confident voice.*

Hollis gripped Haedren by the elbow, intent in turning him towards the door. He pulled his arm from the thief's grasp, maintaining the contest of wills until the greatest among Olm's servants averted his gaze. It was only then that he turned on his heel, with a smug smile upon his face.

Haedren was gone before any of us woke the following day.

The Adder root must have worn off soon after, as that was the last entry until the following day. Through Hollis's memories however, Stephen remembered the details of that night; details that Jeff had left out. Haedren retired to his room upon returning to the 'Mermaid; leaving his comrades to discuss the strange events among themselves. None could bring themselves to admit the same shadow that Theamon commanded had fallen upon their once devout companion. Even Hollis doubted Silvermoon's recollection, having not seen it for himself.

Hollis found Haedren outside the stables, preparing to leave alone. It was obvious Haedren had wanted to do so without notice. His former comrade turned his cold gaze upon him. Hollis's vision dimmed before going dark. He remembered waking; a small crowd gathered around his prone form. Hollis was never sure if Haedren had spared his life or if others had come upon the scene and spooked the man.

Stephen's cell phone chirped softly beside him. He shifted his eyes to its screen, revealing that he had spent two and a half hours reading the journal and reminiscing. After closing the journal with a soft snap, he returned it to his duffel and zipped it quickly. Climbing the stairs as quietly as he could manage,

Stephen walked to the bathroom, his eyes searching the dim depths of the bedroom he shared with his wife. She would be rising very soon, and he intended to be showered and on his way to the florist before she asked any uncomfortable questions.

The scalding water kneaded his tight muscles with firm, warm fingers. But his mind refused to stop wandering to Hollis's newly discovered memories. The morning following Jeff's journal entry, the three of them did indeed leave the city. Silvermoon, Mika and Ret pursued Haedren south toward Utel while Hollis and Marcus searched the Great Library for some clue as to what had befallen their companion. It took them many days to follow a winding trail from one book to another, often across subjects and even sections.

They were able to find anecdotal evidence of similar phenomenon occurring. Any historical mention of personality changes so drastic to border on possession could only be found in transcripts of oral histories written much after the events themselves. Any others were purely the fodder of myth and legend. It was said that Sharroth, the Father of Lies and the closest thing Taerh had to an actual devil figure, could possess people who surrendered their will to him for short periods of time., But the cage in which his fellow gods had imprisoned him prevented him from exerting any real or lasting influence over them..

One scholar theorized that there were personalities so powerful that in death they could possess another being. Theamon was powerful, of that there could be no doubt, but both he and Marcus didn't believe that even the Hand of Lies was puissant enough to corrupt an honestly good soul as Haedren, even when combined with his weakened will.

"Stephen!" Ronni's voice pulled him from his own thoughts like a face full of ice water; chills raised on his arms despite the heat of the shower. Hollis's memories had caused him to lose track of time and he was now squarely in the path of his wife's ire.

"Are you trying to lose your job? I can't support this household by myself."

"I am going in late."

"Obviously. Why can't you think of anyone besides yourself, Stephen? A man provides for his family; he puts it before foolish things."

Heat began to rise in Stephen's chest, filling his face with fear and shame; but in the back of his mind, he could feel another presence, just as he had in Taerh. From somewhere, a sense of calm like a cool mountain stream tempered the fire. He felt a small smile not quite his own come to his lips as he slowly reached down to turn the water off.

"Don't you have anything to say for yourself?" Her tone picked up tempo as she sensed blood in the water, "God, I swear ..."

He opened the curtain with the same deliberate pace, "You swear what, Veronica?" His voice was soft, but firm. She was forced to lower her own to hear his words.

"I swear that I don't know why I ever thought you'd change."

"I do not know either. I never promised anything of the kind." The words were his, but the tone and deliberate delivery were Hollis's.

"What? How dare you?"

He brought his finger to his lips with fluid grace and said, "Shh...you have had your time to express your misery. Ten years as a matter of fact." A surge of panic was building in him; rather than accomplishing his goal of avoiding this conflict, hushing her would only make the matter worse. "It is my turn to address some of your concerns; much past due, if you want my opinion." A reassuring feeling overtook him; a feeling that these little conflicts could not be held at bay forever. Eventually, avoiding confrontation ... constantly giving ground would lead them down an ever-worsening path.

"What are you trying to say?" Ronni's voice began to rise

again. Her lips pulled back to reveal an angry sneer, narrowing her blue eyes to slits.

That sense of panic began to fill him again; he felt naked and exposed, both literally and figuratively. He was still standing there, dripping wet, bare as the day he was born; his wife pressing that advantage as she always had. Again, he could feel Hollis in the back of his mind, his presence brought comfort to his manic thoughts. With no intention of his own, he felt the smile turn into a gentle smirk, the sense of calm contentment spreading through his body, "I am saying that you complain a great deal; you seem to have an issue with who I am...who I have always been. Tell me, dearest wife," the last two words slipped from his lips with a sugar filled purr that didn't attempt to mask his sarcasm, "Why would you marry a man you disliked so completely?" Just as Jeff had written, it was as if he and Hollis were two sides of the same coin. When Stephen withdrew in fear and doubt, Hollis surged forward. The thief wielded his word and tone like sword and dagger, denying Ronni any advantage.

"I never said I disliked you, Stephen." She rolled her eyes as her voice became patronizing.

"Yes, Veronica. Yes, you did, in every glance and every passive aggressive comment." She opened her mouth to retort; but Stephen interrupted her, "I could theorize why you would want to be with someone you do not respect. Daddy issues? A sense of self-esteem that can only be fueled by the subjugation of those around you? A genuine need to just be fucking unhappy? In the end, I am just too tired to be your therapist." Stephen saw the effect these carefully considered; but quickly uttered words had on her. Where she began the argument in a position of strength and aggression, her posture now changed to a defensive one. He hoped she didn't see his hand quiver as he pulled a towel from the rack beside the shower and began drying his face. The gesture in its apparent casualness sought to take away another advantage she had over him. If he demonstrated no discomfort in his vulnerability, Hollis could remove another weapon from Ronni's emotional arsenal.

He could feel the frustration radiating from her, where a moment ago there was only anger, "Are you saying I need therapy? I'm the one that needs help?"

Stephen slid the towel from his face to wipe the water from his chest, watching her through hooded eyes, "I said that I was too tired to be your therapist. In any case, I am not the one to give you what you need. I doubt I ever was." He rubbed the towel down each arm in turn, drying them with economical motions. His anxiety rose again, but still words flowed forth as Hollis rose to the fore again, "As a matter of fact, I think the only person that can help you is you, my dear." His reflection used this term of endearment, coupled with a low, almost tantalizing tone to parry any return stroke... pushing her further off guard.

Her face tightened into a knot as her hands balled themselves into fists at her sides. She was speechless for a moment as the easy target that had always been her husband became less so before her eyes. "What's that supposed to mean?"

He rubbed water from each leg with increasingly steady hands before draping the towel over the shower rod, "It means: if you want to be happy, you have to want to be happy." He felt a chuckle escape his lips, "Seems a pretty straight forward concept when you think about it."

As soon as it left his mouth, he felt that he had over stepped. Despite how she treated him, she was his wife; at one point, their relationship had been good, they had loved and appreciated each other. For those times...those moments, he felt he owed her more respect.

She clenched her teeth so tightly, he heard her jaw click, "Don't speak to me in that tone of voice or ..."

He felt Hollis's opinion beside his own; she had long since abandoned any respect for him, if she ever felt it. He stepped out of the tub, stopping a breath short of her. "Or what? You take less care of my feelings than you do strangers on the street and then take offense when I speak to you without the deference you seem to believe you deserve? Respect is earned, Ronni." H smoothly stepped around her and into the cool dimness of the hallway, "Apparently so is disrespect."

"That's right, Stephen, walk away from your problems. It's my fault for marrying a boy and not a man."

He felt himself turn with such speed that she gasped and took a half step back. Stephen, for a moment, feared that his reflection would escalate the conflict to the physical level, but he felt his brow furrow momentarily in a calculated gesture before nodding slowly to himself, "I suppose it is." He ran his hand over his two day's growth of beard, wiping the last of the moisture from it. "At one point, we were in love, right Ronni? I mean it wasn't always like this." Hollis faded into the background smoothly. He looked into her seething eyes; his own almost pleading, "We were happy once, weren't we?" He waited a heartbeat before turning on his heel and walking into the bedroom.

He heard her footsteps behind him, "I don't even remember, Stephen." In her tone, Stephen could hear a trace of trepidation. It was replaced almost immediately with venom. "But I know that you refuse to grow up... refuse to be a man." Her lips curled back over her teeth as she emphasized the final word.

He froze, his own anger intensified by that of Hollis. "What is a man, Ronni? Is it supporting his family financially? I work a job that crushes my soul to give you the things you think you so richly deserve. Not to mention the financial opportunity to work in a field that makes you feel fulfilled. I sacrifice my own happiness for yours. That is a pretty adult thing to do. Or do you mean a man in the sense of what things I like to do outside of my fifty hour a week grind?" Stephen felt his voice rising and took a deep breath to calm himself, knowing that words and actions that came from emotions, especially rage, would lead him down the wrong path. Hollis and he agreed on that point.

She sneered, "You play games."

Pulling open his dresser drawer, he withdrew a polo shirt, placing it on the bed behind him as he raised an eyebrow, "As opposed to what, watching other men play games on TV? Drinking and smoking in a bar somewhere to try to forget that I hate my job...wipe away the knowledge that my wife doesn't respect me?" Stephen opened a second drawer and pulled out a folded pair of boxer shorts, "If I make you unhappy... if I am indeed the source of your misery, I am honestly sorry, Ronni." He pulled on the boxers and then walked to the closet to get a pair of pants. "There are things beyond our little world, our little problems. We live in a nice house ... we have food on the table and clothes on our backs." He pulled the polo shirt over his head slowly, enjoying the feel of the cotton against his skin, "Others do not ... others have to fight for everything they have, which may not be much."

Stephen turned, again running his fingertips along the stubble along his jaw, "Alan is dead, Roni. Mike is most likely not far behind. I, for one, refuse to continue ... well ... whatever it is we're doing here." He walked through the door, stopping momentarily beside her, "I have better uses for my time."

CHAPTER THIRTEEN
AN ENLIGHTENING DISCOURSE

S tephen pulled into the strip mall's almost empty parking lot, with his mind still racing. He felt so free now that he spoke his mind, the doubts that had been his constant companions for as long as he could remember no longer snapped at the edges of his consciousness. It was as if for the first time since dropping out of college six years ago, he was at peace. A small chuckle shook him for a moment as he thought of the irony that lay within the uncertainty that faced him in the nights to come; he was finally at peace with himself. For his entire life, he had felt out of place, just a half step out of sync with those around him. Now, sitting in this deserted parking lot, he seemed to know his place and more importantly, his path forward.

He took a steadying breath and stepped out into the already building heat of the morning. Stephen pulled the duffel bag from the back seat before making his way towards the building. He could hardly contain his excitement, despite the momentous tasks ahead of him. He forced himself to walk towards the florist at a reasonable rate, even as a feeling of amusement washed through him; no doubt his reflection derived no end of entertainment from his child-like anticipation.

It was due to this sense of anticipation that he almost missed the second shadow that passed in front of the frosted glass window that fronted the shop. Hollis didn't. With every nerve on fire, he pushed the door open.

Samantha stood behind the counter, looking up as he entered, "Ah Stephen, how nice of you to visit." She smiled at him softly, "Am I to assume that I may cease looking for another solution?" He nodded lightly, his eyes taking in the interior of the shop. Since the room was lit by desk lamps on tabletops scattered randomly rather than overhead florescent lights, it seemed more shadow than not. A heavy scent of flowers and rich dirt hung in the air, filling his senses almost to bursting. It recalled the intensity of Taerh; but seemed more cloying than clean, as the air there did. "That is for the best, I believe." Her smile brightened, tension that he hadn't noticed previously, dissolving from her frail form.

He couldn't say that he heard the soft click of a closing door; but it seemed that he could feel someone leaving through the back of the shop. He felt that if she had wanted him to know about it, she would have told him and left that question unspoken. "So, where do we start?"

She laughed lightly and said, "Direct and to the point. I do not wonder why Jeffery and Alan both befriended you. They were also anxious to get to the root of things." Her smile faded from her lips, "In Alan's case, it led to dire consequences."

Stephen again nodded. "In my case, you must understand the sense of urgency. You had said that both were still alive on their side, and I would rather rescue them while they remain so."

Samantha held up a thin finger, "That is correct, son. As I said, I am too old to reflect any longer, and thus have no way to bring them home." He frowned slightly, trying to reconcile how someone long dead could be restored to life. She obviously misinterpreted the gesture and extended her arm and laid her hand on his forearm. For a split second, a wave of panic raced through him, but it passed quickly. "Do not fret, son, we will bring them home."

Stephen forced a smile to his lips, "That is certainly my hope." She squeezed his arm with a strength that belied her age.

He continued, "So again, where do we begin?"

She shook her head, "Why, of course, the beginning." She gestured for him to follow her to the back of the store, without turning to verify that he had, she continued, "Tell me what you remember of your reflections? How many times have you traveled to Taerh?"

He trailed along behind her, "Just a few times ... I remember some issues in a desert city ... Oenigh; but when I woke this morning, we were preparing to travel through the Expanse to Drunmarch, the Dwarven City-State."

The rear of the store was even dimmer, lit by only a single floor lamp with an antique lace shade that seemed to hide more light than it revealed. The air here was thicker, free of the circulation provided by the front door. It wasn't exactly unpleasant but lent a feeling of claustrophobia to the otherwise open space. She tilted her head, "We?"

Stephen nodded distractedly as he took in the eclectic clutter that made up the room, "Yes, in escaping from the Emir's dungeon, Hollis .... I freed a fellow prisoner. She offered to accompany me through the desert."

She nodded, "That is good." She smiled but it seemed that the smile took a split second to reach her eyes. "Do you remember why you were traveling to Drunmarch?"

He nodded, "Hollis had a letter from Renthroas with him, saying he thought his father was there."

She leaned in more closely, as if trying to focus. "I see." An expression crossed her face too quickly for Stephen to read it, but he felt a flash of concern as Hollis's instincts pressed upon his consciousness. "Sometimes when reflecting, you can access your other self's memories. The next time you reflect, see if you can," she made quotes in the air, "'remember' where and when he

159

received this letter. It would be much easier if it worked both ways but your reflection, sadly stays in Taerh when you wake."

Stephen frowned, saying only, "So the connection between myself and Hollis is only when I am reflected?" Even as he sat there, he could feel Hollis with him and could feel the thief's agitation growing.

"That is correct. If I could contact my reflection, I am sure I could have found Jeffery before now. It has been a source of great frustration for me." She watched him with tranquil eyes, "I want you to drink tea made from three leaves of Adder root this evening before bed. That should be enough to reflect completely. Hopefully you can maintain some of your consciousness during the reflection. Try to remember everything you can from you time on Taerh so we can analyze it when you wake. The key to these remembrances is to not try too hard. If you focus too intensely, you will never quite grasp them. It is more like watching something from the corner of your eye; try to remember without really trying." She took his silence for confusion and continued, "It is easier done than explained; just try to remember my words and I am sure it will come to you."

Perhaps it was Hollis's suspicious nature; but Stephen felt it prudent to keep the fact that Hollis's consciousness stayed with him after waking from a reflection to himself. "Could you answer a few questions for me, Samantha?"

She nodded slowly, "Of course, Stephen."

"The last time I reflected, it seemed like more time passed in Taerh than here. I was asleep for seven hours; but it seemed like seven days passed on the other side. Is that normal? How does that even work?"

She chuckled lightly, "That is one of the great mysteries of reflection. Time passes differently here than on Taerh; sometimes it seems like only a few moments pass in Taerh for every hour you sleep, sometimes when you reflect, it will be as if you lose a week there during an eight hour day here. Jeffery had an idea, that

160

there was some mathematical way to determine the time lag based on how often you reflect and the time between reflections here. To be honest, all of it goes above my head."

Stephen frowned, "I saw some of the math in one of Jeff's journals and I understood next to nothing of it."

Samantha shrugged, "I know a professor in New York City that could perhaps have a look at it, if you like. Do you have the journals with you?"

He nodded, indicating the duffel by his side. "They are right here. I am trying to work my way through them to make sense of the whole situation. I have only flipped through that one, but you are welcome to it, if you like."

She smiled again, "That would be wonderful. Hopefully by early next week, he can have a look."

"The journals are pretty organized, but Jeff was embroiled in something that I only half understand. Did he ever speak with you about what was going on in Taerh?"

She shook her head, "Not nearly enough, I am afraid. What do the journals say on that subject?"

"He and the original group's reflections defeated a man by the name of Theamon, but the fight took a lot out of everyone, especially someone called Haedren, whom to my knowledge does not have a reflection here. Is that possible? Does everyone here have a reflection there and vice versa?"

Again, she shrugged, "I am not sure, but I had always thought so...or at least assumed as much. When you are done with them, may I read them as well? Jeff never shared them with me."

"I see no reason why not. Perhaps you will find something I have not."

"Perhaps I can start with the newer journals and work backwards, while you work forward. It would give us two sets of eyes at double the speed."

Hollis's paranoia flared again, as she seemed very eager to read the journals... journals that Jeff had declined to share with her. Stephen dismissed it, as Samantha was only trying to help, "Of course." He reached down and unzipped the bag, pulling out three of the seven journals he'd taken from Jeff's trunk, "Take these and see what you can find."

She took the books in both hands, placing them on her lap. "Thank you, I will read them over this evening and perhaps we can speak again tomorrow." Her left hand rested on the leather-bound cover of the topmost journal, caressing it with a finger.

"Do you know anything about this Theamon?"

Samantha slowly nodded, "A bit. He was the Hand of Lies but fell from Sharroth's favor at some point." At Stephen's frown, she continued, "The Hand of Lies is Sharroth's servant on Taerh. He or she is imbued with a measure of the god's power and acts as his... well...hand in all things on the physical plane. There is one hand for each of the gods of Taerh. The Hand of Dawn serves Olm and the Hand of the Lady serves his twin sister Umma. The creator, Galen, set forth a single law before retreating from sight: *No god shall personally interfere with the affairs of mortals.* The Hands are the gods' way of circumventing that law."

Stephen nodded, remembering the scene from Jeff's journal involving the Hand of Dawn and Haedren's words to him. "How does a hand fall from grace? Are they not the vessel of their chosen god?"

She shook her head, "From what I understand, vessel is not quite an accurate description. Each hand draws his power from his god, but they are still men and women with their own free will. Sometimes, if a Hand fails to serve their master, his or her favor can be taken away, but, again from what I understand, Theamon was able to maintain some, if not all, of his power when Sharroth withdrew his grace."

"Could Sharroth not just strike him down Old Testament style?"

"Due to the fact that Umma and Olm have their brother trapped in a cage of sorts, he simply lacks the power to do so, even if he wished to violate Galen's Law. All the Father of Lies can do is invest another Hand and turn his worshippers against his fallen vessel. But that became moot when Jeffery and his companions slew Theamon. Do you have the journal, perhaps, that describes the battle?"

This time, Stephen could sense her eagerness as well, but again, dismissed it. "I do." It took him a moment to pull forth the second journal he had read. When he did, she added it to the pile in her lap. "Perhaps with your knowledge of Taerh, you can piece together more than I did."

She smiled, "I will certainly do my best."

"Thank you, Samantha. For that and, well, everything." His eyes were drawn to the four books in her lap and the particular way her finger traced a pattern not present on the leather-bound surface. The pattern was consistent, drawn over and over as she spoke with him; but he couldn't for the life of him recall the exact shape of it. "This whole situation is a lot to take in and I fear it would be more so if I had to go through it alone."

She ceased tracing the unseen pattern long enough to place her hand on his thigh, squeezing it gently, "No gratitude is necessary, Stephen. We are aiding each other in this; in the end the only thing that matters is the result."

"I can't believe we are going to get Jeff and Alan back."

She nodded, slowly placing her hand back atop the journals, "Of course."

Stephen replayed the conversation in his mind as he drove to work. Something seemed more and more off about the entire interaction. He could no more put his finger on what precisely invoked these feelings as he could recall the pattern Samantha had drawn on the plain leather journal. He was sure that Hollis's suspicious nature added to his sense of discomfort, but the thief's feelings seemed more like a conscience than an alien consciousness. He set aside his worries as he traded the bright summer sunshine for the shade of the parking garage.

He'd almost shaken the feeling by the time he emerged from the elevator into his office space. That same sense of dread fell upon him like an anvil made of ice, taking his breath away. This time the dread was tempered by a sense of calm...a new calm, confidence. As Stephen walked through the office, he felt trepidation warring with conviction.

He was, greeted by smiles and waves as he rushed between the padded labyrinth of cubicle walls to his own taupe-colored cell. He quickly pulled his laptop from the bag that hung from his shoulder and placed it on the desk. Tossing the bag into the space between it and the floor, he sat down with a soft exhalation of breath.

As the computer booted up, his eyes shifted to the small analog clock that sat on an eye level shelf. It had been a gift from a grateful client and represented the fact that his job was not all bad. There were people who appreciated and valued both him and his hard work. A smile came to his face; he might enjoy his days in the office were it not for the man whose signature graced his pay checks. As if on cue, Jared's voice interrupted Stephen's internal conversation.

"You're aware, Stephen, that we begin work at 8am here, aren't you?"

He felt his shoulders slump slightly as the full weight of his unhappiness settled upon them. "Yes, Jared, I remember. I left you a message this morning, as I had some things to take care of and am glad to take personal time for them."

Without turning around, Stephen could sense the smug smirk that was painted across his boss's lips. "A message does not constitute permission. If you want to take time off, you need to get approval from me or Gladys."

Taking a deep breath, he turned his chair to face Jared, "I

called, but you did not answer. Your sister is off again this week."

A look of anger crossed his boss's face. "My sister works twice as hard as anyone else, which is why she is your supervisor. Or have you forgotten that?"

Deep in his heart, he wanted to rise and confront the man. He wanted to let the tyrant in an overpriced suit know exactly what he thought of him. It was fear that kept him in his seat. "Of course, I haven't forgotten that."

He thought to himself, *How could I? You remind me every chance you get.*

"Good. We hired you when no one else would. How long were you out of work?"

Stephen shrugged nonchalantly. He didn't want to deal with this anymore but there was nothing he could do.

Jared persisted, "How long, Stevie?" he stressed each word like a physical blow.

Looking around him, Stephen spotted a half dozen clients and co-workers transfixed on the conversation. "Six months," he muttered, too quietly. He guessed what was going to happen before it did.

Cupping his thin hand behind his ear, his boss leaned in and asked again, "How long?"

"Six months."

Jared nodded. "Six fucking months. That should've told me something. Sometimes I wonder to myself why I didn't take that as a sign of your worth to this company. But I didn't... I hired you anyway. I gave you a chance when no one else would, and you thank me with mediocrity."

From deep within him, Stephen felt something spark to life. At first it was only an ember. The man took it for embarrassment, "I do my job."

His boss raised an eyebrow, a sardonic smirk blossoming on his lips, "Poorly ... you do your job poorly and yet I still give you the chance to better yourself...to do better for yourself." The ember flashed again, flaring into a burning anger. "I doubt you can, however. Once a loser ..." In a sudden motion, Stephen spun in his chair; he wasn't convinced it was completely of his own volition.

The rage continued to build in Stephen's chest as his eyes ran again over Jared's form, seeing him as if through a new perspective. Despite his height and perceived power, his new impression of the man was small and petty, driven more by fear and jealousy than any true strength. Alongside the burning, a desire built. At its root, it was no different than the impulse that pulled at him every time the man spoke to him. The departure came in the voracity of the feeling. The sneering grin plastered across his face was no different than the one worn so confidently by the Emir's master of torture in his time of triumph. The expression could easily be replaced by one painted in crimson by the kiss of cold steel across his throat. Stephen was shocked by thoughts filling his head, not quite his own but not completely alien. Despite being seated, Stephen had to grip the arms of his chair to fight a sense of vertigo that rolled through him like a wave. Hollis's thoughts filled him like a rushing tide until he feared he would drown in them.

"Are you listening to me, Stevie?" Stephen fought to hold onto his very identity as Hollis's instincts, honed by decades of fighting for his life threatened to sweep it away. "Jesus," he heard Jared mutter as the man turned on his heel. "Your support tickets better be up to date by the end of the day or we're going to have to have a serious discussion about your continued employment."

The man's threats simply mingled with the myriad of thoughts that swirled in Stephen's mind. Their mocking tones were lost amid the sights and sounds of the thief's memories. The harder Stephen fought, the harder it became to resist the press of recollections that weren't his own. Amid the assault, he couldn't help but question why this hadn't happened on the other side... within Hollis's mind on Taerh. Like a sudden flash of lightning in a blue sky, the answer came to him: he had never felt Hollis struggle against his intrusion. In treating the ingress as an intrusion, Stephen had inadvertently turned the thief's presence into a struggle. Just as Stephen fought for his identity, so too did Hollis.

Taking a deep breath, Stephen filled his lungs to capacity. He felt the cool air grazing the depths of his chest before exhaling slowly. As the air left his body, Stephen focused on expelling with it the fear and doubt caused by the swirl of these new feelings. As he breathed in again, he tried to open himself to the validity of each one of them...to accept Hollis's sentiments as his own... simply never considered. A sense of equilibrium slowly began to return, moment by moment and breath by breath.

Stephen wasn't sure how long he was sitting at his desk, simply breathing. He no longer felt his heart beat at a staccato inside his chest. With that sensation came awareness of his surroundings once more. His co-worker, Cliff, was standing behind him.

"...you alright, Stephen?"

Slowly, he turned his eyes to the man behind him and nodded tentatively. "I'll ... I will be fine." The statement was only meant as a platitude, but he felt deep within himself that it may be truer than he'd intended. Stephen, having surrendered to the influence of his reflection, felt a sense of calm settling across his shoulders like a gauze shroud. He repeated, "I will be fine," this time with more vigor.

The rest of the day passed uneventfully. It was filled with phone calls and hard work, but Stephen navigated it from within his placid armor of contentment. Jared didn't seek him out and the man wasted no further energy on the tyrant in the corner office. As he climbed into his car, his thoughts turned to the dictator that ruled over his days as much as his wife did his evenings.

Just as Ronni's pettiness paled in comparison to the life and death struggles that Hollis faced in the pursuit of rescuing his friends, so did the ego driven machinations of the owner of Horne and Horne Consulting. Hollis knew that bullies and common thugs alike often wilted beneath the glare of true conviction, but Stephen had never shown his employer that level of confidence. The thief respected his reflection's principles, values that he had neither the will nor latitude to adhere to.

A small smile came to Stephen's lips as he pulled through the security gate and onto the street. Not for the first time, he realized that he and Hollis were undoubtably stronger together than apart. Despite his lack of confidence, Stephen possessed a strength that those around him were unaware of. Despite the stones and arrows cast at him throughout his life, he clung to a dogma that seemed to him had gone out of style with courtly love.

What Stephen lacked in conviction; Hollis made up in spades. Having relied on himself since his misspent childhood on the streets of Oizan, the thief's faith in his own abilities sometimes bordered on arrogance. Combining the thief's cunning and confidence with his reflection's steely integrity and enduring fortitude undoubtably made them a formidable team.

As he passed through the familiar toll booth and merged onto the New Jersey Turnpike, Stephen allowed his mind to wander. Normally, he left the tribulations of his day behind him as he did the congestion of the city. That should have been true on this day as well, especially with the uncertain future of both himself and his friends that rode on his shoulders. But the weight had settled like iron onto his soul. As he tried to block Jared's pointless posturing out of his thoughts, he felt something within him bringing it to the forefront of his mind again and again.

With the memories of the inequities visited upon him by his boss ran through his thoughts like a World War II propaganda film. There, in these recollections, his shame was laid bare before the eyes of his reflection. Shame passed through him as he felt his cheeks color in embarrassment. His time spent in Taerh had given Stephen a respect for Hollis; he feared that the thief's opinion of him would be shattered as he became aware of how he had allowed himself to be treated. Like a knife, a sense of sympathy sliced through his regret. Instead of the disgust he expected, Stephen felt his reflection's barely contained rage.

Hollis's anger seemed to permeate every cell of the man's body. Images of alley justice flashed in Stephen's mind. The thief didn't possess Stephen's same strong morality. Hollis's feelings were heady in Stephen's heart; it would have been simplicity itself to allow himself to become swept away in them. He felt the excitement of his reflection's promises pulling at him. *One well-placed knife in the darkness and his problem would be solved.* The hair on his forearms rose with the exhilaration of it all. *He could do it. Hollis could show him how.*

With a sudden motion, Stephen pulled at the steering wheel, muscling his car onto the shoulder to a chorus of angry horns around him. He slammed the car into park and closed his eyes against the rush of emotions. Once again, he felt buffeted by the personality that was Hollis's consciousness. He rested his head on the back of his hands he desperately tried to find the core of himself amid the tempest of passions. Stephen focused on not fighting Hollis. Rather he accepted his reflection's sentiments, with a steely resolve, he reshaped them according to his own principles.

Just like in Taerh, a sense of calm descended, crushing beneath it both the rage and shame. He felt Hollis's awareness integrate into his own. Something needed to be done with Jared Horne; but whatever it was needed to be approached carefully and with forethought. A plan formed in the reflections' mind. A smile widened the corners of his mouth, one that he wasn't sure was entirely his own.

CHAPTER FOURTEEN
A HISTORICAL LESSON

The scorching air stung Hollis's lungs as he and Aristoi waited out the teeth of the day beneath the oasis's stand of date palm trees. The cultivated trees provided protection and shade for the less hardy fruit trees that grew beneath their canopy. The thief leaned against the rough surface of the trunk as he watched the breeze raise gentle ripples on the water before him. Beside him, the Kieli woman sat tailor-style among the soft undergrowth sheltered by the trees above them. She diligently splinted his hand and wrist with strips of cloth ripped from the thief's cloak and wood from those same trees.

The days without medical attention had made it necessary to separate the misaligned bones before they could be reset properly. Aristoi worked quickly and efficiently but every moment, his hand descended further into a nebulous mass of pain. Once the last knot was tied, she carefully laid his hand on the sandy ground. "I make no promises, but you certainly have a better chance of regaining some use of it now."

He appreciated the woman's methodical, clinical approach to caring for his hand, but his admiration did nothing to halt the agony that had taken up residence there. Hollis nodded briefly, forcing a tight smile to his lips. Closing his eyes, he allowed the swaddling heat to seep into his body in the hope that it might do something to ease the throbbing in his hand. The thief focused on the breath he drew in slowly before expelling it, forcing everything around him to fade into the background. For moments uncounted, nothing existed for Hollis but the sensation of his breath and the sweltering breeze that moved sluggishly across his skin.

When the pain in his hand had dwindled to a steady ache, his eyes flickered open. Aristoi lay a handful of feet from him, her head cradled on clasped hands as she watched the palm leaves sway in a torturously slow dance. Hollis gingerly turned to face her, and the woman's dark brown eyes shifted to meet his.

"I will not say that I do not appreciate the company, but the Expanse is an unforgiving place when you want to be here. I cannot imagine traveling through it driven by a sense of obligation."

Aristoi raised an eyebrow. "You travel to the Stone City?"

Hollis nodded. "Drunmarch, correct."

She shrugged., "Then our arrangement is more convenience than obligation. Before my ... delay, Drunmarch was my destination as well."

"How did your path lead you through Altair's tender mercies?"

"Suffice it to say that I asked the wrong questions." The thief raised an eyebrow, encouraging the woman to continue. "I sought information, fairly bargained and paid for. The seller either never had that which I sought or was unwilling to part with it. I suppose it was easier to have me arrested than explain which one it was."

Hollis nodded. "It is not an uncommon outcome."

A sly smirk graced Aristoi's face. "So I am coming to learn. Yourself?"

The thief shook his head smiling mischievously. "A matter of pride...no more, no less."

"It is curious how often that seems to be at the root of most issues. Your business with the dwarves?"

Hollis's smile faded as a host of scenarios rushed through his mind, none of them ending particularly well for him. In the end, he decided that if the Kieli had wanted him dead for one reason or another, there were easier and more comfortable ways to accomplish the task. "Two *friends of mine were bound for Drunmarch and asked that I meet them there. What is it that you seek there?"*

"Legend tells of a place of power located in the depths of the Stone City. I need to see it for myself."

"A pilgrimage of sorts?

"Of sorts." A silence lingered for the space of a few breaths as it became obvious to both that despite their shared trials, neither was ready to share all their secrets. Aristoi broke the lull, "Do you know why they call it the Expanse?"

"I had always assumed that it was due to its size."

"That is true, but it was not originally league upon league of this accursed grit." The woman took a handful of the dark sand and let it slip through her fingers. "In the Age of Legends, all of this was fertile land. It was said that raising crops here was simply a matter of dropping a fist full of grain at your feet."

Hollis scrutinized the wilderness of emptiness that stretched into the distance beyond the palisade of date palms, "Legends often make outrageous claims. That is what makes them legends."

"What would you say if I told you there is proof that this particular legend is not so outrageous?"

The thief turned his gaze back to his companion, "What kind of proof?"

Aristoi murmured through her sly smile. "The dwarves remember a time before the First King...remember and have documented it."

Hollis raised an eyebrow, "Please do not take offense; but it was always my impression that the Kieli ..."

"...do not read?" The Songspear finished his thought. With a small shake of her head and roll of her eyes, she showed that she was more amused than aggrieved. "There is a stark difference between not relying on a thing and being incapable of it." Sheepish in his embarrassment, the thief seemed to be at a loss for words. "Do not feel overly abashed, you are far from the first northerner that has assumed such... and I assure you that you will not be the last."

"Have you seen the accounts yourself?"

Aristoi nodded. "I have. I came across them in the Grand Archives within the Mantrian capital of Saintril." Hollis found himself intrigued despite never taking an interest in much beyond what was immediately before or behind him. "According to the dwarven narrative, what we know simply as the Expanse was once known as the Verdant Expanse and at its center stood the Sovereign Tree. The Verdant Expanse was considered the garden of Umma herself."

Again, the thief swept his gaze over the landscape beyond the oasis. "She does not strike me as much of a caretaker."

Chuckling softly, the woman continued, "She tended it with devoted hand until the coming of the shadow. Are you familiar with the story of First King?"

"Enough. The gods installed a friendly dictator...one man above all others to enforce their will."

It was Aristoi's turn to raise an eyebrow, "That is quite a simplification." Hollis shrugged. "There is power in remembering one's past, steeped though it may be in myth and legend."

"If you say so."

The Kieli shook her head. "The gods Olm and Umma saw their greatest creations turning upon one another just as the elves had. Fearing that the strife was encouraged by the whispered words of their hated brother, Sharroth, Olm showed himself to the humans, delivering unto those gathered a code of laws to follow."

Hollis watched her through hooded lids.

"They were simple." She held up the last finger on her hand. "The gods give unto to you that which you deserve. Do not take that which does not belong to you." Aristoi added a second finger. "The bond between lovers is sacred. Do not tempt one heart from another." Raising a third, she continued, "Live your lives bathed in the light of truth. Do not practice the dark art of deception." Aristoi held up four fingers. "And most importantly, that which the gods have brought to life shall not be taken by any but them. Do not rob your neighbors of their lives."

Hollis muttered, "I will point out that a good deal of those take food from my mouth and everyone like me."

"Many agreed with you, Northerner. Those of pure heart followed these dictates. Those who had already accepted a measure of the void into themselves, disregarded them as they saw fit." She watched the thief as she spoke, visibly trying to keep the judgement from her eyes, *"A few, truly lost individuals accepted these four tenants as a pattern to throw down the Siblings and allow their own master to rise to replace them."*

"Sharroth?"

The Kieli nodded. *"The Father of Lies. The laws did not have the effect that Olm had intended. With no leader to follow, each human chose their course for themselves, allowing those who had accepted Sharroth's whispers to have an equal effect on mankind as did those with pure hearts."*

"Some value their freedom of will." Deep within his conscious, Hollis felt his reflection pushing back against his cynicism.

"The Sibling Gods decided that the humans must have a leader, to whom they could pass their wishes and see them done. Umma found the most perfect of mankind and gave him a measure of her breath of life, and with it a share of her wisdom and power. So was born Jaeth, the First King."

Hollis remained silent as conflict waged within his hear between Holli's cynicism and Stephen's curiosity.

Aristoi continued, *"Jaeth searched through Taerh for others who shared his righteousness and desire to bring peace from chaos, finding three individuals who met his expectations from all of mankind."* The woman's eyes became unfocused as she lost herself in the story. *"He dubbed these as his Heralds or Mouhn in Ancient Taerhian. To these men and women, he taught the Baenu...the language of creation itself."*

The thief perked up. *"So, the Heralds were always mages?"*

Aristoi nodded her head slightly and continued, *"The Mouhn traveled throughout the Cradle, spreading the word of the Siblings and helping their fellow man bring peace to their communities. The three were sworn to never rule, but instead guided and enlightened those who sought order."*

"Someone must have forgotten to tell the Risen about that part." Hollis smirked at his own joke. One of the current Heralds, the renowned necromancer sought to bring the peoples of the Cradle under his boney hand.

"Through the strength of Jaeth and the wisdom of the Mouhn, mankind flourished, and their hearts resisted the whispers of the Lord of the Void. For tens of generations, peace reigned in the Cradle, Jaeth's descendants ruling from the Ivory City of Aeth and those willing to take the mantle of Mouhn walking the land to bring wisdom and justice to the people."

"Until..." Hollis finished.

Aristoi nodded. "Through the centuries, Sharroth watched impotently as those who accepted him into their hearts declined until only the foulest continued to do his bidding. His fury was indescribable. With Sharroth's guidance and a measure of his own void soul, the thaumaturge Yost, created a weapon of power."

"Soul Drinker." Even in the teeth of the day, the sweat that glistened on Hollis's skin turned cold. He saw in Aristoi's eyes that she shared his trepidation.

"Soul Drinker. Xentus Ingae in Ancient Taerhian." Taking a deep fortifying breath, she continued, "The pristine silver blade drew into itself the light that surrounded it, living or otherwise. Its hunger was so great that it could draw the very soul from beings struck down by its gleaming edge."

Another shiver ran through the thief's body.

"Suitably armed, Yost hunted down the Mouhn one by one, stealing not only their lives but also their souls as Xentus Ingae absorbed their selves into its silver depths. The people grew afraid as those on whom they depended disappeared, victims of the ever-growing wave of despair that swept the land. Mankind cried out for help first to the descendant of the First King, Brose, and then to the Siblings themselves. Brose sent forces to search for the murderers but the Father of Lies always cloaked his faithful in the shadows from which he was born. Even Olm and Umma failed to discern the source of the attacks, the void forged sword masking its master from even their sight."

Hollis gave words to his reflection's curiosity, "What of the people? Did they not rise up to protect the peace that had preserved their way of life?"

"Fear makes people grasp at anything that promises safety, and mankind reached out for something to calm their minds. As always, Sharroth was there to whisper lies in their ears...into their hearts. He promised that any who did his will would be spared from the fate destined for the First King and his followers. It is said that weak wills make the strongest enemies; it was as true then as it is now. As the years passed and the dark acts continued, more and more of mankind accepted the Father of Beast's promises and stood behind his faithful. Soon Yost, an army of believers at his back, began his crusade against the First King."

The story struck a sensitive chord within Stephen; he could see the parallels between it and how he had bought the safety of his own way of life.

"War swept across the Cradle as the forces of the Father of Lies carved their way north, leaving destruction and ruin in their wake. When it became obvious that the crusaders rode under the protection of Sharroth's void born shadow, Olm left the boughs of the Sovereign Tree and took the field to oppose them. This, however, was precisely what the Lord of Beasts had hoped for. With Olm gone, Sharroth changed his shape to that of the Lord of Justice and entered the Sibling's home. Umma, unable to pierce the illusion, accepted him as Olm. When she was at her most vulnerable, Sharroth struck, impaling her on a weapon made of his own void fueled shadow. Olm heard his sister's scream and flew to her aid, leaving his faithful to their fate. Once their god abandoned them, the forces of the First King collapsed. Brose himself was forced to flee from the field and into the safety of Aerh's ivory walls."

Hollis found himself impressed by the power of the Songspear's storytelling. He was swept into her tale, despite himself.

"As Yost's army began their siege of the Ivory City, Olm and Sharroth battled beneath the shade of the First Tree. The Lord of Justice found himself weakened by the blow he himself had struck to the faith of those who worshipped him, while Sharroth's strength swelled at the victories of his own worshippers. If not for the timely intervention of Umma, still weak from her wounds, the Father of Lies would have bested Olm. Together, the Sibling Gods set Sharroth back on his heels; but just as the two believed they had their wayward brother in hand, the Master of Beasts draped a cloak of void over the Tree itself. The power held within its bark was drawn forth by the void as heat is sapped on a frigid day. With all the might he could muster, Olm struck out with his light, burning away the void. The First Tree, so weakened by the essence sapping effects of the nothingness caught alight as well. Within the resulting raging inferno, the three fought on, their anger and passion blinding them to all else."

"Together, Olm and Umma were finally able to drive Sharroth to the ground and were prepared to deliver the final blow to their despised brother. The Sibling Gods turned from their defeated enemy to see the ruin that was once the Grove of the Sovereign Tree. All that remained of the lush groves and verdant hillsides were ash and soot."

Before Hollis could contain his reflection's curiosity, he blurted out, "What became of Sharroth?"

"The Sibling gods cast him into a cage made of his own hubris, sentencing him to dwell forever within a prison of ash and shadow."

Through force of will, Hollis was able to push Stephen's questions from his mind. "All of this was in the dwarven account?"

Aristoi shook her head. "Just the part about the existence of the Verdant Expanse in the time of the First King."

The thief raised an eyebrow. "And everything else?"

The woman smirked slightly., "Legends have their purposes as well."

Hollis slowly shook his head.

"Now that I have answered your questions, answer one for me."

Hollis cocked his head. "How could I do any less?"

"Alone as we are in the solitude of the Expanse, I cannot help but notice that you still maintain your distance in the still of the night."

"That is not a question."

"Is it not?" The thief let out a brief sigh. The woman spoke again, "Do I intimidate you?"

Hollis chuckled and shook his head, "It is not that. Truth be told, I find it rather arousing. There is a certain appeal to closing your eyes next to a woman and not being completely certain you will ever open them again."

"Then what?"

"You have placed yourself in my debt. I could never be certain that anything that occurred would not be out of obligation." The thief wanted to believe in his heart that he would feel the same was it not for Stephen's influence, but truth be told, he was not convinced.

"Many would not concern themselves with that."

"I am not many."

"So, I am also coming to learn."

CHAPTER FIFTEEN
A TYRANT'S REWARD

Stephen's eyes flickered open in the pre-dawn light of his own bedroom. After the overpowering heat of the Expanse, the cool depths of the room felt good on his skin, despite the increasingly diffuse quality of the time he spent outside of Taerh. Ronni lay beside him in the shadows, her breathing deep and steady. Rolling from the bed to his feet with a smooth motion he would have believed himself incapable of a week ago, he stalked into the hall.

With steps softened by instincts not quite his own, Stephen descended the stairs into the kitchen. After starting the coffee and placing two slices of bread in the toaster, he crossed into his office as he waited for them to brown. On the low circular coffee table sat the grey canvas bag the held the journals that had so changed his life. Next to the bag was the empty cup that had previously contained the Adder root tea he'd drank the night before. He reached out his hand but paused as his mind vacillated between the promise of the journals and the weight of the day before him.

After a moment, he picked up the cup and returned to the kitchen. As he washed it, his thoughts returned to what lay before him at work. Once again, trepidation rose in him like the tide; his strategy was so filled with risk that it bordered on reckless. Like a sympathetic hand, his reflection's presence soothed his apprehension, but it didn't make the plan any less perilous.

Not for the first time, Hollis's initial proposal occurred to him. While murder may be justified under certain circumstances in Taerh, Jared Horne did not constitute such a circumstance in this world. Again, Stephen rejected it out of hand. While expedient and at some level satisfying, the thought of dealing with Jared in such a violent and final way disturbed the man on a visceral level. Impulses like that reminded Stephen that he and his reflection were decidedly different in some very fundamental ways.

$\sim$

Stephen took a deep breath to fortify himself before stepping from the elevator. He smiled politely in response to a few unheeded pleasantries as he stalked through the tangle of cubicles. His first stop was the server room to prepare for the inevitable conflict to come. After ensuring that everything was in place, he walked to his desk and sat down.

Mindlessly, he unpacked his laptop and turned it on, at a loss as to what to do while he waited for his employer to arrive. Blessedly, he did not need to tarry long.

"I see we decided to come to work on time today, Stevie. Perhaps there is hope for you yet." Jared's low voice felt like motor oil in his ears.

"So it seems." Stephen's mind spun around in panicked circles. Each breath eroded his conviction. His reflection's presence eased itself around his fractured thoughts like a down comforter, bolstering his resolve.

"Gladys wants an update on your open tickets by nine am. She's a busy woman, so don't waste her time."

Before he could stop himself words, more Hollis's than his own, flowed from his mouth, "That is impressive, considering she works less than half as often as anyone else." Around hm, Stephen saw heads peek around cubicle walls.

A wave of crimson began in Jared's cheeks and radiated outward until his entire face was bright red. "Excuse me?"

Stephen rose from his chair slowly, his eyes locked onto Jared's. Something passed through Jared's eyes as he took a half step back: Stephen saw that it was confusion, as Jared suddenly became less sure of himself.

His reflection's influence continued, "No offense, but she has been out of the office more than in it for as long as I have worked for you."

Jared's eyes broke contact with his, shifting right and left quickly to judge who was listening to their conversation. Men like his boss depended on the fear of those around them to keep people better than themselves in control. Stephen had without thinking, placed him in a situation where he needed to reassert his control quickly or risk losing it completely. Fear built in Stephen's heart and his mind began searching for a way to placate the man; but he found that he didn't truly wish to. His reflection's words and feelings were indeed his own; just free of the false sense of fear for a man whose only authority lay in an implied agreement and Jared's own mind.

Jared read the moment of indecisiveness in Stephen's eyes and began, "Remember who can fire you with a word, Stevie..." His words were clipped short when Stephen and Hollis's shared resolve cemented. It seemed an arbitrary place to draw a line, but that line had been drawn and this battle would need to be fought at some point. This moment was no better and no worse than any other. Although Stephen's resolve was truly out of practice, Hollis's was tempered in life and death situations and its edge was hard as steel. Somewhere in Jared's subconscious, his monkey brain registered that, and it knew fear.

Again, holding the man's eyes in Hollis's steel gaze, Stephen spoke with soft but measured tones, "I am not fond of that. If you don't mind, I prefer Stephen." Jared attempted to break eye contact again; but Stephen took a small step to the right in order to maintain it. "I am very aware of our respective positions, Jared. I work hard for you; I and the other people here allow you to collect a great deal of money with little to no actual work on your part. That is what you pay for. Perhaps in the past we were willing to also sell you our self-respect for that same wage; but I am no longer willing to make that trade."

Panic filled Jared's eyes as they shifted left to quickly get away from Stephen's. Silence surrounded as everyone within earshot hung on their words, both coworker and client alike. The silence hung for a moment as he could sense Jared's mind reeling. Stephen had put him in an untenable position. He could fire him for insubordination; but everyone heard the truth in his words. He could alternately back down and lose a measure of the power that he'd developed over years of institutional conditioning.

"In the server room now. I want to speak to you in private."

"Of course." Stephen suppressed his smile; a private conversation was exactly what his reflection-conscience had wanted. A part of him began to feel the least bit sorry for the man. He was so used to brow-beating people into submission, he had no idea that he was being moved around like so much of a stringed puppet. As Stephen mentally reviewed his plan, a slow burning sense of uncertainty overtook him. Hollis's experience and calm confidence had made it seem easy; but as the moment of execution approached, he was beginning to feel trepidation. His knowledge of Jared combined with his reflection-conscience's keen understanding of human behavior told him that the events he was about to put into motion would go as planned; but there were so many ways it could go wrong.

He led the way, swiping his key card through the reader and eliciting a soft beep as the magnetic door lock released. He turned the handle and then paused for the shortest of seconds. So lost in his anger was Jared, that he surged forward at the Pavlovian beep, expecting Stephen to already be moving. The resulting collision and exaggerated stumble looked to any observer as if Jared had shoved him from behind, complete with a flat palm teasing a solid thump from the door out of proportion with the force exerted.

As the lock clicked back into place, Stephen turned to face his boss. This time he made no attempt to hide his smile as once again Hollis and he acted as one. So blinded by his fury, Jared began to roar, "How dare you? I hired you when you had no other place to go! I gave you a place, a paycheck when a monkey could do your job!"

With the sense of calm emanating from his reflection, Stephen looked around the server room. He gave ground to the man's furious advance, bumping a keyboard tray with his elbow as he passed it.

"I'm not going to fire you; but you are going to wish I had. When I'm done, you are going to beg me to." A glint of maliciousness crept into his face as he advanced. "If you quit, you can't collect unemployment; so, you'll do anything I want you to and thank me for it. If you don't, you'll be living on the street." The box-cutter that had been on the edge of the tray started to tip as he passed. Reflex caused him to catch it before it fell to the floor.

Stephen reversed his backwards momentum, closing the distance between them in the span of a deep thought, dropping his right forearm so it was parallel to the floor and even with his stomach. "I am afraid none of that is going to happen." He'd tried to prepare himself for the pain, remembering the way Hollis's hand felt under the chisel; but all the preparation in the world couldn't compare to the sharp agony as the tip of the blade entered the flesh of his arm beneath the elbow. Stephen, drew his arm from left to right, opening a deep but superficial gash. With a shallow, steadying breath but before Jared could react, he impaled his left arm twice on the tip of the blade, opening a shallow cut from the last when he retrieved his arm. Flexing the fingers of his right hand, he turned his head slightly to compose himself as best he could while reaching behind him and picked up the wire-cutters from the small desk there.

In the moment, he tried to calm his mind and allowed himself to run on the instinct he knew was there. The Stephen of a week ago would have been crippled by doubt; but those feelings faded beneath his newfound confidence. He focused on appearing calm and cold, despite his dread.

Confusion and anger warred for control of Jared's face as he dropped the box cutter as if it were a snake. "What the fuck are you doing?"

With a sudden movement, Stephen snapped the cutters open, conveniently spreading blood along the floor and the front of the server rack. He then stepped in closer to Jared, so their bodies touched, pressing the sharp tip and cutting edge of the wire cutter against his neck. "Five pounds of pressure." The words were delivered slowly to hide his doubts.

"What?" Jared stammered as he tried to retreat; but his most direct route away from the tool pressed his back to the server rack.

"It takes five pounds of pressure to puncture your carotid artery. It's really the thin layer of muscle that causes most of the resistance; but I am sure you do not really care about the whys and wherefores." Stephen pressed his forearm against the man's chest, making sure to spread the blood seeping from the wound onto his shirt. "The important fact is that once it is punctured, you will be unconscious in five seconds and dead within two minutes."

Jared closed his eyes, the reality of his situation finally settling upon him like a heavy coating of snow. When he opened them again, he was square in the gaze that was very little of the Stephen he had come to know.

"You very casually threaten the lives of those under your purview but seem to wilt like a flower under the summer sun when others do the same. From the outside, I am sure it would not paint you in the best of lights."

"I ... I never threatened to kill anyone." His tone was almost pleading.

Stephen quirked an eyebrow, "Did you not? I watched you fire good men and women because they challenged you or wanted things you promised. You fired Andrei because you thought his accent was too thick." Stephen's soft smile turned into a frown. "Each of them had a family ... people that depended on them. I know you enforced that ridiculous non-compete clause, effectively blacklisting them. You ruined lives, Jared. Why?"

The man's face was already pale with fear. "I have the right to fire someone."

The edge of the cutters dug slightly into the flesh of his neck; a drop of blood traced a thin line of crimson down into his collar. Stephen repeated his question, "Why?" Jared clenched his teeth but remained silent. Stephen felt himself falling more and more into the part he had to play as he held up his left arm, "These are what they refer to as defensive wounds. The story I intend to tell is that you came at me with the box-cutter on the floor. The one with your fingerprints all over it. I was forced to defend myself and, in the scuffle, you were stabbed in the throat."

"You will go to jail... "

He shook his head, "Not likely. Between the obvious sign of a struggle, these defensive wounds and that rather nasty shove, my tale is actually pretty convincing." *He has to believe I am prepared to kill him, otherwise all of this is for naught,* he thought as he seized Jared's eyes once again, "But then tales usually are when there is only one person telling them. I will ask you again: Why?"

He felt Jared's breathing quicken as the reality of his situation continued to dawn on him. He closed his eyes and exhaled. "Because I could, alright? Because I could!"

"Now that wasn't so hard, now was it? Unfortunately for you, that does set a very dangerous precedent. Herein lies the danger of tyranny."

He scraped the edge of the cutters along Jared's throat, riding the wave of the role he was playing. The words came more easily now, more convincing, "Herein lies the danger of a 'civilized society' where victims and tyrants alike live without consequences."

Jared listened quietly, his eyes shifting around the room before blinking slowly.

Stephen continued, "There are two ways with which to lead; Machiavelli covered it rather succinctly in The Prince: you can rule through love or fear; the author himself counseled both if you can manage it. However, most people today remember only that given a choice between the two, he advocated fear allowing for the fickleness of love." Stephen released a slight amount of pressure, still maintaining eye contact through the building pain in his forearm. "The problem with choosing a path based purely on what fits your world view the best and not truly understanding the motivation of the line is that you tend to find your mistakes coming home to roost." A soft smile came to Stephen's lips as he saw in Jered's eyes the same fear that filled him every morning for almost as long as he could remember. "You see, while love...let us call it loyalty...is indeed a fickle thing, when it fades, it leaves apathy in its wake. When fear fades...and it always will because threats lose their teeth the longer they sit upon the mind, it is replaced by desperation in equal measure. This in itself has cast down more tyrants than any army ever will."

"You're insane." It was a whisper but with only the drone of cooling fans surrounding them, the words rang clear.

Stephen shook his head. "I am not sure I am...indulge me for one more moment. You rule through fear; rather than engendering loyalty in your employees...rather than motivating them to do their best for you because they want to see you, the company and themselves succeed, you cultivate in them a cold unreasoning dread. Your employees break their backs because they are afraid of what you will do to them...and by extension the ones they love. Does that sound correct?" Jared simply closed his eyes. "I am not saying it's your fault...well, not completely...you are indeed a small and petty man; but in times past, your behavior would have been kept in check by a real fear that someone or a group of someone's would reach the end of their tolerance...move to a point where they could not become more afraid...and rise up to depose you. In Machiavelli's time, that most likely would mean at the end of a sword." He tapped the edge of the cutters against the man's throat softly, "Or a convenient substitute. But in a 'civilized' society, that fear is removed because violence is not an answer that the collective conscience accepts. People like you abuse your power because there is no check or balance to prevent it." His voice developed a harder edge, "Because you can."

"Are you going to kill me?" Although Jered meant to sound brave, his voice trembled.

Stephen shook his head. "Not unless I have to. I am neither tyrant nor murderer, but I refuse to be your victim any longer. In a perfect world, this would be a 'Come to Jesus' moment for you... that experience that alters your perception and causes you to change your life. Both of us know how truly naïve that is. I am going to take that box-cutter with me as well as get these stitched so there are pictures to document our little discussion." He withdrew the edge from the man's throat and backed away before bending down to scoop up the box cutter in a plastic bag. "If your reign of terror comes to an end, this is the last anyone needs to hear about it. Now let us talk about some time I would like to take off ... "

CHAPTER SIXTEEN
A CURIOUS CONFLICT

As Hollis sat by the campfire, looking out into the unbroken darkness of the desert night, he let his thoughts wander. He felt Stephen's apprehension about the consequences arising from his actions in the server room. The workings of his reflection's world still both amazed and disturbed him. In Taerh, if you did not maintain what was yours, there were a plethora of people who would take it from you...along with much more. He did, however, appreciate the idea of a place where the thief's constant focus on survival would be unnecessary. In spite of the man's almost institutional level of placating those around him, Hollis genuinely liked Stephen.

Even before they found each other, Stephen had been different than those around him. He lived by a code of honor that, based on Hollis's interpretation of Stephen's memories, was considered antiquated by those around him. He toiled for a woman that neither respected nor cared for him because he had made a promise before family and friends. In order to maintain home and hearth, he bent knee to a petty dictator that, were the situations reversed, Hollis would have left bleeding and forgotten in an alley long before. Stephen never stole and only lied when all other options were exhausted. He seemed to treat those around him with respect and kindness, despite how they treated him. To endure the indelicacies visited upon him by those who declined to adhere to his principles and not slip in his insistence upon them demonstrated that he had an inner strength that even those close to him were never privy to.

As he sorted through his impressions of his reflection, Hollis felt the man's presence in his mind. His thoughts and feelings swirling among his own, finding the common ground the two men shared and seizing on them. Where their experiences dictated their opinions differed, it seemed the edges softened leading to compromises that neither realized they were making. The longer either remained reflected, the closer they drew leading to something that was at the same time neither of them nor both.

Hollis was so lost in his thoughts that he did not realize that Aristoi was beside him until the woman spoke. "Another day, perhaps two and we will be at the gates of the Fair Folk. Do you believe that your friends still remain within their halls?"

The thief turned slowly, hiding his surprise before he began slowly, "Perhaps...It certainly would make things easier."

"You never did tell me what they sought in Drunmarch...what drove them to brave the misery that is the Expanse." The Kieli woman stirred the smoldering fire with the tip of her spear.

Hollis shrugged non-committedly. "I have given up trying to guess the hearts and minds of men...even half men such as Ren." A touch of guilt teased the edges of his conscience; Aristoi had proven herself a stalwart companion both at the prison and in the days following their escape. She had been granted plenty of opportunities to betray Hollis's trust as they traveled through the inhospitable wastes that made up the Expanse; but never had the thief doubted the woman's intensions to repay her freedom.

Aristoi chuckled softly, "I can certainly agree with that...I suppose we will find out soon enough at any rate. At least we can expect a welcome respite from this accursed sand and perhaps a good meal or two. The dwarves have a reputation for hospitality so long as you do not bring darkness to their door. I will admit to anticipating a first-hand experience with the Fair Folk."

Hollis cocked his head, glad for the change of subject, "I have heard them called that not a few times; descriptions do not paint them as particularly pretty or pale."

His companion laughed in a short burst and said, "They are neither assuredly. They earn the title for their disposition. It is said that you could more easily rouse a rock to anger than a Dwarf."

"I have heard that Drunmarch spans the length of the Grey Spine Mountains; one would think it difficult to carve such a kingdom with such a gentle bearing."

Aristoi shook her head, "Do not mistake their slowness to anger with weakness...or even kindness. Dwarves live much longer than we do and tend to do everything slowly as well. By all accounts, they are single minded and stubborn once their minds are set upon a course. Dwarves do as dwarves do, with little concern for the words or actions of others."

"You would think that, given the worth of Dwarven steel, someone would have tried to carve themselves a piece of the stranglehold they keep upon it."

She nodded slowly. "A few have tried; but the speed at which they grow angry varies inversely to their fury once they have been roused. The entirety of their race lives beneath a mountain, out of which they have carved a city the size of a small kingdom...by hand. At their disposal is a strength that would put any four men to shame. I heard a tale of a princeling of Utel, a second son that sought to create himself a kingdom among the Grey Spires. I suppose when faced with his lifestyle being dependent solely on the whim of his older, inheriting, brother, he thought the anger of the Fair Folk was an acceptable risk. He was wrong. The little princeling took ten thousand men to the gates of Drunmarch; only those wise enough to flee before the thousand or so Dwarven home guard survived. At any rate, the prince never did need to worry about his inheritance."

Hollis shook his head. "I am suddenly glad I am not Uteli."

"Their ire has faded; but for a hundred years the flow of steel stopped and any man who dare lay a foot upon the Grey Spires would suffer the same fate as the prince's mighty army. Slow to anger, slow to forgive."

Like an itch at the back of his skull, a feeling of unease touched Hollis's senses before he heard the soft sound of leather on sand. He raised his hand, curling it into a fist before touching his ear and indicating the darkness. From the tilt of Aristoi's head and the woman's scowl, the gesture was unnecessary. "Tell me more about the Fair Folk. What changed their opinion of outsiders?" Hollis continued to speak as he shifted against the broken stone arch, his right-hand dipping smoothly into his boot, retrieving the knife sheathed there.

"Eventually, the greed of the few overcame the anger of the many." Aristoi was clearly more focused on the darkness outside their firelight than her words. "As it always does." Her spear continued to stir the ashes of the fading fire. "Although they are slow to forget, the influx of human wealth bought a good deal of forgiveness."

Hollis nodded slowly, his eyes straining to make out a trio of figures fifty yards behind the woman; they were only deeper patches of shadow in the desert night. "When it comes to greed, it would seem that we are not so different, human and dwarf." He scratched the skin beneath his eye with three fingers of his left hand as he nodded ever so slightly towards the approaching figures. A burning pain raced along the back of his freshly set hand, causing his entire forearm to erupt in a crimson cloud of agony. He winced at the suddenness and intensity of the sensation, and his comrade visibly frowned.

"It would certainly seem that way," Aristoi agreed as she tapped four fingers of her own left hand against her chest. She leaned back against the palm tree as she gripped again the shaft of her broad bladed spear.

Hollis felt the intoxicating mix of fear and excitement rise in his chest, old friends both. With his knife gripped in his right hand; he cautiously flexed the fingers of his left to coax some feeling other than agony into it. The figures behind Aristoi were now within thirty yards and were beginning to fan out in an obvious effort to flank the woman. He had to assume that the four behind him had similar plans. There *was a slim possibility that these men were simply being cautious and meant them no harm; but that possibility grew slimmer by the moment. The thief placed the knife onto his lap, adjusting his grip from hilt to blade with one smooth motion as he indicated himself and the area behind his comrade.*

The Kieli nodded, tightening her grip on the dark wood.

With a swiftness that surprised Stephen as much as the men surrounding them in the darkness, Hollis rolled to his feet, his right hand becoming a blur as he did so. The left most figure disappeared, a sickening gurgle the only evidence of his position. Before the man's dying gasps reached his ears, the thief had drawn his short sword and moved past a rising Aristoi.

His comrade's hands firmly gripped her spear as she rotated her body, using the weapon as a pivot point to rise with astonishing speed. She continued her spin, bringing the weapon to bear on the men that a moment ago had been approaching Hollis's unprotected back. The movement coaxed a soft hum from the broad head of the spear, but the sound hung in the air, becoming deeper and richer as Aristoi closed the distance between herself and the four men in the darkness. The hum formed itself into a wordless tune emanating not from the weapon, but from deep within the woman's chest.

Hollis now understood why the spear had been so important to the Kieli woman. In her homeland, magic was practiced differently than in the North. Owing to their tradition of oral history, songs there held knowledge...the knowledge of untold generations before them. A group of men and women, led by the Herald known as the Branded, took that to its natural progression. Rather than the words and gestures that were used by thaumaturges north of the Expanse, the Songspear's bent the forces of the universe through songs of power passed down to them from their ancestors. The puissance of Aristoi's words marked her as a member of that elite group.

The thief saw the effect the deep, haunting tone had upon the remaining pair he faced. Their movements, having become more tentative as their comrade died, choking on his own blood, now came to a

195

stop. He could fell some of his own confidence wavering as the sound seemed to settle into his bones. In another few seconds, the feeling had faded from him as he closed upon the nearer of the two. The man was wearing boiled leather armor and was armed with a Granatyrian longsword. Hollis's ivory hilted Uteli sword surrendered the length advantage to his opponent's weapon, but its responsiveness mated with the thief's own reflexes easily overcame that handicap. Before Hollis shook off the effect of the building melody rumbling forth from Aristoi's chest, he was inside his guard and pressing down onto him hard. The man worked his straight bladed weapon deftly, his two-handed grip lending it a measure of dexterity that a one-handed one would not offer. To his dismay, he required every ounce of it.

Aristoi was standing in the middle of a circle of leather-clad assailants, the rumbling hum still hanging in the air. Her spear probed the space between herself and her four attackers, as she slowly backpedaled to keep the quartet from flanking her completely. They kept their distance, seemingly confident on the fact that eventually, the Kieli would find herself on less sure footing or make a misstep, allowing them to close the circle.

As it turned out, they should have focused less on her spear and more on the melody she wove around her. Hollis could not place when the foreboding notes morphed into the words that oozed from her lips like honey from a hive. He heard each word sung clearly, although they fled from his mind as soon as they reached his ears. The thief knew magic when he heard it.

Those words fell upon one of the attackers moving to close the circle around Aristoi like physical things, his shoulders visibly slumping as their weight settled upon him. It was this man, not the Songspear, who stumbled, the two feet of steel tipping the spear that freed him from the weight of the Kieli's words. As the sand greedily drank his opponent's blood, the tempo of her words increased. They moved from the slow, methodical dirge to a staccato, almost frantic allegro as her movements mirrored the rhythm. Aristoi sprang forward in a rush, with her spear leading the way. The swordsman in her path quickly reversed direction, *his sword parrying furiously to ward off the spear's deadly steel-laden kiss. He was too busy preventing the weapon from finding a home in his gut to notice that that where his feet had glided across the hard-packed sand, now its accommodating surface flowed over the toes of his boots. Each time he lifted a foot, the sand was more reluctant to release it.*

Hollis's nearest opponent tied his blade against the hilt of his own sword. His left hand itched to drive a knife into the man's ribs but he could tell from the burning that echoed along his palm and forearm that there was little chance he could grip a knife much less exert enough pressure to drive it home through flesh and muscle. But instead he stomped his heel hard down on the man's foot and cleared his sword from his opponent, allowing his elbow to lead. To his credit, the man attempted to pull away, avoiding a blow to his chin, although the point of Hollis's elbow connected solidly with his forehead, opening a nasty, although superficial wound above his right eye. The wound bled almost immediately. A slow smile came to his lips as Hollis rotated to his left, attempting to remain in the field of the soon to be compromised vision as the man's companion entered the fray.

Hollis continued his rotation until he faced his opponents head on while thrusting towards the man with blood streaming into his eye. His intention was to keep him too busy defending himself to properly wipe the crimson river from his face. It did not take the man's comrade long to realize Hollis's plan of action, at which point he pressed the attack on the thief. He waited until Hollis once again stabbed at his bloody companion before swinging high and fast, seeking Hollis's throat. It was not until he had committed that he realized the thief's thrust was a great deal of noise and very little substance and the voracity of his attacks was more a function of his half blind opponent's over reactions than the attack itself. Unable to reverse his momentum, the man impaled himself on the broad blade of Hollis's short sword as he disengaged from his feint and brought it to bear in half the space of a breath. He moved past his critically wounded foe, instinctively pushing the man from his weapon with his free hand. His own vision dimmed as the agony in his broken hand screamed to life once more.

197

By the time Aristoi reached the border of the greedy sand, her current opponent had sunk to his mid-calf in it. He simply could not move deftly enough to avoid the spear's deadly touch. Her first thrust bisected the man's hip, cutting through flesh and muscle with equal ease. The second thrust was to his chest as he fell and surely sealed the man's fate; although the Songspear followed it up with a third as her opponent sank into the continually deepening sand. Aristoi turned to face the remaining pair of men as the desert claimed the body as its own.

Aristoi spoke a single, unrecognizable word. It hung in the air as the sand surrounding the quickly cooling body of her foe returned to the hardpack conditions it had been moments before. His grave would forever remain unmarked, untended and ungrieved. The word began to ungulate, the sound pulsing slowly at first. The two men closed upon the Songspear with renewed urgency, giving the area before her a wide berth. Aristoi turned and took a single step back onto the now firm sand as she brought her spear to bear upon her pair of opponents.

Hollis shook his hand slowly, as if he could shake free the pain that reverberated there, his focus wavering for a moment. That lapse in attention was all his half blind opponent needed to take the initiative. His opponent wiped the blood from his eyes quickly before launching a pounding assault with his Granatyrian sword. The weapon's superior length and weight pushed the thief back onto his heels, his short sword meeting and redirecting the force of the larger sword. The first of two vicious overhead slashes drove Hollis's blade to the side; the second opened a long but shallow gash along his left forearm as he dove out of its path. Without conscious thought, he tried rolling to his feet, using that same arm as leverage. The burning pain of the laceration combined with the ever-present throb of his broken hand caused it to give under him, although he struggled slowly to his knees.

The man was on him in a second, raising his blade for a third, inevitably fatal swing. Gritting his teeth against the inevitable pain, Hollis cupped his hand and pistoned his arm forward through the hard pack. He scraped less sand than he had intended for, but as his entire arm dissolved into agony, the small amount he cupped in his palm arched through the air and into his opponent's surprised eyes. Putting the pain in his arm out of his mind, he launched himself at his momentarily blind foe. The two men fell to the sand as the thief drove the point of his broad bladed sword into the leather clad man's midsection again and again. He stabbed him an additional two times before he realized he was pressing an unnecessary advantage against a corpse.

Aristoi swung her spear from side to side, attempting to keep both men at bay as she seemed to try to shake off the fatigue that comes with spellcasting. Hollis had seen Marcus suffer from the same exhaustion on more than one occasion. He saw her draw breath, as if to sing, but waver as no doubt her strength continued to wane.

As the gazelle feels the cold hands of inevitability settle upon it as the pride hems it in, so too did the shadow of dread fall upon the Songspear. She thrust her spear at the man to her left as he became too bold. The man danced backwards, only taking a scratch to his leading leg, but the man to her right pressed in, forcing Aristoi to give ground or face the keen edge of his blade. She slashed to her right, halting an advance from that side, only to have the opponent on her left force her back again. The two men fell into a comfortable rhythm, each one swooping in as the other defended against ever weakening attacks from Aristoi's spear. Her mouth pulled taut into a grimace; that grimace turned upwards as she saw a shape as quiet as a shadow sliding across the sand. Its left hand was held tight against its midsection; but in its right a short, broad blade reflected the pale moonlight.

Some men would hesitate to stab another man in the back, denying him the chance to defend himself. Hollis was not one of those men. So intent upon his prey was the man in front of the thief that he neither saw nor heard his approach. The thief felt Stephen's consciousness cringe as his blade entered his opponent's lower back, just below the kidney at a forty-five-degree angle. Hollis and his reflection felt the sword scrape against vertebrae as it pierced both lung and heart. He allowed his wrist to bend as the man fell to the ground, his own weight pulling him free of the weapon.

The man's partner turned, his eyes wide as the man's death rattle filled the air around him. He took a step back, trying to face Hollis without losing sight of Aristoi; but his moment of indecision cost him his life as the weary Songspear drove two feet of steel into his belly, knocking him from his feet with the violence of the thrust. Before he could struggle free of the spear tip, Hollis finished him with a thrust of his own between neck and collarbone.

Hollis squinted into the darkness surrounding their camp, verifying that no further threats loomed there. He could made out the single retreating figure a hundred yards beyond the firelight. Taking a quick accounting of Aristoi's labored breathing and his own aching hand, Hollis decided that giving chase to one figure with such a lead would be folly. "We missed one," he stated slowly, nodding towards the west.

Aristoi sighed softly, trying to catch her breath, "Very little we can do about it now, I suppose."

"Indeed." Hollis bent down to wipe his sword clean on the cloak of a fallen man. A bulging purse caught his eye, "Although, I believe we are compensated for our evening's labors." He held the jingling leather burden aloft.

The Kieli woman used the haft of her spear to roll another man onto his back and tap the pouch at his waist. "At least there is that."

The thief opened the pouch and poured its contents into his hand, by the combined fire and moonlight, he realized that neither the men nor their coinage hailed from Oenigh. The pouches were filled with round Granatyrian silver Nobles and gold Imperials, not the square silver Sultans and gold Raja of the desert city. "The good news is that we most likely have escaped the Emir's justice for the time being." He tossed one of the silver coins to his companion. "The bad news is that his justice may be the least of our worries."

"From bandits?"

Hollis shook his head slowly. "These men were too well armed...too well paid for bandits." He rolled a gold coin along the knuckles of his right hand, making the light dance on its surface. "Bandits' pouches are filled with the spoils of whatever victims they come across. One *would expect a hodge podge of coins from every kingdom. These men were paid in Granatyr silver and a lot of it...silver that they have not had the opportunity to spend yet."*

"Not bandits...Mercenaries. But why would they be in the Expanse? Why would they have ambushed us? The paltry coins in our purses were surely not worth the risk."

Frowning, he said, "They did not just happen upon us and our money was not their objective." Dropping the coins in his own purse, Hollis continued, "They struck at the target or targets that they had meant to...that they had been paid to." He regarded his comrade for a moment, "Anything you want to tell me?"

Aristoi shook her head slowly. "No...certainly not about these men. I have only briefly passed through the Stewardship and certainly made no enemies who would be willing to pay Granatyrian silver for my head. You?"

"I have made plenty of enemies, some of which have the means to hire sell swords; but none that would go to so much effort." He flipped the gold coin into the air, watching it arc into the moonlight before deftly snatching it again. "That means we are missing something."

"A big something, by all accounts."

He nodded, "We should be to Drunmarch by sundown tomorrow. Perhaps my friends may have a missing piece or two. Are you sure you want to continue to walk by my side? Tonight, you repaid any debt you may owe, at least in my mind."

Aristoi shook her head, "Perhaps in yours, Hollis. In mine, however, there is still a balance owed. I continue to walk as long as there is a road before us."

Hollis shrugged. "Suit yourself."

It took them an hour to gather the bodies together, properly search and sort the belongings of the men who had fallen. Aristoi burned the bodies as Hollis replenished their stores from those of the dead. Both felt the weariness of the day compounded by that of the battle settle upon them; but neither could sleep. When the sun rose, silently, they began travelling east.

~

Just before noon on the second day, they came upon the first Dwarven sentries. Their day's travel was through narrow, high walled switchbacks that seemed to meander aimlessly through the approach to Drunmarch itself. The four dwarves were simply there as they turned a corner, as if by magic. Three sat upon low rocks and the fourth stood before them, seemingly amid a story. They must have been speaking Dwarven, because neither Aristoi nor Hollis could understand a word they said.

Effortlessly switching to the Trade Tongue, the leader turned to face them. His snow-white beard partially hid a wide smile, "Good day, travelers. May I inquire as to your business in the Stone City?"

Each Dwarf stood just shy of five feet tall but easily carried Hollis's mass on this abbreviated frame. Their arms were easily the diameter of one of the thief's legs, ending in a beefy hand. He wondered how such stubby fingers and thick palms could be used to practice the fine craftsmanship the Fair Folk were known for. While they all possessed thick beards of varying lengths, there was no more than a dusting of hair on their any of their heads. All of this, Hollis took in stride, as they were common in the descriptions of the Dwarven race. What took him off guard was the softness of his voice. Although it was a deep, bass rumble that emulated from within the leader's barrel chest, it seemed to never rise above a whisper. The thief felt the words more than heard them. Aristoi nudged him carefully as the Fair Folk spoke again.

"What do you seek within the Kingdom of Drunmarch, my friends?" the Dwarf repeated.

Hollis recovered quickly. "Two comrades of mine set out for Drunmarch from Oenigh perhaps two months ago. We were..." He smirked in the Songspear's direction before continuing. "...Delayed. We were hoping to reunite with them."

"Were your friends members of a caravan? Traders perhaps?"

Hollis shook his head. "No. They were here on personal business."

He raised a bushy eyebrow. "Is that so? That business would be?"

Hollis responded smoothly, "Personal."

The Dwarf shrugged lightly, "Suit yourself. Two months is a long time for an outsider to remain in Drunmarch. How can you be certain that they remain within its depths?"

"I am not, to be completely honest. Perhaps you can aid me in that regard."

"Perhaps, perhaps not. Men come and go with great frequency. Despite the variations in..." He nodded toward Hollis's dark-skinned companion. "...shading, they tend to blend into one another."

"If you had seen them, you would remember. The younger of the two is a half breed; he has the golden hair of his mother and the sharp ears of his father."

The Dwarf scowled for a moment and then said, "A half elf? It is true; I would remember one like this, had I come across him."

One of the other Fair Folk spoke up, his rumble of a voice less deep and more passionate, "I was with the group that brought the half man into the city a few months back." His beard was short but thick, no more than an inch in length although it fully covered his chin and cheeks.

The leader spoke a few words of question in the language the two shared. The younger Dwarf's reply was short but adamant. His elder turned back to Hollis, "We know of your comrades. We will bring you into the Stone City."

A feeling of calm filled Hollis as he watched the interplay between the two Dwarves. Although he did not speak their language, he could almost understand what passed between the two. The sense of calm continued to fill him as he became lost in their conversation. Although the words were lost on him, their expressions and body language spoke volumes. He saw the sadness that hung in the younger Dwarf's eyes and felt the irritation through the elder's nervous scratching of his beard. At least, he'd thought so at first, but it was not irritation at all. Was it fear? Not quite, but unease to be sure.

The leader turned to his companions, speaking to them in their language; they each rose from their stone seats and gathered their things from the ground near it. None of them met Hollis's eyes. The

203

youngest spoke again, his words tinged with sadness, he was met with a sharp command from the leader. The older Dwarf turned to Hollis, "Follow us. We will be inside by nightfall." He also would not meet Hollis's gaze.

Hollis had always had a way with people, a knack for sizing up what it was their hearts most desired or most feared, but this was different. The tiny cues that once may have been beyond his notice now were spread before him like a flower. As suddenly as the calm understanding had come upon him, it faded. As the feeling faded, he felt l his heart rise in his throat.

"Is there something I should know?"

The leader nodded. "Yes; but you will not hear it from me." His eyes met Hollis's for a moment. "I am truly sorry." He turned and joined his comrades. "We have a good deal of distance to travel if we are to reach the gates before dark."

CHAPTER SEVENTEEN
A FORLORN CONCLUSION

Aristoi watched Hollis pace when they waited in the empty audience chamber. He lost track of how many times he had crossed the room before she extended the butt of her spear to gently halt his momentum, "Wearing a trough in the stone will do no one any good, my friend." The thief's eyes shifted from the floor to the wooden shaft. They slowly traveled along its surface, settling on the brown depths of the Songspear's own. There was no humor in Hollis's gaze; it was simply empty. She let the spear's end drop to the floor once more, "As you will, Northerner; but blame me not when the soles of your boots are thin enough to read through."

Hollis's frown deepened for a moment, but his trance was broken, "What keeps them? We have been here for hours."

"Less than half that," Aristoi corrected softly, nodding to the 'sky light' above them. "The sun is just barely setting now."

Hollis himself wondered at how even though they were at least fifty yards below the mountain; the dwarves were able to bring in light from outside. "Seems like longer," was all he said as he looked up at the glass panel above them. Like on the slopes outside the city, a strange calm settled upon him. Gone for the moment was any concern outside that immediately before him. He saw that the glass hung below an image of the dusk sky; but that view was tilted ever so slightly toward the front of the room. His eyes scanned the edge of the glass and found a slight lip on one end. A small, satisfied smile came to his lips as he muttered, "Mirrors."

Hollis felt Stephen's consciousness inside his mind again. It was then, as the calm faded and his reflection's concern for Alan and Mike... Ren and Rhyzzo...came flooding back, that he realized that Aristoi was staring at him. She had been speaking the entire time. "Pardon?" he asked.

The Kieli scowled at him "I said you are beginning to cause me to worry. If your friends are indeed still here, it does not bode well that we were not brought to them directly. If they have sinned in some way and we are being called to task for their actions, both of us will need to be at the peak of our wits to find a way out of it...and this place." Hollis remembered that the Songspear had business within Drunmarch but assumed that she stayed by his side out of her sense of duty.

He shook his head in dismissal. "If they meant us harm, they would not have allowed us to keep our weapons." He indicated the spear that the Kieli casually rested in the crook between shoulder and chest. "It is much worse, I fear. If Ren and Rhyz were in trouble, they would simply have denied even giving them entrance. Something has happened to them; our escorts basically told us as much."

Aristoi tilted her head. "You speak Dwarven?"

"Of course not. It was plain as day on their faces...in their actions."

"Was it?"

"If you know what to look for."

The Songspear squinted at him, "And you do...know what to look for?"

Hollis brushed aside the question with a casual shrug of his shoulders, and by extension the increasing unease with his fits of understanding., "Apparently."

Aristoi cocked her head, as if preparing to press the point, but the scrape of stone on stone drew both of their attention. A slight Dwarf shuffled through the door, flanked by two armed guards. He was a full hand below five feet and looked as if he weighed no more than a hundred and fifty pounds; this made him positively scrawny for one of the Fair Folk.

"You may call me Luciius. I am sorry to have kept you waiting." He approached the two men, his guards stopping a polite distance away. "There was much debate as to who would be best suited to discuss these matters with you."

Hollis interrupted, "Which matters are those?"

Nonplused, Luciius continued, "As the one entrusted with the care of your companion, it was decided that I would be the most appropriate."

"Care of? What happened?"

The Dwarf held up a stubby finger, "My friend, alacrity and under-standing are seldom boon travelling companions." Hollis squinted at him but kept his tongue. "It is best that we start at the beginning." He began walking towards the door he had emerged through a moment ago, "Please follow me and trust that once our walk is done, all of the questions you entered with will be answered." The thief nodded and turned to follow as Luciius continued in his slow, breathy drawl, "That is not to say that their resolution will not spur further inquiry."

The two guards fell in behind Hollis and Aristoi, still maintaining a comfortable distance from the two of them. The corridor beyond the door was softly lit by globes affixed to the stone walls; inside each was a small blue flame capping a brass tube of some sort. Hollis recognized them in Stephen's memories as similar to 19th century gas lights; despite it being technology two centuries old for his reflection, the thief still marveled at the concept. The corridor itself was level and intricately carved from the grey rock of the mountain, although it was obviously smooth from use.

"Your comrades approached the gates on the 6th of Narsfree, requesting entry. Much like yourselves, they claimed to be in search of a lost comrade." Luciius spoke slowly, almost as if he were tasting each word individually. The Dwarf's lack of urgency irritated Hollis to no end; but he held his protests for the time being.

"They claimed to be in search of a Man known to us, one Alexei

207

Silvermoon." Ren's letter had said he was in search of his father., According to Stephen, so was Alan. He was reflected when he entered Drunmarch. "Lord Silvermoon was a member of ... "

Hollis interrupted, "I am familiar with him," with more fervor than he had intended.

The Dwarf regarded him coolly for a moment before continuing, "The Home Guard was unaware of Lord Silvermoon's presence in the Stone City; but to be thorough, messengers were dispatched to verify that he was not within Drunmarch. Your comrades were resolved to wait and found lodgings in the West Gate Tavern." The corridor opened into a large chamber, the ceiling of which was thirty feet above their heads if it was an inch. A ledge ran around its circumference, with five corridors leading from it, like spokes on a wheel. A banister was carved from the stone itself, preventing unfortunate falls from the walkway. I was obvious to Hollis that Aristoi was as amazed at the level of detail in the stonework. The vertical railings themselves were no wider than the thief's thumb with bas reliefs carved into them the size of his pinky nail.

Luciius led them halfway around the chamber as he continued, "Drunmarch is very sizable, so it regrettably took nearly three days for the Entrance Masters to confirm that he was, indeed, not within our borders. An apprentice was sent to inform your comrades of such. The Inn Master of the West Gate Tavern does not remember either of them leaving their rooms; but when the apprentice called for them, they did not respond." He turned into a new corridor that appeared very much like the one they had just left.

"He, of course, fetched the Inn Master." The Dwarf turned to regard Hollis, "You must understand that we take the privacy of our visitors very seriously. It is the height of impropriety to barge into a chamber that has been rented in good faith." The thief nodded quickly, resisting the urge to hurry Luciius's narrative. "There was some discussion as to whether or not to press the issue. We sincerely regret the delay, hindsight being what it is."

Feeling a sense of dread rise in his throat, Hollis blurted out, "What happened?" The corridor ended in a staircase that wound around another massive chamber. Hollis could not make out anything more than vague shapes at the bottom. The gaslights here were replaced by torches held in iron sconces and the scent of burnt pitch and incense hung in the air like wet wool, heavy and sodden.

Luciius stopped and turned to face him. "I was called for immediately; but sadly, there was nothing that could be done for him." The Dwarf took Hollis's hand in his beefy one, the torchlight glinting in his eyes. "Your companion had passed beyond my skill to aid him before I arrived. I knew him not; but please believe that my heart aches for his loss."

Through the shock and confusion, Hollis see the Dwarf's sincerity in his tear-filled eyes. He repeated, "What happened?"

"Alacrity and understanding are seldom—"

"—Boon traveling companions," Hollis interrupted, "You mentioned that. What happened to Renthroas and Rhyzzo?"

Aristoi laid her hand on his shoulder, squeezing lightly before speaking, "Pardon my interruption, but Luciius, you said 'him', not 'they'. Both of his companions were not lost?" Hollis nodded shallowly in gratitude.

Luciius shook his head, "They found the half elf in the chamber, with no sign of his comrade."

Before he could continue, Hollis snapped, "Rhyzzo. Renthroas. What happened to them?" He squeezed the Dwarf's hand harder than he had intended.

Luciius seemed to not notice but extricated his hand with far less effort than the thief would have expected. "The Home Guard was summoned, of course, and the Western Gate shut within moments. His captors tried to hide from us, but none may keep hidden from the Fair Folk within the Stone City. Each of us knows Drunmarch as we know our own minds. They fought to keep your human comrade from us, but we take hospitality very seriously and are not easily dissuaded." He frowned sharply. "I do fear that some of the Home Guard practiced a little more enthusiasm than was strictly necessary. None of those who held your companion survived to be questioned." He turned and led the men down the staircase after pulling a torch from the wall, "I wish to offer my apologies a second time."

Hollis followed along as if in a trance; Aristoi engaged the dwarf in conversation to give her comrade a chance to compose himself. "Rhyzzo is safe then?"

He saw Luciius's head bob. "He is indeed, although, I fear that the circumstances of his abduction may have affected him. We took him in, of course, as it was a lapse in our hospitality that led to the situation in the first place." As they reached the base of the stairs, the light shed by the Dwarf's torch brought the nearest shapes into clarity. Beautifully carved, the short, squat pillars stretched into the shadows like a miniature stone forest. They were grave markers.

Hollis knelt on the freshly turned earth before a pillar like those that surrounded it. The only thing that differentiated it from the ones around it were the words 'Renthroas Halfborn' carved among the flowing characters that he assumed was the Dwarven language. Even amid the crushing sadness that sat upon his heart like the mountain in which they stood, the thief marveled again at how the blunt, thick fingers could manage the delicate loops and fine detail in each of the letters before him. Even though his friend's name was written in the same hand, the written form of Trade Tongue appeared awkward and out of place among them.

Both his memories and those of Stephen flooded his consciousness. His recollections were of Renthroas; child of two races but a member of neither community. Hollis remembered watching the scrawny, stubborn boy grow into a talented, quick witted and compassionate man. His heart could have held no more pride or love for him if he were the thief's own son. He heard his wry chuckle as if his friend was standing beside him now. Although it was the closest the half elf came to true laughter, it was full of warmth and humor, nonetheless. If he closed his *eyes, he saw his cherubic face framed by a halo of golden hair, too wild and unruly to be subdued by cord or ribbon. Despite the tears that threatened to rush down his cheeks, a soft smile came to his lips with the thought.*

The second rush of memories was alien to him; but felt familiar all the same. Stephen's memories of Alan mingled with his own. He saw in his mind's eye a boy of no more than twelve frowning down at a table studying the clutter of paper and dice that covered it. He remembered how that same chubby face thinned as he grew, transitioning from raptly listening crouched at the top of the stairs to sitting around the table as an equal. He saw the look of pride on the boy's father's face when he first made honor roll; it was a pride that reverberated in his own heart. Memories of late nights spent agonizing over his marriage were only made bearable by the unwavering support of best friend, despite the decade difference in their ages.

As the days passed, it was becoming harder to tell the difference between himself and Stephen that he felt as if he were burying Alan for a second time. In this moment, beset on all sides by his loss, it was nearly impossible to tell where he ended, and his reflection began. Beneath it, simmered an anger that warmed his belly. Someone was responsible for his friend's death, both of their deaths. His anger was intensified by the fact that he could not vent his fury upon their murderers, slain by dwarves more possessed by honor than sense; but deep inside, he knew that while the hands that took his friends from him were beyond his reach, those truly responsible were certainly not in that Drunmarch corridor that day.

Aristoi watched Hollis pace when they waited in the empty audience chamber. He lost track of how many times he had crossed the room before she extended the butt of her spear to gently halt his momentum, "Wearing a trough in the stone will do no one any good, my friend." The thief's eyes shifted from the floor to the wooden shaft. They slowly traveled along its surface, settling on the brown depths of the Songspear's own. There was no humor in Hollis's gaze; it was simply empty. She let the spear's end drop to the floor once more, "As you will, Northerner; but blame me not when the soles of your boots are thin enough to read through."

Hollis's frown deepened for a moment, but his trance was broken, "What keeps them? We have been here for hours."

"Less than half that," Aristoi corrected softly, nodding to the 'sky light' above them. "The sun is just barely setting now."

Hollis himself wondered at how even though they were at least fifty yards below the mountain; the dwarves were able to bring in light from outside. "Seems like longer," was all he said as he looked up at the glass panel above them. Like on the slopes outside the city, a strange calm settled upon him. Gone for the moment was any concern outside that immediately before him. He saw that the glass hung below an image of the dusk sky; but that view was tilted ever so slightly toward the front of the room. His eyes scanned the edge of the glass and found a slight lip on one end. A small, satisfied smile came to his lips as he muttered, "Mirrors."

Hollis felt Stephen's consciousness inside his mind again. It was then, as the calm faded and his reflection's concern for Alan and Mike... Ren and Rhyzzo...came flooding back, that he realized that Aristoi was staring at him. She had been speaking the entire time. "Pardon?" he asked.

The Kieli scowled at him "I said you are beginning to cause me to worry. If your friends are indeed still here, it does not bode well that we were not brought to them directly. If they have sinned in some way and we are being called to task for their actions, both of us will need to be at the peak of our wits to find a way out of it...and this place." Hollis remembered that the Songspear had business within Drunmarch but assumed that she stayed by his side out of her sense of duty.

He shook his head in dismissal. "If they meant us harm, they would not have allowed us to keep our weapons." He indicated the spear that the Kieli casually rested in the crook between shoulder and chest. "It is much worse, I fear. If Ren and Rhyz were in trouble, they would simply have denied even giving them entrance. Something has happened to them; our escorts basically told us as much."

Aristoi tilted her head. "You speak Dwarven?"

"Of course not. It was plain as day on their faces...in their actions."

"Was it?"

"If you know what to look for."

The Songspear squinted at him, "And you do...know what to look for?"

Hollis brushed aside the question with a casual shrug of his shoulders, and by extension the increasing unease with his fits of understanding., "Apparently."

Aristoi cocked her head, as if preparing to press the point, but the scrape of stone on stone drew both of their attention. A slight Dwarf shuffled through the door, flanked by two armed guards. He was a full hand below five feet and looked as if he weighed no more than a hundred and fifty pounds; this made him positively scrawny for one of the Fair Folk.

"You may call me Luciius. I am sorry to have kept you waiting." He approached the two men, his guards stopping a polite distance away. "There was much debate as to who would be best suited to discuss these matters with you."

Hollis interrupted, "Which matters are those?"

Nonplused, Luciius continued, "As the one entrusted with the care of your companion, it was decided that I would be the most appropriate."

"Care of? What happened?"

The Dwarf held up a stubby finger, "My friend, alacrity and understanding are seldom boon travelling companions." Hollis squinted at

216

him but kept his tongue. "It is best that we start at the beginning." He began walking towards the door he had emerged through a moment ago, "Please follow me and trust that once our walk is done, all of the questions you entered with will be answered." The thief nodded and turned to follow as Luciius continued in his slow, breathy drawl, "That is not to say that their resolution will not spur further inquiry."

The two guards fell in behind Hollis and Aristoi, still maintaining a comfortable distance from the two of them. The corridor beyond the door was softly lit by globes affixed to the stone walls; inside each was a small blue flame capping a brass tube of some sort. Hollis recognized them in Stephen's memories as similar to 19th century gas lights; despite it being technology two centuries old for his reflection, the thief still marveled at the concept. The corridor itself was level and intricately carved from the grey rock of the mountain, although it was obviously smooth from use.

"Your comrades approached the gates on the 6th of Narsfree, requesting entry. Much like yourselves, they claimed to be in search of a lost comrade." Luciius spoke slowly, almost as if he were tasting each word individually. The Dwarf's lack of urgency irritated Hollis to no end; but he held his protests for the time being.

"They claimed to be in search of a Man known to us, one Alexei Silvermoon." Ren's letter had said he was in search of his father., According to Stephen, so was Alan. He was reflected when he entered Drunmarch. "Lord Silvermoon was a member of... "

Hollis interrupted, "I am familiar with him," with more fervor than he had intended.

The Dwarf regarded him coolly for a moment before continuing, "The Home Guard was unaware of Lord Silvermoon's presence in the Stone City; but to be thorough, messengers were dispatched to verify that he was not within Drunmarch. Your comrades were resolved to wait and found lodgings in the West Gate Tavern." The corridor opened into a large chamber, the ceiling of which was thirty feet above their heads if it was an inch. A ledge ran around its circumference, with five corridors leading from it, like spokes on a wheel. A banister was carved from the stone itself, preventing unfortunate falls from the walkway. I was obvious to Hollis that Aristoi was as amazed at the level of detail in the stonework. The vertical railings themselves were no wider than the thief's thumb with bas reliefs carved into them the size of his pinky nail.

Luciius led them halfway around the chamber as he continued, "Drunmarch is very sizable, so it regrettably took nearly three days for the Entrance Masters to confirm that he was, indeed, not within our borders. An apprentice was sent to inform your comrades of such. The Inn Master of the West Gate Tavern does not remember either of them leaving their rooms; but when the apprentice called for them, they did not respond." He turned into a new corridor that appeared very much like the one they had just left.

"He, of course, fetched the Inn Master." The Dwarf turned to regard Hollis, "You must understand that we take the privacy of our visitors very seriously. It is the height of impropriety to barge into a chamber that has been rented in good faith." The thief nodded quickly, resisting the urge to hurry Luciius's narrative. "There was some discussion as to whether or not to press the issue. We sincerely regret the delay, hindsight being what it is."

Feeling a sense of dread rise in his throat, Hollis blurted out, "What happened?" The corridor ended in a staircase that wound around another massive chamber. Hollis could not make out anything more than vague shapes at the bottom. The gaslights here were replaced by torches held in iron sconces and the scent of burnt pitch and incense hung in the air like wet wool, heavy and sodden.

Luciius stopped and turned to face him. "I was called for immediately; but sadly, there was nothing that could be done for him." The Dwarf took Hollis's hand in his beefy one, the torchlight glinting in his eyes. "Your companion had passed beyond my skill to aid him before I arrived. I knew him not; but please believe that my heart aches for his loss."

Through the shock and confusion, Hollis see the Dwarf's sincerity in his tear-filled eyes. He repeated, "What happened?"

218

"Alacrity and understanding are seldom—"

"—Boon traveling companions," Hollis interrupted, "You mentioned that. What happened to Renthroas and Rhyzzo?"

Aristoi laid her hand on his shoulder, squeezing lightly before speaking, "Pardon my interruption, but Luciius, you said 'him', not 'they'. Both of his companions were not lost?" Hollis nodded shallowly in gratitude.

Luciius shook his head, "They found the half elf in the chamber, with no sign of his comrade."

Before he could continue, Hollis snapped, "Rhyzzo. Renthroas. What happened to them?" He squeezed the Dwarf's hand harder than he had intended.

Luciius seemed to not notice but extricated his hand with far less effort than the thief would have expected. "The Home Guard was summoned, of course, and the Western Gate shut within moments. His captors tried to hide from us, but none may keep hidden from the Fair Folk within the Stone City. Each of us knows Drunmarch as we know our own minds. They fought to keep your human comrade from us, but we take hospitality very seriously and are not easily dissuaded." He frowned sharply. "I do fear that some of the Home Guard practiced a little more enthusiasm than was strictly necessary. None of those who held your companion survived to be questioned." He turned and led the men down the staircase after pulling a torch from the wall, "I wish to offer my apologies a second time."

Hollis followed along as if in a trance; Aristoi engaged the dwarf in conversation to give her comrade a chance to compose himself. "Rhyzzo is safe then?"

He saw Luciius's head bob. "He is indeed, although, I fear that the circumstances of his abduction may have affected him. We took him in, of course, as it was a lapse in our hospitality that led to the situation in the first place." As they reached the base of the stairs, the light shed by the Dwarf's torch brought the nearest shapes into clarity. Beautifully carved, the short, squat pillars stretched into the shadows like a miniature stone forest. They were grave markers.

~

Hollis knelt on the freshly turned earth before a pillar like those that surrounded it. The only thing that differentiated it from the ones around it were the words 'Renthroas Halfborn' carved among the flowing characters that he assumed was the Dwarven language. Even amid the crushing sadness that sat upon his heart like the mountain in which they stood, the thief marveled again at how the blunt, thick fingers could manage the delicate loops and fine detail in each of the letters before him. Even though his friend's name was written in the same hand, the written form of Trade Tongue appeared awkward and out of place among them.

Both his memories and those of Stephen flooded his consciousness. His recollections were of Renthroas; child of two races but a member of neither community. Hollis remembered watching the scrawny, stubborn boy grow into a talented, quick witted and compassionate man. His heart could have held no more pride or love for him if he were the thief's own son. He heard his wry chuckle as if his friend was standing beside him now. Although it was the closest the half elf came to true laughter, it was full of warmth and humor, nonetheless. If he closed his eyes, he saw his cherubic face framed by a halo of golden hair, too wild and unruly to be subdued by cord or ribbon. Despite the tears that threatened to rush down his cheeks, a soft smile came to his lips with the thought.

The second rush of memories was alien to him; but felt familiar all the same. Stephen's memories of Alan mingled with his own. He saw in his mind's eye a boy of no more than twelve frowning down at a table studying the clutter of paper and dice that covered it. He remembered how that same chubby face thinned as he grew, transitioning from raptly listening crouched at the top of the stairs to sitting around the table as an equal. He saw the look of pride on the boy's father's face when he first made honor roll; it was a pride that reverberated in his own heart. Memories of late nights spent agonizing over his marriage were only made bearable by the unwavering support of best friend, despite the decade difference in their ages.

As the days passed, it was becoming harder to tell the difference between himself and Stephen that he felt as if he were burying Alan for a second time. In this moment, beset on all sides by his loss, it was nearly impossible to tell where he ended, and his reflection began. Beneath it, simmered an anger that warmed his belly. Someone was responsible for his friend's death, both of their deaths. His anger was intensified by the fact that he could not vent his fury upon their murderers, slain by dwarves more possessed by honor than sense; but deep inside, he knew that while the hands that took his friends from him were beyond his reach, those truly responsible were certainly not in that Drunmarch corridor that day.

Meandering amid that white hot, immediate anger, was a low and simmering one. Samantha had led Stephen to believe that Alan still lived. The more he thought about it, the more he was sure that she flat out told him that he was. She seemed so sure of herself...or at least she had appeared to be. If she were not so confident, he never would have...

A hand on his shoulder shook him from the depths of his own mind; it was Aristoi, "Northerner, the Dwarf is willing to take you to your friend, Rhyzzo. If you need more time ... "

He shook his head. "I know where to find him." He nodded to the stone that marked Ren's grave, "And he is surely not going anywhere." He tried to display humor that he was not feeling; but he knew by Aristoi's sad eyes that she saw through the charade.

"When you are ready, we will be waiting at the base of the stairs. Take the time you need; I will ask him about the history of the city again...That should be good for another hour or so..."

Hollis turned back to the grave, placing his hand flat upon the fresh earth. "I could not save you, my friend. I will bear that until I join you in the Hall of Dawn; but I swear that those who took you from me will dine there much before that." He clenched his fist, allowing the dirt to run through his fingers. "I swear it."

PART TWO

A LIFE UPON REFLECTION

"True heroism is remarkably sober, very undramatic. It is not the urge to surpass all others at whatever cost, but the urge to serve others at whatever cost."

-Arthur Ashe

CHAPTER EIGHTEEN
REFLECTION'S ACCORD

Luciius pushed on the edge of the heavy stone door and it swung open smoothly and without apparent effort. The room he revealed was dim but not quite dark, only lit by a few gaslights scattered around it. Equally scattered about the room were Dwarves. A few were seated at a low table playing some sort of game involving six sided tiles, while others were seemingly napping in overstuffed chairs. So lost in shadow was the far corner of the room that Hollis almost missed the slim figure sitting there.

The thief stepped past the Dwarf and out of the light cascading into the room from the corridor. He squinted, attempting to quickly adjust his eyes to the dimness of his new surroundings. Even as he did so, an excitement rose in him. Before his eyes identified the figure, his heart knew who sat there. He was at Rhyzzo's side in the space of two breaths.

The man did not react when Hollis called his name; nor did he even flinch when thief laid his hand upon his shoulder. He shook his friend's shoulder hard and called his name again with the same response. Hollis looked up quickly, his eyes seizing upon Luciius, "What is wrong with him?"

The Dwarf shook his head slowly, closing his own eyes, "I have said that I believe the shock of his capture and your half-born comrade's death had their effects upon him." "He was like this when the Home

Guard brought him to me. As far as I can tell, there is nothing physically wrong with him. He will walk where you lead him and eat what is put before him; but sadly, when left to his own devices, he simply sits quietly absorbed in his own thoughts."

Luciius approached the two humans, pausing only to whisper lightly in the ear of a dwarf that had taken interest in the situation. The heavily bearded observer returned to his game placidly. "At first we thought it was the Malaise. It is something that affects the Fair Folk when they do not have a task to devote their time to." He swept his hand to indicate the rest of the room. "It is a kind of depression that we can fall into once our purpose comes to an end. It falls most heavily upon artists and craftsman, less so upon those whose purposes are more fluid. I think it comes from..." The Dwarf stopped, clearly realizing the human was less concerned with the psychological issues of Dwarves than he was those of his companion. "We attempted to treat it as we would the Malaise; sadly, to no effect."

Hollis looked down at his friend, seeing the face of Mike in the slack expression of Rhyzzo. "Are you sure it is nothing chemical?" He frowned slightly as he realized there was no equivalent word in the Trade Tongue for chemical and he had instinctively used the English word. He clarified, "Perhaps a poison of some sort?"

Luciius shook his head, "We fed him Mole Weed immediately, followed by a week-long course of dried Prickle Sun. Neither prompted the least change."

Hollis knew that Mole Weed was a mushroom that had powerful anti-venom properties, like chotachand or mongoose plant that Stephen remembered reading about. Prickle Sun was new to the thief; but Stephen's memories held an image of Echinacea, which possessed some use as a natural antibiotic. He continued to be impressed by the Fair Folk's grasp of medicine, rudimentary though it might have been. "Will he respond to non-physical stimuli?" Again, he used the English word for which there was no translation. In response to Luciius' questioning look, he rephrased, "Does he respond to loud noises? Powerful Smells? Bright lights?"

The Dwarf shook his head, "We tried most of that, except for the scents. I had not thought of that. I really must..." He drew his attention back to the matter at hand, "No change. He reacts to prodding, eats when he hungers, sleeps when he is tired, relieves himself when he must; but other than that, he seems lost."

Hollis nodded absently, the back of his hand going to Rhyzzo's forehead. His friend did not react to the touch at all. The skin there was warm but not hot. His fingers found a pulse at his friend's wrist; it was strong and steady. Hollis thought he felt a hand at his own wrist; but when he looked down, there was nothing besides Rhyzzo's motionless form. "He is not running hot, nor does he have a quickened heartbeat."

Luciius shook his head. "Those were among the first things we checked...as I said, he seems to be in good condition besides the obvious."

The thief raised an eyebrow. "The obvious seems to be a fairly large besides..." He half felt a sharp pain in his shoulder; but it seemed so far away.

A cold feeling came over Stephen suddenly as he tried to calculate how many days he had spent in Taerh. He had almost forgotten that he shared time between the two places: Here and there. He felt the pain again and just out of range of his perception, he could almost hear someone shouting.

As he focused on it, the words became clear as the pain intensified in his arm. 'Stephen!'

He winced as she shrilly called his name again. Slowly, almost as if he were trying to claw his way out of a pit filled with cotton, he murmured, "Why are you shouting?" The pain in his arm intensified with staggering rapidity as his eyes flickered open. They went to Ronni's manicured nails digging deep impressions in the tender flesh of his bicep.

"I thought you were dead," she exclaimed as she hit him hard in the chest with the flat of her other hand. "What's wrong with you?"

The strike took him by surprise and elicited an exhalation of breath from him. His own right hand reached up and extricated his arm from her talon like grip; watching as the impressions reddened before his eyes. "Well, I am not dead. I can attest to that, at the very least."

She frowned as if something sour had taken up residence under her tongue, "Isn't this your on-call weekend for work?" She stood up from where she had been kneeling beside the couch, "If you lose this job, so help me ... "

He rubbed absently at his bicep. "Help you what?"

"What?"

"You were in the process of threatening me." Stephen sat up, flexing the fingers on his left hand as he continued to rub his arm with his right, "I am not working this weekend; but please continue."

A small smile must have come to his lips because she snapped, "I'll make your life miserable."

He could not help the chuckle that escaped his lips, "Miserable? What does that look like?" He swung his legs outward and placed his feet on the floor, "Perhaps you can let me know a little more vehemently how disappointed you are in me." He shrugged as he pushed himself to his feet, his head clearing quickly. "You are truly exemplary at it now, but I have faith you can step up your game."

She stopped, her mouth hanging open before she regained her composure, "Vehemently? Exemplary? Are you too good for contractions now? Who are you trying to impress?"

He laughed softly, realizing that Trade Tongue tended to be quite a bit more formal than was English and he had fallen into using its structure if not the language itself. "Obviously no one."

"Is something funny?"

"That's not the question you should be asking." He was going out of his way to use the contraction. It felt awkward in his mouth, as Trade Tongue did not contain that particular concept, "The question is, When's the last time we truly laughed, Ronni? I mean, put all the petty crap on the shelf for a while and just enjoyed ourselves?"

She pinched her face further. "There's nothing to laugh at, Stephen...no reason to enjoy ourselves. Your job is hanging on by a thread; with it hangs our life...our house, our marriage, our future." Ronni sighed and said, "Tell me, what's there to enjoy?"

Contrary to her intended effect, his smile only dimmed, "That's the point, my dear. That job kills me a little more every day. I do not ... don't pay the mortgage with money; I pay it with my soul. You work in that damned boutique because it makes you happy, even though you could and should contribute more to our *house ,our marriage, ,our future*, if you got off your ass and went back to accounting. For fuck's sake, they won't even give you full time. I work my fingers to the bone every day, to give you the liberty to find your joy, all while you are feeding off mine."

"A man provides for his family."

He stepped close to her, close enough that he could feel the heat of her breath on his neck, "That is right, I do." In his anger, he slipped into the more formal structure of Trade Tongue. "It is a sacrifice I would gladly make if you understood that...respected that; but you do not." His lips pulled back in a sneer of disgust. "Do you even know what goes on outside your reality television and perfect Rockwellian ideal? People have real issues...life and death issues that have nothing to do with your entitled little life."

"What do you know about life and death? You spend your time playing make believe like a little boy."

He turned to retrieve his duffel bag from the coffee table, "More than you ever will." When he turned back to her, she was silently staring daggers at him, "We can add it to the long list of things you have no idea about...starting with who or what I truly am."

She let out an enraged, formless yell and lunged at him. It took him by surprise; rather than shocking him into inaction, as was no doubt her intent, his reflexes took over. That was unfortunate for her. He hooked his left thumb under her right arm pit, exerting enough pressure on the nerve cluster found there to cause her to instinctively turn away from it. His right hand reached for a knife that was not there before he understood what had happened. He removed his hand from her arm as quickly as it had found itself there.

As he moved past her, he repeated, "...No idea."

Stephen regretted putting his hands on his wife, even in self-defense. He'd not raised his hand in malice nor had he harmed her; but something about the exchange left a bitter taste in his mouth. Too much time in Taerh had too sharply honed something inside him. Reflexes that kept him alive in Hollis's world did not serve him so well in his. He sighed as he realized how blended the edges of them had become. He no longer truly considered Taerh exclusively Hollis's and Earth exclusively his.

Truth be told, he felt much more at home in the vibrant air of the other world than he did breathing the pale air of his own. It occurred to him that he was less and less noticing the intensity of stimuli on Taerh; but instead only noticed how washed out everything was while awake. No fewer than twenty people had tried to end his life there in the few days he had been reflecting; but it was quickly becoming the only place he truly felt alive.

He was so lost in thought that he nearly missed the turn into the strip mall's parking lot. He forced his car into a lower gear, providing gentle pressure to the brake as he abruptly turned the wheel. As his car bumped into the lot, the car behind him displayed his displeasure through a long blaring blast of his horn.

Stephen lifted his hand in a gesture of apology, but the man had already sped away.

Stephen pulled his car between the painted lines of the parking spot and turned it off with a smooth twist of his wrist. Normally, an exchange such as that would have at least raised his heart rate; but his hands were steady and his thoughts clear. He noticed that the interior of the car was warming quickly as the air conditioner ceased to run. He sat in it for a moment, letting the heat wash over him and shook his head. Even the stifling heat was threadbare.

He turned in his seat to pull the duffel bag from the backseat floor into the passenger seat; as he began to sit back up again, he noticed the frosted glass door to Samantha's shop open. A man stepped out into the morning sun, shading his eyes against its glare. His instincts told him to remain hidden for a moment longer; the man couldn't have seen him as his eyes were no doubt still adjusting. He listened carefully.

Stephen could see the sidewalk clearly from his awkward position; but he was sure the man didn't notice him. He was thin almost to the point of absurdity. His tee shirt was draped across his frame like a scarecrow and his jeans, which seemed to hang from his hips, held there by some unknown force, pooled at his ankles around an oversized pair of thick soled black shoes. A pair of dead eyes were deep set above dark, bruise-like bags. His patchwork beard sprouted randomly from his chin and cheeks. Stephen took an immediate dislike to him, which he attributed to Hollis. Stephen, at his base, liked most people and was not known to be quick to judge anyone. His reflection, on the other hand, tended to size up a situation quickly and surely. This was not a situation that the thief felt good about. His suspicions were further intensified when the man tucked a pair of clear bags into the hip pocket of his jeans.

From the other pocket, the man drew a pack of cigarettes and a chrome lighter. He drew a cigarette from its depths and threw the pack on the roof of a dented Toyota Camry. He watched him smoking absently as he swiped casually on his phone, feeling more and more foolish by the moment. However, he didn't stir, even to adjust around the parking brake that was digging into his hip.

Stephen's side was burning by the time the man climbed into his car and pulled out of the parking lot. He sat up slowly, like a spring uncoiling until he was upright. His mind had nothing to do while he waited like a voyeur for the man to leave but contemplate what he had stowed in his pocket. It could have easily been marijuana; but Samantha did not strike him as a common drug dealer. She could have been for all he knew; but it was not the impression he had gotten from her. He wished he had gotten a closer look at the bags' contents; all he had seen was that it seemed to be a plant of some sort, green and leafy. Was it adder root?

He reached for the duffel bag; his hand poised above the cloth handles. For some reason, he was thinking better of bringing it in with him. He could always come out to get it should the contents be needed; but once she saw the bag, he could not deny having it with him. His thoughts turned to their last meeting; it occurred to him that he had provided most of the information, while she provided not much more than deflections. He swung the door open and stepped out into the morning, with the bag still on the passenger seat.

"I shall be right with you..." Samantha called from the back room as the bell above the door jingled softly.

"Take your time", Stephen responded, his eyes sweeping the shop. Flowers in various states of preparation lay on the counter. Several vases dominated the small tables scattered around the room. His senses were alive with the cloying mixture of fragrances and incense; the air seemed a physical thing it was so close around him. Not for the first time, he drew a comparison in his mind between the shop and Taerh.

"Ah, Stephen, what a surprise," the woman cooed as she parted the curtain that separated the back room from the shop proper.

His eyes dragged across the counter as his lips pulled into a smile, "I wanted to speak more about our shared interest." The smile froze on his face as he spotted a small stack of clear bags, lying amid a pile of smallish dark green leaves. A shiver ran through his spine; it *was* adder root. It took all his willpower to keep his shock from his face, "Did you have a chance to review the journals I left yesterday?"

She nodded lightly. "I took them home with me and read some of the older ones last night; but have come up with very little of use. Perhaps once I move on to the newer ones, the narrative will become clearer." She motioned him to follow and parted the curtain. "Were you able to peer into your reflection's memories last night?"

He followed her slowly, his eyes darting to the right as he passed by the counter. The bags indeed did lie beside a bundle of fresh adder root. He shrugged briefly, his mind still spinning. *Who was that man? Was she also providing him with mentorship in the ways of reflection? If so, why would she not mention someone who could possibly help him?*

One would think that two reflections working together in Taerh would be more effective than both working alone.

"Stephen?"

He lied without knowing why, "No, Ma'am. I tried but they just wouldn't come."

She clicked her tongue softly. "I told you not to try; that may be your problem."

"Perhaps. When I am in the moment, I think I get carried away. If I had someone with me to keep me grounded, maybe it would be easier." He was fishing a little bit. He watched her back as he walked through the curtain. He saw her tense slightly but relax immediately.

She sat in her high-backed chair before responding, "That, indeed, would be ideal; but sadly, besides you and your friends, I know of no others that have seen Taerh."

It seemed he was not the only one keeping the truth close to his chest; but he smiled to himself. Perhaps she had known more accomplished liars than Stephen; but obviously not more accomplished than Hollis. He felt his reflection's steady nerve settle on him. "That is truly too bad. You said that adder root demanded a cost you could no longer pay. What, exactly, does that mean?"

Annoyance crossed her features but then it melted into her normal kindly countenance. "Reflection splits the mind's focus. Adder root intensifies this effect to a great degree. Signals can get lost, leading to the rhythm of the heart becoming irregular or breathing to stop all together. It takes a physical toll like sleep-apnea on the reflecting party. I have had a few heart attacks over the last few years and one particularly bad stroke scare. I fear my next journey to Taerh will be my last."

A cold flash of panic washed through him, "Does it affect your other self?"

Samantha shook her head, "No. It is a function of the adder root, not the act of reflection itself."

Worry gnawed at Stephen's mind, *Could this just as easily happen to me?* "Is there anything that can be done to minimize the risk?"

She shrugged. "It is possible to reflect naturally, but it is unreliable. When not under the influence of adder root, the body tends to wake up if it is in peril. This makes it safer on all counts. While being under the effects of adder root, it is impossible to wake until the herb wears off."

Stephen nodded, finally understanding why Ronni had issues

with waking him that morning. "Are you able to reflect naturally?"

She shook her head. "I have not been able to do so for at least a decade."

"So, if you wanted to reflect, you would need to use the root."

She nodded, "...and that would seal my fate."

"I'm sorry, Samantha. That must be terrible."

She simply watched him beneath hooded eyes before speaking again, "That is why I am so interested in your time there."

He smiled lightly. "I imagine. What do you want to know?"

Her eagerness got the best of her for a heartbeat as she leaned forward, "Have you...I mean, has your reflection reached the Stone City yet?" She sat back, hoping to cover her excitement; he didn't let on that he'd noticed.

"Yes. It is a fantastic place; they are an amazing people."

"Were you able to find Alan?" Her mouth turned downwards as he inhaled to answer her question; but it was a split second too early. Stephen normally wouldn't have noticed; but Hollis did, so his reflection did as well.

An idea came to him quickly. It was a risk, but in an instant, he decided it was worth bearing a bit of his very real sadness. "Yes, as a matter of fact I did. Once I reached Drunmarch, I was told that he'd been killed by a group of men."

"I am so sorry; I truly had no idea when this started, I swear." Her response was too quick, too practiced. Stephen could feel Hollis's experience in the back of his mind. The only people that reacted so rapidly ... so smoothly were people who already knew the information you were supplying. Hollis had seen many people express condolences with this same fluidity; all of them were liars.

Stephen's stomach tightened when he thought of his friend lying still beneath that mountain; but he pushed it from his mind. He consciously forced himself to not lock eyes with her. The eyes held the portal to the soul; but a liar's true barometer was in the body language. Her hands remained relaxed, casually resting on the arms of her chair. Neither her posture nor demeanor changed as he made his revelation. He raised his eyes slowly, looking not into her own but at her face, as Hollis was trained. Rather than the widening of the eyes that signifies surprise, her lower eyelid was tight with a pair of defined lines between the brows. She had known of Alan's death before he stepped into her shop and was angry.

"You had no way of knowing. The men who killed Alan are dead; but Hollis is very close to discovering the identity of the person who was pulling their strings." He smiled sadly down at her, placing his hand over hers. "I have to thank you. Your faith in us finding him certainly buoyed my spirits despite the eventual outcome."

She broke eye contact as he saw small wrinkles form as one side of her mouth pulled up momentarily. Through Hollis's eyes, he saw that she wasn't feeling the sadness of Alan's death; rather she was struggling to hide her contempt. Stephen marveled at the experience of seeing the interaction through the eyes of his reflection.

"You are most welcome, of course. What of your other friend? Mike was his name, correct?"

"He is alive but nonresponsive. I may be alone in my search for Alan's murderer. I owe him that much at least. I would like to perhaps have the latest journal so I can study up a bit on his last few entries before tonight."

She shook her head. "I have given them to my friend in the city already. I could have them back for you in a few days. Do you think you can hold off until then?"

He smiled smoothly. "Of course. A few more days of planning can certainly not go amiss."

"I'm sure you said you had the journals at home? Could I have misheard you?" Stephen asked. *Why had she lied to him three times in as many minutes?* He was convinced she was sure that Alan was dead before he'd told her; she was clearly put back on her heels now that Stephen had led her to believe he would be pursuing his killers. He saw her eyes darting to the side table where her phone lay, when she thought he wasn't looking.

"I think you did, dear. They're with my friend, but you can have them soon."

He was tempted to press the matter; but resisted the urge. If he confronted her, he knew she would only deny it, perhaps by back-pedaling a bit. On the other hand, if he gave her enough rope to hang herself, he knew he would get to the root of her deception. Purposefully, he shifted his eyes down and to the left. "I will try again tonight to access Hollis's memories...or I should say not try again."

Samantha exhaled in relief; it was subtle, but he saw the relaxation in her shoulders and widening of her nostrils. "Good, dear. As I said, it is not easily explained; but you will get it." She laid her hand on his wrist and smiled at him. I It was the smile from the spider to the fly. "I have faith in you."

Every inch of him wanted to snatch his arm from her grasp; but he turned his gritted teeth into a smile of his own. "Thank you, Samantha. You have no idea how much that means to me."

CHAPTER NINETEEN
BETRAYER'S CLARITY

B y the time Stephen had pulled his car into the hospital parking lot, he'd calmed somewhat. His mind still reeled with the events in the flower shop, but he was thinking more clearly now. A quick glance at the clock told him it'd be two hours until hospital staff would admit him to see Mike. He opened the car's windows and pulled the journal he'd been reading from the duffel bag.

April 27, 2008

I came to my senses on horseback, riding hard. I saw Mika's back thirty yards ahead of me, bent low over the neck of her mount. To my right, rode Roger's double; I saw his knuckles were white from gripping the reins. In a rush, Silvermoon's memories of the intervening few days came back to me.

Hollis had reported seeing Haedren leaving the Inn two days prior. Mika, Ret and I left in pursuit, while George's double and Hollis remained behind to see if they could find any clues to what had befallen our friend in the Great Library. The priest had at most an hour lead on them us; but even though we had been riding as hard as our horses would allow and long into the night, they we had not been able to catch our comrade. Silvermoon had seen sign of his passage and every town we passed through claimed to see the lone rider, although he did not stop in any of them.

Each of us felt equal parts betrayed and confused. After his miraculous recovery in the Hall of Hand in Oizan, he had seemed a different person entirely. Hollis claimed Haedren had attacked him outside the Virgin Mermaid, ostensibly to keep him quiet. Silvermoon had significant history with the priest of Olm and never had he demonstrated devotion to anything besides the will of his god. Kind and generous, this change in him left all of us without explanation.

The next few days passed in a blur, the three of us only slept in fits while our horses recovered. My heart went out to the beasts, but something told me it was a necessity. As the sun colored the sky a glowing amber on the third day after coming to my senses, we charged around a bend in the road and there in the center was our lost comrade.

Ret pulled his horse to a stop through pure determination and upper body strength. The creature brayed in frustration and anger; but Haedren did not so much as flinch. He simply remained planted on the packed earth; his massive mace held in two hands before him. Gone was his ever-present tabard, adorned with the stylized chalice of Olm. In its place, he wore a simple leather jack over his chain mail hauberk.

Mika and I stopped our own horses with less violence and urgency than had Ret; she remained mounted while I leapt to the ground. My horse stomped anxiously, but I brought a small amount of balm to his fear with a kind hand. That hand never strayed far from where my bow was tied, unstrung across the saddle.

"Five days," Haedren began in a breathy low voice. "Five days you have harried my every step."

Ret dropped to the dirt road, pulling his sword from its scabbard. "That is because you run from us, Olmite."

His brow furrowed as the priest digested the Rangor's words before speaking slowly, "Do you have any concept of how little sense *that makes, Northman? You chase because I run...I run because you chase."*

"A little," Ret retorted, with a touch of self-consciousness.

I stepped up beside Roger's reflection. "You made an attempt on Hollis's life outside the inn." While it was clearly a statement, my tone was a question.

He nodded. "That I did. To be completely honest, the boy has always gotten under my skin. His conscience was too slow and his mouth too quick for my liking."

Mika spoke up, "So you tried to kill him?"

Haedren shrugged. "It seemed to be the appropriate course of action at the time." He took a moment to study each of us before continuing, "You would have been better served to have brought him and the spell caster."

Ret snorted. "I need no aid to lay you low, priest. If you will not return of your own will, you will do so tied across my saddle."

I placed a hand on the Northman's arm. "You are not yourself, Haedren. Return with us and we will find someone to get you the help you need."

He laughed loudly, the first sound above a whisper that had emerged from him to that point. "Help? I have never felt more like myself, if I was to be bluntly honest. To think of all those years, I labored under the yoke of another's will rather than seeing to my own needs...my own desires." He shook his head, "I have a great deal of time to make up for."

Mika nudged her horse forward a few yards, her sword drawn and low along its flanks. "We have heard those words before, but not from your lips. You are not the man I knew..."

He regarded her. "You, of all people, should understand my point of view, Mika. Your spirit has always chafed under the weight of these two. The warrior turned farmer, and the petulant, overgrown child."

When he turned to nod in Ret's direction, he was met by a ham sized fist. "Enough of your words! You will accept our aid, even if I must beat it into you!"

241

I stepped forward, catching the Northman's arm as he pulled it back to strike again. It required all the strength at my disposal to prevent its forward momentum. Ret's look of betrayal would have been humorous had the situation not been so dire.

Haedren raised his left hand to his face and rubbed at the blood trickling from his split lip with his thumb. Pinned to his cloak was a broach of dark steel, a skeletal cameo of radiant silver emblazoned upon its surface; it caught the light of the fading sun and reflected it back three-fold. Just as on another road, in another time, it seemed to be the sole spot of light in the dimness that was quickly becoming noticeable.

"I know that brooch, although not how you came to wear it."

Stephen saw the brooch clearly in Hollis's memories, and not simply from the events leading to Theamon's death. Years before that lonely road, he and his companions had retrieved that same brooch for a young noble. The man felt the thief's frustration at not recognizing it on the night of Theamon's death, although Gorack had knocked him senseless by that time, so he felt that allowances could be made.

It stood out in the thief's mind as it was the first time he had travelled with the trio; despite the dangers involved in retrieving the item, it was one of Hollis's most treasured memories.

He followed my gaze with a wide smile. "It was just lying there, and the Fallen Hand had no further need of it." He caressed it as one might a lover, "We dispatched him...brought an end to his twisted schemes. Why should we not benefit from our hard work?" He withdrew his hand, placing it back on the shaft of his mace. "Too long have the fruits of my endeavors gone to those who had no part in them. Beginning with the so-called Father of Justice, who has survived on his laurels for far too long."

I put my entire weight into holding Ret back. "You gave your life to the ideals of the church; why degrade a life's work now?"

242

"A life's work is only decided when you have given your life to it. I have ample time to live one more suited to me...certainly more to my liking."

Mika called from her horse, "This is not you, Hae. The brooch has plied you with promises as sure as a maiden is plied with wine. That is all they are, though, promises. In order to make them fact, you must buy them with the currency of your values, your soul...everything that makes you who you are. When they are gone, all you are left with is whispers in the night."

He nodded appreciatively. "Impressive words. Not many give you the credit you deserve, Mika. Between the oh so endearing humble-ness of the reluctant archer, the unrestrained machismo of the beast man and the smooth charm of the boy-scoundrel, we were both always overlooked. When was the last time you did something for yourself? I mean really for yourself, not part and parcel of one of Silvermoon's crusades or Ret's 'honor filled' campaigns?"

"Enough, Haedren!" I snapped.

He raised an eyebrow. "I disagree. You lead me no further, Alexei. I will let you know when I have had enough." He chuckled slowly, the sound full of pride. "But were I you, I would not hold my breath."

Ret lunged forward and took me by surprise, pulling his arm free from my grip. His bulk charged past me, powerless in the moment to stop him. I swear he slowed slightly before he crashed into Haedren... just enough so our comrade could bring his mace around. The dull thud echoed into the trees; but to his credit, Ret plowed through it. The two men went down in a heap.

Haedren struggled against the overwhelming power of his oppo-nent; but Ret easily pinned his wrists to the dirt. "Stop squirming, Haedren", the massive man grumbled. "It will do you no good."

Mika climbed down from her horse, and dug into her saddle bag, "Hold him still, Ret. I have some rope here somewhere."

With her back turned and his own bulk hiding the brooch from the Rangor's view, I was the only one who noticed the shadows gath-ering around it. "Ret, no", I began, already knowing by the rate at which my former companion's form was disappearing, that I would be too late. "Let him go!" I yelled, already moving towards the melee.

Ret looked up at me with his self-assured smile; that smile turned suddenly into a grimace of pain as his own hand and forearm were lost in the darkness. The words he no doubt sought to throw my way turned into a grunt as the agony hit him. He released Haedren like the man's arm was a snake; when his hand emerged from the darkness, blood flowed from numerous bite marks. The edges of each were already darkened by gangrene.

Even worse than the viciously infected wounds were the shadows that clung to his skin like honey, seeming unwilling to release his flesh from their grasp. They spread slowly towards his elbow in a viscous trickle, moving against the pull of gravity. Wherever they ran, they left his skin savaged and infected. Haedren kicked out powerfully, toppling the larger man onto his back, and began to rise.

Stepping over my bow and hooking it behind my right knee, I allowed muscle memory to take over as I strung it. Mika had turned and redrawn her sword, "Release him from your sorcery, Haedren. I do not want to kill you."

As I pulled an arrow from my quiver, I saw him smirk. "That my dear, is where we differ. I feel ambivalent about the whole situation. I could leave you here to tend his wounds or set you beside him. It honestly means very little to me." He locked eyes with me as I drew the shaft to my cheek. "Very little indeed."

There was something in those eyes that I will never forget. It was more than malicious. I knew he meant every word that fell from his lips. The years they we had spent together were as dust in a windstorm to him. He would slay us here as casually as a child crushes a spider. I felt a despair take hold of my heart; it was suffocating, as the power of it knocked the breath from my lungs. I did not realize until later that my vision was dimming in proportion to my optimism.

Mika rushed past me, raising her sword as she did. Haedren lifted his mace in two hands, the shadows creeping out and flickering along the shaft of his weapon. Mika swung again, putting all her weight

244

into the second stroke. When she withdrew the blade from the shadows that covered Haedren's mace, the metal was pitted and flaking. Her momentary shock allowed our opponent to take the initiative.

His mace knocked her sword aside and his foot slammed into her stomach. To her credit, she recovered quickly and gave ground so the kick did not have the effect it could have. I watched as passionlessly as if it were happening in a dream. Even as he shifted his grip and brought the weapon over his head to crush her from above, I still could not assemble the ambition to intervene.

Mika stepped closer to him, taking the strike from the haft on her shoulder rather than the flanged head on her skull. She had her longsword in a half-handed grip, one gloved hand halfway up the blade, intent to drive the point of it into Haedren's gut. He twisted away at the last second; combined with the all too solid strike to her shoulder, Mika's blow caught in his chainmail before running along his ribs. She had drawn blood for sure; but the superficial cut would not trouble him overly much.

She did not press the advantage, as I would have expected. Instead she took a step back, obviously favoring her left shoulder. Haedren, on the other hand, simply laid his shadow clad left hand on his ribs. They clung to his skin as they had to Ret's; but where their passage on the Rangor revealed tortured flesh, they only revealed Haedren's unblemished skin.

The three figures were almost lost to my sight as the ponderous weight of hopelessness threatened to crush me. As if underwater, I heard Ret trying to regain his feet, biting back cries of pain. Just as it had when Theamon's spell had me in its grasp, the world slowed to a crawl as a feeling of calm settled about my shoulders. Where it touched, the despair fled. The road slowly brightened into focus. I saw the Rangor pushing himself up to one knee behind Haedren. Mika was quickly giving ground as the priest swatted her blows aside and pressed her injured shoulder with strikes of his own.

Still in the cloak of peace, I picked up my bow from where I had

245

not realized it had been dropped and plucked an arrow from my quiver. In one smooth motion, I pulled the feathered nock to my cheek and let it fly. Not waiting for it to strike true, I pulled and let fly another...and another. All three shafts sank deep into the chest and abdomen of our comrade. Lung. Liver. Heart. I drew a fourth arrow as I watched the shadows that had undone Mika's earlier slash ooze across Haedren's stomach and hide the previous three from sight. In their wake, they left nothing but punctured leather and splinters. Hopelessness of the normal sort fell upon me then.

When Ret climbed to his feet, I almost wished the darkness still hid my sight. Both of his arms were savaged, to the bone in some places. The shadows now worked upon his face, crawling unerringly towards his eyes. Mika had bladed her body, so her right side was towards Haedren and her left protected. She had taken a posture reminiscent of a fencing pose, her long sword held in one hand. I could tell it was neither familiar nor comfortable for her; but Silvermoon I had faith in her skills.

I launched three more arrows, aiming for disparate parts of our comrade's body, hoping to split the shadow's ability to heal him. The shadow did indeed split into three smaller patches of darkness, each oozing to a different wound. Mika thrust deeply, forcing Haedren to deflect her sword from his body with a twisting motion. I put another two arrows into him; one buried itself in his kidney, the other found a spot close to his spine.

I was honestly amazed at his resiliency, at the fact that he was still on his feet. Ret lunged from behind him, wrapping his tree like arms around Haedren's chest. Rather than struggling, the priest placidly accepted the embrace. I swear the next arrow I launched sank into Haedren's body; but the shaft protruded from Ret's back instead. It was obvious that Mika shared the same issue, as when she thrust her sword into the priest's chest, it was Ret's lips that foamed with blood.

As the Rangor drove his forehead into the crown of Haedren's head; his own blonde hair began to dampen and turn crimson. "Let

246

him go!" I shouted, as I drew another arrow. When Ret released our comrade, he sank to his knees again as the transferred wounds became evident.

"Do you not see that you cannot best me? I do not need to lay a hand upon you; the three of you are your own worst enemies."

I could not argue with him. It seemed that my reflected state safeguarded me to a certain extent from whatever magic he commanded but I feared that would not be enough. He could kill my other companions with ease, and, despite my protection, I feared I was no match for him one on one.

It was not until the screeching had broken it that I realized that the forest around us had fallen into silence. The cacophony of countless crows filled the air as a dark cloud of the black birds descended upon Haedren. Their beaks carved small but deep wounds in his exposed arms and face; it was all he could do to protect his eyes from the feathered assailants. He stumbled back wildly as he dropped his mace in the dirt. The shadows rushed to the wounds, sealing them as quickly as they were made; but he was on his heels. I searched for an opening into which to launch an arrow but the cloud about him was so dense, I could hardly make out his form.

Then the first bird fell to the ground...and then another; their beaks sticky with viscous shadows. Each time a crow struck too close to where a shadow labored sealing a wound, it latched onto the bird and began devouring it. The muffled grunts of exertion emanating from Haedren morphed into a soft chuckle. "I know not from where you produced this magic; but it too will fail."

A husky voice from beside me muttered, "It is not their magic. It is mine." No more than ten feet from where I was standing, a cloaked and hooded figure exited the trees, flanked by a pair of grey-black wolves. Despite the heavy cloth, it was obvious to my eyes a woman; but the hood hid her face in shadow. "You carry something that does not belong to you, boy."

Haedren swatted away the last of the birds, his entire form dotted with tiny patches of shadow. "All the same, I believe I shall keep it."

The wolves began to growl, low and menacingly, "What you believe is of no consequence to me. That artifact holds a stain that you cannot erase. Whatever it or its former owner promised you, it will never come to pass. Neither I nor any of the other Heralds will allow it." The growls intensified and seemed to surround me until I could feel the rumble in my feet.

"Then pray tell, woman, where are the rest of your ilk?"

As the rumble grew louder, I realized it no longer originated in the wolves' hairy chests; but from the air itself. It was the sound of thunder. "I need them not. That brooch, and by extension you, are affronts to nature. Nature has a way of handling such contempt."

The first bolt of lightning took my sight from me and knocked me from my feet a split second later. I could smell ozone mixed with burned flesh; but through what must have been clenched teeth, I heard Haedren continue, "What the fire burns, the shadow soothes. What the light seeks, the darkness hides. I am at the inception of my power, Herald, while you are nearing the culmination of yours."

"We shall see about that." The light flashed against my sightless eyes again and the crash struck me like a physical thing.

I heard Haedren scream and his body strike the ground. In choking words, he managed, "What was once pure...now become profane...Grapes plucked from loyalty...now becomes the wine of betrayal."

The snarls of the wolves filled the air, drowning out for the moment the drums of thunder. The husky voice snapped, "What are you doing? I am your master...I am your friend..." The sounds of teeth ripping flesh found my ears followed by the crash of thunder again. The snarls morphed into cries of pain and then into silence. The scent of burnt flesh and scorched hair hung heavy. The voice again, "You have only postponed the inevitable, boy." There was no response.

A form crouched beside me, in her husky tones, "He has fled, at least for the time being. Do not concern yourself for your safety or that of your comrades." I felt her thumbs lightly brushing against my eyelids, "What

248

nature takes, it always returns in equal measure." I felt a cooling sensation spreading through my body, emanating from my eyes. "I had thought to catch you earlier, but you and your companions seemed very driven." My eyes flickered open to a familiar face. "I am called the Walker."

I knew her by a different name. To me, she was Samantha.

The cold fingers of dread caressed Stephen's heart as his breath caught in his throat. He reread the line a few times as his mind tried to come to grips with the revelation. The Heralds were the wisest and most puissant users of magic in Taerh. Legend has it, they formed a loose council after Olm and Umma trapped Sharroth in his cage. There are always three Heralds on the council; but they are neither immortal nor invulnerable. When one of their number falls, another is chosen from those who practice their art to replace them. They give their aid and wisdom when and to whom they wish; but have taken a common oath to bring no harm to each other and serve as guardians against any who seek to bring destruction to Taerh. That is not to say that they are the paragons of goodness and virtue; as a matter of fact, the Herald known as the Risen fits more comfortably into the role of villain.

Hollis remembered that the Walker's advice had played a pivotal role in the eventual defeat of Haedren. If Samantha was indeed the Walker, nothing that had occurred thus far was by chance.

The woman at the front desk informed Stephen that during the night, Mike had been moved from the ICU to the long-term care ward. Even though visiting hours didn't begin for another fifteen minutes, she'd signed his pass and given him directions. Stephen wasn't sure it was the easy banter they shared or simply a coincidence, but he was glad for the confidence his reflection shared with him.

The elevator door opened, and Stephen stepped into the hallway, turning left and walking towards Mike's room. He flashed a warm smile to the lone woman sitting behind the nurses' station as he held up his pass. She nodded absently, more focused on the tablet on the desk in front of her than his passage. As he turned into his friend's room, Stephen saw a figure bent over him, injecting something into his IV port. He opened his mouth to excuse himself when he saw the man's powder-blue scrubs hanging from his slim hips and pooling around his thick-soled black shoes.

The feeling that nothing in the last few days was truly by chance returned like a hammer. Samantha's cohort's presence here didn't bode well for either Stephen or his friend. His first impulse was to cross the room and seize the man. The part of Stephen that was still purely Hollis was sure that a moment or two alone with him would shake loose the truth of matters. This time, it was Stephen that saw beyond his visceral reaction. The man was clearly a hospital employee; if he had wanted Mike dead, he would already be so. The thin man was connected to Samantha and he felt that Mike was right where the woman wanted him to be.

He stepped back out of the room, pressing his back to the wall between Mike's room and the next. Quickly, a plan formed in his mind. Out of habit, Stephen flexed his left hand, assuring himself that here he had complete use of it. He heard the squeak of the man's rubber soles as he stepped into the room bordering Mike's and pulled his cell phone from his pocket.

When he heard the sound reach the door of Mike's room, he pressed the phone to his ear and stepped out as well. He turned abruptly to the right and channeled his boss, "I don't care what you had planned. You're paid to work, so that's what we expect of you." Their bodies collided sharply, knocking both back a step.

Stephen brought the hand holding his phone down and held it out before him, "Dude, watch where you're going.", before putting it back to his ear, "No, I'm not talking to you." The man sneered at him and pushed by, lightly shouldering him.

He continued speaking as he brought the phone down from his ear and admired the clear picture of the man's face and name tag on its screen. "I'm glad we have an understanding then." Hector Thompson worked as an orderly in the third-floor children's ward. Ignoring the question of whether the man should be working around children, Stephen was sure he was out of bounds here in the long-term care ward. At any rate, as an orderly, he was not permitted to dispense medication.

The man's own rudeness and Hollis's less-than-honest impulses afforded Stephen an additional opportunity; tucked into his own back pocket was the man's wallet. As he stepped into Mike's room, Stephen opened it and flicked through its contents. Hollis's larcenous impulses took over, guiding the cash into his back pocket before flipping through the mess of business cards clogging the wallet. He found the one he sought almost immediately. It read: *Samantha Marcheur, Florist and Holistic Medicine*. On the back was a handwritten phone number. He tucked it into his back pocket and left the room.

"Excuse me, Ma'am," Stephen spoke softly, as if he were hesitant to interrupt the nurse.

She looked up wearily. "Yes, Sir?"

He leaned over the desk, laying the wallet on the tablet before her, "The young man who was giving Michael Ryan his medication dropped this, I think. He was gone before I noticed; I'm sorry." He pointed with his left hand down the hallway while his right snapped another picture with his phone.

The woman frowned deeply as she opened the wallet to look at the driver's license found within. Her frown deepened as she read Hector's name. "Th ... Thank you, Sir. I'll make sure he gets it. Excuse me for a moment, will you?"

He nodded, "Of course." He saw her pick up the phone as he turned back towards Mike's room; her voice was low but tense. Stephen didn't need to hear the words to understand that she was passing Hector's actions on to her superiors. He was reviewing the picture showing the state of the nurses' desk when she stormed into the room while trying to look casual. He nodded politely and returned to his review; but he saw her replace the half full IV bag with a new one, taking the old one with her when she left. When whatever Hector had inserted into the bag came to light, it would keep him away from Mike for the time being. That, at least, bought Stephen some time.

A smile came to his lips when he found what he was looking for on the image of the nurses' desk. Despite HIPPA and every bit of security advice published in the last ten years, people continued to write their passwords on convenient little notes next to their computers. Obviously, the nurses in the long-term care ward were no different. They were even kind enough to place each of their names next to the appropriate password.

Stephen sat back and closed his eyes; perhaps the game did not belong completely to Samantha after all.

Stephen was sitting at Mike's bedside when his sister and Robert stepped in. "Stephen, how nice of you to come," Nellie murmured, and Robert nodded in agreement. Her fingers were interlaced with his, those of her free hand wrapped possessively around his wrist. He felt a pang of joy for them. Robert could be short-tempered and hardheaded, and Nellie was easily offended; but they were both his friends and he wished them well.

"Thanks, Nell," Stephen responded as he rose from the chair slowly. She smiled at him, reaching out to touch his forearm gently. He accepted the gesture for what it was, a peace offering.

"I have been here for an hour or so; other than a nurse and an orderly, no one has been by."

She nodded, gesturing to the chair he had vacated. "May I?"

He reached out to shake Robert's offered hand, "Of course...I was just going out to grab a coffee. Would either of you care for one as well?" His friend's grip was strong and a touch too enthusiastic, but Stephen let it pass.

"Yes, please." Nellie took Mike's limp hand into her own, laying her free one atop of it.

Stephen raised his eyebrows to Robert in a silent offer. "Cream, with very little sugar," he grumbled, his eyes never leaving the woman before him.

Nellie spoke up again, "Same if you don't mind, Stephen."

"Fair enough. I'll be back in a few," Stephen said. When he stepped into the hall, the woman behind the nurses' station was speaking quietly with one of her co-workers. Both held identical tablets casually against their chests. Medical charts were still necessary holdovers; but those tablets held the prize he sought.

Samantha had casually mentioned her health issues as they related to reflection; it may have been just another in a long list of deceptions. It may, however, be the pearl of truth that always must lie at the root of a deception. From her perspective, it may have been innocuous; but as Hollis knew, no kernel of information is unimportant, no matter how small it may seem. If those tablets held access to a patient record system, they could be Stephen's best chance of determining pearl from sand. If it was, it could be useful should the situation escalate further.

The question in Stephen's mind, was how to separate one from its owner. Hollis's instincts quickly appraised a variety of possibilities. They were too large to be pocketed easily; if there were too many eyes about, someone was bound to notice him lift one from a desktop. They were never far from their hands, so a bump and lift would not work. He continued to observe the nurses' station as he passed. They seemed careless in laying the tablet's down but not so much that one could disappear for long.

As he passed an open door, he could hear a soft chirping from within. When he peered into the room's dim confines, he could see a member of the patient's family gazing sourly at the source of the noise: a machine standing next to the bed. Pasting on his best expression of discomfort, he ducked into the room.

"Pardon me. I hate to bother you; but the machine in my friend's room is making that same noise. What does it mean? It's nothing serious, I hope."

The woman scowled at him. "It's the IV machine. My husband keeps kinking it and the nurses have to reset something to make it shut up."

Stephen nodded, "I see...okay...thank you." Before she could respond, he turned on his heel and walked from the room.

By the time Stephen returned with the three coffees, a plan had materialized in his mind. Normally the situation he needed to fabricate would require a partner; but when you didn't have one, it became necessary to recruit what was required. The soft chirping brought a soft smile to his face as he passed the open door once more. He ducked his head in, "Pardon me. The nurse said if you stopped by the desk, she could take care of that for you."

The woman looked up. "Thank you very much, sir."

He nodded lightly, "It's my pleasure, Ma'am." As he walked towards Mike's room he repeated, "It is truly my pleasure."

When he entered the room, he saw Nellie and Robert sitting close together at Mike's bedside. Balancing the cardboard tray in his left hand, he stepped behind them smoothly. Stephen reached up to open the curtain with his right hand. "Let's get a little light in here, shall we?" When Nellie tipped her chair forward to prevent the hot coffee from being held directly above her head, he swept the thick black cable from the heart monitor under its leg. As he turned, he tapped the plug solidly with his knee. He bit back the grunt of pain as the hard rubber dug under his kneecap; but it succeeded in jarring the plug loose from the wall.

"That's better," Stephen announced as he stepped out from behind them and began to lay the coffees on the tray that straddled the bed. He made sure that both Nellie's and Robert's coffees were a good six inches out of reach of both. "I forgot extra sugar for mine. Start without me." He walked to the door. He heard the voice of the wife of the patient down the hall moving away from him at the sound of Nellie's chair inching forward. As he reached the door, urgent alarms filled the air. The sole remaining nurse left her station and pushed past Stephen.

In her rush, she had left her tablet behind.

CHAPTER TWENTY
REFLECTION'S REVELATION

The tablet pressed against Stephen's spine as he stood up with his back to the wall, watching the nurse recalibrate the heart monitor. At least that was what he thought she was doing; to him it looked like a great deal of pressing buttons and looking displeased. Nellie and Robert stood back from the bed and watched as well.

The nurse looked up when she was satisfied, "You really have to try to be more careful. The cord must have gotten stuck behind the leg of this chair." She pulled the offending object away from Mike's bedside and set it along the wall at the foot of his bed. "This is why we ask that you don't move them."

Robert nodded lightly. "We understand. We'll make sure it stays there, Ma'am."

She studied the three of them with skepticism but didn't comment any further on the matter. The woman turned to Nellie, "Your brother seems to be fine. Let me know if you need anything else." She didn't wait for a reply before leaving.

"Well, that was thrilling. They really should move those cables out of reach."

Nellie had returned to her brother's side; but Robert studied him carefully before whispering, "You didn't have anything to do with that, did you?"

Assuming his best indignant face, Stephen growled, "What are you trying to say, Rob?"

"You have been talking crazy since Alan's death," Robert whispered, trying not to disturb Nellie.

"So that leads you to the conclusion that I am attempting to kill Mike?"

"I didn't say that."

Stephen shook his head slowly. "What is wrong with you?" He turned and left the room. As he walked down the hall towards the rest room, a smile crawled across his lips. He realized that at no point had he answered Robert's question; quite the opposite, he supplied questions of his own, putting the man on the defensive.

Stephen could no longer tell where Hollis's experiences ended and his began, so fluid and complete was the interaction between himself and his reflection.

He felt he should be more disturbed by the sensation but found that he wasn't. It didn't seem to be a loss of himself at any point; rather a discovery of a portion of him that he'd never known was lost. Where only a day ago, he felt his reflection's distinct personality at times, now he seemed to share those opinions seamlessly. He was neither Hollis nor Stephen; but someone new that combined the strengths and weaknesses of both.

Stephen pushed open the door to the restroom and stepped inside. He locked the door, before pulling the tablet from where it was hidden in the waistband of his jeans. As the screen flickered to life, it prompted him for a password. After double checking the appropriate one for the ID already filled in, he typed into the waiting box. He was rewarded by a cheerful, 'Welcome Amanda Reese'.

He quickly checked the time on the tablet before tapping on the icon marked 'Patient History'. He estimated that he had at most five more minutes until the device was reported missing. No doubt, it would take only a few more minutes to locate it via tracking software. He thought it best that it be in its final resting place by then.

He typed in Marcheur in the field marked 'Last Name' and Samantha in the one marked 'First Name'. Thankfully, the name was uncommon; only one result was returned. Quickly, Stephen verified her age and work phone; once he was sure that it was the patient he sought, he tapped on the tab marked 'Personal Information' and took a picture of the screen with his phone. Her address and home phone may prove more useful than her Social Security Number; but one never knew. It was always better to have more information than less.

Once that was done, he tapped on the tab marked 'Medical History'. "She wasn't kidding," he muttered to himself as he ran his eye down the list of hospital visits in the last few years. Most recently, she was seen in the emergency room for a series of Transient Ischemic Attacks, commonly referred to as warning strokes. Each time, she was released soon after with a recommendation to see her own physician. Her list of medications, noted with each visit, were a rogue's gallery of anti-coagulants and those to treat high blood pressure. He made this assumption based on some of the names he recognized. He took another few pictures of these screens with the hope that some quality time with Dr. Google would shed some light on those he didn't know from memory.

He kept an eye on the tablet's clock as he scrolled down to the earliest visits recorded. He estimated that he could browse for only another three minutes before he needed to dispose of the device.

Just less than six years ago, Samantha was admitted to the hospital for a full-blown embolic stroke; blood tests also confirmed that she was in the throes of a heart attack as well. The toxicology tests didn't include adder root, of course; but her levels of triiodothyronine were almost non-existent at the time. Stephen remembered that Mike and Alan both had very low triiodothyronine on the night of the accident. That was too convenient to be a coincidence.

She was placed under observation and given a host of drugs; Stephen took a picture of these as well. A week after being released, Samantha was admitted a second time for a stroke and heart attack; and again, two weeks following that. Each time, her triiodothyronine levels were bottomed out and her blood coagulation was through the roof. Stephen made a mental note to check what other medications they were administering to Mike.

After a year, the attacks became less common and those that did appear seemed to never approach the low triiodothyronine levels of the first few. Each time, the ER physician recommended she see her personal doctor and revisit the medications she was taking. He took a few more pictures of the medications she claimed she was taking for each visit and placed his phone in his pocket.

He tapped the log off menu item; immediately erasing Amanda's ID and replacing it with another from his list. He typed a few typical passwords in rapid succession until her ID became revoked. He then wrapped the tablet in a few paper towels and rubbed his fingerprints from its surface before exiting the restroom.

On his way back to Mike's room, he discretely dropped the wrapped device into the trash bag hanging from an orderly's cart.

~

Hollis's eyes flickered open slowly as the door to the room he and Aristoi shared opened slowly. His right hand reached behind his head to close around the dirk lying under the pillow. He focused on keeping his breathing slow and steady as he shifted it slightly to prevent its feather filled confines from inhibiting his throw. A figure slipped inside, walking past the bed to set a low burning candle on the small desk in the corner of the room.

The thief squinted hard, just making out the thick braids that fell about the figure's shoulders. He sighed heavily. "Aristoi, my friend...we almost had a tragedy there." He pulled his hand, sans knife, from beneath the pillow and sat up. "Rhyzzo and Ren were attacked in their room by parties unknown. That attack left one dead and the other ... whatever he is." The thief stretched lazily. "Perhaps it would serve us both well were you to make a little more noise?"

"You heard me enter, no?"

"I did."

"You ascertained my identity before plunging steel into my back, yes?"

"I did."

Hollis felt the woman's warm smile. "Then what do you bray about? A little suspicion keeps the wits sharp and the mind clear." The thief couldn't help but laugh. His companion continued, "It is past time for you to rise anyway, unless you savor the idea of sharing that bed with me."

He yawned, continuing to stretch as he rose. "I am not sure I could savor anything with your snoring." He stalked across the room, lighting two fresh candles from the one Aristoi had brought with her.

He watched the broad smile as it crept across the Kiel woman's face. "I snore? I believe the only reason we faced so little issues with predators in the Expanse was that they believed the thunder had taken up residence in your gullet."

Hollis scowled and shook his head. "I do not know what you are talking about. I sleep like a baby."

"...a baby dragon," Aristoi added quickly.

"At any rate, and please do not think I am not grateful for a solitary sleep...but what caused you to burn the midnight oil?" Aristoi's smile faded a bit as his eyebrows furrowed. Hollis corrected, "Why are you up so late?"

, "The Dwarf Luciius introduced me to insisted on lecturing me on

261

the history of the Well before he would show it to me. I think the Fair Folk's legendary strength pales in comparison to their love of words."

"Was it worth the lecture?"

Aristoi smiled. "Absolutely. It is the entire reason that I was in Oenigh in the first place. I am on my *Tikha La*. Loosely translated into Trade Tongue, it means 'Long Walk'. It is a rite of passage in Kiel for candidates for the ranks of the Songspear's."

"I had assumed you already claimed membership."

"By virtue of my birth, I was accepted." Her eyes floated to the side momentarily; she was hiding something, but Hollis let it pass. "But in order to learn at the feet of our leader, The Branded, I must complete the *Tikha La*."

Hollis slowly stretched again, scratching at his week's growth of beard with his freshly resplinted left hand, courtesy of Luciius. "The Branded is one of the Heralds, correct?"

Aristoi nodded. "He is indeed. He is the wisest among us; his age and power give him access to songs that no living Songspear has heard. He will only teach those who prove themselves wise as well."

"How does one do that?"

"The Long Walk only ends when the candidate returns with a piece of lore lost to the world."

The thief chuckled. "That seems a tall order."

Aristoi nodded. "That it is. I spent my entire training seeking an appropriate subject to pursue. At the end, I realized it was with me the entire time." She smiled to cover a discomfort whose source was not clear to the thief. "Every Kieli child is weaned on the story of the Well's. We call them Veltim Vilt or Wells of Worlds. Legend has it that every great civilization was birthed in the mystic waters of a well."

Hollis was unable to hide his expression of doubt. "Every people have their own creation myth ... a story to make them feel as if they are special...the universe's chosen. Often, that is all they are, a story."

His friend sighed. "Spoken like a true skeptic. How much history of the Cradle do you know?"

The thief shrugged. "Enough to get by."

Aristoi gestured to the bed as she leaned against the desk. "Getting by is never enough."

Hollis had ever only been interested in history as far as he could use it for his own profit; but his interest was piqued. Stephen, on the other hand, was fascinated by the subject. Had situations been different in his world, he would have finished college with an eye toward teaching the subject. It was now Hollis's turn to wonder at how seamlessly their personalities seemed to flow together.

As the thief sat down on the bed, the Songspear began, "Every kingdom on the Cradle has a history all its own; but what historians often ignore is the history that is not written in their books. Kiel has never abandoned its strong oral tradition. All knowledge is passed from Songspear to Songspear."

Hollis interrupted, "That is why you have no books?"

"Of course, we have books; but we do not rely on them as do the other kingdoms. We rely on the memories of our ancestors, for they have seen where others can only read. It is because of this we remember the time before 'civilization'." She held her hands up, palms facing. It served the same purpose as air quotes in English. "We remember when Kiel was naught but a collection of warring tribes. We spilt the blood of our brothers and sisters for things as petty as tribal grazing rights or marrying into the wrong family."

She watched Hollis carefully. "But amid this chaos, there was one place that was sacrosanct: The Mountain of Fire. It was a holy place, somewhere the chieftains and wise ones could meet to restore order to their tribes. Violence of any kind was prohibited under mutual compact, an agreement that went back through the generations. It was here that the chieftains resolved disputes that had grown beyond their control. The interior of the mountain itself was forbidden even to the most powerful chieftain. Only the wise ones could enter its depths. These wise ones were the predecessors to the Songspears of today; they kept the ways of the ancestors and the knowledge of our past."

"It was one such wise one who entered the Mountain on the Feast of the Darkened Day. His name was Corbane the Singer. He ventured inside with three others to give offerings to the Mountain itself; but emerged alone a changed man. It was Corbane who united the tribes within a decade; it was Corbane who led us from herding goats and foraging on the forest floor to cultivating crops and building the spanning cities that now dwell above it."

Hollis squinted slightly. "And you believe that this Mountain of Fire allowed him to do this … or something he saw while inside?"

Aristoi nodded her head. "After his rise, the Mountain retained its holy status, becoming a place for the members of the Songspear to gather and exchange knowledge. Any Songspear who wished could enter without judgement. I have seen the walls with my own eyes … seen the drawings made by generations of my ancestors as they attempted to depict the wonders, they saw within the waters that filled the Well itself."

"I assume that the well is dry now, just as the one here is."

"Indeed, it is. Far from the cherished libraries in every kingdom are groups that still pass knowledge from lips to ears. They are those who have neither the opportunity nor the freedom to learn what is on the printed page. While your books label their tales legend and myth, I have seen the truth in them. In each kingdom's history, there was a turning point, a time when a strong personality arose to lead their people out of the darkness. Each tale speaks of a place of reverence around which this enlightenment came to be."

"Coincidence?" Hollis asked half-heartedly. He knew in his soul it not to be so.

Aristoi simply studied him for a moment, not responding. She continued, "Unfortunately, the very thing that keeps these stories alive is also their downfall. They excel at catching the spirit of the facts; but sadly, not the facts themselves. All the tale spinners know the Wells exist; but no one can seem to agree on precisely where they are located. Each village seeks to increase their prestige by claiming that it lies within their purview."

The Songspear stood and stretched, seemingly filled with nervous energy. "The one located in Drunmarch is thought to be the first; it is said that on its walls are drawn the prophecies provided by its waters. Those waters went dry centuries ago; but the drawings, etched upon the walls before they did, remain."

"And these drawings are the lost lore you seek?"

The Songspear shook her head. "Not the drawings themselves, of course. I had no problem finding them; I would be willing to bet that the dwarf that showed me would gladly show them to anyone who would sit still for his history lesson." A look of childlike excitement filled the Kieli's face, "They point to something, Hollis. I have compared them to the ones inside the Mountain of Fire. The hand is different ... the subjects are different; but the inspiration is the same."

"So, you are looking to create some sort of codex?"

A lopsided smile crinkled one corner of her mouth. "Better. I am going to find the next Well of Worlds, one that has yet to run dry."

Hollis's attention sharpened. "Something like that would grant unimaginable power to whoever could make use of it."

Aristoi nodded. "Yes. To the right person, it could be of great benefit..."

"Or a tool of great harm. How do you know what it will be used for?"

The Songspear frowned. "If I can find it, my Tikha La will be over. I can take my place among my brothers and sisters."

"Just because we can do something does not mean we should, Aristoi. Are there any tales of the well being used for fell purpose?"

"None that I have come across but seeing as it is recognized as a tool for pulling a people from the mud, I would not imagine villainous acts would be attributed to it even if they should be."

"Are there stories of..." Hollis was interrupted by a soft knock at the door. His eyes met those of Aristoi and then shifted to where her spear leaned against the wall before he pulled his own sword from the scabbard that hung on the bedpost. "One moment." He gestured for the Songspear to take up position behind the door.

265

The thief was greeted by Luciius's smiling, bearded face when he swung the door open. "Good morning, my friend," he chirped.

"A fine morning to you, as well," Hollis mumbled.

The Dwarf clapped him on the shoulder. "I hope to restore some enthusiasm to those words for you. Your comrade has asked for you."

CHAPTER TWENTY-ONE
COMRADES' REUNION

Hollis rushed through the stone doorway, gently pushing past Lucius, but the Dwarf smiled softly and gave ground. Mike's reflection was sitting in an overstuffed armchair, his hands extended towards a roaring fire that burned in the exquisitely carved hearth. He turned and almost made it to his feet before the thief wrapped him in a bear hug. "I do not have the words to express myself," was all Hollis could manage as he pulled his friend to against his body.

"If you do not relax your grip, you will be finding the words for my eulogy."

Hollis released him, his expression turning somber. He sat down in an armchair across from his friend's. "I have visited one friend's grave; I have no desire to repeat the exercise."

Rhyzzo sighed. "I am sorry. I should have chosen my words more carefully. The night is such a blur in my mind. One moment, Ren and I were beginning to turn the tide, the next he was collapsed on the floor beside me." He closed his eyes slowly before continuing. "Things went downhill from there; unarmored and unprepared, it was a forgone conclusion from that moment."

"Slow down, no one blames you. Just tell me what happened, from the beginning."

"We arrived in the Stone City seeking Silvermoon. None had seen him, so we waited as the Dwarves looked into it."

"Why?" He studied his companion's face, looking for signs of another in his eyes, "Why Silvermoon? Neither you nor Ren had ever met the man."

Rhyzzo broke eye contact, looking down and to the right. "You would not believe me if I told you."

The thief turned to the door. "Luciius, can you give us a few moments?"

"Of course. I have some other patients to look in on. I will be nearby, please shout if you have need of me." Luciius backed out of the room and closed the door behind him softly.

Hollis turned back to his friend. "Try me. I have an equally unbelievable tale to spin. Perhaps both are one and the same."

"Stephen?"

Hollis smiled gently, as Stephen's consciousness took over. Hollis felt all of their shared memories in the other world and was in awe of what he saw, though not for the first time, a world so unlike his own. "It is me, Mike. You gave me quite a scare, both worlds."

"I wish I had been frightened...or anything else for that matter. The last thing I clearly remember was the alley. My captors had me trussed up like a Christmas ham and slung between them. Then it all became fuzzy, like everything was made of cotton. I think I may have passed out; I heard voices calling to us...then the sound of steel on steel; but everything seemed so far away. I have no idea how long I was out, although Luciius said it was months."

"He is correct. I would have been here sooner, but I had some delays." Stephen flexed his splinted left hand, trying to keep his face blank so his friend would not worry.

"The funny thing is I think I remember your voice speaking to me through the fog. I could not move...could not see but I heard your voice. I heard Robert as well; but he was with my sister, I think."

"Yes, your injury has sparked something between them. Silver lining, I suppose. You are in the hospital in our world. One of Samantha's friends is an orderly and was giving you something to keep you under."

Mike tilted his head, "Samantha? But she was helping us find Jeff."

"I do not think she was. I think she wanted you on a path of her own choosing...wanted to know where you would be."

"To what purpose?"

"I have not figured that out yet; but I am working on it. Take a deep breath and try to remember anything you can about the men that attacked you. What were they wearing? Did they say anything during or after the attack?"

"Four of them burst into our room; but only armed with thick wooden cudgels. They were dressed in blacks and greys, from cloak to leather. As I said, we were holding our own, since we held steel and they held wood. Renthroas was truly a sight to behold, his sword a shining extension of his arm. Olm was with us that night; we slew two of their number to even the odds and it appeared that we would emerge unscathed." He closed his eyes again. "Then like I said, I heard Ren hit the floor, followed by a loud crack as the man he had been fighting hit him in the head with his club." He opened them slowly, their moisture obvious to Stephen. "He could have done it...Ren could have. Two thugs would have not caused him even a pause. I am not Renthroas Halfborn, not even close."

Stephen rested his hand on his friend's forearm. "I am sure you did your best. That is all he would have asked.".

"One of them struck from the side, clipping me behind the ear. As they tied me up, I lay there, watching Ren's body. He was not breathing."

"And you are sure he fell before he was hit?"

"Absolutely."

"How hard did he get hit?"

"Hard, but not that hard. The two of them argued about it as they carried me. They said that 'he'," Rhyzzo made quotes in the air, "would have their hides. They were meant to capture us both, which explained the cudgels in lieu of steel."

"Their intent was ransom, not murder?"

"I cannot speak to ransom; we were interrupted by the Home Guard before they had a chance to discuss the situation further. I passed out, as I said; and that is all I clearly remember until I woke this morning." Stephen tapped his thumb and pinky on the arm of the chair as he let Mike's words sink in. "I wish I could remember more," his friend said apologetically.

Stephen shook his head, pausing his tapping. "Nonsense, you did fine. It is more than we had a moment ago." He resumed rapping his fingers on the over-stuffed arm, something just out of his mind's reach. When he realized how long the lapse in conversation had drawn on, he stopped. "We will figure this out, Mike...I do not know how Samantha is involved in this; but I know she is."

"She seemed like such a nice lady."

"I imagine she did. Her reflection, however, is the furthest thing from a harmless old woman. In Taerh, she is known as the Walker."

Mike raised an eyebrow, "The Herald?"

"The very same. No matter the motivation, the Heralds always have a plan in mind. We are starting this game at least a few steps behind. It is all I can do to not lose any further ground."

His friend tilted his head, "Do you hear that?"

Stephen squinted and listened carefully turning Hollis's sharp instincts to the task. All he perceived was the crackling of the firewood in the hearth. He shook his head. "What does it sound like?"

"It is sharp and high pitched; too quick for me to get an idea of where it is coming from. It is very regular, like a..."

"Heartbeat?" Stephen finished for him.

Mike pointed to him, "Exactly."

"You may be waking up. I think Samantha's cohort was giving you adder root intravenously," he used the English word as there was no Trade Tongue equivalent, "to keep you under. It must be wearing off."

His friend shrugged, his face becoming placid and unfocused. "It is so soothing..."

Hollis snapped his fingers under Rhyzzo's nose; that brought him back to his senses for a moment. "You cannot tell anyone in our world about Taerh or reflecting. No one will believe you and any that do will not have your best interests in mind." His eyes glazed over again; the thief gripped him by the back of the neck. "Rhyzzo...Mike...tell me you understand."

The man's eyes began to droop, as his speech became slurred. "I understand," he murmured.

Hollis shook him sharply, "Remember, only you and I can know about this."

With that, Mike's presence left Rhyzzo. The man's eyes shot open as a confused smile crossed his lips, "I am not sure what your next words are going to be, Hollis; but I assure you it is much too early in the season for me to entertain proposals."

Hollis had spent most of the morning with his recovered friend. He quickly realized Rhyzzo had no memory of the time Mike was reflected. Just as when Stephen read the journals, he was struck by the difference in Jeff and Mike's experience with reflection and his own. His attempts at teasing out of Rhyzzo any shared memories were rewarded by nothing more than a look of patient confusion from the priest of Olm. One of the qualities Hollis appreciated the most about Rhyzzo was his calm energy. Even during a crisis, he could be counted upon to maintain a cool head and clear mind. Those who did not spend time with him thought him a touch dull, in both personality and intellect; but these people could not be further from the truth.

The thief could count on one hand the amount of times he could remember Rhyzzo wasting a word or speaking simply to fill a silence. If you observed him closely, however, you could see in his eyes that his mind was a contradiction to his appearance. Where he seemed outwardly tranquil and impassive, his thoughts were always working on not only the problem at hand; but several more ahead of it. Hollis remembered playing King's Gambit (a game closely related to chess) with the man; he was amazed with the ease and finesse with which he was able to juggle several scenarios at once, adjusting each according to his opponent's reactions. At no point in his friendship with the Olmite did he ever feel that anything was out of the man's control.

Whether or not perception met reality, this beat a remarkable counter point to Mike's personality. Stephen's friend was a ball of frantic energy; he often seized a misstep or potential obstacle and let it monopolize his entire perception of a situation. He took defeats or mistakes, temporary though they may be, very personally, often allowing them to prevent him from moving forward.

The situation that led to Ren's death was a perfect example of this. Where Mike obsessed on his failure to turn the tide once the half-elf had fallen, Rhyzzo took it in stride. Besides a soft intake of breath and briefly closed eyes, the priest did not dwell upon it. He instead asked pointed questions about the encounter and those that followed. Hollis saw him weighing each against what he knew and calculating his next point of inquiry.

After an extended period of rapid-fire questions and answers, Rhyzzo announced he was growing weary. At no point did he even state a theory or opinion. It was obvious to Hollis that more than rest that the priest needed some silence to put his thoughts in order, and he was glad to provide that to his friend. They parted with an agreement to meet later at the West Gate Inn for dinner. Hollis felt he had every intention of nourishing his understanding of the ambush as much as his stomach.

Despite the series of mirrors that approximated daylight below the mountain, the thief still found that he was unable to accurately judge time in the Stone City. He had found his way back to his and Aristoi's room in the Inn of the Market as the Songspear was rising for the day.

The Kieli was washing her face in the provided basin as Hollis opened the door. "How is your comrade?" Aristoi asked, while drying her face on a linen towel.

"Complicated."

The Songspear raised an eyebrow. "He is free of whatever plagued

272

him, yes?" Hollis nodded absently. "Then, why is it complicated?"

The thief took a short breath and blew it out his mouth sharply before speaking, "Let me ask you a question, my friend. "

"Of course." Aristoi pulled her silk shirt over her thick braids as she listened.

"These people in the stories...those able to make use of the Well's. Do they have anything in common? For example, are there stories of them speaking of places that no one had ever seen? Or perhaps seeing two different people at times?"

"Why do you ask?" the Kieli queried, an eyebrow raised in a sign that she was growing suspicious of him. He found that he didn't like the sight.

"Answer the question first, and then I will be glad to answer yours as best I can."

Aristoi leaned in, curiosity clearly warring with suspicion within her, "Actually, I think you'll find that I asked the first question, one that has still gone unanswered, but very well, have it your way." Hollis chuckled at her words, despite himself. "The stories of Corbane are rife with incidents of his ties to something beyond himself...things beyond that which others could perceive. It was attributed to his ties to the ancestors. A good deal of the wise ones shared the same qualities."

Hollis tried to temper his enthusiasm. "And the other...let us call them Children of the Well?"

Aristoi smiled broadly. "Children of the Well, I like that very much."

He laughed. "Feel free to use it...but what of them?"

"My questions always revolved around the Well itself; but I can remember the same qualities associated with a few other Children of the Well."

"Do you think there is a correlation?" He used the English word again but added, "Connection?"

Aristoi held up her hand. "That is a complicated question, Hollis. The short answer is that I cannot be certain; but it is possible. Again, why do you ask?"

"You would think me crazy." Aristoi shrugged but continued staring at the thief, forcing him to sigh., "I am afraid you will not believe my tale and dismiss it out of hand."

"I can promise you two things. One, I cannot possibly believe your story if you do not share it with me. Two, I am chasing a legendary, constantly moving cradle of civilization ... something that no scholar north of the Verdant Sea would admit much less give credence to." She seized the man's eyes, "I think it is safe to say, I do not dismiss a great deal out of hand."

"Fair points."

"I know, I made them."

Hollis raised an eyebrow but continued, "What would you say if I told you that I believe there are worlds beyond Taerh?"

"I would say that it is plausible if not expected. What kind of narcissist would believe that they were the center of creation?"

"You would be surprised."

"What of these other worlds?"

Hollis took a deep breath. "I am from one of them...Or, rather, I have a friend who is. A friend whose memories and thoughts I see in my mind, as clearly as if they were my own."

It was clear by Aristoi's expression that she was shocked, almost into silence, but instead she said, "Go on."

The thief laughed. "You are not much of a card player, are you? You told me that you would not think me insane."

"I claimed no such thing. I simply said I would not dismiss it out of hand. However, please do not take my initial disbelief as doubt. Your words are unexpected, as you knew they would be. In the short time that I have been in your company, you have given me no reason to believe your words are without support. Please continue. How long have you – or this friend of yours – been on Taerh? How did he come to be here?"

"That is not an easy answer." Hollis frowned as he attempted to compose his thoughts. He was grateful when Aristoi gave him the time he needed. "Let me begin again. Hollis is Taerh-born. Stephen is from

Earth. Thanks to a plant known as adder root, when Stephen falls asleep there, I can feel him with me here. The more it happens the more of him remains within my mind, even when he is not present." Aristoi listened, and his brows furrowed. He was suddenly full of regret, and he knew she would never understand. It was too unbelievable. "I'm sorry, this was a mistake."

The Kieli shook her head, "Stop, my friend. Tell your story. My doubts are my problem to solve. Either you are insane, or you speak the truth. In the first case, you would not be the first nor the last I have spoken to in my quest to finish my Long Walk. In the second, your words may prove to be the end of my quest. Again, please continue."

"I have heard it call Reflecting and know a handful of others who have experienced it. My friends Rhyzzo and Renthroas are two."

"Do you believe that his earlier state is tied to this phenomenon?"

"I do. In Stephen's world, on Earth, Rhyzzo...Mike, as Stephen knows him, was sick. He was being cared for in a hospital. Like an infirmary here on Taerh. But another in Stephen's world has been giving his other self a substance to keep him here."

Aristoi frowned as if concerned. "Why?"

"I have not pieced that together as of yet; but I know it has something to do with the Walker."

, "The Herald?"

"The same. Stephen has spoken to her Reflection in his world. She is the reason that Ren and Rhyzzo came to the Stone City. I also have reason to believe she was involved in the death of Ren's father, known as Alexei ..."

"... Silvermoon. I will say something for you, Hollis. If this is indeed a function of your imagination, you certainly do not aim low."

"I fear this Reflection phenomenon has some connection to the Wells of Worlds that you chase."

"What caused you to come to that conclusion?"

Hollis frowned slightly. "Stephen and I are different when Reflected, somehow better, more like...each of us."

"What happens to Stephen when you are Reflected?"

"That is the amazing thing. I do not cease to be and neither does he. It is as if we are different sides of the same coin, to use an expression from Earth." The Songspear nodded slowly. Hollis turned quickly, "Do you have a piece of paper?"

Aristoi opened her bag and pulled a thick piece of parchment from a bone tube found within. She handed it to Hollis, her wide eyes showing that she was clearly becoming more interested than doubtful.

Hollis tore the sheet in half and drew dots on each half. He held up both sheets. "These dots represent things that make Stephen himself and Hollis himself." The Songspear nodded. The thief placed one sheet in front of the other. "When I am reflected, it is as if I slide into his body and mind." He held the stacked sheets between Aristoi and the candle. The dots on the surface of the rear sheet of paper became visible through the one in front. "At first it was an on or off thing." He pulled the sheets apart. "I was either Hollis or Stephen, but now, even when I am awake," he placed them back together, "It seems we are someone ... something that is neither and both at the same time. I believe that reflection itself may be tied to a plant known in Stephen's world as adder root. When consumed, it brings on slumber during which the sleeper can reflect.

"The common detail in every story of the Well is that those that gaze upon it see inexplicable things in its waters. Those visions could be a metaphor for seeing sights found in the mind's eye of another." She scratched gently at the underside of her chin. "Each of the Children of the Well was extraordinary in some way..."

Hollis nodded, "I have read journals belonging to Ren's father. In them, he describes a sensation of oneness that allows him to accomplish fantastic things."

"Let me speak to the Dwarf that showed me the Well. He is versed in its history; perhaps there is something in his words that can shed more light on this situation."

"So, you believe me?"

"You believe you. For now, that is enough for me."

276

CHAPTER TWENTY-TWO
TRAITORS' AID

Hollis was sitting in the common room of the Inn of the Market and wondering how such a creative people could be so unimaginative when it came to naming things. Everyplace and everything he came across in the Stone City was named simply and with an economy of words. He wished that had not extended to the delicate but flavorful wine sat before him, barely touched. The bartender had called it Bronze Wine, no doubt attributed to its deep yellowish-brown color. He had assumed it to be an imported good, as grapes did not grow very well below ground; but was informed it was a Dwarven invention, made from fermented mushrooms. It did not seem to taste the same after that.

Aristoi had left to speak to the Dwarves about the Well and he had some time to kill until he met with Rhyzzo. The thief was slowly going mad, staring at the dim confines of his room. He had thought to visit Renthroas' grave again, but on his way downstairs, he had thought better of it; he had spent far too much time among the dead in the last few weeks. He had ordered a drink while plotting his next move.

Hollis was unsure when plotting had turned into writing a letter to Maggie, but it felt like the right thing to do for some reason. Perhaps it was Stephen's influence or the losses the thief has suffered in recent days. The room fell silent suddenly, causing the thief to glance up from his work.

The man's rasping cough alone would have piqued Hollis's interest; but his odd appearance also ignited his suspicion. His slight form was lost beneath a thick starched cloak and his face hidden behind the mask of a plague doctor. Stephen remembered reading about such accoutrements coming into prominence during his own world's Black Plague; but being worn for centuries before by different cultures. The thief supposed that given a set of circumstances, such as a widespread sickness, the same fashion could arise in two disparate worlds; but the coincidence seemed a little too convenient.

Hollis pulled further back into the shadow of the huge hearth beside his table and observed the figure from there. The man grumbled something softly to the Dwarf behind the bar, his hand extending to place a coin upon the surface. His hand was delicate, ending in long wisplike fingers. The Dwarf took the coin with one hand, extending the other to indicate where the thief was sitting.

Cursing beneath his breath, Hollis drew a knife from its sheath against his spine and laid it carefully on his lap. The man's stiff cloak scraped along the stone floor as he approached his table. He dropped his head to the left and coughed again roughly before regarding the thief through the shaded lenses that served as eyes for the mask.

"Nasty cough you have there, friend," Hollis remarked.

"It is, is it not?" The man's voice was naturally high pitched, although whatever ailed him had given it a hoarse quality that just made it sound like a rusty hinge.

"You seem to have me at a disadvantage," Hollis nodded towards the bar. "You seem to know me."

The mask dipped once in a slow nod. "After a fashion."

Hollis smiled easily, although simply waited for the man to continue. As the silence drew on, he continued to watch his own reflection in the lenses. If the man sought to discomfort the thief, he was sorely mistaken. Hollis's own eyes held no more emotion than the dead

278

glass, despite the smirk that colored his lips. Casually, he brought his injured left hand up to stroke his mustache and beard.

From within the mask, the voice croaked again, "We have met in another place ... another time."

"I am sure I would remember..." He gestured with his left hand to the man's mask and cloak.

"Objects reflected often times take on distorted appearances."

Hollis frowned deeply. "Remove your mask and allow me to see to whom I speak." A sinking feeling filled his chest as the man reached behind his head and pulled at the leather strap that held the pointed mask in place. Before he had tugged his head free from its confines, the thief knew the face he would see.

"Does this aid your recollection?" Milky fluid filled sores radiated from the right corner of Hector's mouth, disappearing into his sparse growth of beard. A second patch of sores flowed from his hair line and trickling to an end under his left eye; these were an angry crimson, capped with brown crust.

"You have seen better days," Hollis stated, it was all he could do to keep his voice steady when every instinct in his body wanted to pull back in revulsion. He assumed the crusty rash was the beginning stages of leprosy; but he knew the milky one to be syphilis.

"I could say the same for you: Renthroas dead and poor Rhyzzo unable to do much besides piss himself."

The thief spoke through gritted teeth, "Keep their names out of your mouth before I..."

Hector tilted his head, his smile causing one of the larger sores near his mouth to split open. "Before you do what?" The milky discharge oozed into his beard. "I am as much of a guest here as you are. Did the fate of the men who absconded with Rhyzzo teach you nothing?"

Hollis felt heat of his anger rise like a blast furnace within his chest; his hand tightened around the hilt of his knife like a vise. His first impulse was to leap across the table and plant six inches of steel in the man's throat; but he dismissed that quickly as he attempted to seize upon something to cool his temper. The man was unfortunately correct. To the

Fair Folk, a human was a human and a murder was a murder. Slowly, the thief spoke, as if he were tasting each word, "There are always places where eyes are less sharp in every city. This one is no exception."

The man raised an eyebrow, "Is that so, Slender One? Please do not mistake illness for weakness. I know the places you speak of more intimately than any woman that has shared my bed."

A cold hand clenched the thief's heart as the realization hit him that the man spoke the truth...or at least he believed he did. His eyes did not dart or float, nor did his eyebrows rise in fear. Hollis focused on maintaining the man's stare, squinting slightly to keep his own fear from his face.

"If you deliver the vegetable to me, I will leave Drunmarch with him and we never need to see each other again."

Hollis scowled. "You anorexic," he was using the English word again, "little prick!" The thief's raised voice drew the attention of those gathered, Dwarf and otherwise. He lowered his voice and continued, "If you lay so much as an eye on him or me again, I will make whatever cocktail of nastiness you have running through your veins seem pleasant by comparison."

Nonplussed, the man raised an eyebrow. "May I consider that your final thought on the matter?"

"Final as a heart attack."

Hector stood, pulling his plague mask over his face once more. He regarded Hollis for a long second before rasping, "Perhaps we will meet in more intimate surroundings soon."

Through gritted teeth, the thief growled, "I am counting on it."

Hector turned, his stiff cloak fanning out as he did so. The soft scrape of the material on the floor chased him from the common room.

Hollis watched him leave, his eyes so intent upon the retreating form that he did not notice another figure step up beside the table.

A soft throat-clearing sound snapped the thief's attention back to his surroundings. Beside him was a Dwarf dressed in deep crimson and dark grey, the colors of the Home Guard. Once he was sure that Hollis was aware of his presence, the Dwarf spoke, "Would you mind if I sat, my friend?"

"I am not pleasant company at the moment."

The Dwarf laughed, a rich, deep sound. "I have been told that I am tolerable company at the best of times. I am sure I will manage."

The thief tilted his head slightly, recognizing the young dwarf, "We met earlier...in the canyon."

"Yes, I am called Jhorwynn."

Glad of any distractions, momentary they may be, from the uncomfortable conversation he had shared with Hector's reflection, Hollis nodded towards the chair that the man had vacated. "Suit yourself, Jhorwynn."

The Dwarf elected to seat himself in the other unoccupied chair, giving Hector's wide berth. "I could not help but notice your discussion with the Plague Man."

Hollis blinked slowly. "The Plague Man. He actually calls himself the Plague Man?"

Jhorwynn shrugged. "It seems a descriptive enough name. I am unsure if he arrived in Drunmarch with it or it grew around him."

The thief chuckled to himself. "It would not surprise me if the little twit gave it to himself."

"Twit?"

Hollis realized he had begun to mix English and Trade Tongue a lot more, most recently. "Twit...it means fool."

The Dwarf raised an eyebrow. "Then why not say fool? I swear Trade Tongue would be leagues easier to learn if there were not a dozen words for the same thing."

The thief shrugged. "I shall bring that up at the next meeting." Jhorwynn eyed him coldly. Hollis moved on, "Yes, the fool and I had a difference of opinion."

"Be wary, human. I feel he is more than he would first seem."

"You truly have no sense of how right you are."

Jhorwynn shrugged. "He entered Drunmarch with the two men

281

responsible for the abduction of your comrade. I escorted him into the Stone City, just as I did you."

Hollis leaned forward, suddenly intrigued. "Are you certain?"

The Dwarf nodded. "I am. I was also present when the two humans were killed and your comrade recovered, so I did have a close look at them in both cases."

"If he had something to do with Ren's death and Rhyzzo's abduction, why is he not laid beside his friends?"

He spread his hands out before him. "As long lived as we are, the Fair Folk take death very seriously. The magistrates questioned him thoroughly and determined that he was free of any blame besides that of choosing his companions unwisely. He was seen in neither the Inn nor the alley."

"The head does not need to be in the purse for the fingers to pluck out coins."

Jhorwynn nodded. "I understand your sentiment; but I am afraid there is little that can be done...within the city."

Hollis did a double take. This was the first time since he had arrived that a Dwarf had alluded to not following the 'party line' of his fellows. He lowered his voice, "What are you saying?"

The Dwarf also lowered his voice to a whisper, "I am not saying anything; that is the point. However, once you and he have departed, the Stone City takes no interest in what passes between you."

"Why bring this to me?"

He sighed. "I agree with your suspicion that he bears some level of responsibility for the attack on your friends. Unlike some...well all...of my brothers and sisters, I cannot hide behind the traditions."

"Are you willing to inform me when he leaves and how many travel with him?"

Jhorwynn pondered for a moment as he stood and then hesitantly nodded his head.

Hollis placed his hand atop that of the Dwarf, "Thank you, Jhorwynn."

Jhorwynn patted the thief's hand with his free one. The Dwarf opened his mouth to speak but thought better of whatever he meant to say and instead turned and walked to the door.

～

Rhyzzo breathed calmly, his brows furrowed and his steepled fingers lightly tapping his lips as Hollis finished speaking. "Aristoi has gone to the Fair Folk in an attempt to figure out any additional lore that has eluded us to this point."

His friend nodded carefully, grunting non-committedly as his eyes moved slowly from side to side as if he could see the information before him.

"Are you sure you remember nothing after arriving in Drunmarch?"

"Absolutely...however, even that provides value to our discussion. The key to my understanding lies in what I do not remember. I clearly recall agreeing to meet Renthroas in the Virgin Mermaid at the end of Tornsyield; but then nearly nothing until the beginning of Frostdawn almost a month later." The Stephen portion of Hollis translated the Taerh months into Earth ones: October and November respectfully. "If this was the time that your friend was," he sought the word for a quick second, "Reflected, it would lend credence to your story."

"I know it sounds insane."

Rhyzzo shook his head. "Not as insane as one would first think. I mean, who in their right mind would believe their universe was the only one?"

Hollis repeated his response to Aristoi's similar question, "You would be surprised."

He raised an eyebrow but continued, "You say that you remember everything that transpires on both worlds?" The thief nodded. Rhyzzo grunted again but shrugged, "Perhaps it is a function of the frequency with which you move between them. I have no memory of this Samantha and I know The Walker purely by reputation; but if they

283

are, as you say, one person it could bode ill for us and any who align themselves with us."

Almost as if on cue, the two heard a key turn in the lock. A knife appeared in Hollis's hand as if by magic and Rhyzzo's own left hand closed around the chalice shaped amulet at his throat as he raised his right towards the door. His tongue darted out to wet his lips and his brows furrowed with concentration as he no doubt recalled a petition to his god. Neither was needed; it was Aristoi that stepped through the door.

The Songspear seemed to flinch at their less than hospitable reception. "Perhaps in the future, I shall make a mental note to knock before entering."

The thief nodded, "Perhaps that would be best. Aristoi, you remember Rhyzzo. Rhyzzo, this is my boon companion and resident lore master, Aristoi."

Allowing both of his hands to resume their steepled position, the priest smiled slowly. "It is my honor. From what Hollis has told me, I owe you a debt for aiding in his escape and safe passage through the Expanse."

"It is I who owe him a debt for my own freedom." She bowed her head in the thief's direction. "He valiantly ... "

Hollis sighed wearily, cutting the Songspear off before she could begin, "Can we just agree that we all owe everyone some sort of debt and return to the matter at hand?"

The Kieli laughed softly and shrugged. "As you will, my friend." She placed her well-worn satchel on the bed and sat down beside it. "No doubt you have brought Rhyzzo into your confidence?" Without waiting for the thief's nod, she continued, "What the Dwarven lore master, Khem, lacks in brevity, he makes up for in knowledge. It is indeed fortunate for you that I did not come directly to the Stone City when I began my 'Walk. The Fair Folk have enough lost lore to satisfy ten Tikha La; I would have stood beside my brothers and sisters years ago."

"I will consider myself such."

284

"According to Khem, speaking with the weight of his ancestor's knowledge as well, the history of the Wells is associated with more than just change. In every instance of one being used, the right has been bought with blood."

"The three that entered the Mountain with Corbane?" Hollis asked.

"Indeed. In addition, every time that a Well has been used that Khem has record of, seven in all, at least one has paid for it with their life."

The thief's mind turned to the unfortunate deaths of Jeff and his friends. As he opened his mouth to speak, it was Rhyzzo who voiced a question, "What is known of those who gave their lives to empower the Well?"

Hollis turned to the stoic man, "How do we know that it needs to be empowered?"

The priest tilted his head, "A death or two in the process of its use would be acceptable as a coincidence. That would take into consideration jealousy or simple squabbles over who would make use of it." He locked eyes with Hollis. "Seven of seven known triggering of the Wells are simply outside of the realm of serendipity."

The Songspear nodded. "I came to the same conclusion and asked the very same question, Rhyzzo." Hollis sat back in his chair, feeling a little like he had been scolded. "The legends say that each of the known Wells was considered holy ground, just as the Mountain of Fire was. Only those thought to be blessed in some way could enter the chamber containing it."

Hollis spoke up again, "And the surest way to being blessed in the eyes of your fellows is to experience visions." It was not a question. Both Rhyzzo and Aristoi nodded as he continued, "Is it possible that the act of reflection is tied more closely to the Wells than we thought?"

The priest clenched his hand into a fist. "Like a knot."

Hollis turned back to Aristoi, "Did Khem have any additional information on those who successfully used the Wells?"

"Each and every one rose to a place of prominence and power

within their community." Hollis opened his mouth to ask a question; but Aristoi answered it before he could give it voice. "All of them were forces for order; unfortunately, tyranny and justice are orderly in equal measure." The Songspear shook her head. "You were correct, the Well itself can be a tool for as much boon as curse. It depends on the 'Child in question."

"And if the Walker is able to make use of one," Rhyzzo began.

Hollis finished, "With her current power magnified, there would be little beyond her reach." He stood quickly and began to pace. "Walker is certainly not the Risen; she defied the other Heralds to stand with us against Haedren after Theamon's shadow fell upon him."

Rhyzzo's voice, soft and steady interrupted him, "If what you say is true, she also contributed to the deaths of at least two of your comrades as well as my own attempted abduction. How well do you know Walker or her alter ego in your world?"

The thief blew out a breath unconsciously held, "I communicated with the Walker, always through an intermediary, a handful of times during the months spent searching for Haedren; but someone whom I trust unquestioningly spoke highly of her integrity at the time."

"At the time," the priest repeated flatly, allowing Hollis to make his own connection.

"I have not had any interaction with her since word reached me of Haedren's and Silvermoon's deaths." Rhyzzo reached out to clasp his friend's forearm firmly for a fleeting moment before releasing his grip. "That was the beginning of a dark period for me on Taerh as well as Earth. Mika's reflection died only a day later...followed a short time afterward by the passing of Silvermoon's brother, Marcus and his reflection, George." He stopped at the far end of the room to lean against the wall. "I did not deal with any of it well; I am not overly proud of the lengths I went to in order to hide from the pain. It was not until Ren and I found you that things finally began to take a turn for the better."

"I do not seek to reopen wounds that time has seen fit to close, Hollis, but you mentioned that the Walker had a hand in the circumstances leading up to Silvermoon's death and that of this Haedren. Could it be that her intention was to secure the Well, even then?"

"It is possible," he said, his mood clearly darkening.

The priest watched his friend for a moment before remarking, "That time...the years before we met always seemed to be a shared secret between you and Renthroas."

"As I have said, it was a dark time for me...Ren was also at a particularly low point of his life as well. We fed off one another's misery. Until my reflection entered my life, I never guessed the relationship between Silvermoon and Renthroas."

"In your world, they are father and son, correct?"

The thief nodded again. "To my knowledge, neither met the other in Taerh, however."

Aristoi sighed softly and then pushed again, "What do you remember of the interaction between Walker and Silvermoon from that time?"

Hollis thought for a second. "I never witnessed any interaction myself, simply heard about it second hand from Ret and Mika. Jeff... Silvermoon went out of his way to keep me as far from the actual search as he could. At the time, I did not comprehend his reasoning; but after reading the journals kept on my world, I understand that he sought to keep me and my reflection safe." The thief's hands balled into fists. "He believed that if one's reflection was to die, the other would perish soon after. I was young at the time and he did not want to jeopardize what he saw as the potential of a long life."

He swung his fist into the wall behind him. "Little did he suspect how that long life would turn out. If I could switch places with him now, I would without hesitation. Alan would not have had to live without a father and no doubt Jeff would have done a better job at keeping him safe then I have. In some ways, I failed the son as much as I did his father."

Rhyzzo stood up suddenly. "Cease this right now." Hollis locked him with a dangerous glare; but the priest continued as if he had not seen it. "You torment yourself for things over which you had no control...harshly judge yourself based on facts that you neither had nor were capable of acquiring. Your friends are dead...my friend, Renthroas, is dead. These facts are not in dispute. Also undisputed is the fact that in both cases, you had no way to prevent either outcome. Silvermoon...or Jeff went out of his way to keep you safe based on the information he had and motivated by his love for you. Because of that, when he fell, his son had a friend to see him through the ordeal."

Hollis's face softened a bit but remained silent as his friend continued, "It is truly unfortunate that Ren seemed to have been caught in the same cycle of tragedy as his father; but fortune is often a fickle mistress. If you had perished in lieu of Silvermoon, you would not be here now."

"Ren lays cold and lifeless in the dirt; precious little good I did him."

"Mourn his loss, Hollis. Mourn not your role in it. You still draw breath...breath you can use to put an end to those who were truly the cause of it. Renthroas chose to leave Oizan without you...he chose me to travel with him here to the Stone City. Why do you believe that was?"

"Keeping me safe, as his father did, out of some misplaced sense of duty?"

Rhyzzo simply looked at him for a moment before replying, "Look at the road you stand upon rather than the dirt beneath your feet. You truly do have a keen mind when you can remove passion from it. This is not one of those times. As much as he wanted to believe that his father still lived, part of Renthroas knew that the situation was suspect to say the least. He did not want you to accompany him because if things went awry, he knew that you had the best chance to put things right again." The priest's revelation took Hollis aback. "As much of a strike as it is to my ego, he saw me as expendable. In his mind, you simply were not."

Jhorwynn found Hollis in the Market as the reflected sunlight had almost finished its climb to the center of the cavern; the effect approximated the midday sun above Drunmarch. The thief's gaze was locked with that of a silk merchant as they haggled over the price of an expertly tailored cloak.

"Indeed, I will admit that the seams are extraordinary, I can hardly see them against the silk itself..."

The Dwarven merchant snorted. "Almost? I defy you, human, to point out the seam at all, so well is it hidden."

"I agree that were I to hang it upon my wall, it would serve as a marvelous display piece...an intriguing curiosity to delight party guests; but seeing as I intend to wear it...to use it for its intended purpose, twenty five noble is absurd." He was holding ten of the silver coins in his palm. "Ten is the most I could, in good conscience, pay and not seek to hide it from the hazards of the world."

The merchant's face screwed up tightly. "No child has emerged from the womb with skin half as soft as the garment you hold in your fingers. Twenty nobles."

"Indeed, and it would be an insult to a craftsman of your obvious skill to lock away such a fine work in a common wardrobe." A small smirk crept onto his lips. "And, sir, I could simply not live with myself were I to do you such a disservice." He paused a beat, almost as if he were struggling with a dilemma before saying, "It is because I would save you from the slander of another hiding it away that I will offer you fifteen nobles." He fished another five coins from his pouch with practiced fingers. "Take it quickly before common sense gets the better of my altruistic impulses."

The Dwarf shook his head sadly as he reached out to take the coins from the thief's hand. "Were my master here to see the depths to which I have fallen, he would cry tears that would put those of Umma as she wept over the First Tree to shame."

Hollis draped the cloak over his arm. "Then it is fortunate for both of us that his eyes are not upon our transaction." He saw the smile hiding in the merchant's downcast eyes. He would have taken twelve and the thief would have paid seventeen. He turned to face Jhorwynn, "Good morning, my friend."

The crimson and grey clad dwarf carried a cloth wrapped bundle

himself. "Greetings to you as well. If I could speak to you a moment."
Despite their attempts to hide their interest, the Dwarves around the pair
perked up at the interaction. It was uncommon for a member of the
Home Guard to speak to a guest unless it was in an official capacity.
'Fair' as the Folk may be, they were not immune to the siren call of gossip.

"Of course." Hollis gestured to the inn on the edge of the market.
"Lead and I shall follow."

Without reply, Jhorwynn turned on his heel and walked towards
the low building. Even though the longer legs belonged to Hollis, he had
to rush to keep pace with the Dwarf. Once they were free of the press of
the market, he turned to face the human. So sudden was his stop that
the thief had to pull up short to avoid colliding with the broad figure.

"Lord Silvermoon had contracted with Roen the swordsmith on his
last visit."

Hollis raised an eyebrow. "Ten years ago?"

"He paid in full for his commission. As he never returned to claim
it, it was put aside for him or an appropriate representative."

"Again, ten years ago?"

The Dwarf frowned. It is his. Years do not change that fact."

"He is dead...ten years gone; I believe."

"Do you have a relevant point?"

"I suppose not. Please continue."

"Roen passed it into the care of the Home Guard in case he
returned. As you are the closest that Lord Silvermoon has to a desig-
nated representative, it passes to you to do with as you will." He handed
the bundle to Hollis, leaning toward him in a shallow bow. A husky
whisper reached the thief's ears, felt more than heard, "West Gate.
Daybreak today. Five humans left with him on foot."

Hollis took the wrapped object, his eyes squinting in confusion.
Jhorwynn coughed into his raised fist; but it settled in front of his nose
rather than his mouth in the pantomime of a beak. Understanding
dawned on the thief suddenly. True to his word, the dwarf had found a
way to relay Plague Man's departure to him. "My thanks, truly."

Jhorwynn shrugged. "It is the least the Home Guard can do for you. What you do with it is up to you. Our responsibility in this is at an end." He once again seemed like he wanted to say more but turned on his heel and disappeared into the market crowd.

$\sim$

By the time that word had reached Aristoi and Rhyzzo and they returned, Hollis had packed their belongings and was waiting for them in the common room. An ivory-hilted short sword was tied atop his pack; belted around his waist was a Dwarven steel longsword. Through a decade and the barrier of death itself, Jeff was able to give the thief one final gift. It was certainly heavier than his own; but so well balanced that he hardly noticed. Upon unwrapping the bundle, Hollis was again struck by the artistry that the Fair Folk bring to everything they lay their hands upon.

It was forged in a style like Hollis's Uteli 'Tall Knife' but it was almost a foot longer in blade and hilt. The weapon would be called 'Wallin Fahr' in its kingdom of origin; but the cross guard was compact and broad where the Uteli weapon's was normally thin and tapering. A third guard emerged at a ninety-degree angle, thinner but equally broad as the other two, no doubt of use to protect the lead hand when in close corps de corps fighting. The blade itself was solid but slim on cross section with a hollow worked into a good deal of the flat. That accounted for its unusual light weight for the size of the sword and its superb balance.

It was the intricately carved bone hilt that took his breath away. Much like the cloak he had purchased that morning, even the most careful examination could not identify a seam where the two halves were fitted together around the full steel tang. A line of elegant letters wound around the bone, one flowing smoothly into the next. Although the characters bore a striking resemblance to those of the Dwarven language, the words themselves were in English. Carved into the weapon was the message: *If there must be trouble, let it be in my day, that my child may have peace.*

A tear welled in Hollis's eye as he recognized the words. From one of the earliest works of Thomas Paine, it had always been one of Jeff's favorite quotes and one of which he never tired of repeating. All in one expression, it gave the man's loyalty and love for those he held dear. Although the sword itself would have been gift enough, it was not the most profound one Jeff had bestowed upon his friend. Far more precious was the resolve that those simple words restored to the thief. Where both Stephen and his reflection had been lost in doubt, they now found inspiration; where they felt crushed by guilt, they were buoyed by purpose.

His introspection was interrupted by the arrival of his two friends. Rhyzzo carried a thick tome under one arm while Aristoi carried nothing but her spear and ever-present leather satchel. She spoke first, "Has there been a development that precluded us completing our research?"

The priest's silent but questioning glance communicated the fact that the same query weighed on his own mind.

Wrapping his hand around the bone hilt of the sword at his waist, Hollis nodded briefly, "The Plague Man left this morning through the West Gate. He has at least a four-hour lead on us and is travelling with five companions."

Rhyzzo muttered softly, "And thus the packs?" Again, Hollis nodded. The priest sighed, "Have you an idea of his destination? The Expanse is a large pool in which to throw a hook."

"They left on foot; their only choice will be to stick to the trade route between the Stone City and Oenigh. I purchased three camels, which should allow us to make up enough distance to overtake them by just after sunset."

CHAPTER TWENTY-THREE
VENGEANCE'S BITE

As the sun grazed the horizon, Hollis lay upon the uncomfortably warm sand of the Expanse. From beneath the twisted scrub tree, he had a clear view of the six men in their camp. Even a hundred yards distant and in the quickly failing light, the thief could mark the figure calling himself Plague Man by his ever present long nosed mask. From the corner of his eye, he also made out the shape of Aristoi, also prone beneath the branches. Hollis reached out to tap the woman's arm and stabbed the air behind them with his thumb. The two pushed themselves from beneath the tree and stood.

"It seems there are still only six of them," the thief whispered. "If we can remain hidden long enough to close the distance; I think the element of surprise could offset their numbers."

Aristoi nodded silently as they approached the niche in which Rhyzzo waited for them. The priest had a crude map folded in two upon his lap. As he saw them, he held it up for his comrades. "Their camp seems to be only a half league from an oasis. I cannot help but wonder why they did not travel for a while longer to reach it. The risk of traveling at dusk is dwarfed by the advantages of camping within the comfort and safety of its borders."

Hollis frowned. "As much venom as I hold in my heart for this

'Plague Man', he does not strike me as careless; his plan to capture you and Ren proved that."

Aristoi spoke up, "Setting out on foot, he must have had a route in mind. I find it hard to believe that he did not know of the oasis. He set camp where he had intended."

Rhyzzo sighed softly as he moistened his lips with his tongue. His mouth moved soundlessly as he gripped the chalice that hung around his neck. Hollis had always been more comfortable being near Rhyzzo or Haedren communing with their god than users of the arcane like Marcus or Aristoi. When a shaper of magic called their art, one felt it resonating through your soul almost as if everything around you developed a low frequency hum. When a priest called to their god, there were no outward indications of whether the plea was answered or even heard.

The priest spoke the last words in a rough whisper as he rose. "Bringer of Flame, lend me the light of your eternal torch." He squinted into the growing darkness before sinking down beside his two companions. He whispered again, "Thank you, Father of Justice," before speaking to them. "Aristoi is quite correct. Our quarry is indeed camped precisely where he had intended to be."

Both figures tilted their heads, waiting for Rhyzzo to continue. "We were so intent on the path of the man ahead of us that we failed to note those intent on ours. A half score of men, no doubt employed by the Plague Man, are as we speak approaching our position under the same cloak of night that we sought to use to our advantage."

The Songspear cursed beneath her breath, "So much for the charity of the Home Guard."

Hollis shook his head. "Do you believe Jhorwynn had a hand in this?"

"The coincidence of our giving chase on his word only to be caught in an ambush is a little too convenient," Rhyzzo muttered, gripping the symbol of Olm.

"Stunted little son of a bitch."

Aristoi spun the spear in her hands. "Be that as it may, neither his size nor his parentage are going to affect the next few moments one way or another."

The priest spoke again slowly, punctuating each word, "Father of Light, grant unto your children the shield of your justice and the sword of your righteousness so that they may fend off the predations of the dark hearted, as you did Sharroth's chosen at the Tree of Creation."

It was subtle at first; but there began to build in the three a firmness of resolve and lightness of spirit. The fatigue of the day melted from them as spring snow under the sun's gaze. Where soreness from battles of days past had resided, now was only the nervous energy of youth only remembered once it had passed. If he concentrated, Hollis was still aware of every ache, but it was the gauze memories of rain on a summer's day.

The thief cast his eyes around the clearing in front of the small cave. The now familiar sense of calm settled across him like a soft blanket. From this still center his thoughts began to swirl. He noticed little things that should have gone unnoticed. The angle of the last light of the setting sun cast a shadow of the small hill into which the cave was set. Small patches of hard pack dotted the ground spread before him but the largest lie directly in the most obvious route into the mouth of the niche.

A smile crept onto his lips. "We are only going to have one chance at turning this ambush back upon them. Let us make it count. They cannot know precisely where we are or they would have pressed their advantage before now; that means that we have an edge, meager though it may be." He turned towards Aristoi, "How much quicksand can you create?"

The Songspear weighed her answer before speaking, "A patch perhaps three yards on a side; but it will take the space of a few breaths to manifest. If it is to be used as a pitfall, it will be a slow one."

"Someone could get across while it is forming?"

Aristoi nodded, her widening as realization dawned on her. "Yes, but the timing would need to be on a razor's edge. Crossing too late will pull you down with those pursuing, too early and it will be for naught."

"Then I suppose walk the razor, I must. This niche is deep enough for the two of you to take cover. Rhyzzo, how are you with a crossbow?"

"No barn side is safe from me; but that is all I can promise."

"It will have to do. You and Aristoi pull back as far as you can into the cave, such that it is." He used his sword to draw a large X in the sand directly in front of the entrance and winked at the Songspear, "Big enough for you?"

"I find that it is less about the size of the target than the skill of the archer." She chuckled softly before continuing, "I will begin to sing as soon as I see you approach. You will have two deep breaths before the surface begins to pull at your heels; after three you will be trapped with any caught in it."

"Understood. Rhyzzo, as soon as I cross start shooting from the last man forward. I do not want them thinking of moving any direction but ahead." The priest began laying out bolts in an orderly row beside his knee. "If we are lucky, perhaps we can get half of them before the rest fall upon us. Our odds against two of them to every one of us are far better than half again as many." With that he was gone, disappearing into the desert gloom.

Darting from rock to bush in a half crouch, the thief moved like a deeper patch of shadow around the small hill that contained the niche in which his friends were hidden. His gifted sword remained in its scabbard; Hollis having chosen a thin bladed Slazè dagger for such close quarters work. In addition to renewed vitality, Rhyzzo's god had also honed the thief's night vision to a sharpness that rivaled that of the blade in his hand. Even so, he was almost on top of the group of men before he picked them out from the surrounding desert.

They had not the gifts of Olm, allowing him to close on the man closest to him like a whisper and lay blade to throat. Gripping him by the shoulder, Hollis drove the point of his dagger into the mercenary's neck. He twisted it hard as he extended his arm, laying open the man's throat to the spine and showering him with a burning stream of thick, copper smelling liquid. He wiped the blood from his eyes with the back of his knife hand, keeping his firm grasp on the corpses shoulder.

Between Luciius' expert setting of his hand and the Olm gifted vitality, he barely felt any pain.

His companions turned as one, their battle-hardened instincts serving them well. Without a word, Hollis shoved the body to the ground under the feet of the nearest mercenary before pivoting and breaking into a run. The two closest men stumbled over the body of their dead comrade; the other two were able to get clear enough to give chase. The thief expected them to call out to the other group; but for the time being they pursued him in relative silence. It dawned on him that they still were operating under the assumption of surprise. They had intended on chasing him down while keeping their presence hidden from the remainder of Hollis's party.

The thief could not help smiling as he thought about what await them on the far side of the hill. Filled with a vitality he could only vaguely remember from his youth, he had to purposely check his speed to prevent his lead from growing too great. If they felt they were losing him, they would no doubt call for aid. It was important to give them the sense of success to ensure their silence for a moment more. He slowed further as he rounded the hill and felt the wash of the allegro notes build in his chest. Aristoi had begun to sing.

His pursuers were a half dozen paces behind him as Hollis took his first deep breath and expelled it. Twenty yards ahead of him, he watched the sand begin to shift under the soft breeze of the desert night. As he inhaled again, he put his head down and pumped his legs with all his might. By the time he reached the area in front of the cave, his lead had extended to a dozen paces and the sand pulled greedily at his boots. He skidded into the cave and rebounded from the wall with a meaty thump.

A pair of surprised grunts reached Hollis's ears as Rhyzzo's crossbow string sang. The thief's head snapped up, as he hoped to find his pursuers in his baited trap. He was not disappointed. The two who had been in the lead were knee deep in the quicksand and quickly sinking. The priest's aim, while not perfect, managed to catch his target in the meat of his thigh, which caused him to pitch forward into the patch of transmuted sand face first. All that was visible was one of his legs, spasming like the tail of a nervous cat.

Aristoi, the song still on her lips, stepped forward to skewer one of the trapped men in the chest as Rhyzzo reloaded his crossbow. The last remaining free mercenary began to call for his comrades as the thief threw the dagger that was clenched in his fist during the hectic chase. It spun through the air and sunk into the man between his shoulder and collarbone, and his screams for help became more impassioned. The priest's second bolt silenced him forever.

The Songspear braced herself on the haft of her spear and kicked out, catching the final mercenary in the chest as he sank to mid-thigh. The last notes of the song hung in the air as Aristoi stepped back and watched as the sand – only a moment ago thick and viscous – hardening around those who were trapped beneath its depths. Hollis hurried across the patch to drag the only body that remained above ground into the cave. He drove from his mind the fate of those under his boots.

As he dropped the dead man out of sight and retrieved his dagger, the thief nodded towards the open desert. "We have to move; their friends are coming, and this cave will not serve us so well against a concerted assault." Never a planner, Hollis's words would normally have elicited a look of doubt from Rhyzzo, but something in his voice caused him to nod and snatch up the remaining bolts.

Aristoi crouched amid the scrub brush, just beyond the mouth of the cave, her eyes sweeping the night. Hollis moved past her and whispered, "Follow me and stay low." Retracing his now deceased pursuer's steps, the thief led the two men around the hill. Aristoi's woodland honed skills allowed the woman to keep pace with Hollis; the same could not be said for the priest. Rhyzzo seemed to stay low or prevent his steps from scraping along the hard sand but not both; he could do neither with any measure of speed.

Fortunately, the remainder of the mercenaries found the cave at that point and discovered the body of their comrade. As they raised their voices, Hollis gestured for his companions to rush to the place where they had hidden the camels. It was a short run; but their hopes were dashed at its conclusion. All three camels lay dead, their throats slit.

From behind them a voice rasped, "It is not the most secluded of locations; but I suppose it will have to do."

The thief's heart dropped into his stomach as he turned to face the Plague Man. He saw the masked man lean towards one of the five that stood with him and muttered, "Call for the others." As the man did as he was bid, the Plague Man turned back to address Hollis and his small band. "I remember you saying something about desiring a meeting somewhere not under the watchful eyes of the Fair Folk."

A burning anger built in the thief's gut. "I also remember it being termed intimate. You brought almost a score of men, not my idea of intimate. "I suppose you require the eyes of others to," Hollis chuckled in unfelt mirth, "Get your blood pumping, so to speak."

Real amusement echoed in his opponent's voice, muffled by his mask, "Doubtless, your patter has served you well when faced with ruffians and farmers alike, Slender One; but do not mistake me for either. Your babbling is naught but the tapping of rain on a tin roof to my ears; irritating but at the end of the day, of no serious import."

The thief gestured with his left hand as he drew his gifted sword in a smooth motion, "Then let us see if I can prevent you from reaching the end of that day." A familiar twinge ran up his forearm as the blessing of Olm began to fade, and his eyes flashed to Rhyzzo for a second. The shrug he received did not fill him with confidence.

"I have less worry about seeing the sun rise than I do intention of crossing blades with you. What would be the purpose to hiring these men if I sought to sully my hands with your blood?" He gestured to the five men behind him, "Kill him and the woman. Bring the priest to me when you are done." Hollis heard the others approaching. He almost heard the Plague Man's smile in his voice behind his mask. "Your comrades will be here to aid you presently."

The mercenaries leapt forward as one; only the length of Aristoi's spear and quickness of thinking prevented the thief from being carried to the sand. The point took the lead man under his sternum; his own momentum lifting his body over the two men as the Songspear set the butt into the hardpack along the arch of her foot. Hollis only hesitated a split second before dropping to one knee and sweeping his sword across the legs of the closest foe. The edge of the Dwarven steel blade parted flesh and muscle with equal ease. The mercenary crumpled to the sand as the thief allowed the momentum of his swing to carry him to the left, rolling easily to his feet.

Rhyzzo had stepped up beside Aristoi as he drew his own weapon, a finely crafted war hammer. The head resembled the chalice that served as his god's symbol, where the base of the chalice should have been was only a wicked spike. His lips formed an intercession to the Father of the Dawn but ceased almost immediately as his brows furrowed.

One of the remaining three mercenaries laughed. "Do not try to call on our lord Olm, weakling. He will not take sides between his chosen. You will need to win the day through strength of arm." He held up his buckler, upon which a golden chalice was carved.

"So be it," Rhyzzo said, clenching the shaft of his hammer tightly.

The sell swords stepped over the body of their slain comrade, two of them presenting their shields to Hollis and his companions as the priest bent to lay his hand upon the crippled man. The thief heard him whisper to the screaming mercenary. His protests faded when he fell into an enforced slumber. Hollis backed away from the group to rejoin his own companions as Aristoi probed their defenses carefully, her spear darting out, striking raised shield and pulling back quickly enough to not become tangled.

The three sell swords seemed to be in no hurry to engage; the reason became apparent as the other five crested the berm. All eight of them charged as one. The first rank was composed of five men shield to shield, short stabbing swords at the ready. Behind them, the mercenary priest of Olm and two others wielded spears over their comrade's shoulders. Aristoi's own spear kept them honest, trying to buy Hollis and Rhyzzo a chance to come up with a plan to breech their defenses.

Panic seized the thief, stealing his breath for a moment. If the three of them stayed together, the superior defensive capabilities of the shield wall backed by the longer reach of the spearman would prove itself to be unsurmountable. If they split up, drawing the mercenaries away from each other, they would face three to one odds behind what were essentially smaller shield walls. Flight was an option; but with the vitality of Olm quickly fleeing their bodies, it was a gamble as to whose stamina broke first.

Hollis took a deep and steadying breath and he imagined a familiar, soothing calm settling upon his heart. The feeling came more easily than he had expected. The world seemed to slow around him when he noticed things that, until this point, had eluded his eyes. One of the shield-bearers seemed a half step behind his comrades, moving with more trepidation than the rest. The thief saw his face tighten each time the line inched forward. Hollis gestured for Aristoi to give ground as they surged forward again and watched the center of the wall buckle for a moment before the man caught up again.

The spearman closest to Hollis also seemed to have eyes only for Aristoi. When he thrusted, it was always at an angle, towards the Songspear. This not only left half of the shield wall unprotected by his longer weapon but also obscured the view of the priest in the center of the formation. His smile slowly returned, and the thief said, "Aristoi, do you have another song left in you?"

The woman never took her eyes off the shield wall but chuckled softly. "I think I can manage. Do you have something particular in mind?"

Hollis batted aside a spear thrust with his sword, his foot lashing out to keep the shield closest to him beyond short sword range. "As a matter of fact, I do. These gentlemen seem to have a little too much spring in their steps. See if you can do something about that. Rhyzzo, follow my lead."

Rhyzzo nodded once, gripping his hammer in both hands as a deep ululation began to roll forth from the Songspear. It brushed the consciousness of each of them, friend or foe, stealing confidence wherever its notes touched. As quickly as the wave came upon Hollis and Rhyzzo, it passed. It seemed to settle upon their opponents like a wet, woolen blanket. Hollis gestured to his comrades to give ground again, taunting the mercenaries forward. This time, the thief's retreat was only a feint.

As the men surged forward, again the center buckled momentarily. Hollis ducked beneath the outstretched spear, aimed once again at the Kieli and collided with the shield of the chink in the wall. Thrown off balance, the man fell back another half step. Into the gap, the thief thrust his sword twice in rapid succession before retreating himself. The blade bit deeply into the gut of the distracted spearman; he twisted it as he drew it forth, opening a gaping wound in both armor and stomach. The man spilled his intestines like a nest of greasy snakes upon the sand. The second thrust took a surprised shield man under the arm setting the shield, emerging from his shoulder. Another twist of the blade as Hollis gave ground separated arm from collarbone with the sound of a turkey leg being wrenched from a carcass.

The enemy priest drew back his spear and thrust into the thief's back as he attempted to roll free. The weapon dug a deep furrow across his shoulders; but the effect of Aristoi's vitality sapping song and his own forward momentum saved him any real injury. The left half of the formation found itself tripped up on the injured, putting two paces of distance between themselves and the surging right half. The shield wall was momentarily broken, and Hollis's comrades pressed their advantage.

Rhyzzo's hammer impacted the closest shield with the sound of a thunderhead as Aristoi's ever present spear snaked past the line to keep the mercenaries from counter attacking the priest. The shield itself stood firm, of course; but the same could not be said for the arm holding it. The man let out a mournful sound as the shield dropped to his side, still attached to his shattered arm. The Songspear thrust again, taking the injured shield man in the throat and ending his suffering for good.

In a span of three breaths, an equal number of sell swords were removed from the conflict. The remaining five men closed ranks and Hollis noticed the weak link that took up a position on the right edge of the wall. The thief's gambit would not work again; his place in the line would not allow his hesitation to break the formation. Again, they came forward, the magic born fatigue evident in every step.

With his free left hand, Hollis gestured for Aristoi to flank to the right side of the wall, as he moved to his left. Rhyzzo fell back a few steps, forcing a difficult choice on the five men. They would maintain their formation and avoid the fate of the trio of their comrades or separate and forgo its safety. In the end, the decision was made for them.

"Fools! There are five of you and my patience is wearing thin!" The Plague Man's voice became a dangerous growl, "Their weapons should strike far less fear into your hearts then my discipline should you not bring me the priest quickly." The men lunged forward towards Hollis and his comrades. Two sell swords presented their shields to Hollis as they approached. A shield and spear pair similarly circled Aristoi. The mercenary priest engaged Rhyzzo by himself, his spear left behind in favor of sword and buckler.

Hollis's sword held the advantage of length over the short stabbing weapons of his opponents; but their shields hid their torsos from its bite. He tested their line with a couple of half-hearted swings aimed at their thighs and knees; but in each occasion his target would allow his shield to drop, blocking the blow easily. His partner would step forward, leading with his sword, forestalling any chance of a follow up from the thief. He saw that the Songspear's spell still hung over them, sapping their muscles of both strength and speed; but the combination of their shields and teamwork more than made up for it.

The thief hazarded a glance across the sand, hoping that his comrades fared better. Aristoi seemed to be holding her own; the length of the broad bladed spear was more than a match for the one wielded by her opponent, positioned as the man was behind the safety of his brethren's shield. The Songspear thrusted with impunity, keeping both men at a distance but faced the same issue as Hollis in the difficult feat of getting past the shield without inviting a return strike.

Rhyzzo was engaged in a more aggressive duel. His hammer spun and lashed out at his fellow priest; each time he was redirected by the man's swift buckler work. Hollis could see his comrade bleeding from a half dozen small wounds, as his foe made him pay for every time he overextended himself. Each time, Rhyzzo disengaged quickly enough to escape serious injury but unlike Aristoi and the thief, his weapon did not possess the advantage of length over that of his enemy. It was clear he was overmatched, and it was simply a matter of time before he proved himself too slow to avoid an expert cut.

Feeling the pressing need to prevent that from happening, Hollis turned to the matter before him. He took a steadying breath, trying to recapture the steady peace he had felt moments before, but it was shattered as a crossbow bolt streaked towards him. It was only muscle memory that brought his sword up to deflect the deadly missile from its intended destination. Rather than sinking into his leather clad chest, it found a home firmly in the meat of his left shoulder. Letting reflex take over, he allowed his partial parry to rotate him to the left, blading his body to present his right side, sword extended to the two men before him, looking for the source of the deadly missile. He was not surprised to see the Plague Man fitting another bolt into his crossbow.

He let his left-hand fall to his side, vaguely aware of the feeling of profound relaxation in the muscles of his upper arm. He made out the dim light of the setting sun that reflected off a thick paste clinging to the shaft protruding from his arm. Living up to his name, the Plague Man had poisoned him. Hollis's mind churned like the sea as he thrust his sword at one of his opponents and then the other to keep them both at bay. Already he was having issues moving his arm at all, as the poison took effect.

Aristoi's enemies had given up their defensive posture and begun attempting to flank the woman. She back-pedaled to keep them both in sight, but this took her further from her comrades with each step. Rhyzzo's hammer still spun in his hands, but rather than the heavy attacks he had been launching previously, he was furiously parrying the probing strikes of his fellow Olmite. The mercenary priest had rotated around Rhyzzo and was now driving him back towards where the Plague Man finished reloading his crossbow.

Hollis lurched forward, ducking under the deadly missile as it was

304

loosed; but vaguely felt something pierce his bicep as he did. Out of the corner of his eye, he saw the sword belonging to the closer of his opponent withdrawing from a vicious wound in his arm. The fast-acting poison dulled the pain, but he knew it was a wicked wound, nonetheless. The man paid for his success dearly as the thief moved past his shield and drove his own blade into his thigh. The sell sword collapsed instantly to the sand. His companion stepped over his body, preventing Hollis from following up on his advantage.

The thief saw the Plague Man raise his crossbow again and take aim. At the same time, the last mercenary pressed forward in a crouch, his shield protecting most of his body. Hollis gave ground, splitting his attention between the deadly crossbow and advancing sell sword. His steps took him further and further away from the hard pressed Rhyzzo, who was being expertly herded towards where the Plague Man waited.

With a sudden movement, the thief feinted low, aiming his swing at his opponent's unprotected legs. The mercenary shifted his shield to block the blow, only realizing too late that Hollis had meant for him to drop his shield. Deftly, the mercenary brought the wooden barrier up again, deflecting the sword from its intended home in his throat. Unfortunately for the man, it did not shift the weapon's path enough to prevent Hollis's thrust from taking him the eye.

The mercenary slumped to the ground, his own weight pulling him from Hollis's sword. In the instant that the thief's weapon was caught in his now dead opponent, his real enemy calmly fired his crossbow. Unable to deflect its deadly missile, a sharp pain shot through him as it entered his side under his extended arm. Almost instantly, a numbness spread across his ribs as the poison did its work. Despite the mask that covered his face, the thief could imagine the Plague Man's smug smile as he casually reloaded the crossbow.

His eyes shifted between Aristoi and Rhyzzo, who was being driven closer and closer to the masked man. Cursing himself, he made a quick decision and moved away from the eventuality of another crossbow wound. He felt his numb left hand bounce against his hip as he charged to where the Songspear was pressed. In the span of two dozen strides, *the numbness had reached his right shoulder. Given the rate at which the poison was spreading, Hollis estimated that he would have but one exchange with the shield-wielding mercenary who had turned his back on him.*

Allowing his arm to relax and fall to his side, the thief focused all his attention on gripping his sword as if his life depended on it. The man's spear-wielding comrade released a brief shout as he took in Hollis's intended path. The man brought his shield around to foil the thief's attack, but it was too late. He no longer felt his hand but knew his sword would be falling from his nerveless fingers. Crouching low, he lunged the last few feet between them. Hollis caught the weapon between himself and the sell sword.

The pommel dug heavily into the thief's hip as the blade impaled his opponent and both men collapsed to the sand. Instinctively, he rolled away from the dead man, narrowly avoiding another deadly missile from the Plague Man. Hollis felt his breathing quicken as it became harder and harder to draw adequate air. He watched from the ground as Aristoi spun on her remaining opponent. Despite the panic that filled his heart and mind, the Songspear's movements were a thing of beauty and distracted him from his demise, if only for a short while.

With a perfect mixture of ferocity and finesse, the Kieli forced the mercenary back on his heels. So sorely pressed was the man that he committed too fully to an ill-advised thrust. Aristoi dodged smoothly to the side, taking two short steps towards her opponent. This motion brought her inside the other man's guard, turning the length of his weapon into a detriment. The Songspear had no such problem; she reversed her grip and used the shaft to knock her foe's weapon up and out of the way. So focused on retaining possession of his spear was the mercenary that he only noticed the second loop of Aristoi's figure eight as it was too late. The broad blade caught the man in the belly and sliced flesh and leather equally. He sank lifeless to his knees as Aristoi pivoted and charged toward where Hollis gasped for breath.

The thief's vision dimmed. He tried to shout a warning to his comrade about the death tipped bolt that the Plague Man was no doubt reloading but found that his tongue and lips would obey his command no better than his slumping eyelids. As the rest of his body dissolved into insensibility, he was forced to commit all his concentration on gulping as much air as he could. As if under water and from an implausible distance, Hollis heard voices. A flash of cold panic settled over his nerveless body as he heard the crunch of boots on sand.

Cutting through everything, he heard as clear as day the mocking voice of the Plague Man, "As I knew I would, Slender One, I win."

CHAPTER TWENTY-FOUR
FORTUNE'S HAND

S tephen woke with a start, his heart trying to beat its way out of his chest. He gulped great lungsful of air, the over-powering sense of suffocation clinging to him like burial wrappings. In the darkness of his basement man cave, he only heard his breathing and the staccato pounding of his heart. Echoing in his mind were the last words he'd before falling into the velvet oblivion of unconsciousness. "... I win." The nasal, mocking tone would haunt him forever.

In no other reflection had he ever woken prematurely; this fact brought him more fear than the conflict with the Plague Man in Taerh. Had Hollis died in Taerh, causing him to wake up in his own bed? He couldn't make sense of it. The last image of Rhyzzo being dragged away by the man's lackey as Hollis lay fighting for breath on the sand was burned into his memory. Even with his eyes open, the scene played over in his mind like a film.

Stumbling to his feet, Stephen fumbled through the darkness for the light switch, hoping the light would drive it from his eyes. It helped, but not enough.

He was standing in the watercolor confines of his basement, crushed by fear and helplessness. Running his hand over the damp surface of his bald head, he searched for some harbor in the storm of his frenzied thoughts; but there was none. Hollis's presence, a constant companion this past week was gone. Once more, perhaps forever, Stephen was alone.

Questions raced through his brain. *Why could he not sense his reflection? What would happen to him if Hollis succumbed to the poison running through his veins? If he died or was unable to return to Taerh, what would become of Rhyzzo ... Mike?*

If they were correct that the Walker sought to activate one of the Wells by sacrificing his friend, what fate would befall the world that had become more of a home to him in a week than the one in which he was born?

The clock next to his computer read 3:27, but Stephen doubted he could sleep and was not sure he wanted to as he feared what he might find if he returned to Taerh. He took a moment to steady his panicked breathing, focusing on drawing in for the count of five and out for the same duration. Hyperventilating would do no one any good. Once he felt his breathing slow and the drumbeat of his heart faded from his ears, he focused. As he still lived on this side, he assumed so too did Hollis on the other. It was a major assumption but one that would be central to any further progress. One that brought him hope.

Sitting at his desk, he pulled a piece of paper from the feed tray of his printer. After a moment, he located a pen and began to write. Down the left-hand side of the paper he listed: Rhyzzo/Mike, Walker, Plague Man, Reflection, Hollis (RIP?). He paused after writing the last, tapping the tip of his pen against the paper as hopelessness threatened to overwhelm him once more. Although the thief's presence was no longer with him, Stephen still clearly remembered their time together. Alone and beaten in the dungeons of Oenigh, Hollis did not surrender to hopelessness. Even when facing a grotesque and agonizing death, his reflection continued to fight for every breath ... every moment of life. Perhaps he was merely unconscious.

The Plague Man would keep Rhyzzo alive until whatever use

he served was at hand. By extension, Mike would share in that safety as well. The Walker was still a puzzle that wouldn't be so easy to solve. There was no doubt she was involved in every step of this issue from its beginnings with Jeff through Alan's accidental death to his own current predicament. By the moment, it was becoming less and less likely that her involvement was incidental.

Just as he was forced to assume that Hollis still drew breath on Taerh, he was starting to accept the fact that the old woman was more than she seemed. She clearly had more than a passing relationship with the man who had been poisoning Mike since the accident. Both Jeff and Alan had misjudged her. Stephen couldn't afford to make the same mistake.

The Plague Man issue was tied to that of Walker. After their conversation in the Stone City, it was obvious the assassin and the orderly were willing reflections. While it was possible he was working without the knowledge or guidance of Samantha, there were too many inconsistencies in her words and convenient coincidences for all of them to be by chance.

The question was what he could do about it trapped on this side as he was. The last item on his list was the most troubling. Even if Hollis still lived on the other side, the question of how to reach him loomed large. He was tempted to drink another cup of adder root tea but knowing its effect on thyroid levels and what it had done in elevated amounts to Mike and Alan, and even the health issues it had caused Samantha, he was hesitant. Thus both the Hollis and reflection questions had to remain unanswered for the time being. He needed to assume anything he was going to do would need to be done while on this side and his reflection's uncertain fate necessitated that it be done quickly.

Stephen retrieved his phone from the coffee table and began to flip through the pictures of Samantha's medical records. It was the only intelligence he had that she was wholly unaware of. Within it had to lay an answer, if not the answer. Over the last decade, she seemed to rotate through an assortment of anticoagulants; her present medication, Dabigatran, seemed to inhibit the activation of thrombin in the blood stream. Thrombin, as far as he could tell from a quick internet search, was the enzyme responsible for clotting.

In addition, Samantha was prescribed a laundry list of blood pressure medication. Her present pharmaceutical solution was an angiotensin receptor blocker called Telmisartan. It worked by relaxing the muscles surrounding the blood vessels, allowing them to dilate and pass blood more easily. The third and last medication that seemed to be consistent over the last ten years was one to treat the hypothyroidism she presented with each time she was seen at the ER.

Knowing what he did about adder root, he was sure the last medication could combat the drop in triiodothyronine if she were to use the herb. Out of her issues, only the hypothyroidism seemed directly tied to the act of Reflection. He began a more in-depth search of substances that could cause or cure that very issue. After an hour, he'd settled on a likely candidate. Powdered bugleweed sprinkled among the leaves of adder root should offset the effects of her hypothyroid medication.

Bugleweed seemed easy enough to purchase in liquid form via the internet; but Stephen was unsure he had enough time for three to five business days shipping. A smile came to his face as he absently scrolled through images of the plant on Google. He'd taken his wife to a sunflower maze last autumn; it had been a completely unpleasant outing but he remembered a patch of wild flowers near the entrance they had labeled the 'Bee Farm' due to the wide variety of flowers that allowed the local bees to collect pollen. Near the cartoon image of a bee in overalls and a straw hat, he recalled the striking purple flowers that were now clear to him as bugleweed.

His smile faded as the realization settled on him that if his plan worked as hoped, he was going to murder an old woman. It was a truly sobering moment. In theory, preventing someone with evil intentions from gaining the power to bring more harm to the world, any world seems the righteous and noble thing to do. But where theory meets the reality of taking a life is a dark place indeed.

Stephen mentally reviewed each interaction he had had with Samantha, searching for a single instance where he could be sure she was the villain he needed her to be in order to carry out his plan with a clear conscience. At each turn, he found reasonable doubt, that doubt bred a sibling within his heart. He kept telling himself that if she were indeed finished Reflecting, as she had claimed on more than one occasion, the bugleweed laced Adder root could do her no harm. He looked up to the clock again as he came to a decision.

Samantha's shop opened in an hour; he had to speak to her again. He needed to be sure. He reached into the grey duffel bag that sat on the floor and pulled out the most recent of Jeff's journals. Once again, he regretted giving the latest ones to Samantha. After tucking it into the pocket of his oversized hoodie, he made his way up the stairs and into the silent house.

Even after a brief stop at the sunflower farm, which was deserted at this hour, the closed sign still hung in the window of Samantha's shop when Stephen pulled into the parking lot. Driven by habit, he pulled forth the journal that lay like a stone in his pocket.

Flipping to the last entry, he began to read.

February 21, 2010

Today was nigh unbearable; the school day seemed to pass in days, not hours. Once the final bell had rung, I locked my desk and rushed home. Alice had prepared dinner, so I had to swallow a great deal of guilt along with her delicious meatloaf. Feigning a headache, I made my way as quickly as possible to bed. The foul taste of Samantha's tea washed any vestige of my wife's carefully prepared meal from my taste buds.

As I feel gravity's pull upon my eyelids. The adder root's pull upon my very spirit, I sit here trying to compose my thoughts. Walker, Samantha's Reflection, assures us that her mystical attacks upon Haedren have been bearing fruit. Rather than continuing towards Rangor, she claims he's been forced to hide and compose some sort of ritual defenses against her mental incursions.

This has given us some time to breathe and collect ourselves. Before I left my own reflection, waking here this morning, Marcus had been researching the place Walker had called 'The Well of Worlds'. Originally, we'd believed it a singular place, while in actuality, it is only singular in the fact that only one Well can exist at a time. The currently active one is believed to be in the depths of a mountain at the center of the tundra called the Sea of Snows. We have come realize that it is Haedren's destination, just as it had been Theamon's.

The lore of the Well is based in a great deal of hearsay and oral traditions, so Marcus had complained that it involved wading through a great deal of flotsam and jetsam to distill the details that were most likely factual. As the Adder Root takes effect, I can feel Silvermoon's memories filtering into my foggy mind. Marcus has found several accounts, all from different sources, that seem to agree on some commonalities between the various tales of the Well of Worlds.

The first of these lends credence to our assumption that while there have been several Wells over the history of Taerh, only one exists at a given time. Each of these accounts seem to point to the fact that the Well only remains until used, at which point a new one will form.

The second commonality is that each Well forms in an area ripe for enlightenment; it seems to act as a spark to ignite the area's development. They are holy places, and those who frequent them are seen *having gifts from beyond themselves. These gifts normally take the form of some sort of prophecy.*

The final commonality is that while there are tales of multiple individuals visiting the Wells in their function as a holy place, all stories of their use involve a single person. That person is depicted as someone of great power and wisdom; not all, however used these gifts for the welfare of their fellow men.

I will have to speak to Samantha when I wake. Perhaps she or her reflection, the Walker, can provide more clarity on the subject.

The root's influence must have taken over him at that point, because the narrative came to an abrupt end. It was clear now, that Jeff trusted Samantha as Stephen once had. No doubt, it had led to his death. A rush of anger rose in Stephen's heart, but he forced it down with much effort. Passion wouldn't lead to answers. With his connection to Hollis lost and his reflection most likely dead, he would need to be twice as clever, as he was only working with half of his previous resources.

Stephen closed his eyes and tried to recall Aristoi's words in the Stone City. The Songspear had verified some of what Jeff had written in his journals...or vice versa. These Wells lift primitive tribes out of the darkness and into the light of civilization. They seemed to do so through the actions of one person chosen by the Well itself. To this Child of the Well, it grants extraordinary abilities and wisdom. The later piece could have been simply knowledge gleaned from their more advanced Earth reflection. The former, however, seemed to point to something more supernatural.

The man quickly reread the journal entry and then did so again more slowly. Jeff suspected that Haedren, and Theamon before him, sought a Well located in Rangor, but Aristoi had mentioned in passing that in his Long Walk, he had studied an empty Well in the northern wastes. *Could the Well that the men sought have been used by someone else? Could that someone have been the Walker?* Stephen closed his eyes and pinched the bridge of his nose between his fingers. There were too many questions and not nearly enough answers.

Opening his eyes, the man saw a shadow moving inside the flower shop. Hoping his visit with Samantha would yield more of the latter and less of the former, he climbed from the car and into the warm morning air.

~

The bell above the door announced his entry and Samantha smiled a greeting as she held up a single finger. Her other hand-held the phone to her ear on the end of its ivory-colored cord. Despite the absence of Hollis's presence in his mind, Stephen studied the shop as he imagined the thief would. He noticed things that previously had escaped his eyes.

The shop itself seemed steeped in the past; from the corded telephone to the black and chrome rolodex, stuffed past capacity with index cards, it was clear that Samantha had never allowed progress to push her beyond what she had found comfort in. The counter was clear of both computer and cash register, as she calculated sales by hand and wrote receipts in the same way. His eyes moved casually around the room; her distaste for modern conveniences extended to security as well. While the door had two dead bolts, there was not an alarm panel to be seen.

"Good day, Stephen. To what do I owe this early morning visit?" Her voice seemed to contain honest joy, where in previous meetings; it had only held guarded politeness. She was standing at a small sink towards the back of the main room, scrubbing what appeared to be a lace table runner. Next to her on the sink was a clear bottle that appeared to be soapy water, but his nose picked up the subtle scent of bleach. He smiled to himself at the stroke of luck and prayed it would not run short.

As quickly as he could, Stephen wiped the grin from his eyes and sighed once before drawing a slow deep breath. He'd practiced his part in this conversation during the drive, and he hoped it would be enough to appear convincing. "Something happened in Taerh last night. Something terrible." He reminded himself to speak from the very real emotion of the events. The secret of a believable lie is to mix in a good deal of truth and glue it to the fabrication with strong feelings.

She raised an eyebrow. "Is that so?" Again, time spent beside Hollis paid very real dividends. She was a little too anxious, as the words flowed a little too quickly. Her posture was one of satisfaction not surprise. "Is everything alright?"

Stephen averted his gaze for a moment; drawing on the very real feeling of hopelessness that still haunted the periphery of his heart. It was clear that she'd known about the events in Taerh before he spoke; but he had to continue to play his role. Samantha stepped out from behind the counter and approached him, a soft clucking emerging from her as he spoke, "I think Hollis may be dead." She gasped after a split-second delay. It wouldn't have been noticeable had Stephen not been looking for it. While she'd known about the attack, she didn't t seem to anticipate this new piece of information. This, too, was according to Stephen's plan; an opportunity to allow her to prove her less than pure intentions. She took his hand in hers; he fought every instinct to snatch it back. "That is terrible. How can you be sure?"

"I'm not, but I fear..." He hoped she caught the stutter in his voice and believed it to be emotion at recalling the events. "I woke after only a few hours of reflection. Before I did, he had been shot...poisoned by a man I met in Mike's hospital room. Hector was his name. I think he may have been responsible for the attack on Alan as well."

She squeezed his hand gently. He wanted to shrug her fingers away from his but held himself back from the urge. "Oh dear. Do you have any idea why?" Her eyes studied him from beneath hooded lids.

This was the pivotal instant, the moment where truth became lie, where recollection became deception. "Only that he sought Mike for something. He told me that if I let him take my friend, he would leave me alone." He squeezed her hand with a tighter grip. "I couldn't do that; I couldn't sacrifice Mike for my own ... for Hollis's life." The silence between them seemed to stretch for an eternity. Stephen hoped with all his heart that she would not see through his charade and call him on his poorly acted deception as she'd done so before,

"Of course, you could not, child," she nodded deeply in an attempt to hide small smile of satisfaction from her face. Stephen saw the slight curling of the edges of her mouth before she was able to hide it. "Of course you could not, but what makes you think that your reflection is dead?"

He sensed her excitement as she leaned towards him, "Before I woke, I couldn't breathe. I felt as if I were suffocating. As Hollis passed out, I awoke with my heart in my throat." Encouraged by his success, Stephen fell into the role more fully, "I wanted to reflect again but I'm afraid." He drew a shaky breath, purposely giving her time to interject. She spoke; but didn't call him on his deception.

"You should be. You were wise to come to me before attempting it." She led him through the curtain, into the back room. To his satisfaction, the back door also had two dead bolts but no alarm. "Were you to reflect and your reflection was dead, you too would die." Her words were just a touch too quick, tinged with a touch too much enthusiasm.

He nodded slowly, averting his eyes once again. "But what about Rhyzzo? "

She simply shook her head, "I see no other options. Sacrificing your own life does your friend no good. Perhaps when he is discharged, he should come to see me. Perhaps my advice could aid him in some way."

Stephen frowned. After his discussions with both Mike and

Rhyzzo in Taerh, he had assumed that his friend would wake here; Samantha seemed to already know it for a fact. Stephen reached into his pocket and retrieved his phone to divert her attention. "Are you sure that you have not had any interaction with this man? I believe I saw him outside your shop the other day. It was clear to me that he'd been inside." He had brought the photo of Hector's ID badge to the screen and held it out to the woman.

She took a step back, averting her gaze before shaking her head. All of this happened too quickly once again. "Not that I am aware of."

"Are you sure? It was clear from my conversation with him that he too was reflecting."

She extended her hand and took the phone from him. He saw that her eyes shifted from side to side rather than studying the picture. "I am sorry, Stephen, but I am afraid I do not know him." Samantha pushed his hand away as if trying to push away his question as well. "Do you not believe that there are more important things to discuss?" Her clipped tone and flighty gaze indicated to Stephen that she was continuing to hide the truth from him.

There it was. Not only had Stephen seen Hector leaving her shop; but he had clearly had the adder root and whatever he had used to keep Rhyzzo insensate on Taerh in his possession after leaving. There could only be one explanation for her repeated denials. She was lying to him, knowing that his and Mike's lives were at risk. His heart struggled with conflicting emotions. He felt vindication that his plans to keep her and her reflection from the Well were founded. He also felt an intense pang of betrayal, not just for himself but for his friends who paid for her disloyalty with their lives.

She held the phone out to him. "Send Mike to me as soon as he is able. I fear I was not quick enough to save Alan or Jeffery from death. Perhaps I can be quick enough to aid your friend."

"I thought you said that Jeff could still be alive."

Her eyes opened enough for him to see the whites of them as she looked up and to the right. It was sudden and gone just as quickly; but even the best liars could not hide their true motivations when taken by surprise. Stephen saw the edges of her eyes crinkle as she searched quickly for a lie, "He very well may be but the likelihood becomes less and less the more I hear of this man who killed your reflection." She touched the back of his hand. "I am truly sorry; but I fear whatever the final outcome may be your part in it is over."

He nodded as he placed the phone back in his pocket, more concerned with breaking contact with her touch than the location of the device. He stood slowly, allowing his own disappointment to shine through. "I will speak to Mike when I visit him today." Encouraged by his successful deception so far, he lied again, "I'll ask him to come see you as soon as he can."

She frowned, before continuing, "I am so sorry that your journey is at an end, and such a sad end at that." Her expression mirrored sadness, but instead of the triangular fold between her eyes, there was in its place smooth skin.

"At least I have my life here. That is something." He turned and walked into the main room of the shop. At the curtain he stopped, "Would you mind if I took some flowers for my wife? I see some daisies she would like." The daisies were also near the small rectangular box containing what he hoped were her only living adder root plants.

"Of course, my dear. Let me help you."

He held up a hand. "No ... it's no bother. I see some plastic to wrap them in over here."

"Alright, Stephen. They are over there." She pointed to the wooden table that held the daisies. "Take as many as you like."

He forced a weak smile, "Thank you. You are truly too kind." He crossed the room, picking up the plastic bottle on the sink. He placed the bottle down on the table, blocking sight of it from her with his body as he gathered a hand full of flowers and placed them in the sleeve. "These are looking a little parched, let me give them a little water." Before Samantha could protest, he removed the cap from the bottle and upended it into the planter, making sure to coat each plant and soak the soil as well.

A half-beat too late, the woman realized what was happening, "No! What are you doing?"

He turned quickly, dropping the bottle onto the table, "Watering your plants?" he asked as innocently as he could manage. The bleach was a blessing; the soap was positively god sent. It caused the solution to stick to the leaves and soak into them rather than beading off. The only thing that would have made the situation more perfect would have been the addition of the salt that he carried in his pocket. He had not had time to make use of it, but beggars could not be choosers.

"That is bleach, you fool!"

He turned to stare at the plants. "I am so sorry." With his back to Samantha, it hid his satisfied smile from her eyes. When he turned back, he'd controlled his expression again. "Can you wash them?"

She pushed by him in a rush, wrinkling her nose as she caught the first scent of Stephen's improvised weed-killer. "They are ruined." She turned on him, with murder in her eyes. "How could you mistake that for water?"

In the moments since first seeing the bottle and altering his plan, the man had prepared for this question. He shrugged, purposely widening his eyes and allowing his jaw to become slack to mimic surprise and shock. "I assumed it was some organic plant food. Who would have bleach around plants?"

"I was cleaning linens for this weekend's..." She forced a smile that she clearly didn't feel. "It is not a huge loss; I had just finished harvesting this morning." She nodded to where the already harvested leaves sat. "I should have enough until a new crop reaches maturity."

"For Mike?"

Samantha frowned at him, her true feelings for the man becoming more and more evident in her tense posture and clipped tones, "What? Yes, of course for Mike. Who else would it be for?"

He shrugged again. "Please accept my apologies. Can I help you clean up?"

She shook her head. "Just go. Take your flowers to your wife and try to forget this past week."

Stephen nodded slowly, "Of course." He turned and walked from the shop. It wasn't until he was halfway to the hospital that he allowed himself to truly smile.

CHAPTER TWENTY-FIVE
DESPERATION'S VOICE

The curtains of Mike's room were pulled back, allowing the June sunshine to brighten its confines. He was shifting a brown meat-like substance and congealed gravy around his plate with a white plastic fork.

Joy welled up in Stephen's chest. To avoid rushing to his friend and wrapping his arms around him, he spoke quickly. "It's no lamb shank and mint jelly; but it can't be that bad."

Mike looked up, a smile quickly replacing the frown of confused disdain. "Stephen!"

He began extricating himself from tray and bed when Stephen placed his hand on his friend's arm. "Easy, buddy. I'm not going anywhere, and neither are you." His friend settled. "Do you remember anything while you were out?"

Mike squinted at him. "Are you kidding? The only reason I'm not screaming it from the highest mountain is I imagine the food is worse in the psych unit."

"Good thinking."

Mike nodded, taking one final look at his plate and pushing it to the edge of the tray table, "Not so funny thing? I think it's lamb shank and mint jelly ... I just have never seen it ... brown." His lips pursed at the last word, in a sign of distaste.

"I remember the weevil-infested menu in the Emir's dungeon and the thought of that being lamb makes me queasy."

The two friends shared a cathartic laugh, the tension of the week extending it in both duration and ferocity. After it had run its course, a tense silence filled the room. As Stephen sat down in the bedside chair, his friend asked, "So, did everything turn out alright?"

Stephen took a deep breath and blew it out in a slow exhalation, his mind still racing to put together a way this conversation wouldn't end badly. By the time there was no more air in his lungs he was no closer to a plan, so he began anyway. "Not in any sense. To be honest, after everything you have been through, I was debating not telling you. But then I thought that would be a shitty thing to do. You deserve to know the truth." He glanced over at his friend and it was clear he had Mike's undivided attention, so he continued, "Rhyzzo, Aristoi and I came up with a plan after you awoke. I thought it was a solid one; but it turned out worse than I could have imagined."

"What happened? It can't be that bad." It was clear Mike was agitated and reaching for something he knew wasn't there.

He stared at the linoleum flooring, unable to meet his friend's eyes. Stephen nodded, "But it is. We were betrayed by someone I thought was a friend and led into an ambush. We fought so hard and almost saw the daylight at the other side, but the Plague Man poisoned me, and I imagine escaped with Rhyzzo."

Stuttering, Mike asked, "Is...is...is he dead?" He leaned forward, threatening to tip over the tray table before him. "What will I do if he dies? Will I die? I don't want to die, Stephen!"

Stephen rose quickly and stepped up to the bedside, gripping his shoulder and holding him still. "Mike, calm down. Please listen to me."

His friend peered up at him, his tone pleading. "Please don't let me die ..." He struggled against Stephen's grip, seeking to rise.

Stephen squeezed firmly, pressing his thumb sharply between

his friend's clavicle and his shoulder. Mike winced and surrendered, collapsing back into the bed. He began again, "Mike. I cannot promise that everything will be okay, but I can promise you one thing. If it is not, I will have left every ounce of my blood on the field trying to make it so."

Mike brightened at that. "Hollis?"

Stephen finished his friend's hope. "... is fine and giving chase. He will find Rhyzzo." It amazed him how easy the lie came to his lips. He'd wanted to be honest with Mike; he had wanted the man to enter the next phase of his plan with open eyes. But seeing how distraught his friend was, it was all too clear that if he knew Hollis was gone, it'd only take away the slim remains of hope he already held onto.

The panic did not leave Mike completely; but he seemed to relax. "Do you promise?"

Stephen nodded, "But I need you to do something for me." Mike nodded quickly. He grasped the table in front of him to hide his trembling hands, as if he could physically prepare for Stephen's words. "I know it is frightening; but I need you to go back."

Terror filled Mike's face. "Back?"

Stephen squeezed his friend's shoulder gently. "Yes, back to Taerh. I need to know where Rhyzzo is. I need to know everything that is around him, what he sees, what he feels, no detail is too small."

Mike shook his head from side to side, slowly at first. "I can't ... I don't want to ..." The shaking picked up speed. "No ... Please don't ask me to go back.".

Stephen forced his voice to remain soft and calm, "I know you are afraid. I need you to be brave. The more I ... Hollis knows, the faster we can put an end to it." It broke his heart to see his friend in this state. It further pained him to know that putting an end to *it* involved death and he could not be sure that death would not be Mike's. He reached into his pocket and pulled out the small plastic bag containing the last of his adder root.

Mike asked nervously, 'Why can't Hollis go? Why does it have to be me? You said Hollis was giving chase. Please don't make me do this." I hated watching his fingers trembling as he pulled down his sleeve, as if for comfort.

The contents were half the size that they were just four days ago. Stephen frowned softly but continued, "I'm sorry, Mike, but it needs to be you. Please, you can do this. You only need to stay under for a few moments...just long enough to get your bearings. I will be right here and promise I will not let you stay under more than five minutes."

He saw Mike still debating as he asked, "How much do I need to take?"

"Just a pinch. It won't be even a tenth of the amount you and Alan took the last time."

"What if I can't wake up?" He stared at Stephen with wide, fearful eyes.

It broke Stephen's heart, but he knew he had to do this. "That douche Hector was spiking your IV to keep you under. With me here, you will come right out. I promise." He forced a certainty into his voice that he didn't truly feel.

"Okay, I'll do it."

Stephen pulled out a small pinch of adder root from the bag, "Just chew it and try to suck out any liquid. I'm not going to lie to you, it tastes like week old ass."

"You know what that tastes like?" Mike asked, with one eyebrow raised, before chuckling loudly. Stephen joined him, unable to help himself. For a moment, all of the fear between them was gone. He hoped it'd last.

Stephen scoffed, "There was that one time in college but ..." He laughed again and Mike copied him, then Stephen forced himself to be serious. "Not too much."

He placed the adder root in his hand, "No ... just enough ... now lay back and try to relax."

～

Mike had been under for less than three minutes when the nurse came in to check on him. Stephen had been standing next to his friend and was so focused on watching him that he didn't notice the woman enter.

"Excuse me," she murmured as she gently pushed past him. Panic raced through him as his eyes went from Mike's slack face to the machine that monitored his vital signs. "How long has he been asleep?" she asked in a conversational tone.

"Only a few minutes." He pulled at her elbow firmly. "May I speak to you in the hall? I don't want to disturb him."

She looked between Stephen and the paper emerging from the machine like an expensive receipt. He saw her look from him to Mike, but she relented, "Of course, Sir."

Once in the hall, he searched his mind for some way to delay her examination. The uncomfortable silence lingered, and he watched her shift impatiently from foot to foot as her frustration built. Impulsively he blurted out, "Does this look infected?" Peeling the bandage from his forearm, he revealed the freshly stitched box cutter injury. He winced as the gauze, made sticky by dried blood that clung to the wound. Where it had, the laceration began to bleed.

Her eyes widened in surprise. "Sir, please, you need to keep that covered." He simply held the blood speckled bandage out to her. She sighed and shook her head. "I suppose I can get you a fresh one."

"Thanks," he smiled and looked over his shoulder, noticing Mike begin to stir. "I will be in here." Turning before she could reply, he rushed to his friend's bedside.

"No …" he moaned softly, tension building in his previously lax form.

As he came fully awake, Stephen laid his hand on Mike's forehead. "Easy, brother, I am here."

Mike's eyes blinked a few times before they came into focus on Stephen's face. "He's a monster, Stephen."

"I know. What do you remember? Where were you?"

"Don't make me go back! Please, he's a monster!" The volume of Mike's voice rose; but Stephen resisted the urge to cover his mouth.

Instead he let his hand drop to his friend's shoulder. "Shh, I know. We will put an end to his monstrosity. Just tell me what you remember."

Fear widened eyes settled on Stephen's. "My legs hurt so badly. I was lying in a wagon. Stephen, I think he hamstrung Rhyzzo."

A mixture of anger and pity rose in Stephen's chest as he squeezed Mike's shoulder softly. "He will answer for that." He refrained from adding *I promise*, as there was no sense further betraying his friend's trust. "Do you know where you were? What did the scenery look like? Was there sand?"

Mike shook his head, more calmly now, as he was away from Taerh. "No, I was surrounded by low trees and tall brown grass." He searched for a moment, "Savanna. It was a Savanna."

Stephen nodded, they had made it out of the Expanse and crossed into Slazè. "Can you remember anything else? Sights, sounds, scents?"

"In the distance, I saw a small farm. There was a smell of burning in the air." Panic crept back into his voice, "I think he killed the farmer and his family. Killed them and set fire to their home."

Stephen felt the cold fingers of dread digging into his psyche as his thoughts turned to Maggie. "How do you know?"

"I heard the men driving the wagon talking about it. I think it was meant as a message." Sadness bled through the fear in Mike's eyes. "I think it was a message for you."

Guilt replaced dread; *Those people died because I was not quick enough to stop him*. He drew a deep breath and exhaled slowly; he had to remain focused on the matter at hand.

"But how did The Plague Man even know about her? I don't understand. Did you see mountains, even in the distance?"

Mike thought hard, screwing his eyes shut tightly before nodding. "Yes, in the way distance. They were hard to make out, but I'm sure they were there."

He smiled, trying to keep the sadness and worry from his eyes. "Excellent, you're doing great, Mike. You were lying in the cart. Were you moving in the direction of your feet or your head?"

"My head," Mike answered immediately.

Stephen smiled. "What side of you were the mountains on for the most part? The right or the left?"

Again, Mike thought about it for a moment. Just as Stephen was about to press him again, he spoke, "My left. For a lot of the time, they were on the left." Stephen tried to recall the hand-drawn map Jeff had shown him on several occasions. If the Grey Spire Mountains were to the left of the cart, that meant that they were traveling north as the mountains that held Drunmarch dominated the eastern edge of the Cradle. Whatever plans the Plague Man had for Rhyzzo lay north of the Expanse. Perhaps it bought him a little time.

"You are doing fantastically. Did the Plague Man say anything? Did he give you any clue of where he was headed or what he was looking for?"

Mike sighed heavily and then suddenly shook his head. "I don't want to...he is..."

Stephen finished, "...a monster, I know. He cannot hurt you here. It is just you and me. With a little more information, we can put a stop to him."

"Promise?"

He closed his eyes and lied to his friend again, "Yes, Mike, I promise."

His faith in Stephen set his mind at ease; but it had the opposite effect on the man himself. "He was talking about a woman. He never referred to her by name. It was always 'she this' and 'her that'." Stephen nodded, encouraging Mike to continue. "He never spoke to me; but instead acted as if I weren't there at all. He mentioned something once about 'little men'. One of his men was worried about their reaction to trespassing; but he dismissed the soldier's concern." He saw Mike relax, closing his eyes once more. "That is all I remember, I swear."

Once again squeezing his shoulder, Stephen murmured, "That is enough ... rest now."

Mike was sleeping peacefully, this time sans the effect of adder root, when Robert turned into the room. His surprise was clear. After looking over his shoulder he frowned and in a harsh whisper, "You need to go, now." Looking up from the crude map of the Cradle he'd been doodling on the back of a 'Get Well Soon' card, Stephen raised an eyebrow. "Good afternoon to you as well, Rob." The ghost of a smile touched his lips.

He looked behind him again and then. "I'm serious."

"Normally more than I would like, yes. Pray tell, do you have a reason behind this particular declaration?"

"She knows about the drugs," was all he said.

Stephen exhaled slowly, "Do you mean the perfectly natural plant that I found in Alan's trunk?"

"Save your liberal rhetoric."

"The one that you advised me to throw in the nearest dumpster? The one we both agreed to never mention again, that one? How on earth did she figure that out?"

Robert dropped his eyes, revealing more than words ever

could. "She's also convinced that you gave it to both Alan and Mike."

Stephen frowned in disbelief and stood, tucking the drawing into the back pocket of his jeans. "Well, isn't that delightful. You, of course, tried to dissuade her from this belief? Of course, you did not."

"How am I to know..."

He did not let the man finish, "Because your brother and I were friends, because we are friends, Robert, or at least I thought we were. You could've come to me before you told your girlfriend that I was a drug dealer. You owed me at least that much." Stephen closed his eyes and tried to let the warmth of his anger run through him like the first shock of a hot shower. All of it didn't cool; but he continued anyway. "A day is going to come, Rob, when you see more than what is right in front of you, more than how something affects you. I don't blame Nell, I...even kind of expected it. This week has shaken her world to its core; no one, least of all me, would fault her for seeking to make sense of it all. You, however, simply do what you have always done: focus on nothing but what is at the tip of your nose."

Robert stepped forward in a sudden motion, intent on using his athlete's frame to overwhelm the older, softer man. Reflexes Stephen had feared lost responded in the space of a thought.

As he deftly stepped aside, memories filtered into his mind. At first, they came at a trickle and then, as if a dam had broken, they came faster and faster.

Robert turned, his hands clenched into fists.

He was trapped in darkness, aware of what was going on around him as if he were underwater.

He pulled one of those fists back as he stepped closer to Stephen.

He remembered hearing Aristoi's voice and another. It had been vaguely familiar, but he could not place it.

On instinct, he raised his own hands, his forearms angled

outward to establish a perimeter outside of which blows would either miss or be ineffective.

It had been Jhorwynn, the Dwarf that had betrayed him in Drunmarch. He did not understand the words; but the tone was unmistakably one of concern.

He stepped in and took a sloppy right hook against his left forearm as he drove his shoulder into Robert's chest and knocked him backwards into a chair. Pain raced up Stephen's arm into his shoulder.

His nose felt like it was being crushed and he had felt something pressed over his mouth. Whatever it was had been wet and unrelenting.

Robert looked up at him in shock.

Again, words had been exchanged. He understood virtually none of them; the only one that had filtered through the haze that surrounded him was 'breathe'.

Robert tried to rise; Stephen pushed him back into the chair. "Either through selfishness or stupidity, you have put me in a very difficult situation. You can make it up to me by staying here and watching Mike. No one you do not know touches him. Understood?"

"Why would I do anything you asked?"

"Do it for me, do it for him. Do it for anyone you like, I do not care; but just do it." Without another word, Stephen turned and rushed from the room.

CHAPTER TWENTY-SIX
CONFLICT'S END

The Castor and Pollux Diner served a tolerable cup of coffee, if it was diluted with enough sugar and cream. It also happened to have a patio that overlooked Samantha's shop; that was the only thing that made a third cup of coffee palatable. As he muscled through the bitter liquid, Stephen rolled the makeshift hook pick over his knuckles. It was formed from the same automobile hose clamp that he'd used to make the torque. Fortunately for him, the emergency tool kit that served as his wife's most recent passive aggressive Christmas gift had provided the tools needed to trim the thin metal for the purpose.

From his vantage point, he could clearly see the sidewalk that passed by the florist and the strip mall's parking lot, although not in direct line of sight of the shop itself. Stephen sipped the acidic dregs in the bottom of his cup and was contemplating whether he could survive a fourth when Samantha stepped from the concrete ribbon on to the blacktop on the way to her car. He tucked the pick behind his ear and tugged his wallet from the back pocket of his khaki's as he watched the tan Audi pull slowly from the parking lot and into the mid-afternoon traffic.

He fished out a ten-dollar bill and laid it on the table beside his empty cup before walking slowly towards the rickety gate that separated the patio from the diner's own parking lot. Walking past his Honda, Stephen made his way to the edge of the black-top, where it bordered the rear of the strip mall. Slipping behind the building, he strolled as casually as he could manage to the rear entrance of Samantha's shop.

Momentarily closing his eyes and letting out a soft breath, Stephen surrendered to the influence of his reflection. Hollis's practiced fingers made short work of the door's three locks, despite the makeshift tools. He'd thought to wear the leather gloves he always kept in his car; but as he didn't plan on stealing anything, he thought the attention brought by a man wearing gloves in ninety plus degree heat was not worth hiding his iden-tity. If his plan went as intended, there would be none to complain about a little breaking and entering.

Again, the cold fingers of doubt caressed his heart. *What if he was wrong about Samantha? What if there were reasonable explana-tions for her behavior and omissions?* He reminded himself that if she didn't intend to reflect any longer, the dried bugleweed in his pocket would cause her no harm.

Stepping out of the mid-afternoon sun into the thick tepid air of the shop's back room did nothing to cool the man. Sweeping his eyes across the dim interior of the room, he made out the silhouette of the pair of high-backed chairs in which he began his investigations of the deaths of his friends with the woman that he was here to kill. On an impulse, he crouched down to peer beneath the one in which Samantha had been seated that morning.

Stacked neatly, as if they waited patiently for him, were the four journals he'd left with the woman days prior, including the journals that she promised to bring to her colleague in New York City. Flipping through the journal without looking at it, his mind spun, instinctively trying to manufacture a reasonable explana-tion while rage built in his heart. The only answer to which he continued to return was that she had lied to him, about his friends, about her interest, about everything.

Deep in his psyche, his reflection reminded him of the fact that he had a limited window in which to poison the adder root, but he found his hand reaching out to turn on the lamp nearest the chair. The pool of light drove back the dimness of the room, although the shadow seemed hesitant to retreat from its influence. In deference to his reflection's dire warnings, Stephen did not sit. He flipped forward in the book all the same, running his eyes over the words he found there.

February 7, 2010

Although I only slept for a little over eight hours here, that time translated to almost four days in Taerh. I continue to wonder why time seems so fluid between there and here. I have turned to the writings of Dirac and Hilbert to understand this concept of relative time in both places. I have learned more about theoretical mathematics in the past few months than I had ever done in six years of college, or ever wanted to.

The frustration I feel when trying to understand the phenomenon is nothing compared to that I feel when reflected. Silvermoon continues to search for Haedren after their last encounter at the Crown of the First King. The Walker insists that he searches for what she refers to as the 'Well of Worlds'. When it was not found within the nigh impassable mountain range, she retreated to wherever a Herald calls home to 'contemplate' an alternate location.

The longer we cooperate with The Walker, the more her erratic nature becomes apparent. Sometimes, I believe she is not necessarily of two minds, but two separate people. I fear to bring my worries to Samantha, as each time I do, she becomes visibly upset. Her heart condition prevents her from using adder Root, and her inability to reflect weighs heavily upon her.

The one advantage to abandoning the search for the Well in the

Crown of the Kings is that we no longer need to deal with the various tribes of those damnable pigmies.

Stephen frowned deeply; Mike had mentioned something about 'little men' while he was reflected. Hollis knew of the mountain range known as the Crown of the First King. It lay north east of Oizan and was one of the final savage frontiers on the Cradle itself. Having never traveled that far into the mountains, the thief had no first-hand knowledge of the area.

Again, the weight of his reflection's concern about Samantha's now more imminent return settled upon him. Like a hound on a scent, Stephen pushed it down once more and returned his attention to the journal in his hands. He flipped forward a few pages and began to quickly read.

February 10, 2010

My irritation with the Walker continues to build. Once it became apparent that our comrade had abandoned the Crown completely, she insisted quite vehemently that we turn our attentions elsewhere. It is the Herald's opinion that by finding the Well, we shall also find Haedren. We are forced to rely on her guidance, as the brooch's power puts the former priest's abilities beyond anything that the three of us are capable of overcoming.

George has all but begged me to involve Roger and Stephen, but Roger has made his choice and I cannot bring myself to endanger the boy.

It had never occurred to Stephen that Roger knew the truth of what Jeff was dealing with and had made a decision to ignore his friend's plight. The man had always been standoffish but hadn't struck Stephen as someone who would abandon those in need, especially not his friends. Reflecting on his recent interactions with the man's younger brother, he was less sure of his original assumptions.

Stephen's reflection again pushed against his consciousness. Samantha would be returning soon, and he had yet to even locate her final stash of adder root much less treat it with the bugleweed. Another thought itched at the back of his mind, one that didn't originate with Hollis. He remembered reading another entry in the journals about the Well of Worlds. He quickly turned the pages of the journal, searching for that entry. He found it under February 21st and quickly found the reference:

Originally, we had believed it a singular place; in actuality, it is only singular in the fact that only one Well can exist at a time. The currently active one is believed to be located in the depths of a mountain at the center of the tundra called the Sea of Snows. We have come to the realization that it is Haedren's destination, just as it had been Theamon's.

Stephen recalled that Aristoi had told Hollis about a Well located in the north; that Well was inert and had led the Songspear to continue looking elsewhere. If Silvermoon, Mika and Marcus chased their quarry northward towards it at the behest of the Walker...Stephen felt the icy hot bite of revelation in the pit of his stomach. He snapped the journal closed harder than he'd intended. Any apprehension melted from him as frost on a spring morning. Pulling the bag of dried bugleweed from his pocket, he stalked further into the shop to finish what the woman started the decade before.

CHAPTER TWENTY-SEVEN
CONFLICT'S END

Ronni was sitting on the couch when Stephen walked through the door, wearing her familiar frown, in the same way most women wear a favorite blouse. Her eyes were tight and her jaw set. She was ready for a fight and he simply did not have the time. He told her so, "Ronni, whatever it is that you are angry about, whatever it is I've done, it will have to wait."

"The police were waiting for me when I came home."

Stephen mentally cursed Robert once again. "It is going to have to wait."

"Everyone warned me, they told me you were no good. You're lazy. You're irresponsible."

He continued walking, intent on getting into his basement. The adder root in his jeans pocket pressed against his leg with a steady pressure, just as Hollis's memories pressed against his mind. He repeated one final time, "It will have to wait." If he was going to beat the Walker, he would need the ammunition found in Jeff's journals. If she sought the Well, the key to stopping her lay in those pages. It had to.

She stood in a sudden movement, her voice rising in both volume and pitch. "You're a drug dealer!"

He stopped in his tracks and turned around slowly. "Pardon me?"

"*You are a drug dealer.*" She punctuated each word like a physical blow. "My brother and I always wondered why you were hanging out with those kids. At least now we know. I told the police about your little duffel bag. They took that, by the way."

Through clenched teeth, he growled, "You had no right."

"I had every right. It's evidence in an ongoing investigation. "Plus, the law says half of everything you have belongs to me. I'm sure your lawyer will explain that to you." She laughed; but rather than a joyful sound, it was a mocking one. "Maybe you can get a two for one deal on the drug charges and the divorce."

"You are a selfish, vicious bitch. You have no idea what you have done. So much depended on those books. Your petty vengeance will cost more than you will ever know, not the least of which is Mike's life."

"Bullshit, and don't even think about spending any money on more drugs. My lawyer has your banking information and is tracing every transaction."

"How long did you wait before calling him? Were the cops even to the end of the street?"

Realization dawned upon him in a rush, "It was not today." It was not a question. "How long have you been talking to him? How long have you been paying for your divorce attorney with my money?"

"Our money", she corrected.

A sense of helplessness descended upon him; his mind raced to plan his next steps. Without the journals the knowledge shared between himself and Hollis was all he had. It was not going to be enough. Walker was one of the three most powerful entities walking the face of Taerh. Jeff had seen her call lightning from a clear sky and bring a murderous flock of birds to heel with a thought. What hope did a glorified burglar and a less than glorified keyboard jockey have against that?

340

She misinterpreted the expression on his face, "I need a man, not a little boy. A man who knows how to take care of his family. A man who takes his responsibilities and promises seriously." She stood to follow him. "I've put up with so much; everyone said that I was too good for you", Ronni's lips pulled back into a sneer. "I should have listened." She folded her arms over her chest. "I did my best to make you a man ... to love you; but in the end, you were just not worth it."

"What?" He looked up at her with annoyance. Her words had faded into the background, like the static of a distant radio station.

"Same old Stephen. I am trying to save our marriage and you are in your own little world."

Stephen frowned in disbelief. "Trying to save our marriage? You have been talking to a lawyer for God knows how long, you just got finished telling me that I was not worth your patience, much less your love and what else? Oh, I remember. You essentially turned me into the police on trumped up drug charges. If that is trying to save something, I truly fear for anything you were honestly attempting to dismantle. I have seen woodchippers less destructive than you."

Ronni rolled her eyes. "I don't even know why I even try. Nothing is ever your fault. Perhaps if you took responsibility for your life and didn't always take the easy way out, none of this would have happened."

He shook his head for a moment, as if he could jostle her words into making sense. "Easy way out? If you had any idea what I have been through this week, you would know how very much I would love the 'easy way out'."

"What about me? I find out that my husband is a drug dealer ..."

"Alleged," he corrected.

"My husband has not gone to work in almost a week ..."

"I am on vacation," he corrected her again.

341

"I am facing the trauma and stigma of a divorce ..."

"That you seemingly have been preparing for a while..."

"You have an answer for everything."

Stephen shook his head, "Indeed I do not. To be honest, you are just asking easy questions."

"Is this funny to you?"

The ridiculousness of it all caught up with him: Mike's life and most likely his own hung in the balance and the woman who plotted the deaths of at least two of his friends was coming closer to what he understood to be cosmic power; but here he was, debating the end of something that had been over for as long as he could remember. "No, nothing is funny about this entire situation. "

"That's something on which we agree."

"Well, at least there is that."

"I'm going to my brother's."

"Makes sense. Drive safely."

Ronni snorted and pushed past him into their shared bedroom to pick up her already packed bag. He heard her muttering something under her breath as she swept it from the floor. She stared at him as if expecting him to beg her to stay. He didn't wait to watch her leave.

He was sitting on the couch staring at the ball of adder root in his palm when he heard the door slam. After the small amount he'd given Mike that afternoon, there was still a fair amount of it left. Stephen was fairly sure the police couldn't enter his house without a warrant; but he wouldn't put it past Ronni to give them permission to do so. They were not yet divorced. Even when they found no trace of drugs in his bag, no doubt he would be brought in for questioning. He thought they could hold him for seventy-two hours without leveling charges. There was no way he would have access to the leaves during that time. He simply couldn't afford the delay that proving his innocence would require.

As he'd never worked out the time differential in Jeff's journals, he had no idea how long he would be in Taerh with a night's sleep. He was unsure if the police would even allow him that. Even if he knew how long eight hours on this side represented on the other, he still did not know how long he needed there. Before he could think too deeply about it, he pushed the remainder of his adder root supply into his mouth and bit down.

As terrible as tea made with the leaves was, the raw leaves themselves were so much worse. More than the dull, moldy taste that came with the tea, the leaves brought to mind sucking on a rotten log. The steeping process also seemed to remove the burning, acid sensation that was now building in his throat as the leaves mixed with his saliva. Fortunately, he didn't need to suffer overly long. Even as the burning rose to what he hoped was a crescendo, his eyes slammed shut of their own volition and it, like everything else faded to nothing.

It seemed to Hollis that he had existed in this sort of half-life forever. He heard voices around him, although the words were lost to his understanding. It was almost as if his ears were filled with some sort of viscous, malignant liquid. He felt everything his body was subjected to; but again, it was dull, almost as if he lay beneath a thick leather blanket. The only thing he perceived clearly was the undulating pressure in his chest. It ebbed and flowed at regular intervals, only marked by a gentle feeling of expansion in his upper torso. He fought with all his will to move, to speak, even to open his eyes. He thought he remembered something in the time before the pressure. A fight of some kind.

It all came back to him in a rush of memory. The Plague Man had poisoned him after the Dwarf, Jhorwynn, had sent him into an ambush. The last thing he remembered clearly before the darkness came was Aristoi rushing to him as the sand rose to meet his quickly dimming vision. After that it was all dreamlike: voices he could not understand, touches he could barely feel and then the pressure. He tried to remain calm; after all, if Aristoi had not saved him somehow, he would never know about it. If he were truly dead, he would be standing before Olm accounting for his life under the Father of Dawn's searing light, not floating in this accursed darkness.

What did trouble him, however, was a more integral missing piece. He could no longer feel Stephen; so accustomed to his reflection's presence had Hollis become that now it felt like a part of him had been cut away. He still had the man's memories from prior to the attack but nothing more recent stalked his recollection. He was trying to find the calm place that had served him so well since their bonding when the mist obscuring Stephen from him lifted as if it had never been.

Memories of Stephen's, his actions in the day they had been apart flooded into him and just like that he was whole again.

With effort, he was able to force one eye to open and then the other; slowly the room came into focus. Standing above him, pressing some sort of mask to his face was the dwarf that had betrayed him, Jhorwynn. Raising his hand as if it moved through mud, he grabbed at the Dwarf, who gently swatted the hand away and stepped back. Hollis focused for a moment to steady his hand and pushed the mask from his face. His chest felt tight and breathing felt as if it was through cotton, but he was quickly gaining feeling in his limbs.

He tried to speak but coughed instead, the heavy, salty taste of mucus filling his mouth. He leaned and spit onto the floor. Again, he tried to speak as his eyes searched for a weapon of some kind. "You." Another cough wracked his body. "You betrayed me.".

From deep in his chest, the Dwarf rumbled as he raised his thick meaty hands. "I had no idea that his departure was naught but the beginning of a cunning ambush." Jhorwynn looked genuinely stricken. "I was as much of a victim as you." Beneath the genuinely apologetic tone ran a vein of anger.

As Hollis slowly began to sit up, he watched the Dwarf carefully.

"All the same, why do you not stay where you are until I am able to piece together the truth of the matter?" Jhorwynn nodded slowly, watching him with concern as he wobbled a bit on the stone table. The thief rubbed at his cheek and neck, perhaps more vigorously than necessary, trying to coax the numbness from both face and hand. "What happened?"

"As near as I can guess, the bolts we found lodged in you carried an extract of blissweed. In small doses, it acts as a pain killer; in larger ones it can remove your senses from you to allow dalture to do their work." Dalture was not a word he had heard before. It sounded similar to deltune in Trade Tongue, which meant healer. Seeing Hollis's look of confusion, Jhorwynn stopped to explain, "The Fair Folk have not the attention of the gods, as do the humans. Our healing is accomplished through study and a steady hand." The thief nodded, dalture must be the Dwarven equivalent of doctor in English.

"I understand. On the streets of Oizan, those you call dalture are known as Stitches. Dwarves lack the gods' attention; humans often go without for more financial concerns."

The Dwarf raised an eyebrow in disapproval but continued, "In even larger doses, blissweed paralyzes those affected. It even steals from them the ability to breathe." Again, his face took on a look of compassion. "I would imagine it is a most terrible way to die."

"As close as I evidently came, I can attest for that much at least."

Still holding up his hands, Jhorwynn gestured towards the door. "I must let Luciius know that you are awake. He will want to examine you to verify that there are no lingering effects."

Hollis shook his head. "I have not convinced myself that you were not involved."

Slowly, the Dwarf lowered his hand to the thick bladed knife on his belt, "I am afraid that I must insist. Much is known of blissweed, but I would not take needless risks with your life." He drew the knife slowly. Hollis tensed, his search for some sort of weapon, becoming more desperate. He need not have been worried. Jhorwynn held the dagger out to him hilt first, "Take my knife. Should my words not prove to be true, by my oath, my life is yours." So steadfast were the Dwarf's words, so solid and without passion were his eyes that Hollis was convinced. However, one should never turn down the offer of a Dwarven Steel weapon.

"Carry on," the thief said as he accepted the dagger. He was still admiring the workmanship when the Dwarf returned with Luciius a moment later.

The smaller Dwarf was obviously glad to see him, although emotion is a precious commodity to the Fair Folk, not to be spent recklessly. The dalture's voice was even; but Hollis could see the sparkle of joy in his eyes. "Lord Hollis. My heart leaps to see you back among us."

"Not nearly as happy as I am to be here. How long do you think I need until I am ready to be on my way?"

The low bass chuckle reminded Hollis of rusty gears. "It is your good fortune that you are as sturdy as you are impulsive, Lord Hollis."

"As nice of a compliment as I think that was meant to be, it did not answer my question."

"Blissweed was first discovered by the Slaze tribesman, the pre cursors to the Slazèan people that live today. The tribesman used to ... "

Hollis held up a hand. "I am a fan of history, I assure you, but I do not see this helping me give chase to the man who kidnapped my comrade and tried to kill me."

"Without proper understanding of the toxin that was introduced into your body, you cannot go on to then understand the possible aftereffects of it." The Dwarf nodded as if that should set everything right and continued, "The tribesman used to render it with the fat of the great horned oryx that have roamed the savanna...or the Golden Lake as they referred to it in their tongue...for untold centuries. They approached hunting differently than did their neighbors to the north or the south ... "

Again, the thief interrupted him, "Luciius, please. Jhorwynn, at least send for Aristoi while he finishes answering my question."

Hollis swore that he saw a smile beneath the young dwarf's beard as he nodded, "Of course."

With that he was gone, and the elder Dwarf continued. "They would coat their arrows with this extract derived from the bliss weed plant so that any wound inflicted would eventually incapacitate their prey. All they needed to do was follow at a distance until the creature succumbed to its effects." There was more but the thief was lost in the wave upon wave of words that flowed forth from Luciius. He hoped Jhorwynn found the Songspear soon.

By the time Aristoi and Jhorwynn arrived, Hollis felt like his mind was going to burst from the sheer amount of history, horticulture, anthropology and biology that Luciius had imparted on him. "There may be tightness in your chest that could persist for a fortnight; but so long as you continue to have feeling in your extremities and no lingering dizziness or swelling in your mouth or throat, I would say you have avoided any truly adverse and lingering effects."

The thief hopped down from the stone table, testing his balance before releasing the lip of it, "Thanks, Doc." Luciius frowned at the English word. "Never mind," he murmured and accepted the Songspear's spirited hug.

"I had thought you lost, Northerner. With you, also went my honor."

"...and hope of ending your 'Long Walk'?" Hollis teased.

"Let us not quibble over issues that did not come to pass," she dismissed. The thief saw the relief in the woman's eyes. He did not let himself worry about which loss she was more relieved.

, "Let us adjourn to the tavern, I am on the verge of starving."

Aristoi's eyes drifted to her comrade's ample midsection. "I am not so sure about that."

The thief chuckled once but finished, "And I feel if I do not leave now," he shifted his eyes to the elder Dwarf who looked like he was about to begin speaking again, "I will never be able to." The Songspear nodded knowingly and turned to lead the way.

"Would you mind if I accompanied you, Lord Hollis?" It was the bass rumble of Jhorwynn.

"Only if you drop the 'Lord' nonsense. Hollis is just fine."

As the Dwarf followed, he intoned, "As you will."

~

Despite the urgency that pulled at the edges of his mind, Hollis wolfed down half of the lamb stew before speaking. Both Aristoi and Jhorwynn watched him with a mixture of expectancy and impatience. Settling back, his hand on his stomach, he shifted his eyes up to his companions. "I believe the Walker is making her move."

Jhorwynn frowned deeply. "I thought your issue was with the Plague Man?"

"Just as he was behind Renthroas' murder while never actually raising a hand against him, so too does the Walker pull his strings."

"There is a difference between setting accounts with that eccentric and pitting yourself against one of the Heralds."

"Indeed, there is. This is not your fight, Jhorwynn; you can walk away with neither judgement nor ill feelings."

Aristoi laid her hand on the Dwarf's forearm in agreement. "Our path is not yours."

Hollis, not for the first time, looked at the Songspear with amazement. "Our path is not yours either, Southerner. As I lay poisoned in the sand, you settled any debt you may have owed me."

The Kieli dismissed his words with a wave of her hand. "Do not begin this again, Northerner. I alone will make the determination when my debt has been discharged."

The thief opened his mouth to continue the argument; but instead simply nodded appreciatively at the dark-skinned woman. He turned back to the Dwarf, "You owe neither of us any such debt."

Jhorwynn ran his thick fingers through his beard and he shook his head, "On that account, you are incorrect. It was the Home Guard that allowed that man and his cohorts into the Stone City. It was under our not so meticulous hospitality that your comrade was slain. We allowed him the freedom to leave with no repercussions from his actions."

Hollis felt the weight of conscience upon his shoulders. He did not relish the thought of facing a Herald and the man who nearly ended his life, not to mention any mercenaries he chose to bring along with only the Songspear by his side. Aristoi's magic was puissant and certainly not to be discounted; but the Walker's was on a level higher by magnitudes. Even without the Herald's presence, the odds would lie heavily in the favor of the Plague Man and his paid swords. A dwarf warrior could help balance those odds; but could he truly ask that of anyone, much less someone he barely knew?

He made a hard decision and spoke his mind before he could change it, "You are responsible for neither his sins nor the oversights of the entire Home Guard, Jhorwynn. I will not let you take either upon your shoulders."

"I do not seek to make right his trespasses. I do not desire to undo the Home Guard's inaction." The Dwarf slammed his fist into the wooden table, causing it to shake as if struck by a hammer. His voice raised slightly, the vibration of it rolling through the Hollis's chest like thunder, "I chose to circumvent tradition by aiding you in your vengeance and broke a sacred oath in doing so. Those actions almost led to your death and delivered into a villain's hands a prize undeserved. It is for that I seek to repent. It is that I swear to make right."

Hollis raised an eyebrow, "Even against the Walker?"

"Against the god's themselves if that is what is demanded. But that does not mean that I do not seek to understand how a murder in the alleys of Drunmarch led us into conflict with a Herald."

Hollis looked to Aristoi; the Songspear began to summarize their path thus far with brevity and alacrity. To his credit, the Dwarf followed with admirable acumen, interrupting seldom and always with well thought inquiries. Jhorwynn did not so much as blink when the concept of multiple worlds was broached; like Aristoi and Rhyzzo, he also was perplexed that anyone could be so vain as to believe themselves

349

the center of creation. Even burdened by the immensity of the task ahead of him, that made Hollis smile.

When the Kieli had finished, the dwarf thought for a long moment and then spoke, "What makes you believe that the Walker is moving now?"

Hollis took a quick breath before beginning, "I spoke to her reflection in my world. Between her demeanor and some timely counsel from beyond the grave, the situation has raised the hair on the back of my neck."

Jhorwynn raised an eyebrow, "We give chase based on your scruff?"

The thief regarded him from the corner of his eye but continued, "She was too anxious... too quick to dissuade me from reflecting again... too enthusiastic to aid Rhyzzo's reflection. In her every gesture, I could see impatience with a road too long traveled." Hollis shrugged. "I have no concrete proof, but I know in the depths of my heart that wherever the Plague Man travels, the Walker will be waiting for him at the end."

Aristoi pursed her lips. "Have we any idea of where that end may be?"

"I spoke to Rhyzzo's reflection on my world. He told me in which direction they travelled. As best as I can figure, they are headed north through Slazè towards Granatyr."

"There is much between here and there," Aristoi said as she dug into her bag. She laid a map drawn on thick parchment on the table. She traced her finger along the King's Road north from Oenigh to Oizan. "She could rendezvous with him in any of a dozen Inns or public houses; and that only assumes they stick to the well-traveled route." She looked up, worry shadowing her face. "We have nearly no chance to intercept him before that happens."

Hollis studied the map, trying to fight down the sense of hopelessness that again threatened to overwhelm him. He turned inward in an attempt to find that calm place that had served him so well recently. As the peaceful feeling fell over him like a down blanket, a smile crept onto his lips. "Perhaps we do not have to." He was not sure if it was his words or the scoundrel's smile splitting his goatee that piqued the interest of his fellows. "In my world there is a saying: *You have to learn to see the forest for the trees.* It means that sometimes we grow too mired in the details to appreciate the situation as a whole. We know what she desires; no matter where they meet or what path they take, it will always lead them to the Well."

"So, it is as simple as locating a holy site whose entire purpose is to remain hidden. Why did you not mention that sooner?" Her sarcasm was a physical thing.

Jhorwynn's huge hand covered the bottom of the map. "If they head north, what they seek cannot be to the south, correct?"

Hollis nodded and pointed to three points on the map, indicating large cities in Slazè, Granatyr and Utel. "According to the legends, civilization springs from the Wells like roses under a gardener's touch. One would not be found in areas already blessed by one of its predecessor's influence."

Aristoi leaned in, picking up on Her companion's momentum. "That would exclude Mantry as well. I have seen the depleted well in the Rangor, so we can remove the Northlands from our list."

Like an itch he could not scratch, something tickled at the back of Hollis's brain, but he dismissed it as his eyes fell on a small mountain range in the northeast corner of Granatyr. Pressing his finger against the map, he asked, "What do you know of the Crown of the First King?"

Aristoi shrugged. "They offer nothing besides a natural defensive barrier between the Granatyrians and Mantry. Between their height and the savagery of the land that lie beyond them, they remain unexplored for the most part."

The dwarf squinted for a moment. "I remember Luciius saying something about an ill-fated quest a century or so ago. His mentor had led an expedition to find what he believed was a lost tribe of Fair Folk; but all they found was a savage tribe of small humans."

Remembering Jeff's description of their issues while searching for Haedren in the same area, Hollis began to laugh. Both Jhorwynn and Aristoi looked to him as if he had lost his mind. He ran his finger on the map from south to north along the Grey Spire mountains, under which

351

Drunmarch was built, "Friend Dwarf, if we left now, how much time could we make up if we travelled through the Stone City to its northern gate? I know that gate is closed to any not of the Fair Folk; but I believe the Home Guard could make an exception seeing the circumstances. Could we get ahead of a wagon on the King's Road?"

Comprehending the thief's train of thought, Jhorwynn nodded, "Of course, even with their two-day lead, we could reach the Uteli border three days ahead of them. Why?"

Hollis clapped his friends on their shoulders. "Because I know where they are headed. I know where to find the Well."

CHAPTER TWENTY-EIGHT
DESTINATION'S COST

T he sounds of combat had died down moments before the first glow of torchlight on stone was visible. The sweaty and bloody state of the surviving mercenaries bore silent testimony to the ferocity with which the pigmies had been forced to defend their sacred ground. A twinge of guilt burned at Hollis's heart; he tried to rationalize that the results would have been the same whether or not he benefited from their deaths. It almost worked.

The masked form of the Plague Man entered the chamber beside Samantha's reflection. The luminous glow of the Well itself threw her features into sharp contrast. The Walker wore her years far better than the old woman from his world had. The Walker's r eyes still bore the wrinkles that came from watching the passing of the decades, but they were smoother than Samantha's, somehow less harsh. Her hair was braided in the way of the Kieli and tied back with a simple leather thong. The hood and hem of her ivory cloak were speckled crimson, no doubt from the conflict at the entrance. Fastening it at her throat was an oval of flat black metal that Hollis knew all too well. Fear like ice settled in Hollis's belly.

Silvermoon...Jeff had kept him far from the final conflict with Haedren; the thief never knew what became of the cursed artifact of Theamon's evil. Had he known, he would have found it and destroyed it. He immediately knew these thoughts for the lies they were. He had not known its fate and had not wanted to. Hollis had felt its icy touch once and was only spared from it by a timely interruption.

Behind the masked man and the Herald entered the priest from the desert and another sell sword dragging Rhyzzo's limp body between them. The way his limp legs dragged y along the stone sickened Hollis's stomach. Mike was correct; the Plague Man must have hamstrung him to prevent escape. It was just another sin to be held against him when the time for accounting came. After a clear order from their masked employer, they dropped him and fanned out to search the area surrounding the glowing water of the Well.

The three diverse companions were tucked into an alcove high above the mercenaries' heads, hidden by the hourglass meeting of stalagmite and stalactite. Despite the ample protection from prying eyes, they remained low in their perch. Hollis counted four mercenaries in addition to the Walker and the Plague Man. In any other circumstance, his heart would have sung at the promise of only two to one odds; but it did not make a whisper on this day. When they had finished their search, they returned to where their companions stood.

Walker spoke softly, "Put him in." There was no doubt in Hollis's mind that it was Samantha's voice – because he felt Stephen bristling – but somehow more. Her voice carried a measure of power and authority. The thief found within himself a desire to rise to her command but fought the urge and turned to his comrades. Jhorwynn slowly rose to his feet, a wicked hammer-backed axe clutched in his thick right hand. On Hollis's right, Aristoi uncoiled like a cat in a sun beam, her ever-present spear held against her body. The thief came to his feet as well, laying his hand on it but not drawing out Jeff's last gift to him. He was not sure who moved first, but the trio rushed forth as one. The Songspear and the thief hit the stone floor in a roll to absorb the impact; the Dwarf simply dropped to his feet and continued to move, as if he had fallen ten inches rather than ten feet.

To their credit, the men depositing Rhyzzo in the Well reacted first, dropping him and charging forward. Aristoi surged towards them, knocking the priest back into the water and blocking the second from reaching Hollis. The thief moved past the developing melee, running towards his true target. The Plague Man let out a barking laugh as he drew his thin bladed Slazèan dueling sword. Something dark and viscous clung to the blade. Hollis wished he could have watched the man's face when he dropped into a baseball slide under the assassin's first probing thrust and came to his feet three strides beyond him. He drew his gifted sword as he attempted to bull rush an unexpecting Walker.

The Herald stumbled back a few steps; but a moment of confusion was all the thief was to receive from her. As she raised her hand, Hollis almost felt the power she drew into herself. Rather than shy away from such a display as any rational person might, he threw himself forward. He swung his blade two-handed from right to left, forcing her back onto her heels. Deprived of her concentration, he felt a measure of the power disperse into the ether.

The Plague Man barely recovered his wits enough to deflect the Dwarven steel axe and had to hastily side step when it became apparent that he was not strong enough to redirect the weapon completely nor was his weapon sturdy enough to take the full force of contact.. He gathered his wits momentarily as Jhorwynn's full swing had set him off balance. The two remaining mercenaries quickly rushed to their employer's aid.

By the time the priest had climbed out of the Well, Aristoi had marked his partner with a score of minor wounds. The Songspear rotated to her left and struck again at the wounded man. Still feeling the effects of previous thrusts, he leapt back to collide with his emerging comrade. Quickly withdrawing and then suddenly thrusting, Aristoi caught the sellsword again. This time the broad blade struck him in the upper arm, bisecting muscle from bone.

Rotating left again, the Kieli drove her spear into the mercenary's chest beneath his useless arm. She used her spear as a lever to throw the dead man under his companion's feet. Strafing right with two long strides, Aristoi probed experimentally at the remaining mercenary's defenses. To his credit, the priest remained calm, content to parry and move until he was clear of his partner's corpse.

The Walker was forced to forgo her magic and focus on defending herself from Hollis's unrelenting assault. He struck as if his life depended on not giving the Herald a moment to breathe, mostly because it did. "Well done, Stephen. I had not thought your reflection could be so heroic. Stupid, but heroic nonetheless." He lunged forward, dropping the blade at the last second and slicing at her thigh. She allowed her own sword to sweep the blow to the side, "No clever quip? No oath of vengeance?"

He allowed his blade to be turned; but twisted it to ride along hers, thrusting towards her heart. She once again gave ground, which he greedily took. He wasted neither energy nor breath on engaging her verbally. But in his haste to not allow Samantha's reflection any space, he left a hole in his defenses, which she took full advantage of. He saw the blow coming too late; but turned with it so most of the force was dispersed by his leather armor. His chest felt like it had been struck by a club; but he was able to trap her blade against his aching ribs. Corps de corps, he struck out with his wide cross guard; he felt her nose break under the blow.

The Walker drew her blade along the arm that had trapped it, opening a deep gash along its length and withdrew again. Hollis saw her trying to gather her wits in the moment but was distracted by the sudden pain. Despite the tears that blurred her vision courtesy of her broken nose, she weaved together a minor effect with a few muttered words of power that fled from his mind as they reached his ears. Waves of heat washed over the thief as he swung his sword one-handed to drive her back once again. The blast furnace like incalescence stole his breath and singed his skin instantly.

The Plague Man withdrew as the sibling- pair of sell swords closed ranks between him and his Dwarven adversary. Each of them was armed with a heavy wooden shield and a broad, straight bladed Granatyrian sword. Jhorwynn paused for a half beat when they locked shields in front of him. Where others faced with such increased odds may have withdrawn or thought to flank their opponents, the Dwarf simply planted his feet and swung his broad axe. He aimed for the center of the man's shield, striking it true and with the sound of distant thunder. When he pulled the weapon free, the shield briefly came with it before buckling into two pieces.

The woman swung her sword in a strong horizontal cut. The Dwarf shrugged his shoulders, putting his upper arm between the steel and his neck. To her credit, the sword cut through Jhorwynn's leather sleeve cleanly and cleaved deeply into his flesh. More to his, the Dwarf only let out a harsh grunt as he turned his axe's recovery into a vicious overhand chop. Already extended from her own swing, the weapon took the woman between neck and collarbone. It came to rest six inches above her pelvis and remained in her dead flesh. The color drained from her brother's face as he took an unconscious step back, allowing Jhorwynn to pick up the dead woman's sword in his ham sized hand. From deep in his chest, he rumbled, "Do not fear, Human, you shall join her soon." His eyes never left the quickly retreating form of the Plague Man.

Aristoi's remaining opponent was more skilled than his comrade had been. He fought well, not wasting motion or effort. Any time the Songspear's thwarted attack left even the smallest opening, he launched a lightning riposte with his thick bladed sword. Each time, Aristoi dodged the thrust or rolled aside; but the sell sword came closer with each strike.

A low hum built within the Kieli's chest as she began to sing. Her foe pressed forward suddenly, clearly intent on disrupting her spell. What he didn't seem to expect was that a Songspear's spells were as natural to them as breath itself. Aristoi had explained to Hollis that they required no more concentration than putting one foot in front of another. She blocked the mercenary's overhead cut with the shaft of her spear and kicked out hard, the song only growing bolder.

Her foot caught the man in the thigh, knocking his leg out from beneath him and forcing him to his knees. The spear whirled in the Songspear's hands as she prepared to drive it home in the kneeling man's back. The heavy weight of exhaustion seemed to stun her, almost causing her to double over in clear pain. Her opponent took the opportunity to drop his shoulder and roll away from the blow. Although she ceased singing, the song continued to hang in the air.

It was then that Hollis's voice screamed out to her. "Aristoi, stop!" It was too late; as Theamon demonstrated on that lonely road all those years ago, it took far less concentration for a true master of magic to bend another's effect to their will then to conjure one from nothing. He felt the unknowable words of power that bubbled from her lips rush past him to profane the Kieli's song.

He continued to press the Herald, relying more on instinct than his sweat-blinded eyes at that point. She turned away his quickly weakening blows, gaining distance for herself with each passing moment. His stomach rolled with the telltale symptoms of heatstroke and his skin stung at the slightest touch of the still cave air.

He wiped his eyes with the back of his hand for what seemed like the hundredth time and saw the wicked smile painting her lips. It worried him far less than the shadow that concealed her sword arm and half of the weapon it held. Blanketed in its inky depths, the speed at which she beat back his attacks left no doubt that she had called upon the brooch. He pressed forward with the last vestiges of his remaining strength, hoping to break her artifact fueled reflexes. Her sword moved as if by its own will, parrying his blow to the side and slicing deeply into his hip with a vicious return stroke.

He tried to find his calm place and thrust again, aiming for her heart. Again, the darkness wrapped blade deflected his own, riding up its length to sink into his own shoulder. His cross-guard prevented it from sinking more than a few inches but the pain pulled from him a frustrated, only half muted moan. She had turned his own strategy back on him. Without the ability to catch his breath, his peace remained out of reach.

With neither shield nor ally, the dead woman's brother caused little more than a pause in Jhorwynn's pursuit of the masked man. The Dwarf simply met the sell sword's swing with an aggressive parry, backed with his race's immense strength. The man's weapon flew from his hand as Jhorwynn dropped his shoulder and struck him squarely in the chest. Fueled by his forward momentum, the blow knocked him off his feet. Skull met with stone with the sound of a splitting oak tree.

The Plague Man stopped at the mouth of the tunnel leading out of the Well. His eyes widened at the distance eaten by the Dwarf's short, pumping strides. Considering his options, he drew a thin stiletto as he turned to face Jhorwynn. The same viscous substance clung to the dagger's blade. The Dwarf rushed him with arms outstretched in an attempt to carry him to the ground where his superior strength would no doubt win him the day.

The masked assassin clearly had other plans. He shifted his weight as if to turn to flee again; but reversed it smoothly to dodge out of Jhorwynn's reach as he came within an arms breath. As the Dwarf collided heavily with the wall, the Plague Man drove his poisoned weapons into his side before dancing away. As Jhorwynn faced his attacker, he did not bend to recover his stolen sword. He simply drew a broad-bladed Dwarven steel dagger, the mate of the one that rode on Hollis's own belt.

The Dwarf snarled, "Continue to sting, little hornet. You will find your venom of no use today."

The masked man chuckled, keeping his dueling sword between himself and the Dwarf, "Even the cave bear will fall under the assault of the hive, brute."

Jhorwynn pulled his helmet from his head and rocked it back and forth, a tight smile carved in the depths of his beard. "You will wish it was only a cave bear you face." With a speed that belied his mass, the Dwarf lunged in under the man's guard, using his free hand against the stone to add to his momentum. The Plague Man dropped the tip of his blade, skewering his opponent's bicep cleanly; but the blow did not slow his advance. His arm pinned like an insect, Jhorwynn's dagger opened a deep dash across the man's leg from groin to hip. It was all the Plague Man could do to disengage from the Dwarf as he reached out with his speared limb to grab him by the cloak.

Jhorwynn stood up quickly, continuing to pursue his quarry as he flexed the fingers of his left hand. The man bladed his body, sword held before him. He sidestepped the Dwarf's next rush, opening a shallow furrow along his neck as he did so. As he pivoted, Jhorwynn seemed to lose his footing for an instant. It was subtle; but Hollis knew the Plague Man had seen it as well because he smiled.

Hollis saw Aristoi's shoulders sag under the weight of her own stolen song as she back- pedaled under the relentless attacks of her opponent. Within the space of a few moments, she and the man had traded places. The mercenary had forgone defense to press his advantage and it was all the Songspear could do to avoid the man's deadly blade. Out of the corner of his eye, he watched as Jhorwynn and the Plague Man fell into the rhythm of matador and bull. Even from his distant vantage point, she saw the Dwarf's movements losing their steadiness as the masked assassin used his reach advantage to poke and prod his shorter opponent.

Hollis watched Aristoi draw inspiration from this display. Her opponent's next overhand chop was met with her raised spear shaft; however as soon as the blow lost most of its momentum, the Kieli released it and stepped to the left. He saw as another wave of fatigue threatened to bear her to the ground, but she doggedly reached out for the man. The mercenary hesitated for a split second, and it was enough for Aristoi to snake her long arms around the man's throat and interlock her hands. The man threw himself backwards into the wall; but he already felt his consciousness slipping away. A moment later, the Songspear allowed the man's unconscious body to slump to the floor and retrieved her spear.

Hollis almost felt relief when the sweat ceased running into his eyes until the headache began at the back of them. He swung at the Walker once more; but stumbled as waves of dizziness washed over him. Her shadow covered sword drove into his thigh as she stepped away. His body, too long fueled by will alone, betrayed him and he collapsed to the ground; Silvermoon's sword slipped from his fingers. The thief tried to rise but it was all he could do to gasp for breath as his heart pounded in his ears.

The Herald caressed the brooch at her throat, a look of profound satisfaction on her face. Hollis watched helplessly as she took in the battlefield, such that it was. Jhorwynn had finally laid his hands on the Plague Man and looked as if he were unwilling to let go. His opponent continued to frantically stab the Dwarf in the shoulders and arms as he closed his hands around the assassin's throat. The sound of cracking cartilage filled Hollis's ears. Aristoi cautiously approached her fallen friend and the victorious Walker, stubbornly resisting the pull of exhaustion that gripped her entire being.

One word escaped the Walker's lips; although it was whispered, it resonated through the cave, through each creature present.

Clearly a word of power, it's meaning was clear: "Cease."

CHAPTER TWENTY-NINE
FAITH'S PROMISE

Relieved of the will to do anything beyond collapse breathless to the stone, Hollis lay in a heap at the Walker's feet. Out of the corner of his eye, he saw Aristoi standing statue still, her spear held loosely at her side. Silence reigned after the Herald's proclamation; the thief shifted his head to take in the pile of human and Dwarf that was Jhorwynn and the Plague Man. The voice that Stephen had come to know as both mentor and foe broke the stillness.

"That is much better." Samantha's reflection casually walked to the Songspear's side and relieved her of her weapon, tossing it in the direction of the tunnel. "I will admit, Stephen ... or should I call you Hollis? I imagine that it does not matter much in either case." She stepped over to examine the Dwarf and her associate, the left side of her mouth turning up in contempt. She continued as she moved back to stand over the thief. "I will admit that you surprised me, boy."

Hollis met her eyes and muttered, "Now you have been lied to by the best."

She chuckled lightly. "So, I have. So, I have, indeed." She crouched beside him and laced her fingers deeply into his thick goatee. She forced his head back uncomfortably, "Tell me, what you hoped to accomplish? This could not possibly be how you envisioned this day ending." She gestured around the cave before continuing, "Surely, you did not believe you could best me in combat...magical or otherwise."

He shook his head as best he could in her grip. "It was never about beating you here, Walker."

The Herald raised an eyebrow. "Do tell me what it was about then?"

He tried to chuckle, but his parched throat turned it into a raspy cough instead. She released her hold and waited patiently for him to catch his breath. He opened his eyes again, meeting hers. "It was about getting you here...about keeping you here."

"And why would you want to do that?"

"Because as soon as you Reflected, I had you beaten there...where you are just an old woman."

The amusement drained from her face. "What are you talking about?"

It was Hollis's turn to smile. "Did you think I killed your adder root crop to stop you from using it?" She did not respond; but it was clear to him that was exactly her impression. "On the contrary, I wanted you to use it to Reflect. I just wanted to make sure you used the adder root you had already harvested, the root I had chosen for you." He took a short gulp of air, allowing the significance of his words to sink in, "The leaves that I had laced with bugleweed."

Her lips pulled back in a sneer, "You poisoned me?" As his vision began to dim, Hollis was unsure if she felt more anger or fear.

The thief allowed his head to settle onto the warm stone. "That I did. You put too much faith in the ways of Taerh and not enough in those of Earth. I read your hospital records. I know why you could not reflect any longer. I surmised about the drugs you kept for the day you would do so again." He coughed again; but composed himself quickly. "The bugleweed will have countered their effects. Your last visit to Taerh is a one-way journey."

She stood up slowly. "I underestimated you, son. I would make a mental note to never do so again, were you going to survive the night."

Hollis rolled over in an effort to not lose sight of the Walker. "You can still do the same. I recognize the brooch at your throat. I have seen people, good, honest people bent into shadows of themselves under its sway. I know it is the artifact that put you on this path, not your choice. Cast it aside now and be free of it. If you wake now, perhaps you can call 911 before the root kills you."

She stopped at the edge of the Well. "You should have remained silent. At least you would have retained my admiration in death." Reaching down into the water, she pulled Rhyzzo's floating body towards her. "There will be no waking for me. I made use of sufficient adder root to remain reflected for a week. I had to be sure that, as you say, this visit was indeed my last."

"Then there is no way to save your life; but you do not have to leave a stain of shadow upon the world as your legacy. Cast aside the brooch, deny Theamon's spirit the satisfaction of calling you tool."

The Walker regarded him for a moment before her form began to shake. It was subtle at first but quickly built into great, wracking tremors. At first Hollis thought she wept; but when the cackle emerged from her throat, his hopes were dashed. "Me? A tool to this?" She pulled the artifact from her cloak and held it out to him. "This trinket only holds sway over the weak of mind, those without the will to resist the basest of flattery. It was useful for sure; but compared to the gifts of the Well it is smoke and mirrors." She cast the brooch aside; it skidded along the floor to bounce to a stop against the wall.

"If it was not the influence of the brooch..."

"The Walker had power thrust onto her, given freely and without price. She never earned it and she never appreciated it. As the decades passed, she made peace with her eventual end as an extension of the nature of things. We are born...we age...we die...a cycle older than time." Her lips pulled back to reveal clenched teeth. "But I did not want to die. As she aged with grace, I did so with resentment. The power to break the cycle lay at her fingertips; but she refused to make use of it. You ask me what influenced me to walk this path. It was my own influence. Tonight, the Walker ceases to be. Tonight, I send her to her grave and take her place."

Hollis slumped back to the floor, defeated. She had subsumed her reflection rather than making peace with it as he had. There was no route to victory through a woman who literally fought for her life. As he lay upon the quickly cooling stone, he closed his eyes and surrendered to his fate. At least if he was going to die, it would be in Taerh, in the place he had come to love. In his acceptance, he found the calm place he sought.

Suddenly, the situation was brought into stark clarity. Samantha's subjugation of the Walker was not uncommon; as a matter of fact, Jeff, Alan and Mike had all done the same thing.

Stephen and Hollis were the exception rather than the rule.

In Jeff's journals, he wrote about the moments when he and his own reflection reached an accord. It was in those moments when Silvermoon shook loose from Theamon's spells...to drive away the shadows cast by the brooch. He slipped into his own cloak of peace. From the bastion of his placid place, Hollis felt the chains of the Herald's words loosen. She had turned her attention back to the unconscious Rhyzzo. Slowly, he rose.

As the sound of boots on stone reached her ears, Samantha turned, confusion evident on her face. She issued the command of power again. The thief felt the power break against the armor of calm he had woven around himself like waves on the shore. She raised her voice, repeating the word of power a third time. The tendrils of her command forced their way into his mind, testing his will but for the moment, he proved the stronger.

Drawing the broad bladed dagger from his belt, his steps picked up speed. He felt her drawing her power as he reached within a dozen paces. Words of power that Hollis could not comprehend resonated in his chest, but the effect was not aimed at him., Cracks began to split the stone at his feet. Like pale snakes, vines slithered towards him. Hollis leapt over a pair that sought to converge on his ankles and charged towards the woman. She dodged to the side, escaping his grasp as his momentum carried him into the luminous water.

The vines lunged at him from the stone surrounding the Well itself;

they wrapped themselves around his limbs before he could claw his way to the surface. The wooden tentacles sprouted wicked thorns, impaling him at wrist, ankle and knee. Despite himself, Hollis released a cry of agony. The dagger fell from nerveless fingers; he watched it sink into the water.

"Perhaps you will take a measure of my admiration with you to the grave after all, Stephen." She drew a wickedly curved knife from her own belt. "It will be a mercy to put you down now; I will save you the pain of experiencing my rise to power once I finally receive the blessing of the Well." Even mired in such a life and death situation, Hollis was taken aback by her statement.

"Was not one Well enough? Jeff's death...those of Beatrice and George?"

True confusion seized her countenance; it was replaced almost immediately by a joyfully malicious smile. The mocking notes of her laughter played across his ears like steel on glass. "Is that why you sought me out? Why you did not heed my warning? You are far more of a fool than I had ever imagined." Like a stream of cold water, realization flowed through the thief; she had not killed his friends, at least not directly. She had not made use of the Rangor Well, but if not her than who?

Samantha approached him slowly, holding the knife before him. "I cannot help but wonder if the gifts of the Well would be multiplied when I feed it your blood as well as that of the priest." Samantha shrugged, her wicked smile melting into a self-satisfied smirk, but it was wiped away when the Dwarf's thick fingers closed around her shoulder. Jhorwynn pulled her from the water like a ragdoll and tossed her aside. She slid to the place where Aristoi waited with her spear raised. The Dwarf slumped to one knee as the poison finally overcame his people's legendary constitution.

Hollis watched helplessly as the Herald extended a finger and hastily drew a glowing symbol in the air between her and the Songspear. The weapon passed easily into the vibrating glyph; but did not emerge from the other side. Samantha quickly scooped a handful of small stones into her hand, drawing her power again. When she opened her fingers, they were launched unerringly at Aristoi. The thief saw several of them exit through her back in tiny eruptions of blood, flesh and shredded cloth. The Kieli stumbled backwards, bringing her hand up to the rapidly spreading crimson stains on her chest.

Climbing to her feet, the woman said mockingly, "Now, where were we?"

Samantha's lapse in concentration allowed the thief to snap off enough of the larger thorns to wiggle free of the vines. He searched franticly for his lost dagger, a plan coming to mind. The side effects of the adder root would not act quickly enough to prevent the woman from killing him and Rhyzzo to make use of the Well. The only way to buy enough time for the poisoned root to put an end to her was to take that from her as well. He had already made peace with his death; it was a simple matter of sacrificing himself to the glowing waters. and in doing so, deplete them. He could only hope that somehow making use of the Well gave Rhyzzo enough protection to prevent Mike's death on Earth.

His eyes shifted to where Rhyzzo had been floating, blessedly unconscious throughout the battle. The priest clutched the edge of the Well with one hand, the Dwarven steel dagger firmly in the other. "Stephen," he said softly in English. "I've always been too afraid of failing to even try...well really anything."

"Rhyzzo...Mike," the thief said soothingly, "give me the knife quickly." Samantha was approaching. He saw her out of the corner of his eye, but he focused on keeping his voice calm.

His friend continued in English as if he had all the time in the world, "You were always so unafraid." Despite the dire situation at hand, Hollis laughed. It always seemed to him that Stephen's life had been defined by fear. "At least that's how it seemed to me," Rhyzzo avoided the thief's gaze. "You took every hit that life gave you and always seemed to get back up."

"Hand me the knife, Brother." The woman was within a dozen paces.

"But that wasn't what was truly courageous, though. The bravery came when you decided each morning to not let the world take your smile, or any of ours." As their eyes met again, Hollis saw through the fear in his friend's. "Over my life, Stephen, I seemed to perfect giving up until it was almost an art form. I think that inspired those around me to give up on me as well; but you never did. You were one of the few people that actually believed in me...and I paid you back with fear."

Hollis felt an edge work its way into his voice, "Mike." He forced his tone to soften as he continued, "All is forgiven. May I please have the fucking knife?"

Mike and his reflection seemed oblivious to anything beyond himself and Hollis. "I was even too afraid to take all of the adder root you gave me in the hospital. I stashed half of it under my pillow. I sat there in my bed trying to convince myself to take the rest...to come and help you."

The thief opened and closed his hand a few times, "You made the right choice now. I have no hard feelings. Now, seriously, give me the knife. She is coming."

"I have been afraid all my life, Stephen. Despite both your words and your example, I let fear control every aspect of it."

"I forgive you, Mike." Hollis was finally within arm's reach of his friend. Mike's Reflection lifted the knife out of the water. The weapon was within inches of the thief's fingers.

"I knew you would overlook all the times I was afraid...please forgive me for being brave just this once." With a sudden smooth motion, he drew the blade across his own throat. A crimson fountain emerged from him and spilled into the luminous water. Where it mingled with the glowing liquid, the later lost its glimmer.

A blinding radiance filled Hollis's vision in inverse proportion to the Well's fading brightness. He closed his eyes against it but that did not dim the assault. He heard, as if from a great distance, a voice crying out in anguish. To his surprise, the light was neither painful nor unpleasant. It took from him his pain and his worry, leaving in their place an embrace of serenity that made his previous states of communion with his reflection seem hectic by comparison.

CHAPTER THIRTY
MEMORY'S CARESS

S urrounded by bliss made light, Hollis made out shapes in the luminous depths. The images came to the fore as the brilliance dimmed, leaving his sense of well-being intact. He saw the concerned face of a man he did not recognize as hands lifted his unresisting body from where he lay in a quickly cooling pool of crimson. The man spoke words the thief did not comprehend; the meaning of those alien words was unmistakable as his perspective turned to the still body of a young woman. Her body from waist to mid-thigh was coated in a ruby sheen. A wail emerged from his throat unbidden.

That same wail hung in the air as his surroundings changed to that of a pale green tiled room. The man who held him was swathed in a blue apron and face mask. The seamless change from his own memories to those of Stephen was disconcerting for a moment but the feeling passed almost as quickly as it rose in him. He was passed into the waiting arms of a similarly clad woman who gently washed the blood and mucus from his frail body. Hovering nearby was another figure that Stephen recognized from his own childhood. Intervening years had taken from the man's head a good deal of his hair, replacing it in equal measures with weight around his middle, but he still recognized his own father. The easy smile Stephen remembered from his childhood came to the man's face.

Stephen's perspective melted into that of Hollis; his own father's kind countenance was replaced by the harsh sneer of Hollis's. Hollis knew that look well and raised his arms to cover his face as the slap came. His forearms took most of the brunt of the strike, but his jaw ached just the same. The gesture simply infuriated the man further. "How dare you raise a hand to escape your punishment?" The man's tone instantly dropped into a low, dangerous whisper, "I pray every day to any of the Three that will listen to wake to a world where you were pulled limp and cold from your mother. I lost the only thing I loved that day." Hollis lowered his arms a fraction, his eyes meeting those of his father. The man's hand struck out again, causing the young boy's ears to ring and his head to swim. "So, I am left with you." The last word was hissed out from between clenched teeth, dripping with contempt.

The tone of the word changed before Hollis's perspective shifted once again. "...you. Happy birthday, dear Stephen. Happy birthday to you." The sweet song surrounded him like a warm blanket, drawing a stark contrast to Hollis's own childhood. Surrounding him as well was a feeling of love the thief had never experienced before. Stephen felt a smile come to his lips as he swept his eyes over the loved ones gathered around him. His fifth birthday was one of his most treasured ones; his father's parents had travelled from North Carolina to attend. The scent of melted wax and angel food cake filled his senses.

That sweet smell of reminiscence soured into a heavy scent of refuse and urine. Hollis sat on the damp cobblestones; his arms wrapped around his knees. As he raised his head, he took in his surroundings through one half open eye. The other was swollen closed, an effect of the punches the man had rained upon the boy. With every breath, daggers of pain lanced his ribs where his father's kicks had landed once he had been driven to the ground. The thief never discovered what became of his father after he had fled the hovel the two shared. Despite the vicious beatings and truly hateful words showered upon him, he was still Hollis's father. Deep inside himself, in places he was never proud of, the thief hoped the knife he had driven into the man had brought his reign *of terror to an end. Misery and anger warred for dominance in the young boy's heart.*

Misery and anger dulled as Stephen's father gently dabbed at his face with the peroxide- coated gauze. His kindly gaze soothed the sting of the damp cloth on his skin. The paragon of patience, the man silently continued to tend to Stephen's wounds. As his father knew he would, the boy found his voice, "There were three of them." The man nodded his head, placing the vaguely pink square atop the vanity and opened a band aid. His eyes never left those of his son. "I avoided them; but they came after me anyway." At the time, Stephen was too preoccupied by his own thoughts to notice much beyond them. From the vantage point given by decades of distance, he now saw the agony written on his father's face.

Stephen's memory of his father's visage melted into one more familiar to Hollis. A young Slazèan man stood above him, a proud smile worn on his lips. Hollis recognized his mentor, Seran; the man was the first person in his life to show him that he had even a modicum of worth. Beyond the shirtless man lay another boy, a few years Hollis's senior. The boy's chest rose slowly but feebly; each time it fell, small crimson bubbles formed on his lips. A strong hand gripped the thief's chin, turning his eyes to meet those of the man before him. "You established how far you were willing to allow him to push you, Hollis." Something glinted in the man's eyes, although at that point in his life, it was a stranger to him; he would come to know it as pride. "Tomas's fate was of his own doing. We do not make threats, we make statements. If people do not accept each word from your mouth as fact, you will repeat the same fight over and over again until it is you lying broken upon the ground." Despite the grim circumstances, a sense of pride rose in the thief's heart; for the first time in his young memory, he felt as if he belonged.

Hollis's surroundings faded as another set took their place. Three other boys sat near him, within the close confines of the cabin, whispering among themselves. Sitting there beside his summer camp friends, Stephen never realized how much he missed the simple feeling of belonging. A sweet relief rolled through the man's heart; it was a mixture of joy and longing. As his eyes passed over each of their faces, the feeling intensified, almost as if he were experiencing the moment again. Their names sprang to mind of their own volition: Paul. Ivan. Patrick. It was here among those who truly understood him and liked him for who he was, that he felt truly himself. Each summer was an ever so brief respite from the torment of the school year. The physical abuse he experienced in his early school years had become less and less common as his tormentors turned to methods that were harder to prove. Their words actually stung more than the covert slaps or playground scrapes ever could. In some way, Stephen preferred physical torment to the daily ridicule; for some reason, pain seemed to bother him less as time passed.

The dim interior of the cabin morphed into that of a torch lit subterranean room. Figures went about their own training in the smoke-veiled confines of the large chamber; but Hollis only knew the mass of agony that was his thigh. His ankle pressed uncomfortably into the small of his back as his right leg was bent in half, held in place by his equally contorted left arm. This test was simply the latest of many that the apprentices had been subjected to over the previous week in a bid to claim the final promotion from apprentice to lesser journeyman. It was meant to approximate requiring the necessity to remain completely still, often in uncomfortable positions for long periods of time.

He was surrounded by a half dozen other youngsters, all but one laying in various degrees of the fetal position, rubbing furiously at one limb or the other as they tried to massage away the pain. The torchlight brought into stark relief their tear dampened faces. Across from the young thief was the last remaining apprentice left standing beside himself. He had only spoken to Toni on the few occasions that their groups had trained together. Each of those interactions had him convinced that, despite the apprentice's delicate features and lilting voice, that Toni was indeed a boy. His Tigris Island ancestry was plain to even the thief's untraveled eye; the people who called the southern

374

island chain home tended to have smoother features. Hollis's friend, Allister, insisted that Toni was instead a lithely muscular girl; his argument that he just knew was far from convincing, however.

Hollis looked past Toni to the small knot of lesser masters that watched the examination. Among the ranks of observers, Seran's deep, olive colored skin stood out from the crowd of Granatyrian natives. His mentor chatted calmly with another master; at first glance both seemed disinterested in the display before them. That, however, could not be further from the truth. Seran flashed Hollis a quick wink as he passed a shiny silver noble to the man that stood before him, his ever-present confident smirk etched upon his face. Any ideas of falling to the stone floor and giving Toni the victory fled from him as dust from a strong breeze. The man Seran spoke with was none other than Edrich Dhole, the Guild Master's own protégé. Toni, in turn, had been sponsored by Dhole; this made the apprentice virtually royalty inside the guild halls.

It was more than Hollis's desire to make his mentor proud that stiffened the thief's resolve. Somewhere deep inside him, resentment flared. A deep and enduring anger, the source of which Hollis could not identify flashed in his heart. Although none of the apprentices dared lay a hand on him since the unfortunate incident with Tomas years before, he felt a wash of victimization all the same. Although, the two had barely met, Toni had reminded him on a visceral level of other youngsters. In a rush, faces that Hollis did not recognize sped through his mind. Stephen recognized the young faces, stained with contempt and venom. Laid out before both of their perceptions were the visages of Stephen's childhood tormentors. Both of them watched as peace settled over Hollis and the pain faded into the background. At the time, Hollis had simply been thankful for the respite from the agony that allowed him to outlast Toni and secure the rank of journeyman that day. Both he and Stephen now recognized it for what it truly was.

Both men felt the sensation of satisfaction and pride sour into trepidation and fear as the scene changed yet again. Stephen recognized the entry hall of Pope Innocent XII Regional High School. Despite being forced to wear a uniform that must have been designed to be unflattering on anyone no matter their size or body shape, Pope Innocent marked a milestone in Stephen's young life. Not only did it open his eyes and mind to an entirely new world of knowledge, it was also where he first met Jeff. Young Stephen was battered from all directions as he made his way through the halls; small for his age and seemingly unable to put on weight, he bounced like a tumble weed on a windy day through the mass of new students. Stephen remembered the rush of excitement and sting of uncertainly that quickly overcame his first day nerves. Eventually, the young Stephen found his way to the classroom marked on his schedule as 'Home Room', room 212. As he stepped into the open door, he felt as if he had crossed into his own home. At the time, he had not known what to make of it; even after all these years, Stephen knew who he would see at the front of the classroom. Mr. Jeffrey Reese.

Stephen saw Jeff's bushy beard and close-cropped hair, causing a wave of sadness to seize his heart. Unbidden, a flash of memories of Stephen's friend barraged both men's psyches. With effort and a small amount of regret, Hollis reigned in the wild stream of consciousness reminiscence and brought the memory at hand into starker focus. Young Stephen took a seat in the front of the room, setting his backpack on the ivory tiled floor. That is when he felt the tapping between his shoulder blades; the boy turned only to have his ear sharply flicked by the student behind him. Stephen felt a crimson rush expand from the point of impact as the minor discomfort turned to shame.

As he turned to face forward again, acceptance of his fate settling upon him like a wet snow, Jeffrey was standing before him with a stern expression on his previously face. The man simply pointed to Stephen's tormentor and then to the classroom door. Young Stephen felt his embarrassment cool as for the first time in his memory, outside of his own home, he felt the embrace of safety. Jeff favored him with a smile and a small wink before turning his eyes to the class as a whole and beginning to speak in a low determined rumble, "I cannot speak for any of the other teachers here; but in my classroom, in my presence, bullying of any kind will not be tolerated." As much as Stephen attempted to hold on to that moment, the scene shifted again, escaping from his mental grasp like smoke.

"... tolerated. Your discretion in this matter is not only expected, it is mandated. I repeat that carelessness of any kind will not be tolerated." Although six others stood before the massive desk behind which Guild master Hlorn sat, his eyes bore into Hollis'. The thief remembered the pride he had felt months prior, not only to be standing among the other newly minted journeymen but also that as he did so, Toni continued to scrub floors and fetch meals with the other apprentices. At the time, the rush of feelings seemed out of place; but as Hollis and his reflection watched this excerpt from his life, given the context from Stephen's own memories it made perfect sense. Before they had officially met, each was having an effect on the other across the space of their respective worlds.

A smile bloomed on Hollis's lips like a poppy at the morning's first light. His regret was immediate as Hlorn rose from his seat and struck him across the face in one fluid motion. The thief staggered backwards a step, with his cheek cupped in his palm. His youth gave him courage unfettered by sense. When he raised his eyes to meet those of the guild master again, the grin still rode upon lips stained crimson with his own blood.

Hlorn brought his hand back again but was interrupted by a voice behind the gathered journeymen, "Pardon the interruption, Meister Hlorn, but as requested, I have decided upon which one suits my needs best." Hollis took a half step backwards to regard the man belonging to the voice while still keeping the enraged guild master in his peripheral vision. Dressed in green hunting leathers so dark, as to appear black, was Alexei Silvermoon.

The forester stepped in the room with an economical stride and placed himself between Hlorn and the boy, his back to the distressed man. "Are you certain, Lord Silvermoon? The youth has a great deal of things to learn," Hlorn's voice dropped to a dangerous growl, "I intend to take a personal interest in his education."

Silvermoon smiled and favored Hollis with the same wink that

Jeffrey had shared with Stephen before turning to face the guild master. "I am indeed. The task with which my companions seek aid requires a particular mindset; to that end it is best that he have no habits to break...good or bad." A moment ago, Hlorn had seemed a wrathful giant, towering above young Hollis. Standing before Silvermoon's muscular frame, but the man seemed frail and impotent. The smile remained but reminded the boy more of a beast revealing its teeth than the comforting gesture that the two had shared a few seconds prior. "That will not be an issue, will it, Meister Hlorn?"

In a small voice, the man responded, "Of course not."

Almost before Hlorn had finished speaking, the forester replied, "Excellent." Turning on his heel, Silvermoon called over his shoulder, "Come along, boy. We have much to do." As the memory shifted into another, both Hollis and Stephen felt a contentment fall upon them. Whether on Taerh or Earth, their friend was the same.

"... much to do, Stephen." Jeffrey's voice, or perhaps it was Silvermoon's, settled upon his ears before the memory had fully formed in their mind's eye. The man half sat on the weathered oak table looking expectedly at Stephen. Or was it Hollis? He was beginning to lose track of to whom the memory belonged and who was simply the witness.

"I have been giving it a lot of thought, Mr. Reese."

"Jeff." Seeing the boy's confusion, Jeffrey elaborated, "Stephen, when we are outside of school, please call me Jeff."

Stephen and Hollis's identities reluctantly uncoupled as each fell into themselves again. Stephen heard his own voice say softly, "Alright, Mr. ... I mean Jeff." Again, the man smiled reassuringly at him. "I have given it a lot of thought. My last character was a thaumaturge; I would like to play one again if the group is alright with it."

From their position, removed from the situation as they were, the men saw that Jeffrey's smile dimmed for an instant before he responded. "You could do that; but George is already playing Marcus. Do you know what the group is missing, however? A thief." Stephen felt his lips purse slightly; the man noticed and placed a reassuring hand on his shoulder. "We could use the Tolkien term if you like ... "

"Expert Treasure-hunter?"

"That is the one. I have a character all rolled up if you think it would save time." He slid the character sheet across the table to Stephen. "I think you will find it more than adequate."

They watched him turn the piece of paper around so he could read what was written there. "What a peculiar name: Hollis. But I like it, I think." Stephen and his reflection's senses dimmed as their perceptions faded to darkness.

"Hollis." The whispered sound of his name in the darkness jolted the young thief to his senses. Beside him in the blackness crouched Mika, further away, he made out Silvermoon's silhouette as well. The woman's voice was at his ear, the stirring of her breath raising the tiny hairs found there. "They outnumber us three to one. We will have to find a place to ambush them away from the homestead."

Even a hundred yards away from the house, the thief heard the sobbing of the lone survivor. A harsh voice shouted something in a guttural language that Hollis could not understand. The order was followed almost immediately by a thunderous slap; the crying stopped. "That will be too late." Young Hollis rose from his crouch smoothly as water over glass, but a strong hand fastened about his wrist.

Mika shook her head slowly. "The woman means nothing to you, boy. You will not risk your life and those of your comrades for someone you have never met." Hollis remembered sliding back to one knee, not sure if it was the iron grip of the woman beside him or that of confusion on his mind. Never in his life had he contemplated putting anyone's needs before his own, much less his safety, and none had ever done such for him. Stephen, on the other hand, often put others before himself. It was yet another example of how the man had affected his life years before he had first Reflected. She spoke again, so close to his ear that felt the heat of her body against his. "Haedren would say that if it is in the Father of Dawn's plan that she survives, she shall greet another of his children."

"Do you believe that?"

Mika paused for a split second too long before saying, "You have to

379

walk your own path, Hollis. None can walk it for you. What I believe should be of no concern to you."

The corner of young Hollis's mouth turned up. "You are avoiding the question, although I do appreciate the advice."

The woman's lilting chuckle sent a tingle across his skin as her fingers slid from his forearm to his bicep. They lingered there a little too long to be unintentional. Stephen's thoughts recoiled at his own memories of Beatrice, always prim and proper and how they conflicted with Hollis's memories of the more immodest Mika. When his father had died, Beatrice had held Stephen as he wept, a surrogate for his mother that had passed earlier that year. Compared to her reflection, the Mika of Hollis's memories was downright predatory. "Advice, free though it may be, is normally worth what you pay for it."

Hollis remembered enjoying her attention; but was having issues recalling precisely why. Beatrice had been like a mother to him. To Stephen. The thief found himself having more difficulties separating his reactions from those of his reflection. Despite the fact he knew his Mika was not Stephen's Beatrice, his heart was not as discerning. Neither of them noticed as the scene before them changed again.

Young Stephen stood before a polished mahogany casket; its lid closed to the world, as he had felt shut off from it that afternoon. He had blamed the thick haze of incense that hung over the funeral parlor's viewing room for the tears that welled up in his eyes; but now, just as then, he knew the truth. His mother's still form lay hidden in the cocoon of wood, never to be seen again. The sense of finality had weighed so heavily on him that day. Stephen's sense of loss, decades separated from the loss itself was mirrored by that of his reflection; despite never having met his own mother, the thief mourned as if he had lost her as well. Tears blurred the room before him, turning candlelight and cherry wood into a kaleidoscope of light and dark before his eyes.

When they cleared, he found himself at another funeral, Maggie's husband's pyre set against the moonless night sky. Grief had turned to guilt like the flow of the tide against the beach. The woman sobbed softly, her face buried in the young thief's shoulder and his arm wrapped around her waist. Although the two stood close together, they could not have been further apart in that moment. Stephen felt that, knowing the skill and ferocity that he and his companions could bring to bear, that the three of them could have overcome the orc's superior numbers if they had made a stand at the farmhouse. But it had been Hollis in that field and not himself. His head swam as the fire flared suddenly, blinding him momentarily.

When his eyes cleared, he lounged against a thick tree root; the campfire snapped and popped softly as he felt the warm pressure of another's body against his own. He felt the woman's breath at his throat before he heard her words. "Why couldn't we have gotten together sooner?"

Young Stephen pressed his lips against the top of Ronni's head, breathing in her apple-scented shampoo. Both Hollis and Stephen recoiled; but the memory continued to play on as it had decades before. "You were dating Scott." Stephen remembered the waves of frustration that had rolled over him each day at school seeing them together. In that moment, he had been truly happy.

Ronni exhaled violently, the sound more of a growl than anything else, "Don't say his name." He felt her sneer against his shoulder, an expression that in the following years he would get to know well. "If he wants that slut Lucy, let him have her." The girl tilted her face up to young Stephen. "You won't leave me, Stephen, will you?" Her fingers laced into the hair at the back of his head, drawing his lips to hers.

At the time, young Stephen had been carried away with the intensity of the moment. With the wisdom hard won from years of experience, he saw now that she had been sore from Scott's rejection and simply sought to never suffer the same pain again. "Of course not." Hollis...or was it Stephen, it was becoming hard to tell again... inwardly smiled at the thought of the couple's final conversation. Ronni had spoken to a lawyer, but it was him that had truly left.

He felt her fingers tighten in his hair. "You better not." In the dim light of the campfire, her smile had been sweet. He saw it now for the hard expression it truly was. A log cracked in the campfire and fell amid a surge of sparks.

Those sparks blended into another burst in another place, in another time. "You had better not," Maggie lay beside him, with her rough, field-hardened hand upon his chest. "If you know what is good for you, Hollis."

The thief held the small piece of ice, dripping from the ceramic bowl that held the grapes that had served as their repast between vigorous lovemaking. Hollis raised an eyebrow. "Maggie, my dear, if there is one thing you should know about me after all these years, I do not now, nor have I ever known what was good for me."

"Obviously," she grumbled playfully. In her tone, he heard what his younger self had not – an intense sadness and yearning. She rarely asked him to stay with her, simply when he was leaving. Deep inside, both knew the other's answer and leaving it unsaid cushioned some of the pain. He found himself questioning why his answer should have ever been no. All he had wanted his entire life was love and happiness; here in this woman's arms he could have had both in equal measure. A dizziness swept over Hollis; those were Stephen's desires, not his own. He spent his life chasing fame and fortune, excitement and adventure. But why? What good was everyone knowing his name when no one truly knew who he was? You could not buy the things that mattered: respect... joy...love. Excitement was simply a bandage, a fleeting replacement for happiness.

Regret washed over him like waves upon a rocky shore. He had spent years avoiding his loneliness and filled his time with diversions from his own truth. Stephen realized that while the events and motivations differed, the stories were the same. Rather than face the true enemy before him, he chose to flee it each and every time. For Stephen, that enemy was his own doubt and sense of self hatred. For Hollis it was anger and self-hatred.

In their introspection, they had failed to notice that the scene had changed once again.

Stephen sat in Jeffrey's man cave, his leg thrown casually over the *arm of an over-stuffed chair. Before him a young Alan held back tears with great effort. Hollis heard his own voice, Stephen's voice speaking softly, "They feed on your pain. The more you react, the more likely they are to continue to act that way. Don't let them know they get to you." Stephen cursed his younger self's advice. He wanted to scream, "Fight! Make them earn every joy they derive from your pain. I will show you!" However, Stephen had never been a fighter, not until Hollis had come around. His head swam as he tried to sort his thoughts, feelings and identity from that of his reflection.*

In the wash of disorientation, the room darkened, his perspective focusing on a singular point. "... will show you how. Leave your life behind, Renthroas. It is only half lived anyway." The dim-basement had given way to a manicured courtyard. The only illumination came from the lantern held casually in the teen's hand.

Renthroas's frown deepened, "Half lived? So, you have come to mock me as well?"

Hollis shook his head. "Not at all. Truth is hard; that does not mean we should not face it. You belong in the west with your father's people as much as you do here, among the judging eyes and half hidden whispers of those who will never accept you." The anger of the boy's expression turned maudlin, but the thief continued, "Truth can be your ally or your enemy; like either, you need to decide how you are going to deal with it. An ally can take advantage of you often enough so as to be indecipherable from their opposite number and an enemy can teach you more effectively than even your closest friend." Hollis took the lantern from the boy, placing it on the cobblestones at his feet. "In the end, the choice of whether to be the victim of your truth or its architect lies completely within your own hand." The thief held his own open one out, palm up, "All that remains is the will to seize it." Slowly, he closed his fist. "If you allow others' truth to determine your path, you will always be a slave."

"But I have a place here."

Stephen heard his own voice in that of young Renthroas.

"A gilded prison of your grandfather's making."

"I am comfortable."

Like the tolling of a church bell, Stephen's past excuses rang again in his mind.

"As is the lamb before it dances slowly upon the spit."

"My family is all I have."

The tolling of Stephen's former truth quieted, muffled by the sure presence of his Reflection. Rather than swaddling the man in the comforting cloak of Hollis's confidence, the edges of each man's outlook blurred. Stephen's doubts were no longer soothed by the thief's point of view; instead, they softened like clay, warm from the oven. He felt the cold, hard edges of his reflection's outlook, shaped by the tragedy and hardships that he had endured, begin to thaw. Just as Stephen let go of the doubts that had plagued him all his life, Hollis released the resentment he had carried throughout his.

Hollis, his hand still held out to the boy, opened it again. "That is because you have not seized what you truly deserve." While the thief's hand was extended to Renthroas, Stephen felt that in this moment of reflection of a time gone by, it was held out to him as well. As the boy took Hollis's hand in budding friendship, the thief's reflection surrendered to the warm wash of consonance.

Just as two notes, seemingly disparate at first glance, blend into perfect harmony when played side by side, the identities of the two men intermingled.

CHAPTER THIRTY-ONE
REFLECTION'S END

Where there once were two, now there was only one. The man that was Stephen and the man that was Hollis were no longer any more real than any of their respective remembrances. The individual that remained was at once both of them and neither. As suddenly as it had begun, the light faded. Rather than the exhaustion he would have expected, he felt refreshed as if he were born anew. His journey through both of his previous lives seemed to be an eternity; but it was as if no time had passed at all inside the Well's chamber.

Samantha knelt at the edge of the now dark water; by the light of scattered torches, he saw her anger. "You may have taken the Well from me; but you shall never leave it." He saw her draw power in great gulps, directing it at him with a single, thundering word of power. He was enveloped in a searing, unending stream of heat and flame. He drew his arms up to shield his face as steam rose from the thief in massive clouds, obscuring her from his vision. The span of four panicked breaths passed before he realized that while he was aware of the flames licking at his clothes and his flesh, he did not actually feel them.

Slowly, he allowed his hands to drop to his sides. The conjured flames flowed over and around him; but when their magic-born tongues came into contact with his flesh, they sputtered and winked out of existence. The sense of serenity which had previously only been experienced in times of great need flowed through him as surely as his own life blood. Samantha's Reflection was standing at the edge of the now depleted Well, her own hands held out before her directing wave after wave of orange flame in his direction. Her face was twisted into a hateful grimace, "You insignificant little shit. I have too far, sacrificed too much for a pathetic street rat like you to fuck it up now!" She switched from English to Trade Tongue and back again as she screamed at the top of her lungs. "Enjoy your victory for the last, agonizing moments of your life!"

Watching her for a moment from within the protection of the solacing cloak of calmness that the Well had gifted upon him, he saw her gasping for breath, more than her frantic screaming should have accounted for. A smile came again to his lips momentarily as he thought of the trap that he had laid for her in his former world. The more he observed her, the more subtle signs became obvious to him. She slurred some of her words, as the left side of her face seemed to be unable to keep pace with the right. Her right elbow angled toward her body. Each symptom passed as quickly as it had come; minutes ago, they would have been too subtle and their duration too short for him to have noticed. Everything around him seemed to take on a new significance.

His eyes darted to where Aristoi was lying bloodied and limp, the last of many victims of the Walker that day. His grey cloak was stained crimson with the blood streaming from the vicious wounds produced by her spell. To even the most trained eye, she would seem to have breathed his last; the fingers on her left hand, trembled ever so slightly against the stone floor of the chamber and the crimson stain across her lips was occasionally disturbed by the passage of air drawn across it.

Relief washed over him; he was not responsible for the death of all of his friends, although even Mike and Jhorwynn wer too many. As he fell into a pit of self-pity, the air around him burned his throat and with his confidence went the protective aura of calm gifted by the Well. Consciously, he refocused himself, casting aside all thoughts besides the task before him.

The burning slowly faded and was replaced by a comfortable numbness.

Climbing out of the depleted Well, he stepped through the wall of vapor. What color remained there, drained from Samantha's face. "It cannot be possible." Her spell faded from existence but, she already gathered power for another.

"Save your strength. You will need it in the hours to come." He paused, crouching to pick up the Wallin Fahr from where it lay upon the stone, before resuming his slow walk towards her. "You have lost the day. The question that remains is how much more are you willing to lose?"

"I have lost nothing. All you have done is postpone the inevitable." Despite her brave words, the woman turned and fled the cave. He had a notion to give chase; but he was not sure how far the gifts of the Well would take him in an extended conflict with a Herald.

The thief whispered, "Run as fast as you like. You will never outdistance that which gives chase, old woman." His gaze settled on Rhyzzo's limp form as it floated face down in the blood-tainted waters. Closing them, he said a brief prayer for his friend's passage to his justified reward before turning to see to his other comrades.

CHAPTER THIRTY-TWO
DEPARTURE'S PROMISE

The sun was rising over the mountains at the Walker's shoulder as she left the farm behind her. The family was kind enough; but she needed a horse and provisions and their kindness went only so far. With the pigmies' Well depleted, she needed to move quickly to locate the next one as it formed. She set aside the burning need for vengeance against Stephen... Hollis...whichever of them remained in control. There was certainly time for that when she knew where to find the miraculous waters. With the power of the Well coursing through his veins, her magic would not be the advantage it had been in the past; but she felt confident that her cunning would be more than a match for his.

A jaw aching yawn flowed through her as her eyes grew heavy. The events of the evening had taxed even her mastery of her art, leaving her drained. Fleeing through the night, dodging the damnable little men did not reduce her fatigue. Thankfully the farmer and his wife were well into their seventies; she was able to dispatch them without having to call upon her magic. Her sword served her just fine in that case.

She felt her blinks growing longer as she fought off the siren call of sleep.

Samantha's head rested against her shoulder at what must have been an uncomfortable angle. Beside her on the side table was a china teacup, the last vestiges of its contents pooled at the bottom. More leaf than water, the substance appeared closer to dark green mud than actual tea. The woman's hands lay peacefully in her lap as she slept.

Her eyes closed against the brightening day, Samantha took a deep breath of summer air and enjoyed the taste of it on her reflection's tongue. The sun was already beginning to warm her back as she rode. Perhaps it was the residual anger from the night before or the dread of another night in the emergency room waiting for her upon wakening in the other world; but her heart fluttered within her chest. She took another gulp of air and it seemed to subside.

A soft and strangely satisfied smile came to her lips.

Her breathing slowly took on a rasping tone, like steel dragged across stone. Each breath became more ragged than the one before it. Her hands, once placid, balled themselves into fists as they curled back against her stomach. Sweat beaded upon her hairline and coated her face in a smooth sheen.

Her smile faded slowly as she raised her hand to her chest, when the palpitations returned with a vengeance. The sounds of the early morning forest were lost beneath those of her beating heart in her ears. Her breathing became shallow and rapid, as suddenly she felt like she was unable to get enough air into her lungs. She rubbed vigorously at her throat as if she could massage the air into it. Looking around, a

sudden rush of anger ran through her at the sight of the scenery, which remained tranquil and majestic despite the fact that she fought for every breath.

~

Samantha's ragged snores morphed into choking gasps as her body rocked gently in the chair. Her hands were so tightly clenched at her stomach that her knuckles were ivory. Small droplets of crimson stained her dress where her fingernails had lacerated the paper-thin skin of her palms. Her eyes moved spasmodically under closed eyelids as her convulsions grew in intensity. One final tremor shook her body causing her left hand to swing wildly.

It struck the teacup, causing it to slide towards the edge of the side table.

~

Pain shot across her chest as she clutched her throat with one hand. Her other hand was bent into a tight claw at her heart as the pain shot down her arm, causing it to spasm wildly.

~

Samantha's last rattling breath hung in the air as the last of her life fled her body. Her hands relaxed as the peace of her final repose came upon her.

The cup teetered on the edge of the table, swaying gently as if in an unseen breeze.

~

She slid from her stolen horse as the day around her dimmed into twilight. She furiously reached for the saddle horn; but her nerveless fingers could find no purchase. It seemed to her as if everything took place in a dream. Deep inside herself, despite her panic, she felt an alien sense of satisfaction. The reflection that she had so long ago subsumed rejoiced in the suffering of her jailer.

∿

The cup began to fall, tumbling end over end to the floor.

∿

The woman toppled from her horse, no longer even attempting to break her fall.

∿

The china teacup shattered as it struck the floor, sending shards of porcelain scattering throughout the small room. The viscous remnants of her last tea clung like honey to the spines of the books Samantha had sought to keep from Stephen.

∿

The woman's body struck the ground with a sickening thump and she lay still as her horse allowed its fear to get the best of it.

The animal fled from the lifeless heap that had once been the Herald known as the Walker.

EPILOGUE
A DESTINY EARNED

"Actions are the seed of fate, deeds grow into destiny."

-Harry S Truman

"Every man gotta right to decide his own destiny."

-Bob Marley

A HOME BY ANY OTHER NAME

Nellie held Ronni's hands between her own as she sat next to the stricken woman. Tears rolled down Ronni's face as she sobbed, "He may have been flawed; but he was mine. He said he would never leave me." She looked into Nellie's eyes. "He promised."

Robert was standing behind Nellie, one hand laid tenderly on her shoulder and an overstuffed duffel bag clutched in the other. He shook his head sadly, "I can't believe he would do that. He knew he had friends who would have been there for him, no matter what." Nellie simply shook her head but remained quiet. "It is just so senseless. The loss of three of the finest people I know within a week. So unfair."

Ronni wiped at her eyes. "Not everybody understood what we had but we were very much in love."

Nellie squeezed her hands. "We know you were. Everyone saw how much you tried to do your best by him."

"I really did. He was such a wonderful man." The words caught in her throat. "And now I'm all alone." Ronni dropped her head onto Nellie's shoulder. "What am I going to do?"

Robert rubbed Ronni's shoulder with his free hand. "It'll be alright."

"He has life insurance but..." She took a moment to compose herself. "But it is not any help. The doctors say that the machines are the only thing keeping him alive...and they are so expensive." A sob caught in her throat. "What would people say if I had him disconnected? People would think I killed my husband."

"Does he have any quality of life?" Robert's voice dropped to gentle whisper, almost as if he were afraid to ask the question.

Ronni turned to look at him, the fact that she had not considered that evident in the confusion on her face. "I don't know. How can I be expected to think about something like that?"

~

Hollis was standing at the open floor to ceiling windows that dominated the outer wall of his room. The second floor of the Virgin Mermaid offered a breathtaking view of the docks below and the river beyond them. Even in the dead of night, sailors and dock workers busied themselves at his feet. He drew a deep breath, carrying the night air into what felt like his very soul.

The journey to Oizan from the Well site took almost a week, slowed as they were by the injured Kieli woman. Between the heady rush of the Well's power and the overwhelming tragedy of the loss of Mike and Jhorwynn, Hollis had overlooked the fact that they were one enemy body short. After the thief saw to Aristoi's wounds, he searched for the Plague Man but in the end came up empty. Without Samantha or her reflection holding his leash, it did not seem profitable for the Plague Man to continue his vendetta. What troubled the thief was the fact that neither of them was able to find the dark steel and bright silver cameo broach that the Walker had cast aside during the combat. Hollis was sure the disappearances were tied together. It was this feeling that prompted his activities tonight.

Behind him, the thief heard the door to his room open softly. Light, almost dance like steps reached his ears as the scent of sandalwood and wine teased his nose. Without turning, Hollis spoke, "You are feeling more yourself, Southerner?"

Aristoi chuckled briefly. "I believe I preferred when you greeted me with bared steel with...well whatever is happening here."

Hollis turned from the window and favored the woman with one of his cockeyed smiles, "To each his own, I suppose." The thief nodded to the pack hanging from his friend's shoulder, "You are leaving." It was a statement.

The Songspear nodded slowly. "Yes, my walk is at an end. I have been away from my home for too long." Despite the firm way in which she delivered the words, beneath her sure voice, Hollis detected an air of hesitancy.

The thief placed a hand on Aristoi's shoulder and squeezed firmly, "That you have. You have repaid any debt you may have owed me, if there ever was one."

"With interest."

"With interest," Hollis agreed.

"What lies before you, my friend?"

The thief nodded towards the open window. "I fear that the letter I sent to my friend while in the Stone City led to her falling into the hands of Plague Man." He stepped over to where his own pack lay beside the room's only bed. "I plan on leaving tonight for Slaze to search for her." Hollis's face tightened as he bit back the dread that boiled in his guts. He did not give voice to his fear that he may find her dead as well, yet another black mark on the soul of the Plague Man ... and his own conscience.

Aristoi opened her mouth to speak, but Hollis cut her off.

"You said it yourself, your path is at an end."

"My walk, but I appreciate the sentiment."

Hollis corrected himself, "Your walk is at an end. You have business south."

A slight nod was the Songspear's only response.

In an effort to take his mind off of the purpose for his own trip, Hollis abruptly changed the subject. "I have heard of a historical work regarding the Wells in a Slazean library, I may see if they are willing to part with it."

Aristoi raised an eyebrow, "And if they are not?"

The thief ignored the question and continued, "While it is no longer needed to thwart the Walker, she all but admitted that she did not make use of the one in Rangor. I cannot shake the feeling that it played a part in the deaths of my friends."

"As you well know, anyone who involves themselves with the Wells pays for the privilege in blood."

Hollis nodded as he pulled free a rolled parchment, "I am intimately aware of that. One life is too many and we have overspent that by magnitudes." He extended the parchment to the Kieli; Aristoi accepted it with a raised eyebrow. "That documents the locations of three dead drops that Renthroas and I have used in the past. Should you have need, leave a note for me at one of them and it will find its way to me. I will do the same." Before the Songspear could speak, Hollis continued, "It is my turn to become the debtor. I owe you more than I can ever hope to repay; please give me an opportunity to try."

Instead of giving voice to the argument that hung in her eyes, Aristoi simply extended her hand. When the thief had taken it, she pulled the man close, "We will meet again, Northerner," before releasing him and turning on her heel. "There is no telling what trouble you may find if allowed to walk alone."

Hollis watched the door close before turning back to the open window. Taking another deep breath of chill night air, he stepped onto the roof and into the night.

~

The room was only lit by the soft glow of the ventilator. Stephen lay motionless in the tiny bed, a mass of tubes and wires. The police had found him an hour after he had begun his Reflection, moments after Ronni returned home and called them. Unable to wake him, they'd called for an ambulance. The paramedics were there when he stopped breathing and they began CPR. The emergency room doctors placed him on life support as they scrambled to determine the cause. The official diagnosis was a ruptured embolism in his brain; but baring a living will or his wife's consent, he remained attached to the machines that kept him alive.

The door opened slowly, and a figure stepped inside, allowing it to shut before approaching the bed. His stained jeans pooled at his thick soled black shoes. He scratched his patchy week's growth of beard as he studied the man in the bed. Despite the clearly marked warnings nearly everywhere one looked, he dug into his pocket to pull out his crumpled pack of cigarettes and chrome lighter.

The flame brought Hector's face into stark relief for a moment before fading. As he exhaled a plume of white smoke, he whispered, "Now, what to do with you?"

About the Author

A child of the 80's, SL Harby grew up playing Dungeons & Dragons and classic video games. An only child, he was bitten early by the reading bug, cutting his teeth on the masters of modern fantasy. His days were spent inside the worlds created by Howard and Lieber, Moorcock and Tolkien.

An eternal Jersey boy at heart, SL Harby lives in South Carolina with his wife and muse, Jessica and their bad ass rescue dog, Tellulah.

Shadows of a Dream is his first novel, representing four years work and a lifetime of dreaming. Visit www.ReadSLHarby.com for more from the author, including short fiction, creator interviews, book reviews and much more!

Made in the USA
Columbia, SC
24 June 2022

61957827R00224